One day
you will come back
(*Un jour tu reviendras*)

Monique Dubois

Publication Data

One day you will come back (*Un jour tu reviendras*) © Monique Dubois, 2019

Book and cover design by Monique Dubois
Rear cover illustration of *homo erectus*: iStock.creativemarc
ISBN: 978-1-940012-27-8

Preface

This novel was inspired by a song, *Un jour tu reviendras, (One day you will come back)*, sung by Mireille Mathieu, released in 1974. The music is from the classic spaghetti western, *C'era una volta il west (Once upon a time in the West)*, by Sergio Leone, music by Ennio Morricone, and released in 1968. The soundtrack was released in 1972 and in 1974 Morricone cooperated with lyricists Alain Lacour and Maria Travia to produce the song. The combination of the haunting melody and the words of longing for what was and the hope to return to, would surely move anyone.

All characters in this work are fictional, any resemblance to people living or dead is purely coincidental. My apologies to the Third Secretary of the British High Commission in Nairobi in 1975/6 for usurping his position, and to those passengers on the trains and boats and planes that I have displaced. My thanks to Yolanda Meyer at Transnet, Jim Davies at the BA Museum, Barry Attoe at the Postal Museum and Bjorn Larsson for their patience in answering my queries.

Contents

My first love

I was twenty when I fell in love. I suppose many would consider that late in life for a first love, particularly because it was 1970, just after the 60s, the swinging sixties when sex and free love was rampant, at least in the media and the films of the time. I had until that time been focused on academics and had already earned my doctorate. I was one of those girls who people either hate or admire. I had shown signs of high intellect when I was very young and progression through school was an adventure. My parents had kept me back from attending grammar school too early so that I was not too young when I went, but they had provided tutors so that I was well ahead by the time I went to the girls' grammar school, to the extent that I sat my O-levels at twelve, my A and S-levels at fourteen and had my two degrees by seventeen, one in mathematics and one in economics and finished my doctorate in mathematics by the time I was twenty. Then I was offered a research grant to study the economics of the minerals industry. So, I was ready to embark upon the next chapter of my academic life. In all that time I had had no time for first boys, and later men, so, my development in that arena had been sadly lacking. My other social skills were similarly lacking. I tended to pedantry and intolerance, mainly because it was hard for me to understand why others could not see what was obvious to me, so was never the most popular girl, either with other girls or boys, and at times with adult teachers.

I forgot to mention before, but my name is, to paraphrase Sylvia Trent and James Bond in Casino Royale, Barclay, Fiona Barclay. I lived with my family in Henley before going up to Oxford for my bachelor's degrees and doctorate. I say lived with my family, that was true until I was eighteen, then Maman and Dad had divorced. Maman was my name for my mother, reflecting the fact that she was French. Dad, it transpired, had decided that his personal assistant, Felicity, was a better package than Maman, so they split. Maman got the house and a one-time settlement of £15,000,000 and Dad went his merry way. I had not realised that we had such wealth, I knew that we lived in a larger house than most, but we had never been particularly indulged with presents, exotic holidays or extravagant living. My brother, James, and I stayed with Maman, when I was not away at college, but we did stay in touch with Dad. After my doctorate and after I had got the grant to continue my studies, I was able to buy a nice house near Oxford, giving me a place to stay that was away from the students and the college life of Oxford, without being so far removed that it was not easily accessible, it was also close to the dojo I belonged to. I had taken up karate in high school after suffering at the hands of some fifteen-year-olds who did not appreciate my particular brand of sarcasm at their inability to do basic mathematics. I had also cut my hair at the same time. It seemed that hair-pulling was a favourite tactic of girls, so I gave them nothing to grab. I had gone home the day of the fight and had hacked off my hair, to the horror of Maman who had then promptly taken me to her hairdresser to repair the damage, or at least neaten it up. Eventually, I let it grow out a little, and now it is about the length favoured by Mireille Mathieu.

When I joined my first dojo to study karate, I also started to track the development of my body, so I weighed and measured once a month from then on, even now I track things. I took the standard measurements of chest, both across the breast measurements and under the breasts, to get a cup size for bras, I measured my waist and hips, and added biceps, forearms, thighs and calves, always in the same place as measured as a fraction of the distance down the bone from the upper joint. I charted all those measurements and still have them. At twenty I was 34-26-35, wore an A cup bra, stood 5' 6" tall and weighed about eight stone six ounces, one hundred and eighteen pounds for American readers not familiar with the arcane Imperial set of weights and measures, and fifty-three and a half kilos for the rest of the world.

I swim, can ride a horse, even to the extent of being able to go a round in a show jumping competition, play tennis on occasion, but am not a great fan, I never took ballet lessons, unlike many girls, but did learn Tahitian dance from my mother, more of the story behind that later, I can also shoot. Dad took me one day to a club he belongs to and I tried out a handgun, a shotgun and a rifle. I have to say that I did credibly well and he was clearly thrilled that I was not just a blue stocking who had her nose always in books. Actually, I liked the gun club, because I could research the effects of muzzle velocity, windage, wind resistance and gravity on bullet trajectories, I set up the measurement devices and fired off hundreds of rounds using different loads and bullet sizes and shapes and actually published a paper on the subject in one of the shooting magazines. That was my first published item, which rather raised eyebrows when I went for my interviews at Oxford. I think they thought I should be focused on more academic mathematic theory and the idea of a girl blasting away at targets was just not something they had ever considered. I kept up my shooting, but only at my Dad's club, I never took part in anything at the college, but I did go and watch occasionally.

My knowledge of karate stood me in good stead when I went up to Oxford as I was able to fend off an acned, spotty undergraduate who suffered from serious WHT, wandering hand trouble for the uninitiated, and another more serious attack. The first time had been at a student party and the offender had decided that I was to be his next conquest. Well, he received two broken fingers and a broken nose for his trouble. After that, I avoided college socials like the plague. The second time had been more serious and I had had to actually hand out a serious beating, which might have led to problems had the initial assault not been witnessed by a senior police officer, who had not been in a position to intervene, but who came to my aid when the local police did arrive.

It happened this way. I had been asked by a professor I knew to give a course on statistical methods, including an examination. Well, one of the students in the class, a well-known member of the college rugby first fifteen, had failed, and failed miserably, and he was unhappy. His real concern was that Daddy, who it seemed was filthy rich, would be less than thrilled with his performance, so one evening he and two friends happened upon me as I was walking home. They cornered me and he made threats and told me that the exam paper was going to be inserted into unpleasant places, after the three of them had finished the job of deflowering me. I had given the requisite warning that I was a karate adept, but he had brushed that aside, assuming that I was trying to bluff my way out of the situation. Then he had taken a swing at me. Fortunately, I had seen it coming and was able to dodge the swing enough that he only caught me with a glancing blow, leaving only a small cut on my cheek from a fancy signet ring he was wearing. After that I went into full attack mode, flight was not possible, so fight was the only option, I was scared, for the first time in my life I was really scared, in truth I was terrified, and that stoked the adrenaline to pure fury that allowed me to move as quickly as I did and to hit as hard. I had just laid out the third one when the police arrived. A particularly unpleasant police inspector wanted to clap me in irons and I was trying to argue my case, when this older man arrived and said that he had witnessed the assault. The police inspector told him that they would get to him later for a statement at which point a warrant card was thrust under his nose and the man paled. My saviour was the Chief Constable of a neighbouring county, no less, he had seen the initial assault from a window in the dining room of the college and made the 999 call to the police to come and intervene. He made it clear that I was the victim and the police then camped out at the hospital where the villains were taken to and when they were discharged charged them with attempted sexual assault.

The ensuing trial was pure theatre, I was required to give evidence and the defence barrister tried to portray me as a femme fatale who had lured the poor unfortunate spoilt rich brats to their doom and had savagely beaten them. Unfortunately for the defence barrister the CPS, Crown Prosecution Service, barrister had warned me of this and I turned up dressed in the exact same clothes that I had been wearing that day which made me look more like a small, prim and proper school ma'am not a lady of the night, and my would be attackers were all of a size that they would easily grace the second row of a rugby scrum. I recounted the incident and the words said to me, my recollection of which was challenged until I recounted the conversations defence counsel had had with his junior from the time I entered the courtroom until he rose to cross-examine me. The conversation brought colour to the cheeks of both he and his junior and choler to the judge who saw from their reactions that my recollection was perfect, including the less than complimentary comments about his Lordship. His Lordship's summing up had been brief and to the point, I was the victim and rich spoilt brats should be brought to heel and taught manners, no matter how well-placed Daddy may be. The jury had taken exactly thirty minutes, I suspect much of which was taken up with drinking tea or coffee, and had come back with a guilty verdict and the clots were now spending time behind bars, for all Daddy's money.

The family house in Henley was quite a pile, set in park-like grounds of about two hundred acres with beech woods and a pond with a small boat house that doubled as an art studio for Maman. The house boasted six bedrooms each with its own bathroom, plus the usual kitchen, dining and living rooms, plus a very elegant library, which was well stocked with a great variety of books, from dry tomes on banking and finance to racy literature like Fanny Hill. It had come to Dad as an inheritance from his father, whom I may have met but do not remember as he died in 1952. Grandpa was a banker and had done an excellent job of arranging things, such that upon his death the Inland Revenue people were not able to garner much in the way of death duties. That notion, of taxing death, always seemed to me to be a little on the macabre side, I could see clerks sitting at desks poring through the obituaries looking for their next victim.

I had said that I had bought a house near Oxford. It was quite a big house for one person, but I could afford it. I had won a generous exhibition to Oxford for my undergraduate degrees, and not being of age to legally imbibe alcohol had avoided the typical student traps of spending too much on beer and wine and had finished with an appreciable bank balance. I had also received a handsome grant to do my doctoral studies and had gone to Dad for advice about money. Dad had followed the family tradition and was an investment banker, which means that he would not lend you the money for a mortgage for your house, but if you wanted several millions to buy a company, he was happy to oblige, having first done his own assessment. Dad taught me to read a balance sheet and a profit and loss statement and to see beyond the published data and make my own judgements. It turned out that Dad was pretty shrewd and I began to see how shrewd while I was working on my doctorate and had gone to him for information on several matters regarding economic theory and practice. He had also shown me how to trade on the markets and I had done fairly well, so was able to amass more funds and with that buy the house outright. Dad had gone with me to look at the house and make an offer and he did the negotiating for me, to my great advantage I might add, he may have stayed with Felicity the floozie, but he did still have my welfare at heart.

My house was on the eastern side of Oxford in the woods. It was a modern-looking house, a lot of glass and was laid out all on one level in a sort of U shape, with the main living room in the middle, bedrooms, two, on one side and kitchen, dining on the other side. The inside walls of the U were basically all glass, all looking out onto a nice green patch. It was unusual for an English house in each bedroom had its own bathroom, with bath, separate shower, toilet, bidet and hand basin. The house had underfloor heating, rather in the Roman style, but done with small diameter copper pipes embedded in the floor and channelling hot water, which came from an oil-fired stove. I also bought a car, a second-hand Mini Cooper S, which meant that I had to get a driving licence. I decided to go to a driving school and take lessons, which I think was a good idea as in under two weeks I was driving tolerably well and was able to pass the driving test. Then I went to a racing driving school and learnt how to skid, do hand brake turns and generally improve on my skills. After that, it was just practice. Driving into Oxford to my office was not overly burdensome and I was fortunate in that I had a space for parking allotted to me.

Apart from karate I also discovered Shaolin kung fu. I had met a Chinese professor of languages who used to practice tai chi near my digs in Oxford and I had got to know her and had taken up tai chi with her as a way of centring myself before each day. She had also instructed me in kung fu, which extended my knowledge of martial arts beyond that of simply karate, oh, and along the way she taught me Mandarin, which was a nice addition to the other languages I spoke, English, French and Italian, and a few words of Tahitian.

But back to my tale. It was Ian Hartley to whom I lost my heart. He was a postgraduate student finishing up his doctorate and I first saw him at a college dinner for staff and graduate students, a sort of last hurrah before the beginning of the official Michaelmas Term. I was seated with a bevy of ancient professors and he was at a much livelier table of post-grads who were determined to have a good time. I was looking at him and admiring his looks when he glanced up and saw me watching him. Our eyes met and it was like an electric thrill ran through me. I think we both had the same thought, because when I turned to my neighbour to ask who he was, I caught a glimpse of him doing the selfsame thing. My neighbour was the chair of the anthropology department and he told me that the object of my attentions was Ian Hartley, recently back from the diggings at Olduvai in Tanzania, and well on his way to being granted his doctorate. Ian was from Rhodesia, that troublesome colony, or ex-colony if you will. He had got his degree at Oxford three years earlier and had been working towards his doctorate. Beyond that, my neighbour was singularly ill-informed, apart from the one item of which he was certain, that there was no Mrs Hartley. Emboldened with that knowledge I approached Ian after the dinner and introduced myself.

"Hello," I said, probably quite lamely. "I'm Fiona Barclay, I haven't seen you at one of these events before."

"Ian Hartley," he replied. "I think the reason you haven't seen me is that I haven't been here, I've been doing fieldwork in the Olduvai. I gather you're a mathematician?"

"For my sins," I confirmed. "But lately, I've been more of an economics person than a mathematician. I'm not often at these dinners, tonight is somewhat of an exception for me."

"Well, I'm delighted you came," he said. "Could we get some coffee tomorrow?"

"That would be super," I said, thinking that I must sound like a giddy schoolgirl. "When and where?"

"What about the Queen's Lane Coffee House at eleven?" he asked.

"That would be great," I said. "I'll see you there."

"I'll be there," he promised.

I went home and called Maman.

"*Mon Dieu,*" she said when she answered the telephone. "Do you know what time it is?"

"I'm sorry Maman," I said. "But I've met a man."

"You have?" she asked, all ears now and irritation over being called late in the evening, gone. "Who, when?"

"I finally broke down and went to one of the college dinners," I told her. "And there he was, sitting with a group of PGs'. His name is Ian Hartley and he's an anthropologist and I'm having coffee with him tomorrow."

"So, tell me about him," she said.

"Well, he's about 180 centimetres tall, probably weighs about seventy kilos, short blonde hair, been in the sun a while," I replied, for the fans of Imperial measures, just under 6' tall and 11 stone in weight.

"I'm not buying him," Maman said, dryly. "And, I don't need the show ring description, I mean what is he like as a person?"

"I'll find out tomorrow," I promised. "Oh, Maman, he's really dishy and when our eyes met, it was like an electric shock."

"Is the date tomorrow just coffee, or have you something else planned?" she asked.

"Just coffee," I said. "I need to know if there's a Mrs Hartley, I've been assured that there isn't, but I need to hear it from him, and I want to know if there are other entanglements."

"I'm so happy for you," she said. "Tell me what happens."

"I will, Maman," I promised. "I love you, Maman."

"I love you Bébé," she replied.

At the appointed hour I went to the coffee shop, and there he was, engrossed in some paper.

"Good morning," I said. "I hesitated to disturb you, you seemed so engrossed."

"Just a paper that may, or may not, cause complications for my thesis," he said. "But I can return to that. Thank you for coming, coffee?"

"Yes, please," I said. He waved to a waitress who came over and took my order and I noted that he asked for another for himself.

"So, Fiona Barclay," he said. "Tell me about yourself."

"There's not much to tell really," I lamented. "I was an early prodigy and have been submerged in academics ever since, and you?"

"There has to be more than just academics," he protested. "The word is that you are direct to the point of intimidation, you have been known to beat up people."

"Ah, I see you've been checking up on me," I laughed. "Well, the beating up, that only happened once, perhaps twice if you count just a broken nose, and I never thought of myself as intimidating, I think I'm a little too withdrawn for that, and you?"

"Well, I'm sure you did some of your own checking, so a quick life story, born in Rhodesia, educated there until college, bachelor's here and now doctorate, I hope," he said.

"Any siblings?" I asked.

"One sister, older," he replied. "She's a resident at Groote Schuur in Cape Town. You?"

"One brother, younger, at Imperial reading mining," I said. "What made you pick anthropology?"

"I think because I was intrigued by the fact that current humans all originated in Africa and I wanted to know more. It has been and is interesting and I think there is much yet to work out to explain how and why we became the dominant hominid," he explained. "Why mathematics?"

"I liked numbers and mathematics," I said. "But I discovered I also like economics; it seems a little more connected to the world than just straight mathematics."

"So, niceties done, any romantic involvements at the moment?" he asked. I spluttered a little on my coffee and thought of an answer.

"I thought I was supposed to be the direct one?" I asked. "But to answer your question, no, and you?"

"No, no wives, girlfriends or other impediments," he laughed.

"I've never been to Rhodesia," I said. "Should I?"

"Definitely," he said. "It's a beautiful country, mountains in the East with trout streams, hot bush country in the West and south, denser forests along the Zambezi and wildlife and game everywhere. My folks have a tobacco farm there, near Mount Darwin, which is in the Northeast part of the country."

"What's Olduvai like?" I asked.

"Warm most of the time, except when it rains, hottest months, December, January and February, coldest, June, July and August and wettest, April," he explained. "Life on the digs is somewhat governed by the weather, particularly in the rains."

"When you're not digging, what do you do at Olduvai," I asked.

"I like the game, so I take trips around Tanzania and Kenya," he said. "It's different to Rhodesia, but it's still Africa. Did you grow up in England?"

"I did," I confirmed. "My family has a house near Henley, so I went to school there until I came here."

"And, what are you working on now?" he asked.

9

"I've got a fellowship to study the accounting implications of asset valuation in mining properties, and to develop a set of algorithms to determine what could be proven, probable and possible in the way of reserves, based on global economic factors and local cost structures. It all starts with ore values found, which in itself is troublesome, because it very much depends on the methods used to interpolate between diamond drill holes," I said. "I know that sounds like a mouthful, but I've actually found it really interesting. I'm engaged by a group of the major mining houses who are trying to see if the standards set by the Institute of Chartered Accountants make any sense, and to fend off forays by the Inland Revenue."

"What do you do outside of college?" he asked.

"I've just moved into a house," I said. "I'm spending my weekends gardening; I'm hoping that I can get the place to a point where it's a quick once around with a lawnmower. You?"

"I used to row for the college in my undergrad days," he replied. "Since I got back from Olduvai, I haven't done much except try and get my thesis in some sort of shape."

"I remember doing that," I commented. "It didn't help that I thought my thesis advisor was actually wrong in some of his pet theories. That made defending my thesis awkward."

"I imagine it did," he sympathised. "Look, what are you doing this Saturday?"

"Unfortunately, I have something on," I said. "I promised Maman that I'd help her with some work."

"Maman?" he asked.

"Oh, sorry," I said. "My mother."

"So, she's French?" he asked.

"She is," I confirmed. "Dad met her in Paris after D-Day."

"What about next Saturday?" he asked.

"Free as a bird," I said.

"Why don't we go for a picnic on the river?" he suggested. "The forecast is for good weather, maybe the last good weather of the year, I'll get a boat and row you upstream a little way to a super spot."

"That sounds like fun," I said. "Where do I go, when and what do I wear."

"Do you know the Osney Bridge?" he asked.

"I do," I confirmed.

"Just find a place to park on the waterfront just downstream of the bridge, and I'll find you," he said. "Meet me there at nine, if that's not too early, wear shorts, shirt, bring a pullover or cardigan in case it gets cold, and you never know, a raincoat as well, my observation is that forecasts out two weeks are hopeless, so you never know. I'll bring food and wine."

"How do you know I have a car?" I asked.

"One of the other grad students commented that you're a menace in your Mini Cooper," he laughed.

"I'm hungry," I said. "Would you like some lunch?"

"I'm on rather a tight budget," he said.

"I'm not," I laughed. "Just bury your male chauvinism for a while and I'll treat you to lunch, or should I say the mining houses will."

"In that case, I'd be delighted," he said.

We had lunch and talked about African politics, wildlife that he had encountered, languages that he spoke, Portuguese, Shona and Ndebele and now Swahili. We also talked about music, books and art, something about which I was woefully ignorant, but about which he either seemed to know a lot, or he was a master at spinning a yarn. I was sorry that he finally had to go and made sure that I had a telephone number where he could be reached. We confirmed our date for the next Saturday and agreed to meet for coffee again on Monday, same place, same time, I gave him my office telephone number and got one where I could reach him, and also told him that I would be in London at meetings for the rest of the week. As he left, I just sat and watched him stride off, turning once to grin at me and wave. It was just magic, I had not had such a delightful lunch in a long time, he was funny, engaging, and as far as I could tell just as interested in me as I was him. I hugged myself with delight, then paid the account and went back to my office to come back to earth and accounting and finance. That evening I called Maman again and related details of my coffee date.

"So, another date for next Saturday," Maman commented. "Are you ready for what may follow?"

"I need to talk to you Maman," I said. "Could I come over this weekend and see you?"

11

"You know that you can come at any time, Bébé," she reminded me. "But to answer your real question, I will be here, and it will be just the two of us, so we can talk."

"Good," I said. "I'll see you Friday evening, Maman. I love you, Maman."

"*Je t'aime aussi. À bientôt,*" she replied.

The rest of that week I was kept busy. I went up to London the day after my coffee morning with Ian for a meeting with the mining houses. It was long and tedious, lasting a day and a half. It was tedious because they all had slightly different agendas and because application of the work was now being viewed from the perspective of Australian, South African and Zambian law and practice, as well as the laws and practices of England and Wales. I asked them for the relevant laws and received promises to have the papers delivered to me in Oxford. At least they were all happy with what I had done to date, in fact, they all thought I was much further along than any of them had imagined. The mathematics were actually not that complicated, it was the interpretation that would be troublesome and the specific agendas of the users. I had gathered data on LME, London Metal Exchange, prices for all the major metals and had found cost data for South Africa and Australia and had been able to show how the algorithms worked. I had also developed a trial algorithm to predict movements in metal prices, three, six and twelve months out. That still needed a lot of work and, more to the point, computer time, which was hard to get at the college. I had made myself familiar with the arcane language used to tell the computer what to do and had become quite adept at running the punch card machine.

On the second day of our session, while other discussions were going on, I looked around the room at the players. Now that I had met Ian, I was taking more of an interest in men. There were fourteen of them, aged anywhere from their late twenties to early fifties. I knew I was biased, but none held a candle to Ian, they were all either too old, too self-absorbed, too shy, too arrogant, and all but two were married. I knew that because I had overheard a conversation at the end of our very first meeting where had been all discussing me, my attributes, such as they were, my age, far too young to have any real-world knowledge, according to eight of them, and my availability. The unmarrieds had both announced that they had no interest in bedding a teenager, as they called me, but two of the older ones, both married, said that they would not mind making a play for me. The conversation had ended abruptly when I had entered the room, and the two Lotharios had had the good grace to colour up a little and wonder what I may have overheard. It turned out that one of the Lotharios had a reputation, because the secretary who was always there taking notes warned me after the meeting. I had then taken the opportunity to beg leave to depart early from the next meeting, explaining that I was about to participate in a karate event and that it could mean that I moved up from the sixth Dan level to the seventh Dan level of black belt. I hoped that the message would be clear, try to assault me in any way and you will regret it.

After the second day meeting, we usually had lunch and, on that day, someone had picked a club where women were not admitted. It caused some red faces and embarrassment, until one of the committee members, Adam Hill, offered to take me to lunch elsewhere. Adam was actually quite nice; he was one of the older members and I think looked at me in a kind of paternal way. He was not one of the Lotharios, and I had in fact heard him on a couple of occasions admonition other members for inappropriate comments. I accepted his offer and we went off to a place on Bond Street, leaving the rest to their own devices. Adam was known at the restaurant we went to and we were seated quickly.

"Sorry about that," he said. "Sometimes people don't think."
"It's fine," I assured him. "I have learned to accept what I cannot change. Perhaps in time, there will be more equality, but for now, it is what it is."
"Still, I'm really sorry you had to go through that," he said. "I have two daughters, both a little older than you, both recently graduated as engineers and both of whom are having difficulties with male attitudes to women engineers, there are times when I'm sorely tempted to get a shotgun and go and mete out vigilante justice."
"I suppose it will take a while before we get full equality," I said. "But for now, I just put it down to insecurity."

"I liked the way you shut down George and David," he said. "Those two are trying hard to boost their balance sheets with improved asset values, they've both got major projects on the books and would like better balance sheets to get better financing rates. I liked the way you shot down their arguments. Tell me, how do you manage to come up with all these algorithms?"

"I suppose to me, it's all very logical," I said. "I've always had a bent for mathematics and the problem is quite solvable, we, as a group, just have to decide what kind of confidence levels and limits we want to impose and what the chartered accountants will accept."

"Well, I look forward to our next meeting," he said. "I've already been able to use some of the concepts you've given us and it's helped a lot."

"I'm very happy to hear that," I said. "Where did your daughters go to college?"

"One did electrical engineering at Imperial and the other chemical at Nottingham," he replied. "They both did very well and both have jobs, but I rather think their progress will be hampered because they're women. Now that I'm faced with the situation in my own family, I'm seeing how much inequality is out there and how much prejudice, and even how my own attitudes in the past were quite biased. I've told my daughters about you and they're both intrigued and would like to meet you one day."

"I would be delighted," I said. "I sometimes find that life in the world of academia is limited and enjoy these sessions, because they're more connected to the real world, not the ethereal world of university professors and their theories. There's also a surprising amount of prejudice and discrimination against women at the colleges still and I suppose it will take time for that to change," I lamented. "There are days when the frustration level really rises. On a completely different subject, do I recall that you said that you came from Rhodesia?"

"I do," he confirmed. "I was born and grew up in Bulawayo."

"That's in the western part of the country, isn't it?" I asked.

"It is," he confirmed. "Why do you ask?"

"I met this chap," I started. "He comes from Mount Darwin."

"That's in the eastern part of the country, towards the north," he said. "It's in the middle of Mashonaland, whereas Bulawayo is Matabele country."

"Have you ever been there?" I asked.

14

"Once," he said. "A long time ago. Who's the chap from Mount Darwin?"

"His name is Ian Hartley," I said. "He's a post-grad at the college I work at, he's an anthropologist and he's just come back from the digs at Olduvai."

"And you've an interest in him?" Adam asked.

"I think so," I said. "He's nice, we had coffee the other day, he told me that his folks grow tobacco."

"That makes sense," Adam said. "We have a fairly diverse set of holdings and among them are several tobacco operations, one in Rhodesia and the others in Malawi. Our Rhodesian farm is near Mount Darwin. I don't know too much about it, I'm really focused on the minerals part of our business at the moment. We should order lunch, have you any preferences?"

"I think the salmon," I said. Adam called over the waiter who had been hovering discreetly and gave our orders. While we were waiting for the food to arrive, Adam told me a little more about Rhodesia and Bulawayo. He, like Ian, waxed lyrical about the country, but he also commented that the Smith regime was on borrowed time and that a change of government was inevitable. He himself had left the country during the War and had flown for the RAF, the Royal Air Force, in Europe and North Africa. After the War he had stayed in the RAF until after the Korean War, then he had left, stayed in London, and had found his niche in the financial markets and had joined his current employer in the late 50s.

"Thank you for lunch," I said, when we were leaving the restaurant.

"So, back to Oxford?" Adam asked.

"I need to do some clothes shopping, for shorts and other wear suitable for a river trip," I said

"My daughters like to shop in London," he said. "Let me quickly write down the names of their favourite shops and perhaps you could try them."

"Thank you, Mr Hill," I said.

"No, thank you, Dr Barclay. I enjoyed lunch and look forward to our next meeting," he said. "I'm curious to see what you have for us next and, perhaps even more curious to hear about Mr Hartley."

Adam left in a taxi and I stood pondering my next tasks. If I was going to wear shorts for my river trip, then I needed to buy some. I wanted shorts that would not make me look like a lady of the evening, with my backside hanging out, but which also did not end at the knee or below, so mid-thigh, they also needed pockets, I had to have somewhere for my car keys, and I had to be able to move in them, I might be called upon to try my hand at rowing the boat. I finally found what I was looking for at a shop that catered to the African safari market. I hoped that would not offend Ian, but the shorts were a nice length, they had pockets and fitted well, they were actually men's shorts, as the women's were hideous. I have a boyish enough figure that a pair of men's shorts still actually fitted tolerably well. I also bought a shirt there, khaki, like the shorts and a jacket in case the weather turned inclement. I decided that sandals would be good, so visited more shoe shops than I care to remember until I found what I was looking for. I had a hat, it was a rather nice straw hat that I bought some time earlier for some function or other. I went to dress shops and bought, for good measure in case things progressed well, a little black dress, after the style made popular by Audrey Hepburn and a red silk cheongsam that I bought from a shop recommended to me by my Chinese professor friend. The cheongsam looked good on me and made me look about six inches taller, it also left little to the imagination, being slit up the sides almost to the waist, my last item was a denim mini skirt that zipped up the front, all the way from the hem to the waist. For underwear, I decided that I would wait until I visited Maman, she and her friend Bridget had a boutique in Henley, Bridget and Brigitte, that sold lingerie. I had not seen the boutique yet, nor met Bridget, so this was a good opportunity to do both.

Shopping done I caught the train back to Oxford and arrived in the late afternoon, just in time to visit my office, collect the mail, then drive to Henley while the sun was still up. As I said before, Maman was French and we, James and I, had been fortunate in that she had made sure that we grew up speaking French as well as English. So now, either of us could pass as a native French speaker. To add to Maman's talents, she was also fluent in Italian and spoke Tahitian as well. When there was just the two of us, I always spoke with Maman in French, but it would be tedious here for me to record all that was said in French, and then give you the English translation, so English it is.

"Fi," she said, when I let myself in, I was fortunate Maman had given me a new key when she had had all the locks changed after the divorce, so could come and go as I pleased. "How are you?"

"Fine, Maman," I said. "And you?"

"All the better for seeing you, I was beginning to get a little lonely rattling around in this big house, now that James has gone as well. Would you care for tea, coffee, wine, something stronger?" she asked.

"Coffee, for now," I said. Maman does make good coffee and she usually serves it with little pastries that she gets from a place in London run by another French woman. I followed her into the kitchen and watched as she worked. I loved watching her, she always struck me as so capable and able to turn her hand to anything, she also had a natural grace about her in her movements. When the coffee was ready, she took it outside to the patio. It was a beautiful late summer evening and it would have been a shame to waste the sunshine. After all, England is not renowned for its sunny days.

"So, Bébé, what's up?" she asked.

"Why should there be something up?" I fenced with her.

"I know you Bébé, I know when you are happy, sad, troubled, but this is new, so, again, what's up, is it your new swain?" she asked.

"It's possible that he's the one," I said.

"Good," she said. "So, what do you need to know?"

"I know we talked about a lot about sex when you gave me the visual anatomy lesson and answered my questions then, but I need to hear it again. Does it hurt, will it be painful?" I asked. The visual anatomy lesson had been very instructive, when I had asked about sex, boys and babies, she had gone through all the details, first the dry details of procreation, pregnancy and childbirth, then she had shown me on herself and then on me where everything was, and had described function and purpose, so that I probably had had a better sex education than ninety-nine per cent of the rest of the girls in England.

"That depends," she said. She then went on to discuss first-time sex and all the ramifications. Maman was always very candid with me and she went through everything in detail. I had learned over the years not to be embarrassed by her candour and always found our discussions along these lines useful. We went on to talk about sex in general, we covered regular sex, oral sex, anal sex, male and female homosexual sex and sex-related diseases and infections, pregnancy and prevention, toys, lubricants and anything else that she felt was related. I had a few questions for her, that mainly dealt with her own experiences. Before I asked my questions, Maman went into the house and came out with two glasses of wine, she handed one to me and took the other herself. We raised glasses to each other in toast and got back to the business at hand.

"Was Dad your first?" I asked her.

"No, it was my cousin Philippe," she said. "It was 1944 and I was just eighteen and Philippe was also eighteen. Philippe went off to join the Resistance after the D-Day landings and the night before he left, he gave me the old sad sob story about going off to war and he might not come back and I fell for it. He and I met up in the attic of our house in Paris and spent the night together. It wasn't the best love making and there was quite a bit of discomfort and he withdrew at the last minute to make sure I didn't get pregnant, so all in all it was very unsatisfactory, I had asked him to stop after he first started, it hurt so much, but he didn't care and just kept going. When I thought about it afterwards, it was rape and I hated him for it and was actually pleased to hear after the liberation of Paris that Philippe was dead. Not long after that, I met your Dad in the hospital where I was volunteering. I was attracted to him and, let's face it, to a British captain miles away from home I must have looked like a million pounds, I was pretty good-looking in those days. He pursued me and, now I think, somewhat on the rebound from my experience with Philippe, I fell for him, he was gentle where Philippe wasn't, he was considerate and experienced. We were married in Paris, then I had to wait until the war was over. When he had been demobilised I joined him in England and discovered that his family had more money than mine had ever dreamed of. We stayed in London for a while and I enrolled at University College and took my exams soon after that for a degree in chemistry. I had almost finished my studies in France during the war, and it didn't take much to complete them in London. I think they were a little surprised, particularly as I scored very highly and finished with the highest marks of the year and a First Class Honours Degree. Then I had you in 1950, and James in 1952, and you know the rest. I think that sometimes the age difference created some issues, he was twenty-eight when we married and I was only nineteen, but we managed. When we first came here, I struggled with English for a while, and your Dad's French was only passable, still is, he never put in the effort to really learn, which is why I spent so much time and effort with you and James to be sure that you spoke French as well as you spoke English."

"Does Dad know he wasn't the first?" I asked.

"He never asked," she said. "It was wartime, things happened. I have no idea how many other French girls he deflowered between Bayeux and Paris and how many half-brothers or sisters you may have. We were being liberated from the Germans and girls were happy to see them go and more than a few showed their appreciation with sex. I never thought much of the Americans, I thought they were obnoxious and overbearing, but your Dad, as British, was polite, good looking and had a modicum of French, so we could at least talk."

"So, because of your experience with Philippe, you place a great deal on the mutual agreement to go ahead?" I asked her.

"Yes," she said. "You both must agree freely, if one hesitates and the other goes ahead anyway, it's rape," she said. "If you say no, then no it is, and similarly if he says no, respect that decision."

"If I come to you with issues about Ian, will you help me?" I asked.

"Of course, Bébé," she promised. "I think you know that you can trust me with your confidences."

"Yes," I said. "I have always trusted you and you have never given me cause to doubt that."

"Bébé, I will never betray your trust, no matter what you come to me with," she promised. "Even if, God forbid, you were to come to me one day and tell me that you and your Dad had done it, I'd probably never speak to you again, but I'd never talk of it. I can keep a secret."

"Are there secrets that we've kept from one another?" I asked.

"Perhaps," she said. "But for those confidences that we've shared, they have stayed secret between us."

"Are there any secrets that you've been hiding that you will share now?" I asked jokingly.

"Only one," she said. "I was never unfaithful to your Dad while we were married. I never told him about Philippe, and he never asked. I think we both decided that what was before, was before and why confuse things with old flames. I did wonder about your Dad years ago; do you remember his early assistant Janet?"

"Janet, yes, big boobs, bottle blonde, short skirts, looked like a tart half the time," I recalled. "Was that her?"

"It was, well I wondered a couple of times, but then she went, left for Australia, I think, and then stability returned," Maman said. "Well, at about the time I was wondering about Janet, I got pregnant and I was so pissed at your Dad that I told him that I was going to France to see my parents, which I did, but then I made a side trip to Sweden and had an abortion. He hadn't even known I was pregnant, so there were no questions. I think after that our relationship was always a little strained."

"I never noticed," I said.

"No," she said. "We were at pains to keep your lives as normal as possible, so never aired our dirty laundry in front of you. Tell me did he ever touch you or try anything he shouldn't have?"

"No," I said. "Whatever else he may have done; with me he was always a loving and caring father. I remember that when he took me to his gun club, there were a couple of real creeps there, and he took me aside and told me never to be alone with them, and that if I felt in any way uncomfortable around them, I should let him know."

"That's good to hear," Maman said. "Do you have any Daddy issues, have any desires for him?"

"Good Lord, no," I said. "I know some girls flirt with their Dads, which I think is really creepy, but I admire Dad for his business acumen and love him as a Dad, but the idea of doing anything else with him is weird, to say the least."

"Are there any secrets you agree to share with me, that I don't already know?" she asked.

"There is one," I said. "I don't know if you know about the great peeing distance challenge?"

"No, tell," she said.

"Well, when we were much younger, James was ten, he boasted that he could pee four feet, apparently he and his chums would have peeing competitions to see who could pee the farthest. So, I challenged him and we went out in the snow, and he peed and I measured, and he did pee four feet."

"I never heard that one," Maman said in gales of laughter. "He never said a word, neither did you, so perhaps you can both keep a secret. I often wondered what he and his chums got up to in the woods behind the house. I shudder to think now what manner of things they got up to. Another drink?"

"Please, Maman," I said. She got up and poured us two more drinks.

"What do we drink to?" she asked.

"A successful relationship," I laughed.

"A successful relationship," she repeated and we clinked glasses and drank our toast. "So, will you tell me all afterwards?"

"It depends," I said. "When the time and place is right and we're in the right mood, then I'll give you chapter and verse, also if it's a total disaster, I'll probably be crying on your shoulder."

"I will be here, Bébé," she said. "No matter what."

"I know you will, Maman," I said. "You always have been. I wonder why so many girls have issues with their mothers?"

"Competition," she replied. "My theory is that it is a very basic biological urge. The alpha female wants to dominate the group, that's me, and the beta female wants to attract the males of the group, that's you, so there is competition. It's the same with sons and mothers. The mothers see the sons as younger and more virile than the current alpha male, so use him to push the alpha male."

"You said you have no feelings along those lines for James," I said.

"I don't," she confirmed. "I'm proud of James and am delighted with the way he is, but I'm not chasing after him every minute, I think I just prefer the company of women."

"Well," I said. "I'll see how this all turns out and then perhaps, we can have another conversation and compare notes."

"I await the day," she said.

"Thank you Maman," I said. "This has been most helpful."

"Good," she said. "Now Bébé, where shall we go for dinner? I'll get us a taxi, so we don't have to worry about drinking too much. There is a couple I know, he drives and she organises, we'll call her and get them to drop us at a restaurant and pick us up afterwards. What I really like about them is late evenings and nights she goes with him, so I feel safer with them than I would in just any old taxi. So, where to?"

"Would the Catherine Wheel do?" I asked.

"Why not?" Maman said. "I'll call them and book a table and the taxi as well."

Over dinner, Maman asked me about my researches. I had just started, but already had requests from several major mining companies for models that would address the taxing issue of ore reserves. I say taxing, for a double meaning, first, it was difficult and secondly, the Inland Revenue Service wanted a better understanding of proven, probable and possible reserves so that they could tax the assets. It all came down to costs and the relative costs of extraction and processing, versus the price realisation when the product was sold. Obviously, movement between the categories was driven by the market value of the product, so it was an interesting model, something that James might find useful in his career as well.

"Would you do something for me?" Maman asked.

"Of course," I said. "What do you need?"

"I need help managing my money," she said. "As you know I got the settlement from your Dad and that has grown to almost £16,000,000, but I need to be sure that I am investing wisely. I have moved most of the money from your Dad's bank into others and I want to get the most out of it that I can. I need some regular income to manage the house and garden and some to spend on holidays and just general living."

"I'm sure that we can work something out," I assured her. "When we get home, perhaps in the morning you can show me what you have and where and I can start working on some strategies to get the most for you. The big question is risk, do you want growth in your portfolio or steady income, or a mix of both? If we talk about it tomorrow then we can agree on risk."

"How have you done with your money?" Maman asked.

"Actually, very well," I said. "I have taken a reasonably high-risk approach and it has paid off. But I don't expect that to continue forever, so am now hedging my bets against future issues and have a strategy in place to protect my portfolio when the markets turn down. For me, it's a series of mathematical models that I have been refining with time."

"How do you like your new house?" Maman asked.

"It's nice," I said. "A little big for one, but small and compact compared with yours. It's close enough to the centre of Oxford, without being in Oxford."

"Shall we call the taxi and go home?" she asked.

At home, Maman asked if I wanted a nightcap, I thought that that sounded like a splendid idea, so asked for a calvados. Maman poured two and then sat by me.

"So, Bébé," she said. "Where do you think this will go with Ian?"

"I don't know, Maman," I confessed. "I admit I am excited about the prospect of a boyfriend, but am apprehensive as I don't know what to expect and don't know what he's really like yet."

"That is to be expected," she said.

"Do you suppose he's experienced in the bedroom?" I asked.

"How old is he?" she asked.

"I would suppose twenty-four to twenty-five," I thought.

"I would say that he's probably had some experiences," she said. "How many we can't know yet, if he hasn't, then you need to look at him a little more carefully."

"Well, as I said, I'm excited and yet apprehensive," I repeated.

"I'm really excited for you as well," she said. "Will I meet him one day?"

"One day," I promised. "If the relationship goes anywhere. I did go shopping today and bought some things, in case we have a dinner date or something."

"What did you get?" she asked. I went out to my car and brought in the packages and unwrapped them for her.

"Very nice," she said of the black dress and the cheongsam. "What's the idea behind this skirt?" she asked, holding up the denim skirt with the front zipper that ran top to bottom.

"You never know," I laughed. "It may come in handy one day."

"And this shirt and shorts?" she asked.

"For the river trip and picnic," I explained.

"They look as if they're men's," she said.

"They are," I confirmed. "I couldn't find any women's that I liked, they were all either far too short, or far too long."

"What shoes do you have?" she asked.

"I bought sandals for the picnic on the river next week," I said.

"But beyond that, I don't recall many shoes that you have that I would consider as a good fit with the black dress," she said.

"I know," I admitted. "I thought tomorrow we might go shopping, I need shoes, underwear and perfume."

"Oh, what fun," she said. "We'll find shoes first then we'll go to the boutique and pick out underwear and perfume for you."

"Okay, Maman," I said. "I'll see you in the morning. I love you."

"Je t'aime aussi. À demain," she echoed.

Bridget & Brigitte

I slept well and was awakened in the morning by music that Maman had playing and by the smell of coffee brewing. I quickly dressed and found breakfast already on the table. After breakfast, Maman suggested we drive to Reading, it was a bigger town than Henley and there were a couple of nice shoe shops there. Maman drove, she had acquired a new Land Rover, a huge station wagon, blue with a white tropical roof. I think she just liked the intimidation factor when she drove it, just tit for tat, because when she drove her Lotus Elan, I think she sometimes felt intimidated by larger vehicles. Before we left, she gave me a garment bag and suggested that I hang my dresses in it. We found a place to park in Reading then walked to the first shoe shop. Inside there were racks of shoes of all colours, shapes and sizes, but fortunately, Maman had a good idea of what we were looking for and when we were finally approached by a sales assistant, with a name badge that said she was Lisa, she issued instructions. Lisa went scurrying off and came back with an armful of boxes. Maman suggested that I change into the black dress so that we could see the full effect. First, we had the court shoes, black, or black with silver. I tried on six pairs and finally found one that I really liked. It had a heel, not too tall that I would have difficulty walking, but tall enough to give me an extra two inches in height. I put both on and walked up and down and Maman smiled in approval.
"What do you think?" she asked, in French.
"Very nice," I replied, in kind. "Comfortable, nice to walk in, they even look nice."
"Is everything okay?" Lisa asked.
"I'm so sorry," Maman said. "I forgot myself there for a minute, if I slip back into French, please let me know. What do you think of the dress and shoes?"
"I think they go really well together," Lisa said. "Your daughter, I'm presuming here, but the likeness is noticeable, shows off the dress and shoes very well."
"Well, that was comparatively easy," I said. "Now what about in red?"
That turned out to be nowhere as simple. There was nothing in the shop that pleased either myself or Maman, so I did not bother changing into

the cheongsam. We settled on the black and silver pair of shoes and purchased those, package in hand we then walked to the second shop.

There we were approached as soon as we walked in the door by a very enthusiastic assistant, who introduced herself as Victoria. Maman told her what we were seeking and in short order, we were presented with an array of shoes, elegant and ugly. I quickly looked over the display and selected six. The rest were removed and returned from whence they came. For the rest, I was looking at them trying to decide which red best matched the dress, when Maman reminded me that we had the dress with us.

"Is there a dressing room that I may use?" I asked.

"This way Madame," Victoria said. She led me to the back of the shop and showed me the rooms, booths actually. I put on the red cheongsam and carried my other clothes with me back into the shop. We tried on red shoe after red shoe until one pair just seemed to work. They gave me a little more height than the black and silver shoes, and even I had to admit the effect was very elegant.

"If I may say so," Victoria gushed. "That is a beautiful dress and you carry it off so well."

"Thank you," I said. "Maman?"

"You look beautiful, Bébé," she said. "You really do."

"I'm not showing too much leg?" I asked.

"Not at all," Maman said. "The dress is supposed to present you in the best light, and this one does."

"Your mother is right," Victoria agreed, and as if to confirm her opinion I got some wolf whistles from young men passing the shop. As offended as I could have been by the whistles, it was in some way gratifying that we had put things together well.

"Now, I just need something for the denim skirt," I said. "Let me quickly go and change, and I'll be back."

"What kind of shoes were you thinking of?" Victoria asked.

"What about plimsolls?" I asked.

"I'll get some," Victoria said. By the time I was back now dressed in the denim skirt, Victoria had an array of flats and plimsolls ready.

"For good weather, you may wish to consider these flats," she said. "And for less pleasant weather, I think you're right, plimsolls would be good." I tried on both, and had to agree that Victoria was right. So, I took both.

"What about handbags?" Maman asked.

"We have a handbag department," Victoria said. "I'm sure you could find something there."

"You can't take us there and help?" Maman asked.

"I don't know," Victoria admitted. She scurried off and talked to an older lady, who came over to see us.

"Normally we don't have assistants from shoes working in other departments," she said. "But if you insist, I will authorise it."

"Thank you," Maman said. "You may wish to consider changing your policies, women do like to put together ensembles and it helps to see the whole, not just pieces."

"I agree," the supervisor said. "I'll pass on your comments to the manager."

Victoria led us off to another floor, where there were handbags, purses, belts and other accessories.

"What first?" she asked.

"I think the black dress," I said. "I don't suppose there's a dressing room on this floor?"

"I'm afraid not," Victoria said. "But if you come with me, we'll use the staff lounge." I went with her and she shooed out the two ladies who were in the lounge and I quickly changed.

"What do you think Maman?" I asked, when we returned. "A clutch purse, a shoulder bag, a sling bag, what?"

"I think go with a silver sling bag," Maman suggested. Victoria went off and came back with seven different bags and an assistant from that department. The decision was quite easy, I picked the one I liked and it met with approval from all. Then we did the red cheongsam. That took a little longer as we debated between red, which we could not quite match in colour, to gold, which went with the brocading on the dress. I picked the gold and again it was met with approval.

"What about the denim skirt?" I asked.

"Something less formal," Maman suggested. "Something like a leather shoulder bag, with a belt to match." Victoria and the department assistant went off and came back with bags and belts. I tried out several combinations and finally found the one I thought worked best.

"Very nice," Victoria said, and the second assistant nodded in enthusiastic agreement.

"Maman?" I asked.

"They're quite right," she said. So, purchases were made and items wrapped, Victoria and the second assistant, who we finally learned was April, were thanked, and we were on our way.

"So, tell me about the boutique," I suggested, as we started out on our drive back from Reading. "I know that you've had it about a year, but somehow I've never visited."

"Well, I wasn't sure how things were going," she said. "But now, I'm quite happy with the results and want to share it with you."

"How did you get involved in a boutique?" I asked.

"Well, I was in M&S, looking at underthings and I saw my friend Bridget there, we were both bemoaning the lack of anything but the ordinary, so we went for coffee and came up with a plan. That was about a month after the divorce. So, I bought a building in town and we altered it to suit our tastes, now Bridget runs it, we call it Bridget and Brigitte," Maman explained, talking about the common places to shop, Marks and Spencer and Woolworths. "It's actually doing very well, there are a lot of women of means in the area who shop with us, we're not as cheap as Woolies, or even M&S, but we offer a personal service that they cannot."

"Ah, I see," I said. "I've never met Bridget, how did you two meet?"

"We met during the divorce proceedings, she was going through the same thing, only her husband had gone off with her best friend, so she was quite bitter," Maman explained.

"I see, so misery loves company," I said, perhaps a little unkindly.

"In this, yes, absolutely," Maman agreed. "We became friends fairly quickly and discovered we had quite a lot in common. She has no children, only the house she got in the divorce and some alimony payments."

"Back to the boutique, who decides what to stock?" I asked.

"Bridget and I have a formal meeting once a month and we go through our lines, what's selling, what isn't, we also go through new lines and see if they would fit. We have been to a couple of fashion shows, that specialise in lingerie and other delicates, so now we know the manufacturers. I buy here in preference to other shops, and I do buy, I take no owner's discount or free samples, that is a good way to go out of business, I keep my own expenses separate from my business ventures.

So, here's the rain that they promised would not come, and I'm hungry, should we have lunch before we go to our shop?"

"Good idea," I agreed. She was right about the rain. It was coming down in buckets, so much for a nice weekend. If I had gone on the picnic with Ian, we would have been drenched in a few minutes.

"I know a little place in Sonning," Maman said. "Shall we try there for lunch?"

"You're driving," I laughed. "You are in the position to dictate."

The pub in Sonning was close to the river but had no views of it, which was disappointing for me. I have always liked the river, the Thames has been part of my life, in all its aspects, from the winter floods to the Idyllic summer days, just floating around. We waited in the car park for a few minutes to see if the rain would abate at all, but that seemed unlikely, so we made a dash for the door and only got slightly wet. Lunch was a pub lunch, a pork pie with a salad which we ate with a cider. The place filled quickly and soon became quite noisy and smoky, so we were glad to leave.

"This place has changed," Maman said. "It used to be quiet, now I fear it has just become another pub with a jukebox and one-armed bandit."

"Things change, Maman," I reminded her.

"They do," she agreed, sighing a little sadly. "So, lingerie?"

"Yes," I agreed. "Drive on!"

Bridget and Brigitte was nicely situated on one of the main streets of Henley and fortunately for us, there was parking for employees at the back, so we did not have to drive around the streets trying to find somewhere to park. The rain had not abated a whit, so we planned our exit and at the right time made a dash for the back door. Inside the shop was an Aladdin's cave of lace, satin and silk lingerie, some more risqué than others, there was also a counter for make-up and perfumes. There were about a dozen women there browsing through things and I counted two assistants making themselves available, but not hovering unduly. I did see two customers having purchases being rung up by another assistant as we entered. A woman, whom I assumed was Bridget, came over as soon as we arrived.

"Brigitte," she said. "How lovely to see you this afternoon."

"Bridget, this is my daughter, Fiona," Maman said.

"Delighted to meet you," Bridget said. "You're the mathematician, aren't you?"

"I am," I confirmed. Maman had evidently been bragging about me.

"So, Brigitte, are you just showing Fiona around or is this a shopping expedition?" Bridget asked.

"A shopping expedition for both of us, Bridget," Maman said. "I'm just in the mood for something different, and Fiona needs some new underwear, that is more lingerie than granny knickers, now there is a possible man in her life. What do we have that is new and exciting, did we get the new lines from Italy?"

"We did," Bridget confirmed. "Why don't you take Fiona to salon A, and I'll bring some, coffee, or would you prefer champagne?"

"Champagne, I think," Maman said. "Fi?"

"Champagne at two in the afternoon, sounds decadent, but why not," I agreed. We went to salon A, which was above the main shop, looking out over the river, it was well appointed with armchairs and a settee, its own loo and racks for clothes. I had seen the usual fitting room downstairs with cubicles, but this salon and the other across the hall that I had seen, must be for special customers. Bridget arrived and an assistant brought champagne and some strawberries. After the assistant had gone, Bridget seated us comfortably and handed around champagne and then got down to business.

"This is one of our new lines," she said, handing Maman a bra and pant set for her to look at. "As I recall you are 36B, 28, 38?"

"At last measurement," Maman agreed. I was surprised then when a side door opened and a woman about Maman's age came in modelling the same lingerie. I supposed it made sense. This way the customer could see it on without the store having to run the risk of soiled goods being returned as not wanted. It cut down on laundry, cleaning bills and wastage caused by items not being available for resale.

"This is Ashley, she is our friend and she models for us," Maman explained to me.

"I think Ashley is almost exactly the same size as you Brigitte, isn't that right?" Bridget asked.

"She is," Maman confirmed. "What do you think, Fi?" she asked, as Ashley pirouetted in front of us.

"Very nice," I said. It was nice too. Black lace, allowing glimpses of what was underneath, I could see her areolae, not distinctly, but obviously there all the same. I could also see the mass of curls that she had above her pubis. The panties were a scant covering, front and back, with spaghetti straps connecting. The bra was similar, lace non non-wired cups, front closure with thin straps. I must say Bridget and Maman had picked their model very well, showing women in their forties lingerie on a model barely out of her teens might have been attractive, but not very useful, the customers needed to see what it would look like on them, not their daughters.

"I like them too," Maman said. "I think one black, one red and one midnight blue, is that possible Bridget, do we have all those colours?"

"Of course," Bridget said. "Why not also try this, a little more daring, but for the right occasion, perhaps just the right thing." It was a bustier with suspenders, matched with panties that were just triangles of a semi-see-through fabric joined together with spaghetti straps. Ashley stripped off what she had on and put on the bustier set, no modesty here, Bridget picked up the discarded items and folded them up, probably for use again in the future. As Ashley spun around and let us see.

"Well?" Bridget asked, as Ashley paraded up and down in front of us.

"May we see the stockings as well?" I suggested, as I sipped my drink and munched on a strawberry.

"Bridget?" Ashley asked. Bridget proffered a pair of black stockings and Ashley put them on, together with the heels she had brought.

"Very nice again," I said. "I'm not sure I could see myself in one, but you never know."

"I think one black, one red, please Bridget," Maman said.

"No white?" Bridget asked. "White would look good against your naturally dark skin."

"White, no, too virginal," Maman said. "Honest to goodness sinful black or seductive red."

"If you wanted to be outrageous," Bridget said. "We have these thongs just in from France." She offered a pair of panties and Maman looked them over, then looked at me and grinned and then at Ashley who nodded her head in agreement, smiling broadly as she did.

"Wait 'til you see these," she said. "I really like them." She stripped off the bustier set and her shoes, but left on the stockings, then put on the new panties. From the front, they looked like pared-down satin panties, but the back was really different, it was just a thong that nestled between the cheeks of her backside. Her breasts hung loose and she cupped them and stood on tiptoe so that she better showed off her backside cheeks and the way that the thong disappeared between them.

"Oh, definitely," Maman said, as Ashley spun around in front of us. "What do you think, Fi?"

"Wow," I said. "You could drive someone wild with those," I added.

"I did," Ashley said. "When I first wore them at home, I thought George was going to pop right out of his britches. After that things got very steamy very quickly."

"I have to have these, Bridget," Maman said. "Let's see, two black, two red, two midnight blue and two teal green, and stockings to match with suspender belts."

"Teal green?" I asked.

"Goes with a darling evening dress that I have," she replied. "Bridget, is there a bra that goes with these?"

"There is Brigitte, it's a simple satin bra, solid, light wiring in the underside for support," she explained. "The suspender belt is also very nice, satin, closure at the back, with the proper fittings for the stockings."

"Good," Maman said. "Same colours as the panties, oh, and we should also get stockings to match the colours as well. Now Fi, what about you?"

"Okay," I said. "Bridget, would you show me some options? And, Maman, I don't wear granny knickers!"

"I can show you some options," Bridget confirmed. "What are you, 34A, 26, 35?"

"Very good," I said, impressed that Bridget must know her business, she had sized me up by look alone.

"I'll be back," she said, as she left, she thanked Ashley and asked her if she would get Anna to join us. When she came back, she was with a different model.

"This is Anna," she said. "Anna is Ashely's daughter and models for us, when she doesn't have assignments with the big magazines. Anna this is Brigitte's daughter, Fiona." Anna was gorgeous, perhaps a little skinnier than me, but I know that is what the big fashion houses like. Anna quickly disrobed, then put on a red thong and pirouetted for us.

"Very nice, Anna," Maman said. "Fi, I can see you in a pair of those. Would you like some?"

"I think I would, red, black and midnight blue, if you have them, Bridget?" I asked. "I'm not sure I'd ever have the nerve to wear them, but you never know."

"We have those colours," Bridget replied. "What else, it's your mum's treat, splurge, spend, be daring, be rash!"

"I don't know," I said. "That black set that Ashley first tried on looked pretty good, I could see myself in those, and what do you have in the way of a baby doll nightie?"

"I will be back," Bridget said. "More champagne?"

"It depends, who's driving Maman?" I asked.

"I think you'd better drive," she replied.

"So, is coffee a possibility?" I asked. This was a new experience for me, personalised service while shopping. I was sure that we would pay for it when the bill came, but Maman had made it clear that this was her treat.

"Coffee, of course," Bridget said. "I'll be back shortly. Any colour other than black? Anna, anything for you?" she asked.

"Nothing for me thanks Bridget," Anna replied. "I'll just get the set that Fiona is talking about and be back."

"Maman?" I asked.

"Whatever you want Fi," she said. "Go to town, be outrageous."

I went outrageous, the thongs, red bra and pants set, the baby doll nightie, a slip for my cheongsam, appropriately slit so that it would not show under the dress. I also got some lace items that left little to the imagination, they were just about see-through, in fact, they were see-through, with no attempt at modesty, as I said, I went with the outrageous. When Anna had modelled them, I had been a little shocked at what I could see, but thought that for the right occasion, they might be just right. Not, that I could see such an occasion in the near future, that would depend on how well things went with Ian, but if I had them then I would not be searching for something suitable when an occasion did arise.

"Now you said something about perfume," Maman reminded me.

"I did, didn't I," I admitted. "Any suggestions?"

"You might wish to try L'Interdit and perhaps Rive Gauche," she suggested. "They're popular amongst younger women. Then, there's always the old standby of Chanel."

"Let's try L'Interdit," I said. "I like the sound of that."

"L'Interdit was created by Givenchy in the late 50's," Bridget said. "Apparently Givenchy created it for Audrey Hepburn, and she has been the face of L'Interdit for a while."

"What about Rive Gauche?" I asked.

"It was created for Yves Saint Laurent by Michel Hy, it's new, only out this year, very hip, very chic and Left Bank," Bridget replied.

"May I try some?" I asked. Bridget dabbed a little on my wrist and I had to admit it was very evocative. I could imagine the Left Bank and an independent, unpredictable woman.

"Try the L'Interdit," Bridget suggested. She dabbed a little on my other wrist and I compared the two.

"I think both would be good, depending on the occasion," I said.

"I agree," Bridget said. "Use both, but pick the one that best fits what you have planned."

"What about makeup?" Maman asked. "I know you don't use much, if any, normally, but you might wish to try at least eyeliner and shadow and some lipstick, perhaps even some nail varnish."

"I know, I know," I said.

"We have quite a selection," Bridget said. "I'll get Anna to come back, she's the real expert." Bridget left for a few minutes and came back with Anna, who proceeded to give me a crash course in makeup, both types and application techniques. She had quite a variety of makes, colours and types and I finished up with some from Yardley, Mary Quant Cosmetics and Cover Girl. Mama was most generous and bought me a makeup case that Anna then filled with all the appropriate things, eyeliner, eye shadow, lipsticks of various colours and a compact case with some face powder. She also added a makeup brush, an eyelash brush and a manicure set. I do not think the latter was a hint about the state of my nails, merely the provision of the best tools for the job. I thanked Anna profusely and she told me that I could always go to her for advice.

"There is one more thing, before we go," Maman said. "Bridget, do you think you could do something with these?" She held up my shirt and shorts. I had wondered what she had been lugging around in the big bag she had.

"I should think so," Bridget said. "I presume these are Fiona's?"

"They're mine," I confirmed.

"Let's see," Bridget said. "Let's get some measurements." She measured me, it reminded me of my own excursions into body measurements, she was very thorough. "When do you go back to Oxford?" she asked.

"Probably tomorrow afternoon," I thought.

"So, what if I drop these off at your Mum's house tomorrow at about ten?"

"That would be super," I said. "You're sure it's not too much trouble?"

"Not at all," Bridget assured me. "We have to have you looking your best for your young man."

"What do you think of my venture?" Maman asked, as we drove back home in the pouring rain. It was still coming down, almost as if the heavens had opened.

"I like it," I said. "It's a market that will never dry up, the only issue is competition from the chains like M&S, the big department shops and speciality shops."

"That's true," Maman agreed. "I think where we succeed is with the personal service, we not only pick out items that women may want, we also offer a service to fit bras to women's figures. Not many of the chains do that. We have carefully picked our staff, we have three young mothers who you saw today and, on the weekends, we have two younger girls come in. We have Ashley as a model, and you met Anna who likes to come in and model for us when she's not busy with photo shoots for the big fashion magazines, Bridget and I also take turns modelling when Ashely is not available. We think Anna likes the fact that her Mum has a job with us and is earning a little extra."

"Can you afford that many staff?" I asked.

"We can," Maman confirmed. "We pay them a reasonable base pay, and then they share in commissions. We had thought to put them on commission only, but thought that unfair, and also thought that it could lead to competition between them and eventually bitchy behaviour, so have a commission element, but it is shared, so that they have the incentive to work together. It seems to be working very well."

"I saw a place near Marble Arch when I was in London this week," I said. "It looked like it was sex toys and such."

"Ann Summers," Maman replied. "It just opened this year. It will be interesting to see how it does, I think there is a demand, so do not be surprised if more Ann Summers shops are opened. I don't think we're going to go there, there are just too many complications, mainly around laws of display and local possible opposition, lingerie is one thing, sex toys is something else."

"Have you invested in any other shops?" I asked.

"Not yet," Maman said. "I'll give this a year or two and see what we learn from it, Bridget and I have some ideas, but we're waiting to see how well we do."

"I presume it pays the bills?" I asked.

"Oh, yes," Maman said. "I lease the space to the shop and all the operating expenses are covered by sales, and Bridget and I share the profits at year-end. At the end of our first year, we each drew £10,000, so not bad for the first year."

"Not bad at all," I agreed. "I had no idea there was so much money in knickers and had not thought that there were that many people in Henley."

"Oh, we have people come from as far away as Oxford, Reading, even Maidenhead, word has got around and they like the personal service. One thing you could do for me," Maman said.

"What do you need?" I asked.

"Bridget and I both noticed a relationship between certain events and then sales, apart from the expected seasonal shopping that you would expect around Christmas and Valentine's Day. Sometimes there was a direct relationship and sometimes sales either slumped or rose after different events, could you put together some kind of mathematical model so that we can plan for the future?" Maman asked.

"I'm sure I could do that," I said. "Can you give me sales by product by month, or week, would be better, then I can go back in history and see what happened when and build a model."

"I have that at home, in anticipation of you coming," Maman said. "We can look over the figures when we get home."

There was a lull in the conversation, so I posed the question that had been nagging at me for some time.

"Maman, if you feel like talking about it, why did you and Dad split?"

"It was you who put me onto the situation," she replied. "I remember you said something one day after you'd been to his office and met Felicity and seen them together. So, I hired a detective and got pictures,

pictures of him in bed with her. How the detective got the pictures I have no idea, but they were crystal clear and there was no denying it. So, I sued for divorce, and as you know got the house and a reasonable monetary settlement."

"But what I don't understand is why he went after Felicity the floozie," I said.

"Felicity the floozie," Maman laughed. "I love that, good one Fi. I thought a lot about it and decided in the end that I was too independent and not submissive enough. I should have got a clue in the bedroom, he always wanted to be on top. He wanted to always be the dominant one. I think Felicity the floozie suited him as she was happy to submit. Your father had many fine qualities, but I think he felt threatened by an independent woman."

"And, how are you doing now?" I asked.

"Actually, I'm doing very well," Maman said. "I can come and go as I please, I have enough money to indulge myself."

"Any love interests?" I asked.

"Perhaps," Maman admitted. "I met this solicitor, Portia, I really like her and we enjoy spending time together."

"I didn't know you had feelings that way," I commented.

"Neither did I until I met Portia," Maman said. "It was quite a surprise to me, how quickly we became comfortable together."

"So, have you?" I asked.

"Have I what?" Maman teased. "The answer is no, not yet, we'll see how things go. So, here we are, home, shall we have coffee?"

"That sounds wonderful, Maman," I said.

Maman parked the Land Rover in the garage, I blessed Grandpa for having the foresight to add an attached garage to the house, with electronically controlled doors, and to make it big enough for future needs, so it would accommodate four vehicles. Maman closed the door and we took our packages inside.

"I'd say that was a successful day," Maman said as she made coffee.

"I suppose so," I said. "It's all a little new and different to me, I've never really taken that much interest in beauty products."

"That's because you didn't have any kind of love interest," Maman laughed. "This is all new and exciting for you, and for me."

"We'll see," I said. "I've only had coffee and lunch with him so far, so don't go marrying me off in your mind too soon!"

"I won't," she promised. "You were never one to have much interest in the other sex, not like James who always seemed to have a least one girl on the string at any time. There were times when I wanted to tell him to be a little more thoughtful, but things seemed to work out without him alienating all the girls around here, or, God forbid, knocking one up, it still surprises me that they all seem to still like him, even though many of them have been jilted by him."

"I wonder what Ian's really like?" I said, more to myself than Maman. "He was really nice when we had lunch and could talk about things other than digs and anthropology."

"If things do progress, what do you plan to do about birth control?" Maman asked.

"I was going to go to the Family Planning Clinic this week and talk to them," I replied. "My leaning is towards the pill, but I need to learn more. What did you and Dad used to do?"

"We used condoms," she replied. "It was sometimes a little difficult because we couldn't predict when or where the situation might arise, so, if you were to search the house carefully, you'd find odd ones in the strangest of places. I know that you know that the pill doesn't protect against any nasty diseases or infections he might have, so for a while at least you might want to consider both."

"Sort of belt and braces approach," I laughed.

"So, tell me again about how you met?" Maman asked.

"I finally broke down and went to one of the college dinners," I said. "I was seated at the high table with all the ancient profs, and there he was at another table with some grad students. I was looking at him, actually thinking that he looked rather nice, which I know you'll find surprising, it's not normally me, and then he looked at me and our eyes met and locked. It was like magic, I felt something that I'd never felt before. I asked the prof next to me who he was and he told me, and think he did the same thing, because our gazes broke for a minute, but when I looked back at him, it was the same thing. So, after the dinner, I went up to him and said hello and told him my name, and told him that I'd not seen him at one of the dinners before. I know it sounds pretty lame now, but I didn't know what else to say. That's when he asked me if I fancied getting some coffee the next day."

"That sounds as if there's something there," Maman said. "I know what it's like, you're not sure whether to continue looking, or turn away in embarrassment, but it's like an electric shock almost. Then what?"

"We just went our separate ways until the next day," I told her. "We met for coffee and exchanged small talk, and I still liked the look of him, so I offered to buy him lunch. We talked between mouthfuls at lunch and talked about everything, I could have spent the afternoon just chatting to him, but we both had things to do. Then he asked me out for today, but I needed to talk to you first, so I made the excuse that you had a job you needed me to do. So, we agreed on a date for next Saturday, for a picnic on the river, if it's not raining."

"And If it does rain?" Maman asked.

"I'm not sure," I said. "I'm not ready to jump into bed with him, this will be my first time, so I want it to be right."

"At some point, you will have to tell him that," Maman cautioned.

"I know," I agreed. "I'll have to pick the time. But I want to get to know him a little better before I go there."

"Are you hungry?" Maman asked.

"Not really," I said. "I wouldn't mind something to drink, though."

"What about some Sauternes and grapes?" Maman suggested. While she busied herself, I was thinking about what we might do on Sunday and decided that I might need to know how to dance.

"Maman," I said. "Would you teach me how to dance?"

"You can dance," she replied.

"I don't mean Tahitian," I said. "I mean modern, European."

"What, throw your arms in the air and gyrate your hips style of dancing, do the twist, or more classic waltz, foxtrot and the like?" she asked.

"I was thinking of the waltz and the others if you would," I said.

"We'll do that tomorrow," she promised. "Does Ian dance?"

"I've no idea," I said. "But let's suppose we do get on and we go to one of the college balls at the end of term, it would be nice to be able to dance and not just shuffle around the floor."

"Shuffling around the floor with the right man has its plusses," she said. "But I know what you mean. We'll go through the basic moves tomorrow and see if we can get you ready."

"Thank you Maman," I said. "I'm not sure what I'd do without you, you've always been ready to help, even coming away to college with me that first year, I don't know if I ever thanked you, but thank you."

"It was a delight," she said. "I love you Bébé, I always will. I know your teenage years were difficult and we did the best we could, but it must be hard to be streets ahead of your class."

"It had its moments," I said. "Are we going to finish that bottle?"

"We might as well," she said. "There's not that much left."

We finished the bottle then decided it was time for bath and bed. I bathed first while Maman sat and chatted with me. It was common for us to do this, one would bathe and the other sit and talk, it was a good time and a good way to spend time together.

"So, Bébé," Maman started. "How do feel about this adventure?"

"I'm excited to see where things may go with Ian," I replied. "But I'm also apprehensive, what if he doesn't like me, what if I find out that he's just a creep, what if we go out on a date and then he never calls me again?"

"It would be easy for me to just reassure you and tell you that he would be foolish not to see in you what I do," she said. "But that would not be honest. One can never tell how another will respond, so the only thing you can do is take it as it comes and see how you like him."

"But what if he just wants to use me and then go his merry way?" I asked.

"I think you should be able to get a sense of that possibility," she said. "But again, it's possible, in which case you have to chalk it up to bitter experience and try not to let it colour your whole view of men in general. There are those out there who are, what did you call them, creeps, but there are more who are not. Sadly, there is also the culture in the colleges of male competition and they make pacts with one another to see who can bed the most. That may be a view coloured by my own observations, and may also be dated, but I fear not, fundamental behaviours do not change, or if they do it's very slowly."

"I've never felt this way about a man before," I sighed. "It's thrilling and yet terrifying. It's all questions, all what ifs, and there's the nagging fear at the back of my mind, what if he doesn't like me?"

"That seems unlikely," Maman said. "He asked you to go for coffee, he asked you to go on a picnic, so he must have some interest. When you had lunch, did you laugh a lot?"

"We did," I confirmed. "He made me laugh, but he was also serious, he was interesting and either well-read, or a very good storyteller."

"That could be good or bad," Maman commented. "You will have the chance to begin to form your opinion of him when you go on your picnic, who is providing food and drink?"

"He is," I replied. "He said he would bring food and wine."

"Do you remember how to row a boat?" Maman asked.

"I think it's probably like riding a bicycle," I said. "Once learnt, then never forgotten. I remember when Dad took us out on the river, I tried and it took me ages to get it right, but James managed straight away. But in the end, I succeeded and managed to row in a straight line, and to row without splashing everyone else in the boat."

"Take a towel with you, in case you do that again," Maman laughed. "But don't take so much that you need a suitcase, perhaps leave a change of clothes in your car. That leather shoulder bag you just bought should be all you need in the boat."

"Okay, enough about me and my issues, tell me about Portia," I said.

"We met on the train," Maman explained. "I was going to London for a meeting with my solicitors about my will, which by the way, you're still in, and she was on the same train. We said hello and I saw her again briefly at the law office, where I learned that she is a partner, then I saw her again the evening of the same day, she was on the same train as me again, coming back here. We got talking and found that we had a lot to talk about, and a lot in common. She had a husband, but he left to go off with his business partner, a man she'd known for years, but who she never suspected as having a relationship with her husband."

"You said that she's a solicitor?" I asked.

"She is," Maman confirmed. "She works for the same expensive legal firm in London that I use, but she works mainly on intellectual property cases."

"And she lives in Henley?" I asked.

"She does," Maman confirmed. "She has a cottage out on the Marlow Road."

"What's she like?" I asked. "And, I don't mean height, weight, et cetera, you told me off about that when I described Ian."

"She's fun to talk to," Maman said. "Makes me wonder sometimes why I ever pursued men. I'm not sure if our relationship will just be friends and companions, or if there's something else there. Like you, I'm excited and yet apprehensive."

"So, will I get to meet her at some time?" I asked.

"I'm sure you will," Maman replied. "This weekend she had some conference in Birmingham, so was away from Friday, she said that she was going to travel back from Birmingham directly to London, so there was no chance for you to meet her. Are you going to lie there all night and let the water get cold, or should I just run a fresh bath?"

"Oh, sorry, Maman," I said. "I'll get out and let you either add more hot water, or run a new bath." That was the signal that chatting time was over and it was now time to clean, dry and go to bed!

The picnic

I awoke early and the weather had cleared up a little and there was actually watery sunshine, so I dressed quickly and decided to go outside and run around the property. Once around was about four miles, so I planned to do two laps. When I started out, I caught a glimpse of Maman, also running, so set off to catch up with her. I had to really push it, but after almost a lap I was coming up behind her. She heard me and looked behind quickly.

"Fi," she said. "If you want to go ahead, please do."

"No," I said. "I'll just stay and run with you." Maman was wearing the minimum of clothing, she had on a bra that I had seen before, it was her own design and supported her when she ran, so a lot less strain on the back muscles and very little bouncing. I had very little in the way of breasts, but even for me bouncing was noticeable when I ran, so for Maman, it must have been really noticeable. For the rest, she had on a brief pair of bikini bottoms that gave her complete movement of her legs. I could not help noticing that her legs were still good to look at and very powerful, I saw that in each stride she took. She really did run with ease and power. It made me wonder what the Olympics and others were thinking when they would not have events for women over 800m. The theory was that women were not physically capable, what rot! I stayed behind Maman for the rest of the way and was feeling a little puffed by the time we went in. I had not done that in a while. Apparently, Maman had, because she was panting less than I was. I checked our time, eight miles in forty-eight minutes, not bad, not bad at all!

We went in and Maman put on some coffee, then asked me if I wanted breakfast.

"Let me just have a shower first and put on some clean clothes," I said. "Give me ten minutes or so." I showered quickly then put on the minimum of clothing, the house was warm enough that I could have easily gone without.

"Coffee or tea?" Maman asked when I went back to the kitchen. She had obviously also showered and was standing there in the kitchen in a dress that zipped up the front, something that I thought would have been worn by Emma Peel from The Avengers.

"I think coffee, thanks," I replied. Maman made such good coffee that it was a shame not to take advantage of the opportunity to have some.

"Did you enjoy the run?" she asked.

"I did," I said. "Cleared my head and set me up for the day. How are you today?"

"Very well," she replied. "I just was enjoying the run around the property, I should get back into the habit myself, I've been lazy the past few weeks. I don't want to go to seed, I've worked hard to keep my figure. It was good to have you just behind me, it kept my pace up and gave me something to aim for, not to let you pass me!"

"I think you look good, Maman," I told her.

"You're not just saying that?" she asked.

"No, not at all," I reassured her.

"Breakfast?" she asked. "I have some muesli, fruit salad and bran muffins."

"Sounds good," I said. "Disgustingly healthy, in fact. So, dancing lessons today?"

"Dancing lessons it is," she said.

We started with the waltz, simple enough, one, two, three, one, two three. Maman put on some music then showed me how to hold my partner and then how to follow. She took the male part and led, while I trailed around after her.

"Try not to stamp on my toes too much," she said as we did our first circuit around the living room.

"Sorry," I said.

"The secret to ballroom dancing is to accept the fact that there is a leader and a follower," she said. "In social occasions today, the male partner, or pseudo-male partner in an all-women gathering, takes the lead and the female partner follows. The trick is to observe and pick up on his moves, the small things he does that tell you what is coming next. The male has to remember the choreography and the female just follow. I know, all very male chauvinistic, but that's the way it is. Now again, this time follow my lead." I did, trying very hard to follow, and I succeeded. I was dancing!

"Very good," Maman said. "You learn quickly and I know you are light on your feet from the martial arts you do. So, what about the foxtrot?"

"Okay," I said.

"The foxtrot timing is different to the waltz," Maman explained. "Think of it as, slow, quick, quick, where the slow steps have twice the value of the quick steps. Does that make sense?"

"I think so," I said. "Could you just spin around the room on your own and let me see?" She did and I got the idea, now the trick was going to be following my leader.

"Now," Maman said. "When you dance with your partner, you need to align your bodies, not nose to nose, but right side of your body, to right side of his, that way he can see where you're going and your feet are less likely to collide. Shall we try?"

"Okay," I said. We lined up and set off. We had a few collisions before I got the idea and soon enough, we were foxtrotting up and down the room. The next trick was to elegantly turn at the ends of the room, or follow the perimeter. After an hour we mastered that for both the waltz and the foxtrot.

"Coffee break, I think," Maman said. "You're doing well Bébé."

While we drank our coffee, I thought about dances and dresses. Did I even have an evening dress. I wondered about the cheongsam, could I class that as an evening dress, and more to the point could I dance in it, or was it too confining. I thought that the answer was probably no, at least for me. If I were an expert dancer and I knew my partner well, I could probably do it, but just as a beginner and with a partner of unknown ability, I concluded that it was not a good idea. So, perhaps an evening dress, suitable for dancing was next on the acquisition list. But that bridge would be crossed when there was an actual need. We were about to start back into other dances, when Bridget arrived with my shirt and shorts.

"Here we are," she said. "Try these on." I did as requested and had to admit the fit was superb, more form fitting than they had been, but yet still loose enough so that I could move.

"Very nice," Maman said. "Thank you, Bridget."

"I am happy to be able to help," she said. "Must dash, see you on Monday, Brigitte."

"*À bientôt,*" Maman replied, then she brought me back to earth with her next question.

"So, what else, rumba, cha cha and quickstep?"

"If you think I can manage all those and remember the others," I laughed.

"Of course, you can," she said. "Now, quickstep, essentially slow, quick, quick, so four beats to the bar, consider it a fast version of the foxtrot. Think of it as the slow steps on your heels and the fast steps on the balls of your feet."

"Okay," I said, hesitating a little, Maman made it sound so simple. Anyway, she demonstrated, then we tried together, and I have to say I did quite well, no feet collisions and I managed to keep to the beat. Next, we tried the rumba, another slow, quick, quick, rhythm.

"Fine," Maman said. "But some movement of the hips would be better. This is a Latin dance and some more movement of your body is needed, think of it as luring your man, by flirting with him with your body, not stiff as a board, but more flexible, with some real hip swings, in time with music of course." I think I got that right, but when she came to spinning me around, I am afraid I made a total hash of things and then collapsed in laughter.

"Let's try that again," Maman said. "This time, just let me spin you around, and remember, you're the one following, so take my lead."

"Yes, Maman," I said, much chastened by her tone. I was probably trying her patience, so focused on the task at hand and managed to execute a spin turn quite nicely.

"Much better," Maman said. "Now, again!" We went around the floor a dozen more times, each time with some improvement, until I have to admit, I was actually enjoying it. Finally, we did the cha-cha. In many ways, the rumba and cha-cha were more fun than the waltz, foxtrot or quickstep. Those latter seemed to me to be about more formal balls, whereas the rumba and cha cha, were just fun to do and not only allowed a little exhibitionism, but expected it. So, more of a chance to show off, have fun and just enjoy the music and dance, something more akin to the Tahitian dance that I was used to. I realise that ballroom dancing aficionados would probably disagree most vehemently, but that was the way I saw things.

"Good," Maman said. "Now I think we take a break for lunch, and then we'll run through all the steps quickly again."

"Thank you, Maman," I said, and I really meant it. I had never taken an interest in dancing before, but she had introduced me to a whole new experience.

We had lunch and then ran through the steps again and I think that even Maman was pleased with my progress.

"Very good, Bébé," she said. "Now, you have the basics, so if the occasion arises, you will be more prepared than most there, the only ones who will do better are those who have taken dancing lessons."

"How did you learn?" I asked.

"We had lessons when I was at school," she said. "After that, it was just practice. So, what do you want to do for the rest of the afternoon?"

"I should get back to Oxford," I said.

"Of course," she said. "I hope the weather cooperates and your date on Saturday goes well," she said.

"I'll call you afterwards," I promised. "We're meeting again for coffee tomorrow, so is that another date?"

"Possibly not," she thought. "More of the still getting to know you process, before the real date. This is the second coffee?"

"It is," I confirmed.

"Well, have fun," Maman said. "I love you Bébé."

"I love you, Maman," I replied.

I collected together my belongings and borrowed some books from her library and then said goodbye and drove back to Oxford. I still had a job and work to do, and I needed to review all the notes I had taken at the meetings in London the week before. I also needed to quickly run a Hoover around the house, it had not seen any cleaning for almost two weeks now, so dust was starting to accumulate. My discussions with Maman had been most useful, but I was still torn between the excitement of the possibility of a real date and the apprehension of whether or not it would go well. All the clothes I had just acquired might just be a total waste of money if things did not go well.

I was at the coffee shop at eleven the following morning, but there was no Ian. I ordered coffee and waited and waited, looking at the others in the shop, particularly the couples, speculating on whether or not there really were couples or just two people enjoying good coffee. I was disappointed that he was not there, I had not really appreciated how much I was looking forward to seeing him again, it had been a whole week since we saw each other. It was almost thirty minutes past the hour when Ian finally did come. I had almost given up hope that he would be there, and was thinking about leaving, but there he was, grinning, flustered and looking more than a little windswept.

"I'm so sorry I'm late, I called your office, but you'd obviously already left," he said. "My thesis advisor was in the mood to debate, discuss and denigrate today and I had a difficult time getting away."

"I'm glad you came anyway," I said, and I was, I really was, I had been looking forward so much to seeing him again and I had begun to despair that this might be a relationship that never really started, but all that had vanished, like a puff of smoke, when he had walked through the door. "Are there problems?"

"A few," he admitted. "Do you remember last week, the paper I was reading?"

"I do," I said. "You said that it might raise some issues."

"It does, or at least in the mind of my thesis advisor," he lamented. "Personally, I don't think that it does, but I'm not the advisor."

"I'm so sorry," I said. "Coffee?"

"Yes, please," he said. "Actually, a stiff drink might be better. So, enough of me, how was your week, were you able to help your mother?"

"I was," I told him "Maman has a boutique and she wants me to create some algorithms that give her leading indicators, so that she can better prepare for movements in sales. I came away with tons of sales data for the past year, all sorted by week, now I need to go back and look at the calendar and see what happened when and try and correlate events to sales trends."

"You can do that?" he asked.

"I should be able to come up with something," I said. "There is often a correlation between events and buying patterns, all I need to do is work out what that is."

"What kind of boutique does your mother have?" he asked.

"It's mainly a lingerie shop, with perfumes and makeup, very much a feminine shop," I told him.

"And it does well?" he asked.

"Very," I confirmed. "Maman and her partner offer a service that the large shops do not, so she has a following and that is growing."

"So, if I wanted to buy you something for Christmas, that would be the place to go?" he asked.

"If you decided that that's what I would like," I replied. "Ah, here's your coffee, are you hungry?"

"I can't have you buying me lunch again," he protested.

"Why not?" I asked. "I'm saving you the cost of lunch, so that you can provide the picnic on Saturday. Aren't you glad we didn't go this last Saturday, it poured and we would have been like drowned rats?"

"It did rather rain, didn't it?" he agreed. "The forecast for this week isn't much better, so we'll have to see."

"We will," I agreed. "But back to lunch, are you hungry or not?"

"I am," he said.

"Fine," I said. I called over the waitress and ordered two lunches, then sat back and watched him as he sipped his coffee, obviously still ruminating on his morning. He must have been putting in long hours, because he was looking tired, he looked distracted, so whatever the issue was with his thesis, it must have been weighing on him. He looked up and saw that I was watching him and grinned, our eyes met and again there was that electric shock feeling that ran through me.

"Sorry to be such a wet blanket," he said. "You're looking beautiful today, I'm so glad I came, I almost didn't come, but now I'm here you have just brightened my day."

"So, I didn't look beautiful last week?" I teased.

"You did, you did," he assured me. "I just meant that it's so nice to see you again, you've just brought a ray of sunshine into my life."

"You think I'm beautiful?" I asked. "It's not a compliment I get very often, people usually have other words for me."

"I know," he said. "Ice queen, iron maiden, and a few others I've heard. But that's because they don't see you as you."

"Why, thank you, Mr Hartley," I said. "I thought it was only Maman who really saw me."

"No, it's me as well. So, tell me about your London trip," he said.

"A lot of meetings," I complained. "But that's why I have the job. The people from the companies all have slightly different agendas, so it's an interesting exercise. I give them my thoughts, the mathematics and the logic, they then have to work out how well that fits their particular situation. I did have lunch with another Rhodesian."

49

"You did?" he asked. "Anyone I might know?"

"I doubt it," I said. "He's from Bulawayo and left in 1940 to join the RAF and he flew in England, and never went back."

"So, he's older then?" Ian asked.

"He is," I confirmed. "We spent some time talking about his two daughters and the challenges they face as engineers. Ah, here's lunch, dig in!"

"Bon appétit," he said. We ate and talked between mouthfuls. I asked him about Africa and the sounds and experiences of the wild.

"There's something about the bush," he said, after chewing for a few seconds. "The sounds, the smells, as well as the birds, and animals, I particularly like the early mornings, when the sun is just coming up and the night time chill goes and the day time heat starts. We should go one day."

"Really, you'd take me to Africa?" I asked.

"I don't know about take," he laughed. "I'm not sure I could afford two tickets from here, but I'd love to show you around one day."

"I'll hold you to that," I said. "I've only been as far as Italy, and that was a while ago. I've been to France a few times, but mainly to see aunts and cousins. How do get to Rhodesia from here?"

"Unfortunately, the options are not that great, one way is to take South African which goes London, Lisbon, Luanda, then Salisbury," he explained. "The other option is BOAC to Jo'burg, then a short trip north. Either way, it's an overnight flight from London south, but you can usually see the dawn come up over Central Africa, which is pretty spectacular."

"How did you get back and forth from Tanzania?" I asked.

"BOAC or British Caledonian or East African Airways to Nairobi, then drive to Arusha, and then to the dig," he explained.

"Are there many people at the dig?" I asked.

"There's usually a few," he said. "Mostly students like me, but there are also the local staff who help with the dig and who cook, clean and all that sort of stuff." As he talked about the dig and the people there, I watched him entranced by the animation in his voice and in his face. He clearly liked what he had been doing. I suppose I had noticed it before, but he did have quite an accent, very similar to that of Adam Hill. I decided that he looked like a younger blond Alain Delon, he had the same kind of features.

"Are you listening?" he asked, interrupting my thoughts.

"I'm so sorry," I said. "I was miles away there for a minute, I was deciding which famous actor you remind me of, and I've decided that you're my Alain Delon."

"Well, I suppose I should be thankful for that," he laughed. "Look at the time, I have to go, I have some stuff to finish and then another session with my advisor. We're still on for Saturday?"

"Weather permitting," I said.

"Well, if it rains, what about the pictures?" he suggested.

"I like that," I agreed. "I'll see what's playing where. Will you call me tomorrow?"

"I'll call, are you in your office all day?" he asked.

"I should be," I thought. "I've a lot of work to do, so don't plan to agree to anything else. I've enjoyed this, talk to you tomorrow?"

"Tomorrow," he agreed. I got up from the table and he followed and then I took the big risk and kissed him. Just a quick peck on the cheek, but enough to make me decide that more would be nice. Something to look forward to on our date. He grinned at me and took my hand and kissed it and said, *"Au revoir chérie."*

"À bientôt," I replied. I left him standing there, his hand against his cheek where I had kissed him and decided that I had been forgiven my inattention, judging by his even broader grin. I wondered about the *chérie*, did he simply use it as part of his farewell, or did he really mean it, did he think of me already as his sweetheart?

When I got home that evening there was a parcel waiting for me. It was from Maman and contained all that one might need for a night of passion and for one who was alone, a very lifelike vibrator. She had written an explicit set of instructions on how to best use that, including hints as to how its use would make eventual sex easier. I tried it out that night and wondered why I had never got one before. I fantasised about Ian and debated with myself long and hard about just when I would invite him to the house, with the aim of bedding him. Perhaps he was having the selfsame thoughts and fantasies, only time would tell. The date on Saturday might answer some of those questions. Perhaps I was indulging in teenage-like fantasies, and was looking to rush things, in my mind, my newly found romantic side was warring with my rational side, and for now the rational won. For all his apparent charms, Ian might be the one, but he might not be, and I was not about to start hopping into bed with every man I kissed on the cheek.

The week dragged on, I made considerable progress on my project and even managed to find some correlations for Maman and her leading indicators, Ian called me on Tuesday and I called him on Wednesday. I also visited the local Family Planning Clinic, where I spent quite some time talking to a counsellor. I think at first, she had thought to just give me some advice on methods of contraception and warn me of the perils of sexually transmitted diseases, but the discussion had gone far beyond that as I asked question after question, seeking to clarify what I had read on the subject. I wanted data, not just statements, so asked about incidence of unwanted pregnancies when using IUDs, diaphragms, condoms, cervical caps, interrupted coitus and the pill, etc., so we talked about all those and I was shown examples of each of the physical barriers and learned about the risks and perils of coitus interruptus. I also wanted to know the broader health risks associated with each method and in the end, I did come away from the clinic with a supply of birth control pills and had started taking them immediately. I had also acquired a goodly supply of condoms of various sizes, recognising that pills alone do not protect against diseases. I was impressed by the job Maman had done in telling me what I needed to know, she might not have had the statistical data, but everything else she had told me paralleled the pitch from Family Planning.

On Thursday and Friday, Ian had gone up to London to the British Museum to do some research, so we missed our now daily calls. He had a reader's card for the museum which gave him access to papers and documents that were in the archives. So, as there was no Ian to talk to, I called Maman and asked her if she would spare me the time and come over on Friday night and stay the weekend. I also got a call asking me to be in London on Wednesday and Thursday of the following week to review some new proposals over the treatment of assets. Maman duly came on Friday and got ready to hold my hand, as it were, as I ventured out for my first real date. Finally, Saturday arrived and with it the sunshine. Early in the week, it had looked as if rain had set in for a month, but as the week progressed, the clouds started to thin and by

Friday afternoon the sun was peeping through the remnants of the clouds, and by Saturday morning the sunshine was actually quite brilliant, with a cool autumn day, giving beautiful clear air, it was probably going to be the last day of the year when a picnic was possible without layers and layers of clothes to keep out the autumn chill.

When I arose on Saturday, I dressed with care. When I had been a teenager at school, it had been easy, school uniform was dictated. Then went I first went up to Oxford there was more freedom, but there were still the gowns to be worn over normal clothes, which were typically knee-length skirts and a pullover in the cold months and a blouse in the warmer months. As a postgraduate I had even more freedom, so had gone to jeans and pullovers. Now as a post-doctoral fellow, dress standards were expected again, so I wore severe suits, that reflected a business approach to things, all very straightforward. Now I was dressing for something and someone else. For underwear, I decided that swimwear might be a good option, as who knew, we might land up in the drink, so I decided on a black string bikini that I had, but had never really used. I did take a change of underwear with me and picked the La Perla that I had got from Maman's boutique, I put on the shorts and shirt that Bridget had altered, then the sandals, lastly, I dabbed on, as the famous quote would say, five drops of Chanel No. 5, but I substituted Rive Gauche. For makeup, I had Maman assist me and we applied eye shadow and eyeliner and lipstick. I decided to forego face powder or blush, I was likely to blush enough naturally without having to rely on rouges. I got myself a towel, in case of rain, or very splashy rowing, a cardigan and a rain jacket and a change of clothes and put them in a bag to be left in the car. When all was done, I looked myself over in the mirror and was quite satisfied, my last items were a pair of Ray-Ban Aviator sunglasses and my straw hat, I put those on as well to see the effect and was agreeably pleased.

"What do you think, Maman?" I asked.

"*Très belle,*" she said. "You look like a film star trying hard not to be recognised."

"You really think so?" I asked.

"I do," she confirmed. "But more importantly, what do you think?"

"I think I look pretty good," I said. "The alterations that Bridget made, make all the difference."

"Nervous?" Maman asked.

"Yes," I admitted. "I'm excited and nervous, I've got butterflies in my stomach like I never had for even orals. I'm half tempted to call it off and hide here."

"No, you'll be fine," she assured me. "Just go and enjoy the day, if it goes nowhere, at least you had a nice day out on the river."

"But what if I make a fool out of myself, what if I say the wrong thing?" I asked.

"You really like this Ian, don't you?" Maman commented.

"I do, Maman," I said. "He's fun to talk to, he makes me laugh, I get goosebumps when our eyes meet, is this love?"

"Perhaps," she said. "Do you think of him often?"

"I do," I confirmed. "I look forward to his calls, and am excited to call him. But how do I know what he thinks about me?"

"You'll find out soon enough," she assured me. "I think he must like you, or else why would he call you each day?"

"I suppose you're right," I admitted. "But all the same I'm still nervous, I don't want to mess things up."

"You'll be fine," she assured me, again. "Now, if you bring him back here this afternoon, I will leave and go home, I wouldn't want to get in the way."

"Thank you, Maman," I said. "I mean it, thank you for everything. I love you."

"I love you, Bébé, good luck," she said as I left the house.

I drove through town to the bridge, my heart a flutter as I thought about the coming day. All our meetings so far had been in public places, this would be the first time we were actually alone together. Once over the bridge, I turned off and took the side roads to the waterfront and found a place to park. There were quite a number of people already there, taking boats out on the river. But not the kind of boat I was looking for, these were narrow boat barges, the kind one can hire for a week for a holiday, and other smaller motor boats, typically for the weekend amateur boater. I walked along the waterfront looking for Ian, and for the first time in my life, I was actually attracting attention, I was getting wolf whistles. As offensive as this was on one level, it did mean that I was presenting myself in a good light for Ian. Finally, I saw him, talking to a couple of other people. He looked up when he heard the whistles and saw me and grinned, an ear-to-ear grin. I walked up to him and gave him the standard French greeting, a kiss on each cheek, and mine were not the fashionable air kisses where you just fake the thing, I actually kissed him, which caused some comments and whistles, and an ooh la la, from the peanut gallery that was the closest narrow boat.

"Morning Fiona," he said. "These are my friends April and Paul, April, Paul, meet Fiona."

"*Enchantée,*" I said, wondering if we were going alone on our picnic, or if he had invited others. My question was answered soon enough.

"April and Paul have the boat that we are borrowing," he explained. "I promised to have it back to them by three this afternoon."

"Thank you for the loan of the boat," I said. "It's very kind of you."

"April and Paul have a pub close to here," Ian explained. "I got to know them quite well when I was an undergrad, I roomed with them then and do again now." Then he went on to properly introduce me to them. "Fiona is a whiz at maths and has a research fellowship at the college. Unlike me, she already has her doctorate and isn't having to deal with an advisor who seems bound and determined to make my life hell."

"So nice to meet you, Fiona," April said. "You've got a lovely day for your picnic. Ian, I've put all the food and wine in the boat already, I've also put in a blanket, towels in case you get wet, and two raincoats and hats. Enjoy yourselves."

"Thank you," I said. So, that was how Ian was managing food and wine, he had his own personal caterer.

"Would you like me to park your car at our pub? I'll put it at the back where we park our own car," April suggested. "It's only a few minutes away, and I could bring it back here at three."

"That would be super, it's the green Mini Cooper, just down there," I said, handing her the keys, and pointing down the street to where the car was parked. I had no idea what kind of neighbourhood this was, but it did occur to me that the car might be better parked off the street.

"Shall we go?" Ian asked. He took my hand, and there was an electric thrill as our hands touched. He helped me into the boat and showed me where to sit and gave me the tiller lines, then he climbed in himself and took the oars. He gave me a quick tutorial on which line to pull to go which way, and the instruction to keep us to the right side of the river in the direction we were facing, so opposite to driving, then Paul shoved us off and waved as we drifted out into the stream. "Have a good day," he said, then I heard April's aside to him, "She's gorgeous, I'd give anything to have a figure like hers." That was a new one for me, no one, apart from Maman, had ever described in those terms before. I did wonder how April had made that judgement, as my eyes were hidden by the Ray-Bans and my face was partially obscured by my hat. I also wondered about her comment about my figure. I had always seen myself as having a rather stick-like figure, some bumps and curves, but not what one would typically think of as in any way voluptuous, not like Maman or her friend Ashley.

As Ian propelled us upstream, I took the time to look at him. He was, like me, dressed in shorts and a shirt, but he had no hat and no obscuring sunglasses. He had well-muscled and tanned arms and legs and he handled the oars with practised ease. He just sat there, rowing slowly, grinning at me, as if he had stolen something of great value, like the proverbial cat that got the cream.

"What?" I asked him, wondering just what this hunk of man could find to grin at so incessantly. Was my hat on straight, had I left buttons undone, was there hair sticking out at odd angles, what was it about me that he found amusing?

"I'm just so happy that you came," he said. "You look particularly beautiful today."

"Thank you," I said. "I tried."

"You look like a film star," he said. "Big floppy hat, sunglasses, the works."

"That's just so that I can hide my face," I laughed. "I'm not used to being seen out in public with handsome men."

"You have a nice tan," he said, looking pointedly at my legs.

"It's not a tan," I said. "It's just me. Mémère Monique, my maternal grandmother, was Tahitian, apparently Pépère, maternal grandfather, was there as part of the French administration and they met, married, then went to France to live. I think those genes from Tahiti passed down to me as well, which is why I'm a little dark. Maman, is a trifle darker than me and the Tahitian shows more in her, she's quite exotic looking, but we still look very much alike. Hold up for a minute there's a boat coming down the river under the bridge."

"Anyone behind him?" Ian asked.

"Not that I can see," I said. "When he's gone, it should be clear for us to go under." We waited and a narrow boat came downriver. It just about cleared the bridge, another foot or two of water in the river and it would not have made it. After he had gone by, we rocked a little in the wake of the boat, then Ian started rowing again and I steered us towards the centre of the bridge. Once clear we went back to our side of the river and continued our slow passage upstream. On our left were allotments, lots of them, I had had no idea they were there and how large an area they covered. It just showed how cloistered my time had been in Oxford until then.

"Could you grow tobacco here?" I asked Ian, indicating the allotments, thinking right after I asked the question, what an inane question to ask. Why was I asking questions about tobacco, when I should be trying to learn more about him. But I was trying hard to get over my shyness and apprehension, normally I was the confident one, taking the lead, taking charge, but somehow this was different, I had not really had a personal relationship with anyone outside my family before, so was in new country trying to discover how to behave and what to talk about.

"No, not warm enough," he replied. "Kentucky in the States is hot in the summer, as is the area around Mount Darwin, where my folks have their farm."

"You didn't want to stay in the family business?" I asked.

"No," he said. "I don't like smoking, never have and I wonder if we're not doing a disservice to people by hooking them onto tobacco, I can't believe it's good for you. Sorry to sound a little preachy, but I've never been a fan, again sorry, but do you smoke, I've never seen you smoke?"

"Never have," I said. "I don't like the smell, particularly as things get old and stale. Back to today and the river, how far up are we going?"

"For now, I thought we'd go up to Godstow, through the lock and stop at the Trout Inn for a beer and a loo break," he replied. "Then, upriver a little farther, I know a nice spot for a picnic. We should be at the Trout Inn by ten, ten-thirty, so after that picnic at noon or so, then a leisurely trip back."

"Hold on a minute Ian," I warned. "There's a boat coming out into the river from the side ahead."

"It's probably coming from the Oxford Canal," he said, as he glanced behind him at the boat ahead. "There's a connection here that links the river to the canal. We'll wait until he's clear." We sat for a minute or two watching the boat and her captain as he made the turns from the canal cut into the river. Fortunately, the river was quite wide there, perhaps made so by dredging, that there was room enough. The captain waved to us as he went by and we started out again on our journey upriver. The banks were now lined with trees on both sides and it was really rather pretty. I was trying to think of things to say to make conversation, but was not sure what to talk about, apart from the weather, Ian's visit to London, or the state of politics in England. I decided that there really was no need, why not just enjoy the day, enjoy the scenery, the company and the experience of being gently propelled up the river, with the sounds of water lapping against the boat and the oars dipping into the water. I just concentrated on keeping us pointed the right way and far enough from the bank that the oar did not hit bottom in the shallows. When the occasional boat did pass us, going upriver, I tried to make sure that I gave it as much space as I could, without getting us into the shallows. There seemed to me to be more boats going downstream, I counted five in the space of fifteen minutes, but they passed us easily enough, leaving just their wakes and the gentle rocking that followed. Fortunately, none of them was in a hurry, so the wakes were small, not big enough to really rock the boat or break over the sides and get us wet.

We went upriver farther and we then had a break in the trees on the right and allotments on that side. Then the trees thinned out on both sides and we went past a small marina, with what looked like boats for hire. We passed under a footbridge and the trees vanished on the right, to be replaced with open meadows, with the occasional cow coming down to the river to drink. I looked at Ian and saw that he was watching me, still with his broad grin on his face, I could not help but grin back, that day was beautiful and I was just enjoying being there with him. When our eyes met there was still that electric thrill, like the first time our eyes had met, but it was now more comfortable, less alarming to me as it had been when it had first happened. We wended our way upriver, until I saw ahead a lock on the left side of the river.

"Is this the Godstow Lock coming up?" I asked Ian.

"It is," he confirmed. "Change of plan, stay to the right and go up that channel on the right, we'll go straight to the Trout Inn without going through the lock." I kept us to the right, past an island, then a weir, then I saw a junction.

"Which way ahead?" I asked. "Left or right?"

"Take the left channel," he said. "It'll take us up to the inn, when we get there, put us over to the right and lay us alongside the wall they have. We'll tie up there and go and get a beer and a loo break."

I steered us up the left channel and we shot under a footbridge that seemed to go from the inn to the island and Ian kept enough way on the boat that I was able to steer us into the bank while he shipped the oars.

"Neatly done," he said. "Couldn't have that better myself, have you spent much time in boats?"

"A little when I was a teenager," I told him. "Dad used to take us out of the river in Henley and showed us the basics."

"Does the basics include rowing?" he asked as he hopped out of the boat and tied us up.

"Some," I replied.

"Would you like to try when we go back downstream?" he asked. "The current will be with you, so it won't be hard work."

"I'll give it a try," I agreed.

"Great, then I can just sit and watch you," he said, grinning even more than he already had been. "Let's go and get something to drink and use their loo."

He held out his hand to help me out of the boat and I got the thrill again as I took it. This time he did not let go and held my hand as we walked up to the inn. It felt natural walking with him, hand in hand and I was almost sorry when he let go to open the door for me. Inside I took off my sunglasses, so that I could see, and I also took off my hat. "Ian, howzit," the man behind the bar said.

"Chris, howzit man," Ian replied. "I didn't know you worked here."

"Worked here for a year," Chris replied. "You back from Tanzania?"

"Just recently," Ian said. "Chris, this is Fiona, Fiona, Chris, he's another transplant, but he's from South Africa."

"Can't trust these Colonials," Chris laughed. "We seem to meet up, no matter what."

"Chris and I met when I first came to England," Ian explained. "We actually met on the boat coming over here and have been friends ever since, I've even forgiven him for being a Boertjie."

"So, what can I get you?" Chris asked.

"Fiona?" Ian asked.

"Do you have something in the line of a white wine open?" I asked.

"We do," Chris confirmed. "We have a Louis Jadot Pouilly-Fuissé, which is very nice, Ian?"

"I'll try some," Ian replied.

"I thought you wanted a beer?" I asked.

"No, wine sounds good," he said. "Can we use your loo, Chris?"

"Of course," Chris said. "It's left and left again, Fiona." I took the opportunity to go off and spend my penny and when I came back Ian and Chris were deep in conversation.

"Chris and I were talking," Ian said. "He suggested that rather than go up through the lock, we just take our boat a little below the footbridge here and pull in to the island and have our picnic there."

"Is that okay?" I asked Chris. "We won't be buying food or drink from you."

"No, man, it'll be fine, you just bought some wine, so you're paying customers," he replied. "We sometimes have events on the grass just over the bridge, but not today and I doubt we'll get many customers today who will want to go across the bridge, so go and enjoy yourselves."

"Thank you," I said, then took a sip of my wine while Ian scurried off to the gents. "This Pouilly-Fuissé is good." I told Chris.

"Glad you like it," Chris said. "Do you work with Ian?"

"No," I said. "I'm in mathematics and he's into digging, as you know. We met at a college dinner and we've been seeing each other for a couple of weeks."

"You know he's nuts about you, don't you?" Chris asked. "I've never seen him like this before."

"Really?" I asked. "I know he sits and grins at me a lot, but he hasn't really said anything yet."

"*Ag*, I'll have to chaff him about that," Chris laughed. "Big, brave Ian, just sitting and grinning, I like that."

"You like what?" Ian asked as he joined us.

"You sitting and grinning like a Cheshire cat," Chris laughed. "Go, have fun, enjoy your picnic. There's no rain forecast, so it'll be fine."

We finished our wine and left to go back to our boat. Ian took my hand in his in the most natural way, and it felt right. Still that electric thrill when he did and still such a joy to hold someone's hand. He handed me into the boat, then untied the line and pushed us off. We drifted downstream a little until he had the oars in place again, then he spun us around and headed off downstream. A little way below the bridge he spun us around again and we started to look for a suitable place to pull in.

"What about there?" I suggested, pointing to a small area that almost might be a cove.

"Looks good," he agreed and he quickly rowed us into the bank and beached the boat. He hopped out over the bow and made our line fast to a tree, then I handed him the baskets of provisions that April had provided, plus the blanket. We found a flat spot under the trees that provided a nice view of the river, had some shade, but also allowed the sun to come through, and spread the blanket out and sat down. Then Ian rummaged through the baskets and laid out the food and wine that April had provided. It looked to me enough to feed the five thousand, but I suppose that was an exaggeration. There was roast chicken, salads, rolls, savoury pastries and dessert pastries and some white wine and some water.

"Well, we won't starve," Ian said. "What would you like to eat?"

"We have plates, why don't you just make me a plate," I suggested.

"I can do that," he said. "Will you pour the wine?" I found the corkscrew that April had put in one of the baskets and opened the wine. It was another very nice Pouilly-Fuissé and April had wrapped it up well when it was cold so it was still fairly cool. I poured out a couple of glasses and handed one to Ian.

"What do we drink to?" I asked him.

"I think to a wonderful day, thank you so much for coming with me," he said.

"I'm thrilled to be here, so here's to us," I said, chinking my glass against his.

"That's good," he said. "I'll have to thank April when we get back."

We ate, we talked and we just enjoyed the place and each other. I looked out at the river and was struck by the sheer beauty of the place, by the way the sun played through the trees and cast pretty patterns of shadows on the grass, by the way the water rippled as it was disturbed by the breeze and by more water coming down from the weir and by the occasional fish that jumped or duck that dived down to dabble for edibles in the shallows.

"This is very *Wind in the Willows*," I commented.

"It is," he agreed. "But sadly, although we might see Ratty and Mole and Mr Toad, we're unlikely to see Otter, they've all but been wiped out by the effects of pesticides like DDT and Dieldrin, which got into the food chain."

"Do you have otters in Rhodesia?" I asked.

"We've two," he replied. "The speckled-throated and the African clawless, I've seen both in different places."

"What kind of bird is that?" I asked, pointing to one wading in the shallows and working its way towards us.

"That's a grey heron," he said. "But look, out past it there are some grebes diving in the deeper water." We both drifted off into silence as we watched the river and listened to the sounds, the birds, the water running and the occasional human sound from the inn.

"More wine?" I asked him.

"Please," he said. "Can you imagine a more perfect day, the sun is shining, there aren't three million people all milling around and best of all there's you?"

"I'm glad I came," I said. "Tell me about growing up in Rhodesia."

"I did that before," he said. But he laid back on the blanket and did go ahead and tell me again about his early life, his trials and tribulations at boarding school in Salisbury and his trips out into the bush.

"So, what kind of music do you like?" I asked.

"I like some of the classics," he replied. "Plus, the Moody Blues, Leonard Cohen, the Who, and you?"

"Like you, some of the classics, I like the Moody Blue as well and I'm also a big fan of Mireille Mathieu and Françoise Hardy," I replied.

"I've heard of Mathieu, but not Hardy, another French singer?"

"She is," I confirmed. "You've never heard of her?" I got no answer so I looked at him and he had fallen asleep, pastry in hand. I sat and watched him, watched his chest rise and fall with his breathing, watched his face as it relaxed as he fell into a deeper sleep. I was sure that he had been working long hours trying to get his thesis done and was probably tired out and this was such a relaxing place, and he had rowed us upriver, then had lunch and two glasses of wine, it was not surprising that he had fallen asleep. I reached over and gently took the pastry from his fingers and heard him sigh, I hoped with contentment. I looked at his face, the lines that were already showing, whether from stress, or weathering I could not tell, those lines gave his face some character, he was not just what Maman would call a magazine cover. I saw his whole body relax and then conform itself to the ground as he slipped into a deep sleep.

I let him sleep until just before two when I gently tapped him.

"What?" he said, waking with a start. "Did I go to sleep on you, I'm so sorry?"

"Don't worry, you looked as if you really needed the rest," I assured him. "We probably need to start packing up and heading back."

"What time is it?" he asked. "God, it's almost two! You shouldn't have let me go to sleep, what kind of day out is it for you, when all I do is sleep?"

"I enjoyed just watching you," I told him. "Really, I had a lovely time, I'd come again." We packed up our things and stowed them in the boat, then he helped me into the boat and then he pushed us off into the stream. We had a little confusion as we switched places in the boat, me to row and him to steer, but we got ourselves sorted out before we ran into any trouble. I unshipped the oars and pulled us around to head back to the inn.

"I need a pee break before we go back," I told Ian. I pulled us up to the inn, unshipped the oars and let us drift into the bank. Ian managed to put us alongside neatly enough that he could hop out and secure the boat. He then gave me a hand out and we both, hand in hand, scampered into the inn to find the loo.

"Hey, Fiona, Ian, how was the picnic?" Chris asked.

"I fell asleep," Ian said.

"Ha," Chris laughed. "You've got the prettiest girl with you and you fall asleep, man, I worry about you!"

"Is it okay if we use the loo?" I asked Chris quietly.

"No, man, it's fine," he said. "You remember, left and left?" I did indeed remember and hurried off to spend another penny at the Trout Inn. When I returned Ian was also back and talking to Chris.

"Thank you, Chris," I said. "See you again one day?"

"I hope you'll come again," he said. "Even if Ian doesn't come, you come, you brighten up the place!"

We went back to the boat and organised ourselves a little better this time and Ian shoved us off. I spun us around and we headed off downriver. It had been a while since I had rowed, and I was probably going to have sore muscles the next day, but I was going to row us back and was determined to show that I could do as good a job as he. Once into the rhythm of the stroke it all came back to me and I settled into an easy row. Ian was right, of course, I was going with the stream, so we made better time going downriver than we had made earlier. We were passed by a cabin cruiser and there were some comments about the fact that I was rowing and Ian was just sitting and steering occasionally. Ian just grinned and waved, he was enjoying himself.

"You didn't tell me that you were good at this," he accused me, after the cabin cruiser had gone.

"I haven't rowed for quite a long time," I said. "I'm surprised I remember how. What are you grinning at now?"

"I'm just happy watching you row," he said. "You make it look so easy, I should have asked you before if you knew how and then you could have rowed us upriver."

"No, that was your job," I said. "Next time you can do all the work."

"Oh, so there will be a next time?" he asked, laughing.

"Of course," I said.

"Well, good," he said, grinning even more, if that were even possible. "You just keep rowing there and I'll just sit here and enjoy the view." I was not quite sure what he meant by the view, the scenery around us or me, was I showing something that I should not be or did he just like to look at me?

We made it back to our starting point at ten to three, and were just beginning to unload the boat when April arrived with my car.

"Good trip?" she asked.

"Perfect," I said.

"Except that I went to sleep on her," Ian confessed.

"I told you that you were looking tired," April said.

"It was lovely," I assured April. "I was happy to just sit and watch him sleep. When he's asleep he's rather angelic, I'm not sure that that would be true if he was awake."

"Too true," April laughed. "I'm glad you enjoyed your picnic."

"Thank you so much for the super lunch, I think we both ate far too much," I said. "But at least I got to work off a little of mine on the way back, not like lazybones there who just sat and grinned at me the whole way back."

"He did, did he?" April laughed. "Typical, I'm glad you had a good time," April said. "Just leave everything in the boat there, I'm going to move it down to our boathouse and I'll empty it there, here are your keys Fiona." She hopped in the boat and was gone in a minute headed downstream somewhere.

"Is there somewhere I can drop you?" I asked Ian.

"No, thanks Fiona," he said. "April's pub is just down the road and I can walk there in a few minutes." Now came the awkward part, did I just say goodbye, or did I say goodbye with a kiss, what? I opted for the safe approach and said goodbye with a quick kiss on the cheek. I do not think he even expected that. He held my hand, not wanting me to go, but I needed to go, I was not ready for anything further, just yet, perhaps after a few more dates, plus I needed to tell him at some time that he would be my first, so that he was prepared.

"Thank you for the lovely day," I said. "I'll call you on Monday."

"Promise?" he asked.

"Promise," I confirmed.

I drove home and Maman saw me arrive.

"You're alone," she commented. "How did the date go?"

"It was super," I said. "We rowed up the river, had lunch, he went to sleep for a while, then we rowed back and here I am."

"He went to sleep?" Maman asked.

"I think he was tired and it was such a relaxing day, that he just fell asleep after lunch and a glass or two of wine. I spent a couple of hours just watching him breathe," I said. "It was actually rather sweet; I was able to really look at him without him grinning at me at the time."

"He was grinning at you?" Maman asked.

"He does that a lot," I explained. "It seems that whenever he sees me, he grins."

"He's got it bad," Maman laughed.

"That's what his friend Chris said," I told her. "We stopped at the Trout Inn in Godstow for a pee break and he knew that bloke behind the bar; while Ian was in the loo, Chris told me that Ian was nuts about me."

"Bébé, I'm so happy for you," Maman said. "You go and change your clothes; I'll make dinner and then you can tell me all about the day."

65

The challenge

I spent my Sunday doing my washing, cutting the grass and other chores around the house. There might well be romance in the air, but the mundane things of life continued. I had the pleasure of Maman's company, so all the chores were done quickly and we chattered away while I was busy. I blithered on about Ian and how much I liked him and how he made me laugh and the electric thrills I got when he took my hand. We talked about first kisses, not the peck on the cheek kind that I had been doing, but a real kiss. Maman told me that I would know when the time was right, and to not rush things just for the sake of ticking it off my list. She went home Sunday afternoon and I was left with an empty house, so I put on loud music and fantasised about Ian.

On Monday I was actually happy to go back to work at the college and get ready for my meetings later in the week in London. Ian called me just before ten asking me if we could meet for coffee. I was thrilled and told him, same time, same place. I finished what I was doing and waited and paced and waited until it was time to go to the coffee shop. I was there first and had ordered my coffee when he arrived. He was not grinning.

"What's up?" I asked him. "No smiles today."

"I'm having issues with my advisor," he said. "But we can forget him for a while, how are you, any soreness from the rowing?"

"A little," I confessed. "I hadn't done that in a while and I used muscles I hadn't used in a while. Coffee?"

"Please *chérie*," he said. I got the attention of a waitress and she came and took his order, then he continued. "I've a question for you, have you ever shot a rifle?"

"I have," I said. "Why?"

"I belong to the rifle club, and we're having an event on Saturday," he partially explained. "It's part of the Freshers' Week events, where we try and recruit new members. Ten of us are having a shoot-out, but with a twist, we each have to bring a girlfriend and she has to shoot as well, and the aggregate score wins, all to show that the club is not just dry, boring, target shooting, but that we do have fun at times."

"That does sound like fun," I said. "When and where?"

"Saturday at nine in the morning, weather permitting, at the small-bore range, which is at the Mayfield Road complex," he said. "The last time I asked if you had done something, you said yes, but you didn't tell me the whole story, so can you shoot?"

"I won't embarrass you," I promised. "I think I can guarantee to hit the target each time, you said small-bore, what are we talking about?"

"We use single-shot bolt action twenty-two rifles," he replied. "Ever shot one?"

"I have," I confirmed. "It's what Dad started us out on. What distance are we talking about?"

"Twenty-five yards," he said. "If you've shot before, we have a good chance of winning, I don't recall any of the others saying that their girlfriends could shoot. We'll give you all a range briefing and basic lesson, then you'll get ten shots for practice, then you'll shoot for money, ten shots each at a separate circle on the target sheet."

"There's money involved?" I asked.

"Just a figure of speech," he laughed, and it was good to see him laugh, I had just discovered that I did not like to see him unhappy. "But I'm willing to wager that there will be side bets, no puns intended there."

"In the interests of full disclosure, I should tell you that in my Dad's shooting club, I'm reckoned to be the one to beat, but I've never shot in a competition outside the club," I said.

"So, is that challenge?" he asked.

"I didn't mean it as one, but if you like I'll try and see if I can outshoot you," I replied.

"Is there anything you're not good at?" he laughed.

"Yes, netball, lacrosse, hockey, all the girls' sports," I replied.

"Why do you suppose that is?" he asked.

"I think two reasons," I said. "First, I never played well with others, I just didn't like people much as I was growing up, outside of my own family. And, second, when I did play it was always with girls two to three years my senior, so I overcompensated by being aggressive, so was frequently penalised, or even thrown out of the game, so no one really wanted me on their team. When I had to play a sport, I was usually the fourth or fifth reserve and spent most of my time sitting."

"Shame," he said. "If you don't like people, why spend time with me?"

"Because I like you, idiot," I said. "You make me laugh, you put up with me and I just like being with you."

"Even when I fall asleep on you?" he laughed.

"Even when you fall asleep on me," I said, remembering fondly the time he had slept. "I spent the time just watching you, weird I know, but it was very nice, I liked watching you breathe in and out and the little twitchy smiles on your face when you were dreaming. What were you dreaming about?"

"No idea," he said. "You should have asked me when I woke up. God, look at the time, I'm sorry, I have to go, I have a department meeting in five minutes. Call me tomorrow?"

"I will," I promised. "The rest of the week is difficult, I'm in London Wednesday, Thursday and Friday morning, so tomorrow we should work out what to do on Saturday."

"Okay, *au revoir chérie*," he said, leaning over and giving me a peck on the cheek.

"À bientôt, chéri," I replied.

At my office, I looked at my schedule for the week and thought that if I rearranged things for my trip to London, I could play truant on Friday and go to Dad's shooting club and practice a little. Then I got back to the work at hand and buried myself in the mathematics of asset valuation. I wished, as I had done many times before, that the college had a better computer and easier access to it. Spending time in the card punch room was not really that productive and the wait times for the jobs to be run were sometimes downright annoying. I never worked how the arcane system of job scheduling worked and used to think that it was probably influenced by who brought what pastries for the computer operators. The college had been toying with the idea of teleprinter access, but that had yet to come to anything. I think the problems lay with the college hierarchy, they were mainly academics who were lost in the ethereal world of literature and classic languages; mathematics, engineering and science were necessary evils to allow them to advertise the college as serving the needs of all. It struck me that the theoretical physics people must have even greater frustrations than me, they depended on computer models to explain their ideas about how atoms worked and what was going on in the clouds of electrons that whirled and whizzed their way around the nuclei.

My Tuesday coffee date with Ian was almost cancelled. I had had a call from the mathematics department head who wanted me to give a lecture to some undergraduates. I wanted to know more and why, so had spent quite some time talking to him about what, when and where and only tore myself away when it was almost eleven. I arrived late at the coffee shop and Ian was already there, idly stirring a coffee and staring at the door. He grinned when he saw me, a delighted grin that told me that today was a better day for him.

"So sorry to be late," I said. "I was being pressured to give a lecture on statistical methods to an undergrad class, the usual prof managed to fall off a bicycle and is in hospital at the moment with a fractured femur."

"Ow," Ian said. "That'll take a while to mend, does this mean they'll want you to step in and help?"

"I don't think so," I said. "I think they have a plan, but just needed someone right away as a stopgap measure."

"When is this lecture?" he asked.

"This afternoon," I said. "I'll need to have a working lunch deciding just what it is I'm going to say. I have to give an introduction to statistical methods, I've done it before, I just need to look over the material I used before and decide how much to change, if anything."

"Maybe I'll come and listen," he said.

"That would be nice," I said. "Mathematics 201 at two."

"Okay," he said. "Now, Saturday, do you want to meet me there?"

"Why don't I pick you up at your digs and we'll drive together?" I suggested. "We're supposed to be going as boyfriend, girlfriend."

"I like that," he said. "You remember where we picked up the boat?"

"I do," I confirmed.

"About two minutes' drive past that, the Billy Goat," he said. "Does this mean that I can tell all and sundry that you're my girlfriend?"

"Yes," I confirmed. "Now, what do I wear, are we shooting standing, kneeling or prone?"

"We typically shoot prone, so wear trousers," he suggested. "I don't want people peeking up your legs when you lie down."

"You don't want?" I laughed. "What about me?"

"I'm just taking a proprietary interest," he said.

"Oh, so now I belong to you?" I asked.

"No, no, that's not what I meant," he spluttered. "I just don't want a bunch of blokes leering at you, you do have rather nice-looking legs."

"Why, thank you," I laughed. "So, how are things with you and your advisor?"

"Not brilliant," he sighed. "This is turning out to be a nightmare, I'm having all my conclusions challenged. I'm not sure where this will end."

"I'm sorry to hear that," I sympathised.

"Ah, well," he said, sounding very sorry for himself. "At least there's you! You brighten up my life."

"As do you," I said. "I must dash, I've got this lecture to think about, I'll be in London for the next few days. I'll pick you up at your digs at what, eight-thirty on Saturday?"

"Eight-thirty, right," he said. "If it's raining and the shoot is called off, we'll go and do something else, perhaps the pictures, I'll check what's showing."

"It's a date," I confirmed, then gave him the usual peck on the cheek and left, perhaps on Saturday, after the shoot, I would actually kiss him properly."

Ian did show up for my lecture that afternoon, he sat in the back and even took some notes. I was disappointed in the students, they all seemed to lack curiosity and the questions were all of the 'will this be in the test' genre, so very little thinking about what I had been saying. I was able to talk to Ian briefly after the lecture then he had to go off to his own appointments. Early the next day I took the train to London. I got a local train to Didcot, then joined a faster train with limited stops to London's Paddington Station. Then it was a Tube ride to the City where our meetings were held. I was intrigued to hear what George and David were proposing now. At our first meeting, I heard them out and it all seemed very logical, but something was nagging at me, something that my brother James would have seen immediately. Then it dawned on me.

"George," I started. "This looks very exciting, but isn't there an issue with open pit mines?"

"I'm not sure what you mean," George replied.

"Well, forgive me if I don't understand the niceties of mining, but in an underground mine you can always sink the shaft a little deeper and come at the ore deposit from lower down, but in an open pit, don't you have to take off everything from the top down? If you have high-value ore lower and low-value ore higher up, don't you have to remove all the lower values before you can get to the good stuff?"

"She's right," Adam said. "You might get away with a little high grading in a pit, but in the end, you can only take out what has been uncovered."

"Dammit," George said. "I thought I'd cracked it. How could I have missed that?"

"You're thinking like an underground bloke," one of the others chimed in. "In our pits, we have to accept the fact that there is often an oxidised and or low-value area high up and we have to remove it before we can get to the high values."

"I can modify your algorithm so that that is reflected," I suggested.

"Thanks," George said. The meeting continued in a similar vein for the rest of the morning and then we broke for lunch. After lunch, we listened to a representative from the Inland Revenue who explained the current regulations and some changes they were proposing. In my view their logic was flawed, so I pointed out why the valuation system they were proposing could be challenged, and that they would likely lose all challenges. He disagreed, but then that was his prerogative. We finished at about four and sent him on his way and agreed to meet the next morning to create some strategies to counter their moves. Then I excused myself and went off to take James to dinner.

I took a taxi to my hotel first and dropped off my suitcase and briefcase and changed into something a little less severe, but which would probably surprise James, a pair of jeans and a crimson blouse. Then I took the Tube to the South Kensington station then walked up Exhibition Road to the hall of residence where James was staying. He must have been waiting for me, because he came out to meet me as soon as I got there. He had a place already selected for dinner that was a short walk away, A French restaurant, a place where I was sure that he would not normally eat as his budget did not stretch that far. It was interesting, for all Dad, and Maman for that matter, was well off, James, and I while I was at college, were on budgets, and tight budgets at that. I had been lucky with the exhibition I had won in that it gave me extra spending money, but James was on the basics, except for an annual grant of £100 from the Overseas Mining Association.

"So, James," I asked. "Now that you've been here two whole weeks, what do you think?"

"I'm glad I came," James replied. "The curriculum is set, first year is all basic stuff, common to many of the engineering courses, and we get extras like mineralogy, classes that are more mining-related come in the second and third years. We also have to go and work in mines in our summer vacs, but they seem to have that pretty organised with the mining houses."

"How many in your year?" I asked.

"Thirty-two," he said. "We've a mix of overseas and home students, from Ghana, Zambia, Indonesia, Malaysia, Australia, Turkey, South Africa and the rest of us are homegrown. You remember my friend George from school, he's in the class."

"What's the hall of residence like?" I asked.

"Not too bad," he said. "At least it's warm, so will be nice in the winter. There's a bar downstairs and a refectory, so won't starve or die of thirst. One rule that is constantly being tested, no girls overnight, women are housed elsewhere. I suppose in time that may change, but it does seem a little archaic. Here we are, after you Fi."

We walked into the restaurant and were shown to a table, I noted that James had put on a tie for the evening, and that all the other patrons wore them as well and concluded that this must be one of those places where jackets and ties will be worn. I took off my coat and sat down. James looked at me and then looked at me again. "You've changed your wardrobe a little," he commented.

"I thought it was time," I replied. "I see you dressed up tonight."

"I was told that no ties here meant no table, so thought I'd better make sure we didn't get turned away at the door," he laughed, then he looked up as a waiter brought us menus and then left us to our deliberations.

"So, Fi, I heard that you've met someone?" James asked, peering over his menu.

"I have," I confirmed. "His name, as if you didn't already know, as I'm sure Maman gave you some information, is Ian, he's a Rhodesian anthropologist. What about you?"

"No one yet," he bemoaned. "But I've only been here a couple of weeks. The male-female ratio here is not the best for dating, probably about ten to one the wrong way, but there is the music school down the road and the French Institute nearby, the challenge will be to actually meet someone. As you might imagine, there are no girls in my class and I've only seen a handful in the common lectures, I think there's a couple in Civil and Electrical. Most of the women here are in physics, chemistry, biology, botany, zoology and mathematics. Back to this Ian, is it serious?"

"I think so," I told him. "You know I've never been one for boys, but Ian is different, I like being with him, he makes me laugh, he grins at me a lot, we went for a picnic the other day."

"That's it for your dates, you went for a picnic?" he asked, looking at me as though I was from the moon. "That's the sum total of your dates?"

"Well, we do meet for coffee often and call each other each day if we can, and we've had lunch together a couple of times," I said. "I'm going with him to the rifle club on Saturday for a boy-girl shoot. We shoot as a couple and aggregate score wins."

"Do the others know he's bringing in a ringer?" James asked.

"I only told Ian this week that I can shoot, so probably not," I admitted.

"Is there money riding on this?" James asked.

"Officially, no," I said. "It's supposed to be an exhibition kind of thing to attract new members during Freshers' Week."

Further conversation was interrupted by the waiter who came back and asked in a very poor ersatz French accent if we had made any decisions. I'm afraid that I treated the poor man badly and launched off into a stream of idiomatic Parisian French, which left him at a complete loss. Fortunately for him, the owner overheard and came over to interpret. We settled on food and wine and then asked the owner about his antecedents. He had come to England just after the War and had established the restaurant. He had enjoyed success and was now thinking of opening another. His greatest challenge was finding staff. His chefs were French, he would bring them over on three-year contracts, but the wait staff and rest of the kitchen staff he retained locally and that, for him was always a challenge. I gave him my card and told him that our cousin, second cousin actually, Dion, was training to be a chef and that one day he might be of interest. I think the card rather surprised him and he looked at me and asked about the Doctor title. I confirmed that I was indeed a doctor of mathematics at Oxford University and that he was welcome to call upon me at my office should he ever be in Oxford. I think he had us pegged for a couple of students living it up for once.

Dinner was surprisingly good and the wine we had selected was very good. The bill reflected that, but I had room enough in my budget for the occasional splurge, and if I could not treat my brother once in a while, I would have thought myself a poor older sister. On the walk back to his hall, we talked about my project and the contacts I was making in the mining industry, one day they might be of use to James, so it would pay for me to at least to be considerate towards them all, and not alienate any. At his hall I kissed him goodbye, in the French fashion, then walked back down Exhibition Road to the Cromwell Road and hailed a taxi, it was late enough that I saw no reason to be riding the Tube alone.

The next day, there were more meetings and things actually went well, I had plenty to work on when I got back to my office. We set the next meeting for a month away, now that I was into the serious business of creating complex algorithms there was no need to meet any more frequently. We finished earlier than I expected, so I went home, there was no need to spend another night in London. On Friday, I decided that I would forego the office and instead drove over to Henley to see Maman and to visit the gun club and see if I could still hit targets. Maman was not home, so I went straight to the gun club. Henry, the range master saw me and waved.

"Miss Barclay," he said. "I haven't seen you in ages, how's Oxford?"

"Fine, thank you, Henry," I replied. "How are you?"

"Busy," he said. "We're getting ready for some clay pigeon shooting tomorrow, what brings you here?"

"I've been invited to partner in a shoot-out tomorrow," I explained. "Boy, girl team, aggregate score wins. I'm probably a little rusty."

"So, what are we talking about?" he asked.

"Small-bore, twenty-two single shot bolt action," I replied. "I think all shots taken from prone, but am not certain of that."

"Why don't I set up some small-bore targets, what range?" he asked.

"Twenty-five yards," I told him.

"Fine, let me get a rifle and some ammunition and let's see how rusty you are," he suggested.

I followed him to the clubhouse, where he collected a rifle, boxes of ammunition and a box of targets, then we walked out onto the range. It was overcast, cool and not much wind, so shooting conditions were pretty good. He left me at the shooter's station and walked out to the twenty-five-yard markers and pinned up three targets. When he came back, he told me, left standing, centre kneeling and right prone. I opened up a box of ammunition and took out ten shells that I lined up on the bench. Then I put on glasses and ear protection and took my stance. I was rusty, out of a possible one hundred, ten times ten, I managed only eighty-two. Next was kneeling and I managed to inch that up a little to eighty-eight and finally prone, I inched up a little more to ninety-two. For someone who had consistently shot one hundred that was a bit of a disappointment to me. I was shooting inconsistently. I actually shot as low as a six on one target, way off the mark.

"Remember your breathing," Henry commented. "And relax, you're as tense as a cat waiting to pounce on a mouse, relax and breathe, now again." I waited until Henry had replaced the targets, then shot again, this time with much better results, ninety-eight, ninety-nine and finally one hundred.

"Better," Henry said. "Just relax a little more and manage your breathing, you've done this before, you'll get back into it quickly enough, just take your time."

I took my time and did several more rotations until I was consistently getting one hundred, and only one ninety-nine. When I was in my teens and had just started shooting, I used to resent Henry's comments and instructions, but over time I learnt that I should listen to him and then I would shoot better. I had not noticed but we had collected an audience, there were several club members who had arrived and who had come to see who was shooting.

"Anyone fancy a go?" Henry asked.

"No thanks," was the general response.

"She doesn't bite," Henry said. "I don't think any of you have met Miss Barclay, sorry, Dr Barclay, she's the daughter of William Barclay, one of our long-standing club members."

"Are you the one that wrote the paper about windage and muzzle velocities?" one of the newcomers asked.

"I did," I confessed. "I was just a teenager then, but the mathematics of it all fascinated me."

"I tried to read it," the man said. "But a bit too erudite for me, I got lost in the math, but I got the general idea."

"Well, I should probably leave you to it, Henry, thank you for the time and the instruction," I said.

"Good luck tomorrow," he said.

I drove into Henley and stopped at Maman's boutique. She was there closeted with Bridget, going over accounts and orders.

"Fiona," Bridget said. "What a lovely surprise. How are you?"

"I'm fine, thank you," I replied. "And you?"

"Fine, thank you," she said. "Have you come to see your Mum?"

"I stopped at the house and you weren't there, so I wondered if you'd be here," I explained.

"Well, we've just finished here," Maman said. "I was thinking about lunch, Bridget, would you like to join us?"

"I would love to," Bridget said. "But I have a date, so perhaps another time?"

"Of course," Maman said. "So, Fi, what really brings you to Henley on a Friday morning?"

"I'll tell you over lunch," I promised. "Where shall we go? How much time can you spare?"

"All afternoon," Maman replied. "Why not the Compleat Angler in Marlow?"

"Fine" I agreed. "I'll drive."

We drove to Marlow and the Compleat Angler and were shown to a table looking out onto the River Thames.

"So, what's up?" Maman asked, when we were seated and had been handed menus.

"Ian has asked me to join him as his partner in a boy-girl shoot-out tomorrow," I explained. "I'm not sure how good Ian is, but what if I'm better, do I let him beat me so as not to wound his male ego, or do I go ahead and shoot as best I can and maybe beat him?"

"That will depend on how secure he is in himself," Maman thought. "If he's secure in himself, then he'll be happy for you. If he's insecure then the male ego could take a bashing and he might be like many men and just sulk."

"But if I beat him, I don't want to have him not want to see me again," I complained.

"I cannot really help you, Bébé," Maman said. "You have to judge how he will react. But think about this, do you want a man who is secure in himself, or one who will object to you besting him at something, will he always have to be the best?"

"I suppose he took it well enough when I was rowing the other day," I thought. "He joked about it, and I didn't get the impression that he was upset at all."

"How is your shooting?" Maman asked.

"I was really rusty," I laughed. "Couldn't hit the side of a barn, but I went to the club and saw Henry and got some practice in, when I left, I was shooting one hundred consistently."

"You really like this Ian, don't you?" Maman asked.

"I do," I confirmed. "Oh, Maman, he's just lovely, the more time I spend with him, the more I like him. I wait for his calls and when he does call my heart seems to skip little beats, I go to the coffee shop and wait for him to come, panicking when he doesn't come exactly on time. I like to hold his hand, and don't want to let go, I'm working up the nerve to kiss him, not just goodbye pecks on the cheek, but a real kiss. Am I in love?"

"It sounds like it," Maman said. "Do you know how he feels about you?"

"As I told you before, his friend Chris said that Ian was nuts about me and he does grin at me a lot, as though he's got something to be really happy about, he calls me *chérie*," I replied.

"It sounds as if the feelings are mutual," Maman said. "Will you bring him over to see me sometime?"

"I will, Maman," I promised. Further conversation was interrupted by a waitress who came to see if we had made our decisions. We ordered and then she asked how we liked England. I think that took us both a little by surprise, but then we realised we had been using French, as was usual for us. Maman handled it well, and told her that we were having a marvellous time. She waxed eloquently about the location and the view of the river, complained only briefly about the weather, but said that it was autumn after all.

After lunch, I dropped Maman off at her boutique, then drove back to Oxford to my office. I checked my messages and there was one from Ian, telling me that the shoot was still on and reminding me to pick him up in the morning. The weather looked promising, overcast again, but no rain forecast, and not much wind. In a way that was not so good, I could probably handle windy shooting conditions better than most, so a calm day offered no advantages. I went to bed that night dreaming of Ian and playing out all kinds of marriage fantasies in my head, all very premature, but still there.

In the morning I dressed to kill, not from a sexual point of view, but dressed for the range. I did make a concession with underwear and went with the La Perla, otherwise, everything else was practical and clothes that I did not mind getting dirty, in case we really did have to shoot prone and the ground sheets were not adequate. I picked Ian up at eight-thirty as agreed and we drove to the range.

"You're looking lovely this morning," he said.

"No, I'm not," I countered. "I'm hardly the picture of elegance."

"Doesn't matter how you're dressed," he said. "You're still lovely. Are you ready for this?"

"As ready as I'll ever be," I said. "Are you?"

"Yes," he confirmed. "I've got money riding on us winning, twenty quid to be precise."

"Who's the bet with?" I asked.

"Alan Bates, one of the other members, he bet that he and his girlfriend could beat the pants off me and anyone I brought along," Ian explained.

"Does his girlfriend shoot?" I asked.

"I think she does," Ian said. "She goes to King's College in London and I think she belongs to their rifle club."

"Well, we'll see how good she is, can you outshoot Bates?" I asked.

"We're usually neck and neck, so it's going to come down to you and whatever her name is," Ian said. "I'm sorry I took the bet, but he pissed me off and I just reacted without thinking."

"We'll see what comes, and if we lose, I'll split the bet with you," I promised.

When we reached the range it was chilly, overcast and there was no wind to speak of. We joined the throng, I was surprised at how many people were there, apparently, it was either a popular event or had been well-advertised. Ian pointed out Alan Bates to me. He came over to us with a blonde in tow. "Ian," he said. "This is Samantha, Samantha, Ian."

"Nice to meet you, Samantha, Alan, Samantha, this is Fiona," Ian said making the introductions. I recognised Samantha, I had never met her but knew her from shooting event reports, her name was Samantha Edwards and her picture was often in the shooting magazines, probably because she was particularly photogenic, she typically shot an eighty. I pulled Ian aside and whispered in his ear that he might want to raise the bet, if Alan was up to it. I pulled a £20 note from my purse and slipped it into his hand, perhaps that was rash on my part, but Alan was bragging so much about Samantha's prowess, that I thought it a bet worth taking. Ian then went off and I saw him in deep talks with Alan, the upshot of which seemed to be a bet taken. Now all we had to do was deliver, and that meant both of us. The range master came out and detailed the rules. The men would shoot first, two tranches of five, and would each get five ranging shots to become familiar with the rifle they had been issued, before they shot to score. Then there would be a coffee break, whilst us women got our briefing and instructions. We would shoot, again in tranches of five, but individually, he made a passing comment that if one of us shot wild and hit another's target, then obviously that could not count, so we would shoot individually, not in groups as the men did. Us women would also get some ranging shots, but as we were unknown quantities, we would get ten ranging shots each before we shot for the targets.

The teams drew lots and we drew number five in the second tranche. So that basically meant we shot last, as we were in the second group and number five which put us at the end. That was fine with me, it meant that we would have a chance to look at all the other scores before I had to shoot. The range master handed out rifles and boxes of ammunition and then went and pinned up targets at the twenty-five-yard mark. The club had provided ground sheets, and the shooting position was going to be prone, so sprawled on the ground we would be. The first five men took their positions and shot off their allotted five ranging shots. Then the targets were retrieved and handed to the respective shooters who reviewed them and made any adjustments they felt appropriate. Then new targets were hung and shooting began in earnest. I had some binoculars with me and went down the row of targets looking at the results. There were eights and nines and quite a few tens. The best was number three. I asked Ian who that was.

"Edgar Spencer, he's the club president," Ian said. "The others in this group have all been members for about a year, but it looks like they're all a little rusty, no one has been practising whilst on summer vac."

At the end of the round, the leader was clearly Spencer with a score of ninety-eight. Then the second group took their positions and I stationed myself behind Ian. I watched as he made his ranging shots and saw that he had picked one particular spot and was trying to see how well he could group his shots so that he could get a feel for the rifle. I was impressed, Ian was actually pretty good. I took a quick look at Alan's target and saw that his ranging shots were also grouped well together. Ian was right, this was going to be close. Then the real shooting began. I watched Ian's target as he made each shot. The first was a ten and I was thrilled. Then the second was another ten, then the third, this was going to be a good result. He made his one hundred and I cheered for him. There was applause all around for Ian and Alan who had both shot well and who had both scored one hundred. We then broke for coffee, which was very welcome. Although time was passing and the sun had to be up there somewhere, there had been no appreciable rise in the morning temperature. The range master gathered us women and went through the rules, then he went through the parts of the rifle and how it operated, demonstrating the bolt action for us. He then issued a rifle to each of the first five and they went to their respective positions, but this time the partners got down on the ground with them as instructors and coaches. Targets were hung and ranging shots fired. I quickly scanned the targets and noticed that number three was better than the others, by a lot. "Who's number three?" I asked Ian.

"That's Pamela Roberts, she's a club member, I didn't know she was going out with Edgar," he replied. We both moved to behind her to watch her shoot. The new targets were hung and firing began. Number one managed to hit the target every time, but the results were not that good. When done she scored fifty, which meant that she did not actually hit a couple of the individual targets, as the minimum score was six for a hit. Number two did about the same, but scored fifty-five. Pamela Edwards shot fairly well and her score was a solid eighty. So, the aggregate to beat was now one hundred and seventy-eight. As Ian had hit his one hundred, that meant I had to shoot a seventy-nine to win. Of the others in the first group, numbers four and five shot and they both scored in the sixties.

Now came our turn. We traded places with the first five and I got down on the ground and Ian joined me. He handed me the rifle and I looked it over, pulled out the bolt and peered down the barrel, not too much fouling yet, just a few specks from the shots fired before, the extractor looked fine, and as this was a single shot rifle, there was no magazine spring to worry about. I asked for some patches and cleaning rods and ran them through to clean the barrel. I noticed that after I had done that, that Samantha also did the same. We waited until it was our turn for ranging shots and I decided not to give too much away by going for a group, but created a face by placing shots just where I wanted them. I picked the spots on the target and whispered to Ian where I was aiming. He gave me precise reports and I made my adjustments accordingly. By the fourth ranging shot, I had the measure of the rifle and was placing shots just where I wanted them. Then we had to wait for those targets to be collected and replaced and for us to each shoot again. The audience had grown a little and as each shot was registered there was applause based on the score, so I knew when the first ten had been hit. When it came the turn of Samantha, she started to get a lot of applause as she several tens in a row, then I noticed the wind flags start to move a little and her next few shots were on target, but not in the tens. Her final score was eighty-eight, I think a personal best for her. So that was now the number to beat. The next girl shot, but she was not in the same league as Samantha, so there was applause, but it was polite.

My turn finally came, and I settled into the serious business of shooting. Ian moved a little closer to me and aimed his spotting scope at the target and gave me very precise reports. They were useful because the breeze had now picked up a little more and I was having to make more allowance for windage. I did what I set out to do and scored one hundred, to a great deal of applause. I was so delighted that I leaned over and kissed Ian. Kissed him on the lips, I did, it was delightful and he responded, particularly when I told him that I loved him. There were ribald comments around us, most of which suggested getting a room somewhere, but I did not care. I was kissing my *chéri* and enjoying every moment of it.

"So," a voice said, which I identified as that of Alan. "Who's the better shot, Ian or Fiona, I think we should find out." That met with general acclamation and the challenge was out there. I looked at Ian and asked, "Do you want to do this?" I was worried lest I offend his male ego and was trying to decide if I would go ahead with this and shoot my best, or let him win.

"Only if you do," he said.

"What do you suggest?" I asked Alan.

"Fifty yards, ten shots, large single target, highest score wins," he said.

"Chéri?" I asked.

"Okay *chérie*," he said. "Let's give the mob what they want, will you still love me if I win?"

"I was going to ask you the same question," I laughed. "Will you?"

"I will," he confirmed. "I love you *chérie*, and I will, even if you win, but no letting me win, you have to shoot fairly."

"You too," I said.

"Okay, okay, enough with the love talk," Alan said. "Ian, you're in four and Fiona you can stay where you are. We've changed targets and distance, so any time you're ready. Do you want to toss a coin to see who goes first or are you going to shoot simultaneously?"

"Simultaneously," we both replied. The distance and the light breeze made things a little more challenging, but in the end, we both scored one hundred.

"Okay," Alan said. "Now, seventy-five yards, same type of target, ten shots each."

I looked at Ian who nodded.

"I need a break," I said. "I want to walk the range to seventy-five yards; Ian are you coming with me?"

"Of course, *chérie*," he said. We both stood up and walked hand in hand down the range. I was interested in the wind to see how it blew, but I also wanted to talk to Ian.

"Is this our first test?" I asked him. "To see if we can compete and still be together?"

"We should just treat it as fun," he said. "No matter what happens *chérie*, I love you."

"I love you too, *chéri*," I said. "You won't be all wounded and hurt if I win?"

"No," he said. "It would only make me love you more. But who says you're going to win?"

"Oh, so it is a challenge," I laughed.

"It is Fiona Barclay," he said. "You told me yourself that you were the one to beat."

"So, let's find out, shall we," I suggested. "We walked back to the shooting stands and took up our respective positions.

"Any time you're ready," Alan said.

We both shot and again to the delight of the crowd it was a dead heat, ninety-eight each. The crowd I noticed had devolved itself into two factions, I had nearly all the women and Ian the men. This had become a proxy battle of the sexes. I also noticed money changing hands and wondered if there were odds being taken, or if it were straight bets.

"Okay, this time, one hundred yards, we'll use one large target each, ten shots each," Alan said.

Ian and I walked the range again, out to the one-hundred-yard marker, hand in hand. I was actually enjoying the day, I knew that whatever happened it would not change how I felt about Ian, or he about me. I think I loved him more for that. We walked back and took up our shooting positions and shot again, the wind was picking up quite a bit now and I had to watch the flags carefully to see when the gusts came. When the targets were retrieved and examined there was some debate as to whether one of my shots was on the ten line, or inside the ten line. In the end, the range master ruled and I won by one point, ninety-seven to ninety-six. I hoped Ian had not let me win and I hoped that he was not disappointed that he did not win.

"Fiona wins," Alan announced to the crowd. Money changed hands and some of the women looked elated, while some of the men looked a little disappointed. I was a little irritated by that, let them try and shoot as well as Ian had. I had beaten him, but just and only after a ruling by the range master, and at one hundred yards in deteriorating conditions. I gave Ian a long consolation kiss, to the delight and applause of the crowd. Ian then collected his winnings from Alan, and suggested that we go and have lunch to celebrate. The range master finally spoke up, after being largely silent all morning, except for his safety briefings.

"How many of you bet against Ian and Fiona?" he asked. Several people either spoke up, or put up their hands.

"You know that this is Fiona Barclay?" he asked.

"Who?" Alan asked.

"You need to read more," the range master said. "If you did, you'd discover technical articles by Dr Barclay about muzzle velocity and windage, among other things."

"So, you're saying Hartley brought in a ringer?" Alan asked.

"No more than you did," the range master said. "I also think, judging by today, that they are truly girl and boy, so they met the terms of the shoot. So, read a little more and you may learn more!"

That set off a buzz of conversation and I did hear Samantha say to the person next to her, "So, that's Fiona Barclay, I'd no idea she was so young."

It looked like the group were planning to go to a pub to have a drink and either celebrate their winnings or bemoan their losses, but I did not fancy that, I wanted to be alone with Ian. I had things to discuss with him, things that were better not said with many other people around.

We walked to my car and he put his arms around me and kissed me. It felt so good to be in his arms and to feel him next to me. It was as if once the ice had been broken by our first kiss at the range then we could not get enough of one another We finally broke and I unlocked the car and suggested that we go for a late lunch. We drove out to Wolvercote and then to the Trout Inn. I had taken a quick look at their menu when we had been there before and had decided that there were dishes that I might enjoy.

"Ian, Fiona, back so soon," Chris said, as we entered the bar.

"Howzit Chris," Ian said. "We've come for a celebratory lunch, we just won forty quid at a shooting event."

"Well, let's get you a nice table," Chris said, coming out from behind the bar and leading us to the dining area. "Too cold to sit outside, so what about here, looking out at the river?"

"Looks good," Ian said. Chris handed us menus then left to go back behind the bar. A waitress came over and took drink orders and said that she would be back for food orders.

"Are you okay?" I asked Ian.

"Of course, why shouldn't I be?" he asked.

"Well, you didn't win," I said.

"Hey, if I had to lose, I'm glad it was to you, it was close though wasn't it?" he said.

"It was," I agreed.

"I'd lose again and again if it meant that you'd kiss me like you did, I wasn't expecting it, but I'm just thrilled that you did," he said. "Oh, Fiona, I love you, I really do."

"I love you," I told him, reaching out and taking his hand. "I think I knew that last weekend, but I was too afraid to tell you, in case you didn't feel the same way." He leaned over and kissed me, and it was wonderful.

"Hey, hey, enough of that," Chris commented as he brought our drinks. "We're a respectable institution, but we could get you a room for the night."

"Okay, okay," Ian said. "Wouldn't want to risk being thrown out for being in love."

"I knew it," Chris said. "I knew it, and you went to sleep last week, think of what you missed."

Our waitress returned and we ordered food then ate. After lunch, we moved into the bar area for coffee. It was quiet there with very few people around. As we drank our coffee, I sat working up the courage to take the plunge to tell Ian how things stood. I waited until the people next to us left then broached the subject.

"Ian, *chéri*," I said. "We have to talk."

"We do?" he asked.

"We do," I confirmed. "It's a rather delicate matter."

"What about? When a girl says we must talk, it usually means that that's it, it's over, tell me it's not over already," he said.

"No, it's not over, it's about me," I said. "I'm not sure how to discuss this, so bear with me."

"What is it, Fiona, you're not dying of some rare disease are you?" he asked in panic.

"No, nothing like that," I assured him. "Well, here goes, if this relationship proceeds and things take their natural course, then we'll end up in bed at some time. You should know that that time will be my first, I've never had sex."

"So, you're a virgin?" he asked. "Okay, for a minute there I really did think you were going to tell me that you had some rare disease, or that there was some other dark secret in your life. But all you're telling me is that you're a virgin, that's a relief."

"I am," I confirmed. "To you, it may be a relief that that's all it was, but it's been really difficult for me to work out how to tell you."

"Why haven't you ever had sex before?" he asked. "I would have thought that there would have been any number of blokes wanting to date you. You're gorgeous, smart, independent, it's surprising that I'm to be your first."

"First love, first hand holding, first kiss, first everything," I said. "I just never met the right man before you, when I first saw you and our eyes met, it was like an electric shock, I probably knew then that you were the one. But what I'm trying to say, is that I'm excited but apprehensive about where things go, so am asking you to be patient and let me pick the time and place, is that okay?"

"*Chérie,* just knowing you love me is enough to keep me going for months," he said. "I know the common thing to say is if you really loved me, we would make love now, or I'd leave you, but that won't happen, I promise *chérie.* This is something that has to be right and right for you. My sister really drummed it into me, listen to what she says, she would tell me, no means no and only go forward when she's ready and she really wants to, let her set the pace. We've only today gone from hand holding to our first kiss, so there is a lot to explore before we get to the bedroom. So, *chérie,* take all the time you want and let me know when you're ready, I will not push, nag or whine."

"Thank you *chéri,*" I said. "That makes me feel so much better. I've been agonising over what to do, what to say, when to say it and terrified that you'd walk away from me if I didn't just jump into bed with you. Now, I'm not talking about months and months, I'm thinking before Christmas, it's a big step for me and I want it to be right."

"I won't walk away from you," he promised. "I'm too much in love with you to hurt you or pressure you into doing something you aren't ready for."

"Thank you for understanding," I said, relieved. I had been half afraid that he would walk away from me, but also half confident that he would stay with me, it had been causing me quite a lot of anxiety. I kissed him as a thank you, then sat back and grinned at him.

"I'm glad that's over," I said. "I've been all sixes and sevens as to how to tell you."

"I'm glad you did," he said. "It could have been awkward for us both to try and get through things if I didn't know ahead of time. I will be guided by you and we will take our time."

"Would you come with me to meet my Maman at some time?" I asked.

"Of course," he said. "You said you and your Mum look very much alike, aren't you worried that I'll fall for your Mum?"

"Don't you dare," I laughed. "Maman is spoken for anyway, she told me the other day that she has met someone, Portia. This is new for her, and for me, I didn't know she had feelings that way."

"It's more common than you would think," he said. "So, when do I get to meet her?"

"What about next Sunday?" I asked. "We could drive over in the morning and back that evening."

"Okay," he agreed. "I'll make sure I've got all my errands done on Saturday and will be at your disposal all day Sunday. So, your Dad won't be there?"

"Maman and Dad divorced two years ago," I explained. "Dad lives in London, one day I'll introduce you to him as well."

"Sorry to interrupt," the waitress said, as she came to find us. "I'm off in a few minutes, could I trouble you to settle the account?"

"Of course," Ian said. "We're sorry we've kept you waiting, we've had a lot to talk about."

"You two make a really cute couple," she said. "How long have you been married?"

"We're not," I said. "We've only been dating a few weeks."

"Really?" she said. "You seem so comfortable together, I would have bet money that you were married."

"Perhaps, one day," I said and smiled at her, while Ian grinned like the Cheshire cat.

We left the inn and, after kissing again by the car, we drove back to Oxford and I dropped him at his digs, again with a pause to get close and kiss, and then I went home. I think I sang all the way home, I sang "*Then he kissed me*", by the Crystals and they probably would have been horrified at my rendition. I was happy, I was relieved and I was looking forward to what would come. Once home I called Maman.

"Fi," she said when she answered the telephone and learned that it was me calling. "How are you?"

"Maman, I kissed him today," I announced, not bothering with the normal mundane talk about health and the weather, but getting straight to the point.

"Kissed who?" Maman asked, teasing.

"Ian, Maman, and oh, Maman it was wonderful," I told her.

"When did this momentous occasion happen?" she asked.

"At the shooting range," I told her. "I had just shot a one hundred so there he was lying next to me, spotting for me, so I leaned over and kissed him."

"Very romantic," she said, dryly.

"It was," I said. "It was just the right time, place and occasion. I'm glad I did, since then we've not stopped. I also told him that he'd be my first experience and asked if we could take things slowly, and Maman, he said he understood and that he loved me."

"So, who won the shooting thing?" she asked.

"Oh, Ian and I won, then we had a challenge between the two of us and I won, barely, but I won," I explained.

"And no bruised male ego?" she asked.

"He said no, and I believe him," I said. "He made no fuss and I think it helped when I gave him a big consolation kiss."

"I'm so happy for you Bébé," she said. "Might I meet him at some time?"

"I was coming to that," I said. "Would next Sunday be convenient?"

"It would," she said. "You're sure you don't want to come on Saturday and stay the night?"

"I'm not ready to be under the same roof as him yet," I said. "Foolish of me, perhaps, but I'm just not ready, I'm not sure I trust myself to not do something foolish, that I'm not really ready for and that I would regret in the morning."

"Well, you take all the time you need," she said. "But don't create something in your head about the perfect time and place, you're likely to be disappointed. Things happen as they happen."

"I understand that, Maman," I said.

"Just take things as they come," she continued. "When you're ready, that is, be spontaneous, if it's the bedroom, fine, if it's the kitchen, or in the bath or on the living room floor, or, God forbid, in the back of a car, just enjoy yourself."

"I'll try and remember that," I said.

"When shall I expect you on Sunday?" she asked.

"Shall we say about ten?" I suggested.

"Ten it is," she said. "I await the day with great anticipation."

"That sounded like a very formal speech," I laughed.

"It did, didn't it," she agreed, also laughing. "I'll see you next week Bébé, I love you."

"Je t'aime, Maman. À bientôt," I said.

Ian meets Maman

The whole of the next week, I applied myself to my job and met Ian as often as we could, for coffee, lunch and even once for dinner. He took me to a curry house, that was well known by students, for its budget meals, which were good, but rather limited. I have long appreciated how fortunate I had been in my upbringing, Maman was a good cook and we had eaten French as well as English meals. Much to the surprise of some of her French friends, she had even made her English dishes so palatable that they had had difficulty accepting that it was English cooking. Ian was quite well known at the curry house and they were really interested in me, I gathered that he had normally eaten there alone and I was the first person he had taken there, so they were curious. Ian was still having problems with his thesis advisor and the pessimistic side of me saw real problems in the future, and I hoped for Ian's sake that his thesis would not be rejected. That could mean extra study, or perhaps even a return to his dig and more research. That would not sit well with me, as it would mean that I would be without his company for a while. Still, I resolved to cross that bridge, when and if it came. I was getting to enjoy his arms around me and feeling him close to me, in fact, I looked forward to our meetings, so that I could enjoy that moment when he wrapped his arms around me and kissed me. I know, all very school girlish, but I had never been in love before, so this was a whole new experience to be savoured and enjoyed and not to be taken lightly or for granted. I called Maman after each date, meeting, encounter, call it what you will, and gave her detailed reports, and she gave me small pieces of advice as what to do and what not to do, which was invaluable. I suppose girls that have a best friend of their own age would probably do the same, but I had no such friend, only Maman, and she truly was, and is, my friend, as well as being my mother.

I was excited to introduce Ian to Maman, I was sure that she would like him, and hoped that they would get along. Maman had always been very protective of me, and I think things would go ill for anyone who hurt me, either physically or emotionally, not that I could see Ian ever raising a hand to me, but if things went awry in our relationship, she would want to know how and why. I was getting to know Ian better, and the more I found out, the more I liked him as well as loving him. He was fast becoming my friend. We arranged for me to pick him up at nine at his digs on Sunday morning, an hour was a little long for the journey, but an early arrival would be fine. Poor, Ian, he wanted to know if he should wear a suit and tie, I think he was actually a little nervous about meeting Maman. I assured him that suit and tie were not necessary, what he wore to college each day would be quite appropriate, so jeans, a shirt and pullover would be fine, plus a jacket in case we went wandering around the estate. I decided that I would wear the denim mini skirt I had, a blue blouse and a leather jacket, plus some ankle boots that I had recently purchased.

I collected Ian at nine on Sunday morning, the sun was trying very hard to peek through the clouds, but it was still a grey day. We drove over to Henley, both complaining about the lack of sunshine, I imagine for someone born and raised in Rhodesia, it must have been particularly depressing. I looked at him and how he was dressed. He had taken me at my word and had on jeans, a plaid shirt and a jacket. I also noticed that he had had his hair cut. He wore it short, probably because it was more comfortable in the tropics with close-cropped hair. He had also shaved carefully, because I noticed a tiny bit of shaving lather on his right ear. I kissed him good morning, then I used my handkerchief to clean off his ear.

"You're not your happy, grinning self this morning?" I said. "What's wrong?"

"I'm nervous about meeting your Mum," he explained. "We're still expected?"

"We are," I assured him. "I talked to Maman yesterday and she's excited to meet you."

"Will there be anyone else there?" he asked.

"She didn't say," I replied. "My brother, James, is in London and I've not met Portia yet, so I'm not sure if she'll be there or not. So, don't worry, you're not on show or trial with fifty family members all asking about your prospects and how you intend to support me."

"All the same, what if your Mum doesn't like me?" he asked.

"Why wouldn't she?" I challenged him. "I love you, I like you, so why should she not at least like you?"

"Because I've come between you two," he suggested. "From all you've told me, you two are very close, more like best friends than mother and daughter, and now I'm in the middle. Do you share confidences with her?"

"I suppose I do," I said. "I go to her for advice when it comes to almost anything outside mathematics and economics."

"So, you've already analysed me, dissected me, categorised me and generally talked about me?" he asked.

"Of course," I said. "But it's all been good, her image of you is of a caring man who loves me to distraction, at least that's what I've told her, I even quoted your friend Chris, who said you were nuts about me."

"He said that?" Ian asked, colouring a little. "I'm not sure I can live up to the paragon you've painted me to be. What if she discovers I've got clay feet?"

"She'll like you all the more, we all have feet of clay to some degree," I told him. "We're here." I got out of the car and opened the massive gates that protected our property.

"You grew up in this?" he said. "This looks like some kind of manor house, it's huge, how much land is there, does this wall go all the way around?"

"About two hundred acres," I replied. "The wall was built in the Twenties by Grandpa Barclay and does go all the way around. I cannot imagine what it cost to build, there's actually about four miles of it, with this gate and another at the back of the property. Grandpa Barclay must have built it before the town fathers started placing limits on wall height, who today could get away with a ten-foot wall, that is stone, three feet thick at the base and almost two feet thick at the top?"

"Has the house been in the family for a long time?" Ian asked.

"No, my understanding is that Grandpa Barclay purchased it when the owner defaulted on loans, he had outstanding. He was in a good position to do that, he was an investment banker," I explained.

"Is your Dad also in banking?" Ian asked.

"He took over his dad's private bank," I said. "I've no idea how much money is involved. But I do know that there is quite a bit of risk involved, so assets can rise and fall quite quickly. I gather that during the Depression in the Thirties, that things were bleak for a while, but that Grandpa Barclay managed to pull off some fancy financial deals and came out of it better than most."

"And your Mum got this house in the divorce?" Ian asked.

"She did, plus a one-time cash settlement," I replied.

"Your Dad must have really messed up," Ian said dryly.

"He did," I agreed. "Maman managed to get pictures, then it was just a negotiation. Dad's not hard up by any means, he's probably made back already what he had to set aside for Maman."

"I'd no idea your family had money," he commented.

"Well, I don't, at least not now," I said. "I suppose it's possible that when my folks both die that I may get something, but I'm working on the basis that I get nothing, so have to earn everything myself."

"I know what you mean," he said. "I've no expectations out of the farm in Mount Darwin, so have to make my own way in life. Shouldn't we go through the gate and to your house?"

"All right, all right, it's your fault that we're sitting here gossiping," I laughed. "Oh, there is just one more thing. Maman and I normally use French when it's just the two of us and we try to remember to use English if there's someone else with us. So, if either of us forgets, gently remind us."

"Do you want the gates closed?" he asked.

"Yes, please," I said. He got out of the car and closed them after us and got back into the car. Then I drove on up the road to the house.

I pulled up to the front door. Ian got out and opened my door for me and we walked hand in hand to the door. I took my shoes off and put them in the box that was there.

"You take your shoes off?" Ian asked.

"Maman preserves some Polynesian traditions, one of which is removing your shoes before going into the house," I explained. "Normally they're just left by the front door, but she didn't want them to disappear or make the place look untidy, so she had this box made, it has racks inside for shoes of all shapes and sizes."

"Okay," he said, and removed his shoes and placed them next to mine. Conventions satisfied, I used my key and let us in.

"Maman," I called. "We've arrived."

"Bébé," I heard her call. Then she came to front door.

"Ian, I'm delighted to meet you," she said, giving him a kiss on each cheek. "Please come in. Did Fi terrify you with her driving on the way here?"

"No," he said very gallantly. "She actually drove very sedately, no speeding, no risky overtaking."

"Liar," she laughed. "Coffee, tea, wine?" she asked.

"Coffee would be super, thanks," he said. I took his jacket and hung it with mine and we trooped into the kitchen. Maman had coffee already on the go, and an array of pastries on the table.

"So, Fi tells me that you're a Rhodesian studying the origins of man," she said. "Wasn't it in the then Northern Rhodesia that one of the early finds was made?"

"There was indeed," he confirmed. "In 1921 a Swiss miner found skull fragments and other bones of an early hominid at the lead and zinc mine that is at Broken Hill, now Kabwe. There's a lot of debate about where he fits, but the consensus is that he was a precursor to homo sapiens."

I poured coffee and listened to the conversation. Maman, in her true fashion, had done her homework and was able to chat about the various hominid forms that had been discovered and how they might all fit into time. Maman was charming the poor man, and he was already lost to her wiles. The telephone rang and Maman excused herself to answer it.

"You're right about looking alike," he said, after she had left the room. "You two are so alike, it's uncanny. I can see where you get your good looks from, what did your grandmother look like?"

"I've pictures somewhere," I said.

"Pictures of what?" Maman asked, when she came back.

"Mémère Monique," I said. "Ian was curious, so I told him I had pictures."

"The album is over there," Maman said, pointing to the counter, she had apparently anticipated such a request, because I knew that the album normally lived in the library. I got the album and opened it and found the pictures of Mémère when she was younger.

"She's beautiful," he said. "The Polynesian obviously passed down to you both, now I understand why Fiona is so beautiful, it's all in the genes."

"Yes," Maman said. "I think we were lucky to take after her and not my father. There are also pictures of Fi growing up, look, here she was five, there seven, there eleven."

"You were really cute," Ian said, grinning at me. "What's the story here, you've got no hair?"

"I got into a fight with some older girls at school," I explained. "I discovered that girls like to pull your hair in a fight, so I came home and chopped it off."

"I was horrified," Maman added. "So, took her to a hairdresser to see what could be done to clean things up a little, that was the best she could do with what was left."

"So, do you have baby pictures of you naked on a zebra skin rug?" I teased.

"No, afraid not," he laughed. "I don't have any pictures with me, they're all back in Mount Darwin."

"Fi told me that your parents have a tobacco farm," Maman said. "You have no interest in continuing that?"

"No," he said. "I'm not a great fan of cigarettes, so won't take over the farm, at least not to grow tobacco. But it did provide for a very good education for my sister and me."

"What does your sister do?" Maman asked.

"She's a doctor, she practises in South Africa at a big hospital in Cape Town," he replied.

"More coffee?" Maman asked him.

"Yes, please," he said. "Fiona told me that the estate here is quite large, how do you maintain it?"

"I have an army of landscapers and gardeners, but much of it is wooded, so does not take too much, beyond cleaning up fallen branches and the occasional tree that comes down in the wind," she replied. "But I still do some things myself, particularly in the kitchen garden. You should get Fi to take you on a tour, while I think about what I'm going to cook for lunch."

I took the hint and got Ian's jacket and shoes and we went for a drive around the property. I took Maman's old Land Rover, the one she used for estate jobs.

"Your Mum's really beautiful," Ian said as we took the perimeter path that followed the wall. "No wonder you're so gorgeous, it runs in the family. You said she and your Dad got divorced, if it's not too intrusive, why, who would walk away from one so beautiful?"

"I'm not totally sure," I said. "But perhaps Dad was having what they call a midlife crisis and was looking for a trophy, or perhaps Maman was just too independent for him."

"Your Mum is well-read, she had obviously done some reading about early man," he commented.

"That's her," I said. "She wanted to put you at ease, and what better way than to be able to talk about what you do? She wanted us to go off and spend a little time together, she's had planned for a week what she'll cook for lunch."

"I like her," he said.

"Just don't go liking her too much," I warned him. "I'm the one you love, remember that!"

"Ah *chérie*, how could I forget," he laughed. "It is interesting to see how you might turn out, I've often heard it said that if you want to know what your girlfriend will look like in later years, check out her mother. Well, I have every reason to be delighted."

"*Cochon,*" I said.

"I'm sorry *chérie*," he said. "Let me make it up to you."

"How do you propose to do that?" I asked.

"If you stop the car, I'll show you," he said. I stopped and he leaned over and kissed me, that was nice but gear levers and such got in the way, so I climbed over them all and straddled him. My skirt did rather ride up when I did that, showing a great deal of leg, and making me feel a little uncomfortable at exposing so much of myself, perhaps I should have worn jeans instead of the skirt. Straddling him was a much better position for kissing in the Land Rover, so I was prepared to live with a little emotional discomfort.

"I love you," he said, when we paused to breathe.

"I love you," I replied. "I'm glad you came, Maman likes you."

"How do you know?" he asked. "She's only spent a short time with me."

"I know Maman," I said. "If she didn't like you, she would have not suggested we take a drive around the estate. She would have kept you close to keep an eye on you."

"Perhaps we should go back," he suggested. "I wouldn't want her to think I'm trying to lead you astray, particularly if she saw you with your skirt hitched up almost to your waist."

"Don't worry about that, I think for quite a while she despaired that I would ever date, so she's happy that I have found someone," I assured him, climbing back into the driver's seat and pulling my skirt back down to a more sober and decorous length.

We drove back to the house and Maman was waiting with some wine glasses.

"Did you have a nice drive?" she asked.

"We did," I confirmed. "When did you plant all those pines by the back gate?"

"Three months ago," she replied. Then she turned to Ian and appealed to him, "You see what I have to deal with, she comes, she stays, she bothers and harasses me, but she doesn't see."

"I think Fiona has had much on her mind lately," he said. "She's been really busy with her consulting project."

"Excuses, excuses," Maman laughed. "Tell me, Ian, have you been in France?"

"I have," he confirmed. "I've been to the caves at Lascaux, I got there by going to Bordeaux, so I suppose I've also been there, I was amazed by the ice age paintings, I've been to Paris once, and spent most of my time in the Louvre and I've been to Nice."

"I've seen the paintings at Lascaux," Maman said. "But that was quite a while ago in 1959, before they closed the caves for a while to restore the paintings. We took Fiona and James with us, do you remember Fi?"

"I do," I said. "I can't say I was a fan of the caves themselves, but the paintings were amazing, I would like to go back and see them again, now that they've been restored."

"I'll take you," Ian volunteered.

"Are you sure you want to?" Maman asked.

"Absolutely," Ian confirmed. "After Lascaux, we could also go to Altamira."

Ian and Maman then had a long discussion about the paintings of Lascaux and Altamira, while I just sat there, watching and listening. Here were two people I loved, getting along, it was wonderful. I gathered up the wine glasses that Maman had been holding and poured out three glasses from the bottle she had opened and handed them around.

"This is really nice," Ian said, taking a sip. "What is it?"

"It's a Sauvignon Blanc from Sancerre," Maman replied. "I have a friend in London who is a wine merchant and brings over nice vintages."

"Tell me," he said. "What was Fiona like when she was growing up?"

"It was a challenge," Maman replied, looking at me fondly and probably recalling the good and bad times of my childhood. "Academically she was so far ahead of everyone else her age, that keeping her occupied was a full-time job. Her social skills didn't really develop until much later."

"Social skills, she has social skills?" he asked, grinning like an idiot.

"Hard to believe, isn't it?" Maman laughed.

"I'm standing here," I protested. "I'm standing here and I do have social skills, I just reserve them for people I like."

"Of course you do, Bébé," Maman said. "I'm just fortunate that you like me, as I think is Ian. Now, would you set the table for lunch; we're having trout almandine?"

"Which table, the one here in the kitchen or the dining table?" I asked.

"I think we should use the dining table once in a while, why don't you set things out on that one?" Maman suggested.

I busied myself setting the table while Ian and Maman carried on their conversation. I noted that it was being delicately steered towards Ian's feelings towards me, and in some sense, to use the old saw, what his intentions were. I heard him describe our first encounter, then our first coffee together, then our first date when he had gone to sleep on me. I think that still rankled with him, no matter how many times I had assured him that I had had a lovely day and had not minded at all watching him while he slept. It is difficult to describe my feelings of that day, I think I developed a deep affection for him then, just watching him sleep and relax. I doubt that many would understand, being focused more on the here and now and the activity of the day, which was supposed to be a picnic, not a time to sleep. Then I heard Ian telling Maman about our shooting match and the moment when I leaned over and kissed him. I peeked back into the kitchen and he was standing by the counter with a huge grin on his face as he remembered it. He was happy again, and I was happy for him. For all his apprehensions about meeting Maman, he was enjoying himself and had relaxed to be his normal self. I thanked Maman for that, she had this uncanny knack of being able to make people comfortable, no matter their social standing, education or background. It was a skill that I did not possess and I sometimes envied her ability. James had inherited that from her, as he also could move easily in any circles, but not me, I was awkward and found it difficult to relate to people socially.

Lunch was superb, Maman was, is, a good cook and likes to try out new things on whoever she can find. Not all her experiments turned out well, but I have to say that for the greater part, they do. After lunch, we had coffee and just chatted. Ian told us about his family and his early life in Rhodesia and the challenges that his folks now faced.

"If you're from Rhodesia, how do you travel in Tanzania?" Maman asked. "I thought the Tanzanians were quite opposed to the Smith government?"

"They are," Ian confirmed. "But my folks kept their British passports, and when I was born registered me with the British High Commission and I also got a British passport. I actually carry two, one just to move in and out of Rhodesia and the other to go anywhere else, so the Tanzanians see me as coming from London, not Salisbury."

"Is that permissible?" Maman asked.

"It's an accommodation that the High Commissioner set up for me, before the declaration of independence he had been a friend of the family for years," Ian explained.

"Tell us about your sister," Maman said.

"Irene?" he said. "Well, she's a little older than me, she's a doctor, surgeon actually, currently at Groote Schuur in Cape Town."

"Do you get on well?" Maman asked.

"For the most part," he said. "Like any brother and sister, when we were younger, we'd fight a lot, but we went to different boarding schools in Salisbury, then she went to varsity at Cape Town. We stay in touch and get on quite well now."

"So, tell me, your mother came from Tahiti," he said to Maman. "Have you been there?"

"Yes," she said. "When I was about fourteen, we went to see relatives, it wasn't long before the War, in fact, we had to cut our trip short and return to France as Papa was needed in his government office."

"What is Tahiti like?" Ian asked.

"Tropical," Maman replied. "Just like you see in the pictures. We were lucky we had been taught Tahitian as children, so could speak that as well as French, it made us more accepted."

"Have you ever been, Fiona?" he asked.

"Not yet," I said. "There hasn't really been the opportunity. One day, I would like to go to see where Mémère Monique came from."

"Do you speak any Tahitian?" he asked.

"Only a few words," I lamented. "I think when we were growing up, we were busy learning English and French, and we only got the odd words when we went to stay with Mémère Monique. Maman was lucky because when she was growing up, they spoke French and Tahitian in their house."

"She can dance though," Maman interrupted.

"What, you mean Tahitian dance, the hips swinging kind of dance?" he asked.

"She can," Maman continued inexorably. She was leading up to me giving a recital, I could tell.

"Maman," I warned. But she ignored me.

"You should have her show you," she said to Ian.

"Maman," I pleaded. Again, I was ignored.

"We have music and she shouldn't have forgotten everything," she said.

"Maman," I whined, and was studiously ignored again.

"Would you?" Ian asked, grinning at me, a grin I could not resist.

"I will if Maman dances with me," I said. I thought, two could play at that game, so she was going to be roped in to dance as well. "Maman taught me, so she's actually much better than I am, she was taught by Mémère Monique who was really good."

"If that is what it takes to get you up to dance, then, yes, I'll dance with you," Maman agreed. "Ian, make yourself comfortable, we'll be back in a few minutes. Let me just dig out the music, when I tell you, play this record."

I went with Maman to one of the spare rooms, and there she had stored away the grass skirts that Mémère Monique had made for us. These were real grass, not the man-made fibres that were being used lately. She had other adornments as well, including some pieces to wear on our heads and belts with extra fringes to be worn low on the hips, to accentuate the hip movements.

"So, what do you suggest we were underneath?" I asked.

"Just what you have on," Maman replied.

"But they're almost see-through," I protested.

"He won't notice," she assured me. "And if he does, he won't mind."

"You bet he won't mind," I said. "You can see just about everything; I'll be on display."

"Don't worry about it," she said. "I'll wear what I have on as well, so you won't be alone in your exhibitionism."

We changed and adjusted things to her satisfaction then paraded back through the house to the living room.

"Now Ian," she called. We waited until the music started then sashayed into the room doing our dance. I was caught up in it, I had not danced for some time and had forgotten how much feeling and emotion was put into the dance. When the music finally stopped, Ian applauded and just said, "Wow!"

"That was an *aparima*," Maman explained. "It's a dance that tells a story and this one is about my mother and her meeting my father and their journey to France. She choreographed it after she'd lived in Paris a few years and taught it to me when I was a teenager. The next dance we'll do for you is the type that tourists usually see, much faster pace, done to drums. When I say ready, please put this record on."

Ian did as requested, and when the drums started, we made our entrance and got into the swing of things, quite literally. I had not shaken my hips like that for quite some time, so was sure that I would pay for it the next day. When the drums stopped, we scuttled off and changed back into our more normal clothes, then rejoined Ian.

"I had no idea that it was so energetic and suggestive," he said.

"Now you know why the priggish British missionaries banned it when they arrived in the early 1800s," Maman said. "Fortunately for us, Mémère Monique's family kept the traditions alive and went underground to avoid the missionaries."

"Which of the dances do you prefer?" I asked him.

"I think the first one," he said. "It has sensuality, but I could tell that there was a story there somewhere. I'm having a hard time with the idea that Fiona the mathematician can also dance."

"What's so surprising about that?" I asked.

"I just never saw you that way," he said. "It just shows how much we don't know about people."

"I don't dance often," I told him. "But that dance is a family thing and I think it's important to preserve one's heritage, I once saw Mémère Monique dance it when I was about six, she still had it and you could see why Pépère fell for her."

We must have just talked for a good other hour, because I realised it was dark outside.

"I'm sorry Maman," I said. "But I have early meetings in Oxford and should be getting back."

"Of course," she said. "You're sure you don't want to stay the night?"

"I'd love to," I said. "But I don't like the early morning drive from here, too many others on the road."

"As you wish," she said. "Ian, it has been a delight to meet you, I hope you will come again. Tell me, are you going back to Rhodesia for Christmas?"

"Unfortunately, no," he said.

"Well, your misfortune is our fortune," she said. "Would you like to join us for Christmas, come and stay a few days, as you can see, we have plenty of space, and I expect only Fiona, my son James and perhaps a girlfriend, so we will not be overcrowded."

"Thank you," he said. "I'd be delighted, if Fiona agrees."

"Of course," I said. "Thank you, Maman for suggesting it."

"Good," Maman said. "Just let me know what day you will arrive, I love you Bébé."

"I'll do that, Maman," I promised. "I'll call you when I get home. I love you, Maman."

On the drive back to Oxford, Ian and I talked about the day.

"Your Mum's lovely," he said. "She's not only beautiful, but she's smart, articulate and a good cook as well."

"I know," I agreed. "I'm very lucky. Just don't get any ideas about her, I'm the one you're interested in!"

"You are, you are, I love you, as you said before, to distraction," he assured me. "I'm still having a hard time working out why your Dad left for someone else."

"Well, Felicity the floozie does have attributes," I said. "I think the main of which, is that she is at the beck and call of Dad and she caters to his every whim. I think Maman became a little too independent for him."

"You've met her then?" he asked.

"Many times," I said. "She is very pretty and very competent at what she does as an assistant. I just have a difficult time warming to her because Maman and I have always been so close."

"It's interesting," he said. "Your Mum speaks English with an obvious French accent, but you don't."

"That's because I learned English from Dad, so I speak English like someone from the Home Counties and French like someone from Paris. When I was growing up, if it was just Dad and me, it was always English, if it was just Maman and me, it was always French and if we were all together, we'd use English during the week and French on weekends."

"Your Dad speaks French?" Ian asked.

"Passably," I said. "That's how he met Maman, he was in hospital in Paris and he was the only British soldier who had any French."

"I loved the dance," he said. "It was so sensual. I could imagine what kind of uproar there would be at the college if you ever did that in public, all the religious nuts would be calling for your execution, or at least excommunication, the conservatives would be running for cover and the hippies would be asking for lessons."

"Well, I'm not going to dancing in public any time soon," I said. "At least not that kind of dance, a waltz or foxtrot I could do, but not the *'aparima*."

"Tell me," he said. "What do you normally wear underneath that grass skirt?"

"Better covering panties than I have on," I laughed. "And normally a more opaque bra of some kind, or a fabric top, but I imagine in the nineteenth century when the missionaries first got to Tahiti, they didn't bother with such things as bras."

"I enjoyed the show," he said, wistfully. "You really are beautiful."

"Just don't get any ideas too soon," I told him, wondering which show he was actually talking about, the dance or the views of my body he got from my sheer underwear. "I'm not ready to make that leap yet."

We both fell silent for a while, me thinking about how much I had shown him and wondering what he thought of a mother-daughter pair that would flaunt so much and apparently have no qualms about it. What he was actually thinking about, I had no idea and could get no clues.

"Just drop me at the road end and I'll walk down to the pub," he said when we got to Oxford and I was working my way through the town to the Osney Bridge. I did that, after I had kissed him good night and thanked him for coming with me to Henley to meet Maman. My parting shot to him was, *ua here vau ia oe*.

103

"What does that mean?" he asked.

"You'll need to find that out," I told him.

I drove home and called Maman to tell her that I was back safe and sound.

"I like your Ian," she said. "I think you've found a nice man there. I hope it all works well for you."

"Why, don't you think it will?" I asked in a panic.

"No, no, Bébé, I didn't mean that I see any problems," she assured me. "I just hope that all stays well and you and he can grow together."

"I'm cross with you for making me dance," I told her.

"No, you're not," she laughed. "I saw you looking at him while you were dancing, you were enjoying the moment and you had him completely entranced."

"Well, I'm sure I'll regret it tomorrow morning," I said. "I think that I'll just get a glass of wine and go and soak in a bath for a while."

"That's a good idea," Maman agreed. "I think I'll do the same. I love you Bébé.

"I love you, Maman," I replied.

I hung up and went to the bedroom, stripped off and went through the dance again, in front of the mirror. Ian was right, it was very sensual, I was pleased that I still remembered it and had been able to do it for him, perhaps one day I would do it for him as I did then, with no clothes to cover the movements. I took a long soaking bath and hoped that the muscles I had used would not protest too much in the morning.

I did ache a little the next day, my hips had not seen that much gyration in a few years. I drove to my office and called Ian.

"So, how are you today, *chérie?*" he asked.

"I have a few aches and sore muscles," I confessed.

"I had a lovely day yesterday," he said. "I just regret that I don't have a movie camera, I would have liked to capture you dancing, so that I could keep the image forever."

"Oh, so you mean, it's already faded from your memory?" I asked.

"No, nothing could erase it," he said.

"So, coffee later?" I asked.

"I'm so sorry *chérie*," he said. "I can't, I have to go to Germany for some research, I'll be gone for three weeks. I leave today, my advisor sprung it on me this morning, we're going together, today, in fact, we're leaving for Dover in about five minutes, we take the ferry then we're going by train from Calais."

"I'm not sure I can survive without talking to you for three whole weeks," I complained. "Is there any way to contact you?"

"I'll let you know," he said. "I don't even know where we're staying yet. And, sadly, by the time I would get your letters, it would be time for me to come back."

"I'll write anyway," I said. "Then you can read my letters when you get back. Where are you going in Germany?"

"To the Neander Valley," he replied.

"That's where Neanderthal Man was found isn't it?" I asked.

"It is," he confirmed. "Neanderthal Man was a parallel to us, but many believe that there was species interbreeding. So, many of us in Europe may well be part Neanderthal."

"Well, come back to me," I said. "I'll miss you when you're gone."

"I'll see you as soon as I get back," he promised. "I love you *chérie*."

"I love you," I told him. *"Reviens à moi."*

"I will, if that means what I think it means, I will come back to you," he promised. "Oh, I talked to one of the linguists here, so, *ua here vau ia oe.*"

"I love you too," I said, delighted that he had taken the trouble to find out what the Tahitian meant.

He was gone, gone for three weeks, I looked at the wall and cried. I had managed to hold the tears back while I was talking to him on the telephone, but now he was gone, I knew that it was not forever, or even a long time, but three weeks seemed like an eternity, and he was still gone, gone away, unreachable in the short term. I dried my tears and got back to work, I had plenty to do, so could stay busy for the next three weeks. It struck me that I had nothing of his, no items of clothing to remind me of his aftershave, no keepsakes that he had given me, I did not even have a picture of him, that was something that needed to be remedied as soon as he got back, and I probably should give him a picture of myself.

That evening when I got home, I called Maman.

"Bébé, what's up?" she said, when she answered the telephone, detecting from the tone of my voice that all was not well.

"He's gone," I cried. "Gone."

"What do you mean, gone?" she asked.

"He's gone to Germany for three weeks," I said, through my sobs.

"That's not so long," she said. "He's coming back, isn't he?"

"He is," I confirmed. "But I won't be able to talk to him for three weeks. Oh, Maman, am I being stupid, dramatic or just idiotic, he's only going to be gone for three weeks, but it seems as if he's going to be gone forever?"

"No, you're not being any of those things," she assured me. "This is your first love and everything is new, even the separation. You'll manage," Maman promised. "Stay busy, that's how I dealt with long separations."

"You know, I don't even have a picture of him," I lamented. "I've got nothing of his, no pullover to remind me of his aftershave, no little mementoes, nothing."

"You should get at least a picture when he returns," she suggested.

"I will, and, I need a picture of me to give him, do you still have your dark room?" I asked.

"I do, do you want some pictures of yourself to give him?" she asked.

"I think that would be nice," I said. "Could I come over this weekend and have you take some pictures, is Portia going to be there, will I be in the way?"

"Portia is coming, and she has said that she'd like to meet you, so this weekend would be a good time," Maman said. "Come on Friday afternoon, bring your nice dresses and underwear, we should get as many different kinds of photos that we can."

"I'll be there, Maman," I promised. "So, enough with my petty troubles, how are you?"

"I'm well, thank you," she said. "In fact, I'm better than well, things are very good at the moment. Portia and I are getting on famously, the boutique is performing brilliantly, thank you for the algorithms, by the way, they've made stocking so much better, my portfolio is performing very well, again thank you. All in all, I have nothing to complain about."

"That's good," I said. "Have you heard from James lately?"

"I have," she said. "He has a girlfriend, I gather that she's South African, in London studying French, where and how they met I leave to you to discover, I have no idea."

"I'll try," I promised. "I'm sorry I called with my stupid problems, I know that's it not that long, but it seems now like an eternity. I've never had these kinds of feelings for anyone, and I've got to like our coffee mornings together and to see him regularly, and to call him every day. I won't know what to do with myself in the mornings for the next few weeks."

"Is there anyone else there that you like?" Maman asked.

"Not really," I confessed. "I get on well enough with Janet who had the office next to me, otherwise it's all strictly business."

"Ask Janet for coffee," Maman suggested. "Just talk to her, talk about the weather, ask her about her researches, if you think you can trust her, tell her about Ian."

"I'll try, Maman," I promised. "I love you, Maman."

"I love you, Bébé," she replied.

The next day I stopped at the Registrar's office and talked to Mrs Harrison who ran things there.

"Good morning, Dr Barclay," she said. "What can I do for you?"

"I was wondering if you had photographs of students?" I asked.

"Anyone in particular?" she asked.

"Ian Hartley, he's a grad student in Anthropology," I replied.

"I don't think so," she said. "Sadly, we don't have photos of our students, it would make my life easier if we did, I've suggested it to the Master a couple of times, but he's waffling. Have you tried the Anthropology Department office; they may have one?"

"That's a good idea," I said. "Thank you, Mrs Harrison."

My next port of call was with the anthropologists, but I had no luck there either. Then I remembered that Ian had rowed when he was an undergraduate, so went to the library and paged through old copies of the college magazine. I finally found a picture that had Ian in it, so asked the librarian for a copy, enlarged as big as her copier would go. Then I cut out Ian from the others. It was hardly the best picture, very grainy and a little blurred, but now at least I had one.

For the rest of the week, I applied myself to my researches and kept myself busy. I did write a letter to Ian, a long, probably rambling letter in which I expressed my love for him and detailed my daily life. I realised that he might not be that interested, but it was very therapeutic for me, it kept me from crying. On Friday afternoon, I finished early, went home and did a few chores, then drove to Henley. When I arrived at Maman's house it was already getting towards dusk and the temperatures were falling, it looked as if we were in for a frosty night. I blessed Grandpa Barclay again for the four-car garage, so I could park my Mini alongside Maman's Land Rovers and her Lotus. I unloaded my luggage and made my way through from the garage to the kitchen.

"Bébé," Maman said, when I stumbled in with my bags. "How are you, how was the drive over, are you cold, are you hungry or thirsty?"

"Maman," I said. "I'm fine, the drive over was slow and damp, the bloody heater in the Mini is playing up, I'm not hungry but I could use something to drink."

"Mon Dieu," Maman said. "Look at the hour, Bébé, please take my new Land Rover and go to the station and meet Portia for me, I'm busy with dinner here."

"How will I know who is Portia?" I asked.

"She'll be the one with the briefcase," Maman said.

"That's not much help. What about other clues?" I asked. "Tall, short, blonde, dark?"

"Oh, brunette, a little taller than you, looks a lot like Claudia Cardinale," Maman said. "Now, please go, I don't want her to wait around at the station. Thank you Dear, I'll have wine ready for you when you return."

I dutifully drove to the station and was in time to park and wander over to the platform before the train arrived. The train pulled in and people got off. I saw her, it had to be her, as Maman had said, she did look a lot like Claudia Cardinale. She was dressed in a dark grey suit, looking very severe, but then she looked in my direction, and smiled and walked over to me.

"You must be Fiona," she said. I admitted that I was, and kissed her in the French fashion for greeting.

"I'm sorry Maman is not here to meet you," I said. "She was busy with dinner, so I was delegated."

"Well, I'm delighted to meet you," she said. "Brigitte has told me so much about you, I feel I know you already." I wondered what Maman had been saying, but assumed that it was mostly good, she had never, to my knowledge, complained about me to anyone outside the family.

"May I help you with your luggage?" I asked.

"No, thank you," Portia said. "This doesn't weigh much." I led the way to the Land Rover and opened the door for her, then took her bags from her and put them on the back seat.

"Maman tells me that you're a solicitor," I said. "She also said that you're a whiz at intellectual property issues, which I suppose is copyright and such."

"It is," Portia confirmed. "We also have a growing environmental practice, which I also head, for my sins."

"Were those sins of commission or omission?" I asked.

"Omission," she laughed. "I wasn't there one day and they voted me in as head. Brigitte said I'd recognise you because you two look alike, you really do, there was no mistaking you at the station."

"Maman told me to look for Claudia Cardinale," I said. "She was right about that too."

"Why thank you," Portia said. "Nice to be perhaps mistaken for someone as famous."

We arrived at the house and I parked in the garage. Portia had been before, that was obvious, she knew the way to the kitchen and knew to remove her shoes at the back door.

"Maman, we're here," I called.

"Portia, *chérie*," Maman said, giving her a kiss. This was not like mine, a peck on each cheek, this was a proper kiss, as I would kiss Ian. I looked at them both and surprised myself. I had wondered how I would react when I saw them together, a lesbian relationship that was so close was new to me. I found that I was happy for them, not offended in any way, or I suppose in the extreme disgusted by the idea, they were just two people who had found each other, and the mutual affection was obvious.

"Fi, would you take Portia's bags to my room for her?" Maman asked.

"Of course, Maman," I said. I gathered up the bags and took them upstairs. When I came down the two of them were locked in a passionate embrace.

"Hey," I said. "As they told me when I kissed Ian at the shoot, get a room!"

"We will," Maman laughed. "Portia, *chérie*, Fiona is out of sorts because she's lost Ian to Germany and anthropology for three weeks, so she's missing him."

"Poor thing," Portia sympathised. "You should tell me all about him, but first let me go up and change, I've been stuck in suits for the whole week, it's time to dress down a little."

"You really like her, don't you?" I asked Maman when Portia had left. It also dawned on me after Portia had gone that we had all been using French, it was so natural for me to talk to Maman in French that I had not even noticed that Portia also was using French, so apparently, she was fluent in French as well as English.

"I do Bébé, she's smart, she's fun to be with, I just enjoy her company," she confirmed, then she grinned at me wickedly and said. "And she's a tigress in bed."

"Good for you," I said. Not rising to that bait. "Now are we going to die of thirst, or do you have the wine you promised."

When Portia came back, I thought that it was as well that Maman had the house heated, because she had on a mini skirt, shorter than the one I had, and a halter top, no bra. I had to admit, that apart from the physical likeness to Claudia Cardinale, she had the rest of the package to go with it, great legs, slim build, still firm breasts. But I did wonder about the challenges of being a female solicitor, even a senior one, in a world that was still so dominated by men, how many of them just saw her as an attractive woman, which to look at she definitely was, but did not take her seriously as a lawyer?

"Is that wine you have there?" she asked. "So, Fiona, tell me about Ian."

"He's a post-grad student," I started, but then thinking about Maman's comment once about not wanting to buy him, changed from a simple description of his physical assets to a more lyrical description of him. "He makes me laugh," I said. "He grins a lot when he's with me, I love him and I know that he loves me."

"But I gather from Brigitte's comment, he's gone for a while?" she asked.

"He went to Germany for some research," I confirmed. "He's been gone for a week now and he'll be gone for another two weeks, I miss him, I miss his laugh, his grin when he sees me, I miss the scent of his aftershave, his arms around me, his kisses, I just miss him."

"She's in love," Portia said to Maman.

"That's why she's here," Maman said. "She has no picture of him nor he of her, so we're going to spend some time tomorrow taking photographs."

"I do have a picture," I said. "I found one in an old college paper, see, here it is." They both looked at it and Maman commented that it was not the best picture and Portia said that he looked like quite a dish. With that, I had to agree, to me he was quite a dish.

"So, what kind of photos are you thinking about?" Portia asked.

"I thought a simple portrait and perhaps some other shots, like me with a rifle, me next to the Land Rover, maybe some others," I said.

"So, essentially a small portfolio," Portia said. "No, boudoir shots?"

"I suppose I could," I said. "But I'm not sure when I would give those to him."

"Well, we can decide tomorrow," Maman said. "Now, it is time for dinner."

Over dinner, we three discussed being a woman in worlds dominated by men and the challenges that that brought. It seemed that Portia had had her share of sexual bullying, but had held her own, much to the chagrin of the bullies. All of us had heard the condescension in the voices of men who had assumed that we would not be capable of understanding what it was they were saying. I was thankful that Ian was not one and that he treated me as an equal, all the more so since our shooting match and the close finale. Portia, though steered the conversation back to photographs.

"So, Fiona," she said. "Do you want a portrait picture for your Ian, or more candid shots, or boudoir shots?"

"I don't know," I admitted. "I've not really thought about it much, perhaps we should do all of them and then I'll see what I like. Is that okay, Maman?"

"It is," she assured me. "But let me show you some examples of what Portia is talking about for boudoir shots." She went off and came back with a folio and started showing me the photographs that she had taken of Portia. There were formal portraits, less formal candid shots and then Portia clothed in only underwear in the bedroom in various poses, some of which I would describe as erotic, some as racy and some as just plain come and get me. She also had some nudes of Portia, which I have to say were very good, Maman really did have a talent.

111

"I think I could try some of these," I agreed. "I'm not sure if and when I might give any to Ian."

"We also have these of Brigitte," Portia said. In the later part of the album were similar shots of Maman. If we had not had the attitudes we had about nudity I might have been bothered by the shots of Maman, but if Portia had taken them, they were every bit as good as those that Maman had taken of her.

"So, boudoir and nudes?" Maman asked.

"Why not?" I confirmed. *"Autant aller jusqu'au bout,"* which essentially means in for a penny in for a pound.

"Good," Maman said. "We'll start after breakfast and see what we can do. Now, I think it's for bath and bed."

Now that could have been an interesting experience. I have described before how Maman and I would chat while one bathed and the other waited. Now there were three and I was embarrassed to think of the idea that Portia would share that moment. However, it did not happen, she left Maman and me to share our moment, then she joined Maman and I went to bed.

The next morning was for photography, after breakfast, and an early breakfast it was. Maman had us in the room she had used as a studio by eight, me to be photographed and Portia to handle lights, reflectors and generally assist. Maman had me pose sitting, standing, kneeling and even lying, on a sun bed she had there. She had me pose in the black dress, the cheongsam, my denim skirt and jacket, jeans, shorts, in fact almost my entire wardrobe. She also had me pose for a variety of semi-candid shots, holding a rifle, dressed in my show jumping gear, dressed for tennis, in a one-piece swimsuit, in my Tahitian costume and a few other ideas that she had Then she told me to pose in my underwear for the boudoir shots. She was good at this, she knew how to make me relax and just let her do the directing, she did have me go through almost my entire wardrobe of underwear, until she found that which she thought worked the best. One of the really good things about having Maman do this, was that I did not have to worry about the pictures ever getting into the wrong hands. Maman would safeguard the pictures and the negatives with her life. She finally did some nude shots of me, it took a little more time to do these, because she wanted the lighting just right, so poor Portia was directed around the room, moving lights and holding up reflectors.

After the shoot, Portia and I went to the kitchen for coffee and pastries, while Maman worked her magic in the dark room. We talked about all sorts of things, but along the way, I discovered that she had more in common with Claudia Cardinale than just her looks. Portia had also been born in Tunis, to an Italian mother and a British diplomat father. She had been raised in Tunis, Rome, Paris and London, thanks to her father's career, so she spoke English, French, Italian and Arabic. She told me that she had not used her French in a while and had worried about losing her fluency, but a short time with Maman had fixed that and she was now as comfortable in French again as she was in English. We talked about her life growing up, her education, her career and even her failed marriage. I discovered that she and I had one thing in common, we had both participated in show jumping events, the difference was that Portia still rode and jumped on occasion and had a horse that she kept at a local stable. I liked Portia, I could see why Maman liked her too, they suited one another and it was clear that she loved Maman. That for me was enough, if they loved each other then what did it matter that they were the same sex. That was a discovery for me, until then it was one of those things that you knew about but had no direct experience of, and often had ill-informed views about what same-sex relationships were all about.

It was well over an hour before Maman came back with her first runs of small prints from the negatives. She brought a small light table and a magnifying glass so that we could look through them and pick ones we might want enlarged. Then there was much debate and discussion. We each went through the strips of small prints and indicated which ones we thought were worth enlarging. That took us until well past lunchtime, almost until three, by which time we were all famished. I was despatched, under protest, to the local fish and chip shop for some rations, fearing that in my absence Maman and Portia would pick out pictures of me that I was definitely not going to give to Ian, at least not yet. When I returned, there were about a dozen pictures on the table that had been enlarged, and I had to admit that they were good, even the more risqué ones, Maman had a flair. I picked out three that I thought that I would give to Ian and asked for copies of them, the rest I would keep for myself. That was the time before colour photography was commonplace, so all the pictures were black and white, or rather, infinite shades of grey. I had my pictures, now all I needed was to get one of Ian.

I kicked myself for not having Maman take some when we had both been at her house, that would have been the perfect opportunity and I said so.

"Maman," I began. "When Ian and I were both here, why didn't you take any pictures?"

"There are times when life should be just lived and enjoyed, and taking pictures captures some memories, but also distracts from the sheer enjoyment of the moment," she said. "You tend to see life through the camera lens and not as it really is.

"So, why pictures now?" I asked.

"Because that is the moment for today," she said. "The experience today is that of posing and being photographed, it is in and of itself something to be enjoyed."

"I admit, that once I got over the shyness of being photographed that I quite enjoyed the experience," I said. "You do have a knack, Maman, of making me relax."

"That is a trust issue," she said. "You have to trust the photographer, and I know you, you could not have done that with an outside studio, no matter how well-known they were, or how good the photographer was supposed to be. I know you trust me, so for you, it worked. That is also why it worked for Portia and me, we trust one another completely."

"I do trust you, Maman," I said. "I always have."

The Humanities Ball

We spent what little was left of that afternoon going through photographs and arguing about which ones to keep and enlarge. Dinner, we had out, there had been no time to cook. Portia did put some more clothes on for that outing, as did I, autumn was well set in and winter was beginning to make itself known with falling temperatures, frosts and fogs. The Sunday we spent just enjoying one another's company, music, dance, laughter, good food and wine. It quite took me away from my self-pitying misery of missing Ian. Portia took us to the stable where she kept her horse, and she organised one for Maman and one for me, and we took an afternoon ride through the woods and hills. I enjoyed that, I had not been on a horse for a few years, but had not forgotten everything, so was able to enjoy the ride. I did wonder about sore muscles that I would have the next day, but it was worth it. I did not stay the night in Henley, but went back to Oxford, in the dark and the drizzle and was happy to get to my nice warm house. Unfortunately, once there I had another bout of the self-pity blues and cried, I cried while I poured myself a drink, I cried while I was in the bath and I cried myself to sleep. Silly, I know, because it was just self-pity, Ian was coming back, and I really had nothing to be sad about, it was just that I had not seen him or talked to him in a week, and I missed him.

The next two weeks dragged by interminably, no Ian, but plenty of work to do, so I immersed myself in the work, staying late at my office, to reduce the time I had at home to contemplate and indulge in bouts of self-pity. I had got over the initial bouts of tears, but I could still feel the blues, as is said. Love, I decided was a two-edged sword, on the one hand, there was the happiness and the thrill of being with someone who meant the world to you, but on the other hand, there was the loneliness and sadness when that person was not there. I had never seen myself as in any way philosophical before, I always had seen myself as pragmatic and logical, so this was all very new. Towards the end of the last week that Ian would be gone, I went to London for a progress meeting with my project sponsors. That actually went well, I had made significant progress in developing the algorithms and now needed more than ever computer time to run simulations to validate the mathematics. One of the mining houses came through and offered me time. It meant that I would have to be in London again the following week, but at least I had the time allotted to me. I was on the train going back to Oxford, engrossed in some of the notes I had taken when I caught the aroma of a familiar aftershave and tears welled up in my eyes as I thought of him, then I heard a longed-for voice.

"Excuse me, Miss, is this seat taken?" he said. I looked up in hope, and there he was, as large as life, in the flesh, as real as he could be and right next to me.

"Ian," I said, almost shouted. "Ian, you're back." I stood up, or I should say I just about leapt up, brushed aside my tears and kissed him. "Oh, it's so good that you're back," I rambled on. "I've missed you so much." We were interrupted by another traveller who remarked that while it was nice to see two people happy to see one another, that he would like to pass further down the train and that his passage would be made much easier if Ian put his suitcase overhead and sat down. Well, in not quite such flowery words, but the gist was the same. I let Ian go and he heaved his suitcase up into the rack then sat down next to me, taking my hand and holding it as though I would be pulled away from him by some unknown agency.

"Oh, Fi," he said. "You're crying, is everything okay?" he asked.

"I missed you," I said. "Then I smelled your aftershave and it made me think of you and I realised again, how much I love you and missed you.

"Well, that was the longest three weeks of my life," he said. "I had no idea time could drag so, God, I missed you." He kissed away my tears and told me again how much he loved me.

"I missed you too, *chéri*, but now you're back, when did you get back?" I asked.

"We got a ferry back today and took a train to Victoria, then the Tube here," he replied. "When we were walking up the platform towards peasant class, I saw you through the window, so let the others go ahead and came to join you. I've only got a second-class ticket, so will have to pay to stay here."

"I'll pay that," I said. "I'd buy you a new ticket, three new tickets, if it meant you could be with me."

"Thank you, *chérie*," he said. "I've almost run out of cash and need to get to the bank."

"Well, how was the trip?" I asked.

"Professor Ambrose, I have decided, is an eccentric dodderer," he replied. "We went on this trip with no fixed itinerary, no hotels booked, just a few appointments at museums. I learned a few things, but not much that will help me with my thesis. I think he's working up the nerve to tell me that there are issues."

"Who else was with you?" I asked.

"Two others from the department," he said. "It made things difficult, because they are both women and when we got hotel rooms, to save money Ambrose only took two rooms, so I had to share with him. Not the most pleasant experience?"

"Do I know these women?" I asked, thinking to myself as I did, that I should not become a jealous possessive girlfriend.

"I don't think you've met them," he said. "They're towards the front of the train, with Ambrose."

"He didn't mind you abandoning them and coming to sit with me?" I asked.

"I told him I'd seen a friend and was going to join her," he replied. "I think that at this stage of the trip, we were each looking for time alone."

"Well, I'm glad you spotted me," I said. "Imagine travelling all the way to Didcot on the same train and not sitting together. I have something for you."

"You do, what?" he asked. I rummaged in my briefcase and took out the envelope with the photographs that Maman had enlarged for me. I had been carrying them around with me since I got them. I took out the three that I had picked out to give to him and spread them out on the table in front of us.

"I had Maman take some pictures of me, so that I could give you one," I said. "Have you got one of you that I could have?"

"Gosh, Fi, I'm sorry, I don't," he said. "These pictures of you are great, do you think your Mum would do some of me?"

"I'm sure she would," I promised, thinking that if she did a shoot of Ian, I would want to be there to supervise, and wondering if men also did boudoir shots. He picked up each of the three pictures in turn and examined them.

"What?" I asked him.

"I'm trying to decide which one I like the best," he said. "I like the portrait, but I didn't know you rode horses, that one's really nice as well, and I really like the one with you toting a rifle. I can't decide which one I like the best, so I think I'll put this one of you armed to the teeth in my office, this one of you dressed to ride in my digs and if I could get a smaller version of the portrait, I'll carry that one with me."

"I'll ask Maman for a small one of that," I promised. "I also have here the letters I wrote to you, you can take them and read them whenever you like."

For the rest of the journey to Didcot, we just sat and talked and he told me of his travels and travails in Germany. The ticket inspector finally came just before we reached Reading and I paid the excess fare, much to the annoyance of the inspector who had to make out a receipt and issue a new ticket. I just sat and revelled in Ian's company and held his hand and kissed him in breaks in our conversation. It was so wonderful to have him back; my life was complete again. At Didcot, we alighted, each with our suitcase and briefcase. We could not hold hands because it is difficult to do so when both hands are busy with luggage. I did have an observation though, when we did hold hands, there seemed to be a natural way that we did it, one hand over the other, if we reversed the position of our hands, it felt wrong and unnatural, when he held my hand it was natural, when I held his hand in felt wrong. On the platform we saw Professor Ambrose, pointed out to me by Ian, he came over to see us.

"I see you met your friend, Hartley," he said. "Introduce us, would you?"

"Doctor Barclay, meet Professor Ambrose, professor, Dr Barclay is a Research Fellow at the college in the Mathematics Department," Ian said.

"Delighted to meet you," Ambrose said. "I must say I was surprised when Hartley left us at Paddington. When did you get your doctorate?"

"Earlier this year," I said. "I was granted the Fellowship in August and have a research project sponsored by the mining industry."

"But" he started, I could see that he was struggling with what to say, he probably wanted to ask how old I was and how it was that someone so lacking in years could have already achieved their doctorate. "When did you first come to the college?" he asked. Ah, that was a clever way to get around the age question.

"I came up for my bachelor's in 1965," I told him.

"And you have your doctorate already?" he asked, almost in disbelief.

"I do," I confirmed. Leaving it at that, I had been thinking of making a snide remark that I had been fortunate in my thesis advisor, but decided against it, partly because as I had not been fortunate in my thesis advisor as my ideas conflicted with his pet theories, and partly because I did not wish to prejudice Ambrose against Ian. Two women then came up to us, I presumed they were the two who had also been on the trip.

"So, Ian, who's your friend?" one asked.

"Gloria Best, Angela McIntosh, meet Dr Fiona Barclay of our own mathematics department. Fiona is a research fellow with the college," Ian said, making introductions all around.

"So, you're Fiona Barclay," Angela said. "There are all kinds of stories about you at the college, you're practically famous. So, you're the one Ian has been pining for the past few weeks."

"There's the Oxford train," Gloria said. We all boarded and found place for our luggage. This was a small local stopping train, with no first-class seats, so Ian and I were sociable and sat with, or at least, near the others, across the aisle, in fact. That left us able to sit and hold hands, and still listen to the conversation. At Oxford, I offered to give Ian a lift back to his digs, an offer he accepted with alacrity.

"Are you busy tomorrow?" he asked, when we were alone in my car.

"No," I said. "I had made sure that I had nothing on, so that if you came back today and wanted to do something tomorrow, then I'd be free."

"Great, look, why don't we go to the Trout Inn for lunch again?" he suggested.

"I'd love that," I said. "Will you let me pay this time?"

"I'm the one asking you out," he said. "I have the funds, I can afford lunch for us."

"You're sure?" I asked.

"I'm sure *chérie*," he said.

"Okay," I said, a little unsure about the true state of his finances. "What time shall I pick you up?"

"How about eleven?" he suggested. "That gives me time to go to the launderette and wash my clothes."

"Eleven it is," I confirmed. I drove him to his digs and we said goodbye, that took a little while as we had three weeks of missed kisses to make up for.

When I finally did go home and was happy again. The self-pity blues were gone, Ian was back, I had been able to hold his hand and kiss him. Life was good, in fact, it was better than good, it was brilliant. I sang all the way home, not "*Then he kissed me*" this time, but "*Something*", and I'm sure the Beatles would have been appalled by my caterwauling. At home, I called Maman. "He's back," I said.

"Good," she said. "Now you can cheer up a little."

"We're having lunch tomorrow," I told her. "He did ask me for one thing, he says he has no pictures of himself and he liked the ones you took of me, so asked if you could take some of him?"

"I'd be happy too," she said. "Why don't you come on Sunday, if you're both not busy? Portia's here now and will be on Sunday and I know she'd love to meet Ian. Tell him to bring a variety of clothes, so that we can get formal and informal pictures."

"Okay, Maman," I agreed. "Thank you for doing this. Now, how are you?"

"Ah, you finally asked after your poor Maman," she said. "I'm in the pink of health, and Portia has moved in with me and we're going to let out her cottage."

"Oh, Maman," I said. "That sounds terrific, I'm so happy for you."

"It's new and exciting," Maman said. "The house doesn't seem so big and empty now. Portia brightens it up a lot."

"I'm sure she does, Maman," I said. "Does she go every day to London?"

"She does," Maman confirmed. "I drop her at the station and pick her up in the evening, like any good suburban housewife."

"Oh, Maman," I protested. "I cannot see you as a suburbanite, as a loving partner, I can."

"I do love her," Maman confessed. "She makes my heart skip little beats, just like Ian does to you."

"Does she love you?" I asked.

"Yes," Maman confirmed. "Apart from the fact that she tells me, she shows it in many little ways. We are both really happy."

"Good for you," I said. "I'll talk to Ian tomorrow and call you in the evening to confirm whether or not we'll be there on Sunday. I love you, Maman"

"*Bon,*" Maman said. "*À bientôt. Je t'aime.*"

I picked Ian up at eleven and we drove out to the Trout Inn.

"Ian, Fiona," Chris said, when we entered the bar. "Back again?"

120

"Back again," Ian confirmed. "We're here for lunch Chris." We were shown to a table and presented with menus and had our order for drinks taken.

"Fiona," Ian began as we sipped our drinks. "Would you go with me to the Humanities Ball this year?"

"Of course," I said. "When is it?"

"In two weeks' time, at the college, on Friday the twenty-seventh, begins at six, dinner at seven, then dancing, ends when we get thrown out," he said. "It's a formal ball, so long dresses and dinner jackets."

"That sounds like fun," I said. "I'd love to go with you. I've never been to any of the college balls, I never had any inclination to go, and never had anyone to go with, so this will be a first. How much is it?"

"Don't worry about that," he said. "I do have enough budgeted for that."

"Are you sure?" I asked. "I could always go halves with you?"

"I'm sure," he said. "Really, I am."

"Fine, but I'm getting us a hotel room," I said, asserting myself a little. "I'm not driving home after the ball, I'd rather spend the time with you."

"Are you sure?" he asked, probably guessing what else that would mean.

"I'm sure," I told him. "We could just stay the whole of the next day and night and leave on Sunday."

"You're sure?" he asked again.

"Sure," I said. "Or, as I've heard you say, sure sure."

"That sounds wonderful," he said. "So, what are you going to wear to the ball?"

"I've no idea," I said. "I have some things I could wear, but do you have a preference?"

"Just a dress that makes you look as amazing as you are," he said. "I don't think it would matter what you wore, you'd still look terrific."

"I presumed there'd be dancing?" I asked. "Can you dance?"

"A little," he said. "When I was at boarding school in Salisbury, they gave us ballroom dancing classes. I managed, but can't say that I'm Fred Astaire. Can you dance, apart from Tahitian?"

"Maman taught me the basics," I said.

"So, we won't look like complete idiots," he commented. "You could always liven things up by doing a Tahitian dance."

"Don't even think about it," I warned. "I'm not having a bunch of spotty undergrads drooling over me."

"Why do you think they would drool?" he asked.

"Because you did," I laughed. "I saw you when Maman and I danced for you, you looked like a big dog, sitting there anticipating a biscuit."

"Okay," he said. "I promise, I won't ask you to dance any Tahitian."

"Thank you," I said. "Now, what are you doing tomorrow, Maman said that she can do a photo shoot for you tomorrow, if you want?"

"That would be super," he said. "Let's do that."

"Good," I said. "She said to bring clothes, so that she can shoot you in a variety of poses and in different clothes. Oh, and I should let you know that Portia, I told you about her before, has moved in with Maman, so she'll be there as well."

"Just as well I did my washing," he laughed. "It wouldn't do to sit for pictures with grubby clothes and an unpressed suit."

Lunch was ordered and delivered and we ate in comparative silence. After lunch and over coffee we had the chance to talk again.

"So, tell me more about your trip," I suggested. He did, he went through it day by day, telling me about the places they went, the museums they visited and the artefacts they examined and argued over. He told me about the squabbles over who would sit where on the trains they took, the pettiness over splitting accounts when they had dinner somewhere, splitting hairs over who had more than one drink and who had dessert and who did not. It sounded like the trip was one long argument. He assured me that it was not, it was just that those items stuck in his craw as he could not see the point of it all. We finally left the inn at six in the evening, after we had indulged ourselves with afternoon tea, that I insisted on paying for. It had been a lovely day, just the two of us chatting away like magpies, making up for lost time. I drove us back to Oxford and dropped him at his digs, with the promise to collect him at eight the following morning, shaven, packed and ready for his day of posing.

I collected Ian, his suitcase and his hat, the next morning at eight and drove over to Henley, I do admit to a little speeding as we were there in just over thirty minutes. I parked in the garage and we went into the kitchen.

"Maman," I called out. "We're here."

"Bébé," she said, as she and Portia came from the stairs into the kitchen. "How are you this morning, Ian how lovely to see you again, Portia, this is Ian, Ian this is Portia? So, Ian, you'd like some photographs taken, have you any particular poses you want?"

"I thought perhaps a formal shot that I could use for a CV," he replied. "Then, just a selection of others, maybe some standing, some less formal, in jeans and a shirt, not a suit."

"Did Fiona show you what we did for her?" Maman asked.

"I have the three she gave me," he said. "There were more?"

"A lot more," Maman said. "Let me get some and show you, Portia, *chérie*, would you make some coffee for Ian and Fi?"

"Maman," I warned, desperately hoping that she would be selective in the photographs she showed him.

"Don't worry Bébé," she laughed." I won't show him the one of you naked on the bearskin rug." Ian looked at her and at me, trying, I think, to imagine me naked on a rug, and also trying to decide if she was joking or not.

"There is no such picture," I told him.

"So you say," Maman teased. "But there are others."

"Maman," I pleaded.

"Sadly, she's right, Ian, we didn't get that far in her photo session, but we could arrange for you to be shot naked on a bearskin rug, I'm sure Fi would appreciate that." Poor Ian, he blushed so deeply at the suggestion. Maman went off to her dark room and came back with a selection of pictures. She had been teasing me, there were no nude photographs, nor any boudoir shots, just a wide variety of formal semi-formal and candid shots. Ian looked through them and showed Maman the types of shots he might like of himself.

That done, Maman suggested that Ian might be more comfortable if I was not watching, and he, perfidious man, agreed, so I was banished to the kitchen to think about what we might eat for lunch. I had lunch prepared and ready to be served when they finally came back.

"Well, how was it?" I asked Ian.

"It was surprisingly fun," he said. "Your Mum is very good at making her sitters relax and just pose."

"When do we see prints?" I asked.

"I'll develop the films after lunch," Maman promised. "I'll have proofs soon afterwards, and we can select those that Ian wants enlarged."

"While you're doing that, could you make a wallet-size print of the formal portrait that I picked?" I asked. "Ian would like one to keep with him."

"How many would you like?" she asked him.

"Three would be super, if that's possible?" he asked.

"Of course," Maman said. "Now, let's see what Fi created for us for lunch.

After lunch, Maman disappeared into the dark room while the rest of us just waited and chatted. I told Portia that Ian and I were going to the Humanities Ball and that it would be formal.

"So, have you a dress?" she asked.

"I'm not sure what to wear," I confessed. "I have the short black dress, I have the red cheongsam, but no formal long dresses."

"I can help you there," she said. "Do you have reason to be in London anytime in the next two weeks?"

"I do," I replied. "I going up to London on Tuesday to run some more computer simulations."

"Good," Portia said. "Can you come to my office at noon?"

"Yes," I agreed. "If I get the runs started in the morning, then I typically have to wait until three to get the results, so have a couple of hours to kill."

"Good, then I'll introduce you to a friend of mine and we'll get you sorted out," Portia promised.

"Thank you," I said.

"Thank you for what?" Maman said as she joined us with strips of prints, her small light table and a magnifying glass.

"Portia's going to help me find a formal dress for a ball," I explained.

"Wonderful," Maman said. "Thank you *chérie*, Fi and I have always fenced over clothes, and it's only now that she's taking any real interest. Now, Ian, look through these and let me know which ones you like." He did as instructed and scanned the strips carefully, pointing out those that he thought he might like enlargements of. I was allowed to look at the print strips and, again, Maman had done a wonderful job.

"So, which one do I get, or can I pick my own?" I asked him.

"You picked, so I pick," he said. "I think these three." He indicated the three and Maman nodded in agreement. She went off and came back telling us that the enlargements were drying. I also noticed that she surreptitiously slipped Ian three print strips. I clearly was not supposed to see that, so pretended that I had seen nothing.

After tea, Maman gave Ian the prints of his pictures and the prints of me that he had requested. He dutifully handed over the prints of himself and I was thrilled. One was a formal suit, but an over-the-shoulder look, which I really liked, another was less formal, just jeans, and a blue shirt and the one I think I liked the best, dressed for the African bush, khaki shirt, trousers, bush hat, sunglasses, holding a tin coffee cup. That one was going on my desk, to me it was Ian, more so than the suited man, or even the Adonis in blue jeans, to paraphrase the Jimmy Clanton song. I thanked Maman and suggested to Ian that we should get going, both of us had morning meetings the next day. As we left, there was a whispered conversation between Ian and Maman and all I caught, was to let her know which ones he wanted. I decided to let things go, perhaps Ian wanted to surprise me with a photograph and had recruited Maman and Portia as willing accomplices.

On Monday I went to the Randolph, one of the older, better hotels in Oxford and told them that I wanted to take a suite for the weekend of the ball. I was shown upstairs and taken around the various suites and picked one out. So that there was no discussion about my ability to pay for the room, I paid for it then and there with cash. The next day whilst I was in London, I presented myself at the law firm where Portia worked.
"May I help you?" a receptionist asked.
"Yes, please," I said. "I'd like to see Portia Harding."
"Mrs Harding is very busy, I'll check for you, who shall I say is here?" she asked, in a very superior and condescending way.
"Dr Fiona Barclay," I said as haughtily as I could. I could give as good as I got. The receptionist made a quick call and then looked at me again, in some surprise.
"Mrs Harding will be down immediately," she said. Immediately was almost right, it was less than a minute before Portia arrived.

"Fiona," she said, as she kissed me on both cheeks.

"*Portia, bonjour,*" I said. "*Ça va?*"

"*Trés bien, on y va?*" she asked, suggesting that we go.

"*Oui,*" I said. Portia told the receptionist that she would be back later. She then hailed a cab and we went to an address in Mayfair.

Even I recognised the name on the door, that of one of London's better-known couturiers, Rachel Adams. We went in and Portia obviously knew the girl at the desk, because she was greeted with respect.

"Rachel is expecting you," she said. "Please go straight through." We walked towards the back of the building and into a largish room, replete with floor-to-ceiling mirrors. Rachel was there waiting for us.

"Portia," she said. "How lovely to see you, you're looking very well."

"Thank you," Portia said. "I'm very happy these days, I've moved in with Brigitte."

"Oh, I am happy for you," Rachel said.

"Rachel," Portia said. "This is Fiona, she's Brigitte's daughter and is in need of a dress for a college ball in Oxford, I was looking for something to wow her young man, who I've met, and who I would describe as grrrr."

"That good-looking, is he?" Rachel laughed. "Well, Fiona, let's take a look at you." She indicated that I should pirouette in front of her while she studied me. "Can we try that without the severe suit?" she asked. I took off the suit and handed it to Portia, and spun again for Rachel in my underwear.

"Hmm," she said. "Good bone structure, nice figure, a little boyish, but could carry almost anything off well. I think I may have the very thing, it's not one of my designs, but I think you'll like it." She vanished through a side door I had not noticed and came back with an armful of clothing.

"This is an Yves Saint Laurent evening ensemble," she explained. "It is a separate skirt and bodice, in block colour velveteen, with puffed upper sleeves on the bodice, very chic, he calls it Rive Gauche. The bodice top laces up, so if things go well with grrrr, then easy to remove. Come, try it on." I pulled on the skirt and zipped it up, it was a little loose at the waist. Then I put on the top and tried to lace it up, Portia took pity on me and did it for me. The top fit perfectly.

"So," Rachel said. "Spin again for me." I did as instructed and she looked at me carefully.

"Good," she said. "A small adjustment in the waist, Hermione," she called and a woman came from the back. "Hermione, would you take the measurements and make the adjustments to the waist for me."

"Of course," she said. After she had measured and marked, I took off the skirt and handed it to her, then put my own skirt back on, then traded tops as well.

"What do I wear with it?" I asked.

"Basic underwear, bra and panties, no need for a slip, no need for stockings or tights, wine red shoes and clutch bag," Rachel said. "If we go and get you some white bra and panties, we'll dye them to match the red in the skirt and the bodice, and don't worry, the dye won't run, even if you go swimming in the Thames. Because it could be cold and damp, I suggest a grey cloak to match the grey in the bodice and the skirt, I can get that for you."

"How much will this cost me?" I asked in horror, a Saint Laurent outfit had to run to a fortune, let alone all the other items

"My treat," Portia said. "The whole ensemble is my treat."

"Oh, Portia, I can't," I said.

"Yes, you can," she said. "This is Fiona's first love, first ball, so I want to make it special," she said to Rachel.

"But how will I get everything?" I asked.

"We'll go and have some lunch," Rachel suggested. "Then you can try on the skirt again when we come back and take it with you. The rest we'll sort out and Portia can bring it to you."

We went for lunch at a fashionable Mayfair restaurant and Portia and Rachel excused themselves and talked legal matters for a while, then they turned the conversation back to me and asked me about Ian. I gave them chapter and verse and, unlike me, I actually opened up about my feelings when he had been away for the three weeks. Apart from Maman I had never really had any female friends and it was nice to spend a lunch time with two successful businesswomen. Back at Rachel's studio, the skirt was ready, so I tried it on again and the fit was amazing. I spun around for Rachel, then took some waltz steps around the floor. I could dance in this skirt. Then, in case I had too much to drink and succumbed to prodding and whining by Ian, I kicked off my shoes and tried some Tahitian hip movements. I confess I got carried away and did the whole of Mémère Monique's 'aparima. I could even do that in this skirt, not quite the same as in a grass skirt, but I could do it.

"What was that?" Rachel asked, applauding.

"Oh, sorry I got carried away," I said. "It's a Tahitian dance that was choreographed by my grandmother, and which I learned from Maman."

"It was lovely," Rachel said. "So sensuous, you do it so well."

"Brigitte danced it for me once," Portia said. "But she did it with a little less on, so no long skirt to constrict the hips. It was sensual enough that censors everywhere would be looking to ban it ever being performed in public."

"I can imagine," Rachel said. "So, Portia, what do we suggest that she wears with this as accessories?"

"Well, Fiona doesn't have pierced ears," Portia commented. "Fiona, how are you with clip-ons?"

"Not a big fan," I said. "They hurt my ears."

"Okay, so we just go with a simple silver choker with a dark sapphire and a matching silver brooch, also set with a sapphire, they'll go with the blue panels of the dress and bodice," Portia suggested.

"I like that," Rachel agreed. "I know just the place, I'll give you the address. It's been wonderful to meet you, Fiona, I hope you have a great time at your ball. When you're in London again, come and see me."

"Thank you," I said. "Portia, I don't know how to thank you."

"Just have a good time," she said. "And, tell me about it afterwards."

I went back to computing and Portia went back to legal matters. For the next almost two weeks I was busy with my research and the project. The computer simulations had been really useful in proving the algorithms, now I had to refine them to take into account the potential variation in market prices of metals. I built into the models the ability to wildly swing the LME prices, so that the user could see the impact and make their valuations accordingly. Ian and I met every day I was in Oxford, except Sundays, when I kept myself busy at my house, either cleaning, doing my washing, or tidying up the garden. With all the leaves off the trees, there was much raking to be done. When I did not see Ian in person, I called him, during the week in his office and on Sundays at the pub. For two people who saw each other almost every day, we seemed to find a lot to talk about on the telephone, but I suppose that was what being in love was all about.

Finally, the day of the ball arrived and I registered at the Randolph early, at about three, along with my beauty team. Maman, Portia and Bridget had all said that they would be there to help me get ready. I thought it was a little overkill, but if it kept them happy, I was glad for their support, just as long as they left when I went to the ball, so that the room was empty when Ian and I returned. I was bathed, had my hair washed, dried, trimmed and brushed, had my nails trimmed, and buffed, both fingers and toes, then had clear varnish applied, then Bridget tended to my eyebrows and also applied eyeliner and shadow. There was much discussion about lipstick, and the consensus was that I needed some, but it should be muted, grey to match the grey in the bodice and the skirt, rouge and other face powder were dismissed as unnecessary. When all the facial items had been done, I was given the wine-red underwear to put on. There was little enough of it, if it were priced by the square inch, it would have been outrageous, and if it was priced by the actual opaque coverage it would have been doubly outrageous. It was lacy, with enough empty space in the lace to be almost see-through. I wondered who had selected it and decided that it was a joint decision by the three who now primped and prepared me. They had prepared for all kinds of eventualities, because there were actually three sets of the red underwear, including the set that Rachel had dyed for me. It felt a little like the Elizabethan era where I was being prepared for the marriage bed, and that was made even more of a simile when Maman produced a care package of condoms, lubricants and other accessories. They had obviously decided that tonight was the night and were taking no chances. Finally, with the undergarments on, hair done, nails done, it was time for the skirt. I put it on and it still fit, like a glove actually, Hermione had done a wonderful job. Then I put on the top and Portia laced it up for me. The finishing touches were a silver choker with a sapphire set in it and a matching silver brooch with a sapphire surrounded by tiny diamonds. I put on the red shoes and grasped the bag and was ready. I was then allowed to look in the mirror.
"Is that really me?" I wondered. The Saint Laurent ensemble was simple, but elegant and it set off the meagre figure that I did have very well.

"It is, Bébé," Maman said, crying. "You will be the most beautiful girl at the ball."

"I agree," added Portia, also in tears.

"Bridget, will you take a picture for me, I can't see through the tears?" Maman said.

"I'll try," Bridget said. "But I'm not sure I'll be any better than you, you do look beautiful Fiona."

Maman, Portia and Bridget dried their eyes, then Maman picked up my cloak and told me that they would wait for me in the lobby. I suspected that what she really wanted was pictures of me coming down the grand staircase that graced the foyer of the Randolph. I let them have their moment. I gave them a few minutes, then left to go and meet Ian. I saw him as I was tripping, actually trying very hard not to trip on the long skirt, down the stairs.

"Wow, Fiona," he said. "You look amazing."

"You look very nice," I said, taking in his dinner jacket, fancy shirt and bow tie. I noticed that he had a coat over his arm, so he had also come prepared for the elements. Maman came over and took his coat, then chivvied us together so that she could take our picture. We were posed on the stairs, by the front desk and in a couple of other places that Maman thought might be photogenic. I wondered what the hotel staff thought about all this, my three beauticians and now pictures.

"Can we go now?" I asked. "Please Maman."

"Enjoy yourself, Bébé," Maman said. "You too Ian, have a nice time at the ball. Ian, we'll put your case in the suite."

Ian helped me on with my cloak, then he donned his coat and we went down the line of my supporters and kissed each of them goodbye, and then walked the short distance from the hotel to the college. There we handed in our outerwear at the cloakroom and went to the ballroom. I was intimidated by the number of people there were there, it seemed to me to be thousands, but it was probably only two hundred or so. Ian and I looked around to see if there was anyone there that he recognised, or for that matter that I might recognise. It showed that my time at the college had been cloistered, as I knew not a soul in that crowd. At last, he saw people he had been expecting and guided me over to the table that had been commandeered.

"Ian," one of the men said. "Glad you could make it."

"Rory," Ian said. "This is Fiona, Fiona, Rory McIntosh, and with him is Angela White, and going around the table, George Wilson, Mary Heath, Henry Bishop and Katherine Roberts."

"Are you with the college?" Katherine asked.

"I am," I confirmed. "I'm in the mathematics department."

"You aren't Fiona Barclay?" Mary asked.

"I am," I said.

"So nice to meet you, I've heard so much about you," Mary said. "I love your outfit, where did you get it?"

"A friend of mine got it for me in London," I said.

"It's different," Angela said. I suppose it was. The other women at the table had on classic ball gowns, lots of spaghetti straps, bare shoulders, low cuts across the bust and flared skirts, so my skirt probably did look a little different and the lace-up bodice was really different. I put them all in the mid to late twenties and learned in subsequent conversation that they were all in the Humanities Department in one way or another, Angela was a medieval historian, Mary a Latin scholar and Katherine a linguist, specialising in French. Of the men, Rory was another anthropologist, George was another linguist but his forte was Polynesian languages, Ian whispered to me that he was the one who had translated my Tahitian, and Henry was an archaeologist. Ian excused himself and went to the bar to get us some drinks, he came back with two bottles of wine that he placed in the centre of the table. He poured one for me and then asked if anyone else would like some. There were some takers, but Rory and Henry both said no, they were going for more serious liquor.

"I heard that you shoot rifles?" Angela said. "Isn't that difficult?"

"Not really," I said. "It takes concentration, but it's simple enough."

"I could never shoot a gun," Angela announced. "Too dangerous."

"I also shoot with a bow," I added. "I use a modified long bow."

"You never told me that," Ian commented. "I've never tried a bow; will you teach me one day?"

"I'd love to," I told him. "You've got much better upper body strength than me, so we could use a longer bow with more pull."

"Was it you who used the Tahitian with Ian?" George asked.

"It was," I confirmed, tentatively, wondering where this might go.

"What did she say?" Mary asked.

"Ua here vau ia oe," George said.

"What does that mean?" Mary asked.

"I love you," George, said grinning. "I wondered who it was that Ian was struck on."

"Does that mean you're Tahitian?" Mary asked.

"Only part," I said. "Oh, and before you ask, I don't do the Tahitian dance."

"Liar," Ian whispered in my ear. I was saved from more interrogation by the arrival of the first course of dinner. Then for the next hour silence reigned, except for occasional remarks.

When the final dinner things had been cleared away the band struck up. The first dance was a waltz and Ian asked me if I would like to dance. I was happy to be with him, away from the others, away from their judgmental looks when they looked at my skirt and top, perhaps I should have cattily told them that it was a Saint Laurent. I wondered about George too, when Ian had asked him to translate the Tahitian, he had to have guessed that someone that Ian knew could speak it, so was there a surprise in store for us later. The waltz, ended and up next was a foxtrot, followed by another waltz, I have to say, Ian was actually a good dancer, better than me and I actually remembered Maman's comments about following, rather than trying to lead. We had just finished the waltz when the tempo and style changed. Convention had been satisfied, there had been the requisite ballroom dances, now it was a free-for-all with more modern music, so the twist and a host of other dances from the sixties. I saw George go up to the bandstand and money changed hands and instead of continuing into the next dance, the drummer started off on a classic Tahitian beat. I saw quite a number of people trying their hand, or more properly their hips, to the beat, but none could master the moves. Then, three girls came from a side door, dressed in typical Tahitian dance attire and gave us a demonstration. Wherever they had been found, they were not Tahitian and were not masters of the moves. I was tempted, I was sorely tempted, to give them a demonstration, but resented the notion of being tricked into something.

"I'm so sorry," Ian said, holding my hand and looking absolutely horrified. "I had no idea George was going to pull something like this."

"Ladies and gentlemen," George said into the microphone, then he pointed at me. "We have an expert in our midst, we should get her to show us how it's really done." The crowd started to whistle and cheer, but I was not having it. Quite frankly I was horrified, dancing for Ian was one thing, being on public display was another.

"Please take me home?" I begged of Ian. "Please, I don't want to be here any longer. Please don't make me stay."

"Of course, *chérie*," he said. Then we walked out of the ballroom, to the jeers and catcalls of the others. I was in tears by the time we got my cloak and his coat

"Why did he do that?" I asked Ian, through my tears.

"Because he's an ass," Ian said angrily. "Probably thought he was being funny or clever."

"You didn't tell him that I danced, did you?" I asked.

"I'm so sorry, I may have done inadvertently," Ian said. "I mentioned that I had seen someone do a Tahitian dance and asked him about the significance of the *'aparima*, I never mentioned your name, and I suppose he made his assumptions and decided that whoever I brought to the ball, had to be the one."

We walked back to the hotel, and by the time we arrived, I had got myself back under control and dismissed George and his antics from my mind. All I wanted to do then was meet him in a dark alley and mete out punishment. I collected the key to our suite and told Ian which room we were in. When we got there, I burst into tears again.

"What's wrong *chérie?*" he asked, holding me tight.

"I wanted this night to be so special," I sobbed. "I wanted us to dance and have fun, then come back here, then have you undress me and make love. But now I'm not sure, I'm upset by what George did, I don't know how I feel at this minute."

"Why don't you go and have a long soak in a bath and relax?" Ian suggested. "Then, we'll see how you feel."

"Okay," I sobbed. I ran into the bathroom and ran a bath and took off my clothes. I had been looking forward so much to having Ian take them off for me and was angry with George for messing up my plans for the evening. The hot bath was soothing and slowly I relaxed and eventually decided that all was not lost, in fact, I got to feeling quite randy, here I was with the man of my dreams waiting for me to decide how things would go and I was wallowing in self-pity again, Well, enough was enough, I was going to have him that night. I got out of the bath, wrapped myself in a towel and went into the bedroom. Ian was sitting staring into space, probably wondering if he should just pack his bags and go home.

"Why don't you have a quick bath, then join me here?" I suggested.

"How are you feeling now?" he asked.

"I'm feeling like I need you," I told him. "I need your hands on me, I want you. I hope you brought enough condoms."

Ian scurried off and I heard him in the bath, so I pulled back the covers on the bed, threw the towel off and draped myself, in what I hoped was a seductive pose, on the bed. He came out soon enough, sans towel, took one look at me and growled.

"Man, you are only beautiful," he said. He was not so bad-looking himself and he did have a beautiful physique, well-muscled and tanned. He came over and kissed me, then we kissed more and again more, then he moved his kisses down my body to my breasts, then lower and lower. For the rest, I have debated long and hard about how much to reveal and in what kind of detail. I know the fashion today is to be very explicit, but I am not prepared for that, so you must use your imagination, but I will say this, Ian brought me to a climax three times in the ensuing hour. First with his hands and fingers, then with his tongue and finally I guided his erect manhood inside me and we both came to a most spectacular climax. Having him inside me was wonderful, I could not get enough of him. We made love again with me on top, with me in his lap, with him kneeling in between my legs as I lay on the edge of the bed, until we both admitted to being tired and fell asleep in each other's arms.

When I awoke the next morning, it was to the joy of feeling him behind me, cuddled close. Then I felt his hand between my legs.

"What do you think you're doing?" I teased.

"Just exploring," he said.

"Well, I think you need to be a little higher," I told him. He moved his hand and I felt him on me, then when I was ready, I reached back between my legs and found him erect, already sheathed and ready, so I helped him find his way inside me. It was a slow lovemaking that was relaxing and just absolutely wonderful.

"I think we should have a bath," I suggested when we were done. "It's big enough for two."

"I like that idea," he said. "I'll go and run one and when you're ready come and join me." Join him I did and I was soon astride him, riding him slowly and trying not to make too many waves, to put water all over the floor.

"Happy?" he asked.

"Ecstatic," I assured him. "Last night was wonderful, and we have the rest of today and tonight here as well. I hope you brought enough condoms."

"I brought a dozen," he said.

"That was either hopeful or presumptuous," I laughed. "But let's see, last night was four times, this morning this is the second time, so that's six so far, in what, ten hours, and we've probably sixteen waking hours left, so say another, eight, that's fourteen total, I think you should get more." I had completely forgotten about the care package that Maman had brought. I had stashed it in my suitcase before I had left for the ball and clean forgot about it.

"I will, after we have some breakfast or lunch," he laughed.

"What time is it?" I asked.

"I think a little after nine," he said. "We got back here around eleven last night and we finally went to sleep around two, so we've had seven hours of sleep."

"I wonder what time they serve breakfast until?" I asked. "I'm rather hungry, it's all this exercise I've been getting, like now."

"I thought I was supposed to do all the work?" he laughed.

"No, you just lie there and let me have my way with you," I told him. I speeded up my ministrations and was rewarded with another mutual climax.

"I love you, Fiona," he said, as we just sat in the warm water and held each other close.

"I love you too," I said. "I'm happy, I'm with you, I'm connected to you in the best way, what more could I want?"

"Breakfast," he reminded me, laughing.

"Spoilsport," I laughed. "Help me up and I'll dry myself, then find some clothes to put on." We made love once more before we both actually managed to get clothes on. Ian had come across me bent over selecting clothes from my suitcase, and one thing had led to another and we had made love on the bed. I am not sure who was the more insatiable, him or me. We both wanted the other so much and just could not get enough of one another.

"Breakfast," I said, quite severely. "We need breakfast!"

"Yes, *chérie*," he agreed. "No more lovemaking until we've eaten."

"We should have thought and ordered breakfast and had it delivered," I said.

"That would have been better," he agreed. "Perhaps tomorrow, we'll do that, we could always call down and get it brought up now. Let's do that." He called the room service number and put in an order for a full breakfast, tea and coffee, then sat back on the bed and just looked at me. "What?" I asked him.

"I was just thinking how beautiful you are," he said.

"Don't start anything," I warned. "There may be a knock at the door at any moment, the room does have dressing gowns, we should at least put them on."

"True," he sighed. "I'm glad we left the ball early, being with you here was much better. I'm sorry it was not what you had imagined."

"So was I last night," I said. "But as soon as we started to make love, all that went out the window, and I thought that we should not have gone at all, just stayed here in bed together."

"It doesn't always have to be in bed," he suggested. "There's a nice-looking couch in the other part of the suite, perhaps we should try there after breakfast."

"Not perhaps," I said. "We will." My further thoughts on that matter were interrupted by a knock at the door. Breakfast had arrived. The maid wheeled in a trolley and set it by the dressing table. I signed for it and thanked her with a small tip and she grinned at me when she left. I poured tea for Ian and coffee for myself, then we tucked into the breakfast. I was hungry and the food went down quickly. After eating, Ian looked at me speculatively and said, "Now what?"

"On the couch," I ordered. He went to the couch and lay back and I climbed on top of him, laying down length to length. He felt so good to be close to, and it was not long before I felt stirrings beneath me, which I put to good use by sitting up, equipping him with the necessary protection then riding him to a climax.

"Are we going to do this all day?" he asked, grinning like the Cheshire cat.

"I hope so," I said. "I can't get enough of you, Ian Hartley, I should have done this earlier and not wasted all that time."

"You weren't ready," he said. "Last night you were. But you're right, I need to go out for a few minutes to a chemist at least."

"Fine, we'll both go, time to get dressed, and this time we really should get dressed," I ordered.

We left the room and saw the maid outside, I told her that we would be gone for an hour or so. I think she went in to make our room as soon as we had disappeared down the corridor. We walked hand in hand down the stairs and out into the street. It was raining, so we turned around and went straight back in again. The front desk took pity on us and offered us a giant umbrella, large enough to shelter two. Well protected from the rain, we quickly found the chemist and replenished our supplies. Then it was coffee time, so we paid a visit to our favourite haunt and got coffee. As we sat drinking, I asked Ian which position he liked best. The poor man, I think I may have actually embarrassed him. He looked around furtively to see if anyone might overhear, then he replied. "You on top," he said. "I just like to watch you, and with me on top, that's not always so easy."

"Good," I said. "When we get back to the hotel, we'll try that again, have you finished your coffee?"

"Let's see coffee or you?" he laughed. "Let's go."

We walked back to the hotel, under the umbrella and handed it in at the front desk and went back upstairs to continue our weekend of lovemaking. It was to be an afternoon of experimentation. We tried different things and decided what we liked. We agreed that we would not dine in our room, but would venture out and eat in the dining room, downstairs.

"Fiona," Ian said. "Why don't you wear the dress you had on last night, I really like it and you look smashing in it?"

"All right," I agreed. "But you have to help me lace up the bodice."

"I can do that," he said. "Because then I'll know how to unlace it."

As I dressed for dinner, Ian watched. He was grinning again, grins of happiness. When I put on the red lace panties, I heard his sharp intake of breath.

137

"What's the matter?" I asked.

"Those panties make things more erotic than simple nakedness," he explained. "I can see, but not quite see, which gets things going in my imagination."

"That's a lovely thought," I said. "What about the bra?"

"Same," he said. "Who would have thought that clothed could be as big as a turn-on as no clothes?" I put the skirt on, then the top and asked him to help me lace it up. Then I watched him dress in a simple blue suit that he had brought. I was probably just as smitten with him as he was with me, and his body was worth looking at. The last thing I did was pin on the sapphire brooch and put on the sapphire choker.

"I didn't really look at those last night," Ian admitted. "But those sapphires are beautiful, they must have cost a packet."

"I've no idea," I admitted. "They were a gift from Portia, as was the skirt and top, underwear, shoes, bag and cloak, the whole outfit."

"You have really nice friends," he said. "Are we ready?"

We were both ready, we did a final check in the mirror then walked down to dinner. Ian had called down and reserved a table, and we were shown to it by the maître d'hôtel. As we walked to our table conversation in the room stopped. Terrified that I had done something peculiar I tried to look over myself to see if there was anything showing that should not be, or if there was anything about Ian that would stop conversation. After we were seated, conversation started up again, I leaned over to Ian and asked, "What was that all about?"

"It's not that often that a truly gorgeous girl walks in here," he said.

"I'm not gorgeous," I protested. "You're only saying that to butter me up and get me into bed later."

"Yes, and no," he said. "To me you truly are gorgeous, but yes I would say or do anything to get you into bed."

"You don't have to try," I laughed. "I have designs on you for later." We were interrupted by a lady who came to the table, "Excuse me," she said. "I have to ask, is that a Saint Laurent ensemble?"

"It is," I confirmed.

"It's beautiful," she said. "And it looks so beautiful on you, quite took my breath away when you came in."

"Thank you," I said, not knowing what else to say, if anything.

"Well, excuse me again for barging over here, but I had to know," she said. She went back to her table of six ladies and then there was a long conversation, with numerous glances in our direction and I heard the names Juliet Berto and Françoise Hardy bandied about. Finally, she came back. "Excuse me again," she said. "So, sorry to bother you at dinner, but we were talking, we can't decide are you Juliet Berto or Françoise Hardy?"

"Neither, I'm afraid," I said. "I'm just a simple mathematician."

"I think you're not being honest with me," she challenged. "But your secret is safe with us, enjoy your evening and, again, so sorry for barging in."

Nice to be mistaken for a film star or singer, but I was not sure that either Juliet Berto or Françoise Hardy would be that thrilled, in fact I would not have said that we looked at all alike. Ian and I enjoyed a rather good dinner, it was definitely better than the one served at the ball, but then that was catering to the five thousand, this was more select. After dinner we walked back upstairs and, in the room, we kissed and kissed again. Then Ian unlaced the bodice he had so carefully laced up earlier and slipped his hands inside around me. From there events took their natural course and we made love on the bed, then again in the bath, then on the sofa, and finally again on the bed. It was such a magical time. We finally went to sleep entangled in each other's arms and legs, face to face. In the morning I awoke first and gently moved his arms and legs so that I could go to the loo. When I came back, he was awake and looked at me with such affection that I almost cried. I went to him and kissed him fully awake, then used my mouth and tongue to awaken him elsewhere, then quickly fitted a condom and climbed on top of him.

"God, what a way to be woken up," he said. "Fiona, *chérie*, you are the best thing that ever happened to me."

"I was thinking the same thing about you," I said. "Now sit up and hold me." He sat up and we made love with me in his lap, his arms around me and mine around him. We took our time, pausing when things became too heated, until neither of could stand it any longer and then we both came to a massive climax together. I cried out in pleasure and afterwards wondered if the people in the next room could hear anything.

"We need to check out of the hotel soon," I told Ian.

"It's been a fabulous weekend," he said. "I'm sorry it's over, but will there be other times?"

"Yes," I told him. "Why don't you come and stay with me next weekend, I can put you to work in the garden in the day time and again in the bedroom at night?"

"Sounds great," he said. "Will we have coffee tomorrow?"

"I will clear my calendar," I promised. "If you have any conflicts just call me."

"I will," he promised. "Now, I suppose we should pack our bags before they come looking to throw us out."

We left the hotel and I drove him back to his digs then drove myself home. Then I called Maman.

"Bébé," she said. "How are you?"

"Well, Maman," I assured her. "Very well."

"Ah, so things went well?" she asked.

"Not exactly," I said, then I went into a long recitation of the evening of the ball and my reason for leaving, but then gave her the other news.

"Oh, Bébé," she said. "I'm so happy for you that it all worked out. And, did you and he make love often?"

"Oh, yes, Maman, we did," I told her. "It was wonderful, I wonder now why I kept putting it off. We tried the bed, the bath, a chair and a sofa."

"And he was satisfactory?" she asked.

"More than, he was wonderful," I said, remembering. "It was all so magical, me with him and him with me, waking up to find his arms around me, watching him watch me get dressed, everything was just incredible. I wore the outfit that Portia had given me, to dinner at the hotel and I was asked if I was Juliet Berto or Françoise Hardy."

"Really?" Maman asked. "How would anyone think that?"

"I've no idea, I can't imagine that anyone could see a likeness to either of them," I replied.

"Well, come here when you can and tell me everything," Maman commanded.

"I will, Maman, and thank Portia for me for the outfit and Bridget for the hair, makeup and nails," I said. "I need some lunch and some sleep, so will talk to you soon. Oh, did the pictures you took of us at the hotel turn out well?"

"They did," she confirmed. "I'll give you some when you come over and I'll have some for Ian as well."

"Thank you, Maman," I said. "Well, I really do need to eat or I'll faint away. I love you, Maman."

"It's all that exercise you've had over the past two days. Let me know when you're coming over and I'll make sure Portia is here as well. *À bientôt, je t'aime aussi,*" Maman said.

Thesis problems

The next week was a busy one for both me and for Ian, I went to London for two days to do more computer runs and Ian went off to the University of Newcastle for some discussions with an expert there. So, we only met briefly on the Monday, the rest of the week we tried hard to telephone one another, but seemed to leave as many messages as have actual conversations. I was disappointed, I really wanted to see him every day if I could and was having to come to terms with the fact that that was not always going to be possible. At least I had his picture, now framed and in pride of place on my desk. What I really wanted was a poster to put up on a wall in my bedroom, so I could indulge my fantasies about him. I talked to Ian on Friday and he was still in Newcastle and not due to return until the Sunday.

"*Chéri*," I said. "How will I survive the weekend without you?"

"Just think of me," he suggested. "Imagine that I'm next to you."

"Perhaps I'll go to Henley this afternoon," I told him. "Then I'll come to the station in Oxford to collect you on Sunday and we can at least spend that night together."

"Would your Mum mind if I came there and spent the night with you there?" he asked.

"She'd be delighted," I replied, confidently. "I'll pick you up in Henley then?"

"Hold on, let me just check the timetable," he said. I heard paper shuffling and then he came back and gave me an arrival time into Henley.

"I'll be there," I promised. "Bring plenty of supplies! We have a week to make up."

"I'm looking forward so much to seeing you again," he said. "I've missed you this week."

"I've missed you too *chéri*," I told him. "I'm longing to feel your touch again and have you arms around me, I love you."

"I love you *chérie*," he said. "I have to go; I'll see you at the station on Sunday."

"I'll be there," I promised. I heard the telephone click as it went dead, and he was gone. Gone, but not forgotten or unanticipated, at least I would get to see him on Sunday and I knew Maman would be thrilled to have him stay at her house with me. I called her and asked her if it was convenient for me to drive over and stay the weekend and also if she minded me bringing Ian for the one night.

"Bébé," she said. "I am thrilled that you are bringing him. I'll put you both in the back room, that overlooks the garden. When will you be here this afternoon?"

"Well, I'm finished here for the day," I replied. "So, I'll go home, collect my mail, set the oil feed settings on the stove, collect some clothes and drive over, so say one and a half hours. Is Portia there?"

"Not yet," Maman said. "I'm going to the station in five minutes to pick her up. We'll be back before you get here. Bring some better clothes, we may go out somewhere nice, so not just jeans."

It only took me an hour to run my errands and drive to Henley, even with the evening traffic.

"Maman," I called when I went into the house.

"Ah, Bébé, you're here," she said. "How are you?"

"Missing Ian," I confessed. "Oh, Maman, I didn't know one could miss someone so much, I haven't seen him since Monday. I miss his touch, I miss his arms around me, I miss the scent of his aftershave."

"That's all, you don't miss anything else?" she teased.

"I miss that too," I said, grinning from ear to ear. "Oh, Maman, it was wonderful, he was patient and loving and there was no pain or discomfort, I enjoyed it so much."

"And did he?" she asked.

"Oh, I think so," I said. "I definitely think so, I'm not sure who was the more insatiable, him or me, I couldn't get enough of him, it was so nice, is that weird or unusual?"

"Not at all," she assured me. "You clearly love each other and what better way to show that love?"

"I do love him, Maman," I told her. We were joined by Portia, who had shed her severe suit that she customarily wore for business for a short skirt and a loose shirt, that she had knotted showing her abdomen and the well-defined muscles that she had. "Portia," I greeted her. "Lovely to see you, did I ever thank you properly for the dress?"

"You did," she assured me. "And, you looked lovely in it."

"I brought the choker and brooch back," I told her.

"Why, they were presents for you to go with the outfit?" she said.

"You're sure?" I asked. "They must have cost a packet."

"Don't worry," she assured me. "They are my gift to you. Now Brigitte told me that all did not go per plan at the ball?"

"I probably planned too much and expected too much," I replied. "But I'm glad we left early, being with just Ian was much more fun."

"So, tell all," Maman commanded.

"You're not going to feed me or offer me anything to drink?" I asked in feigned horror.

"Of course I am," Maman assured me. "It's all ready in the living room, come, we'll drink and eat while we talk."

Talk we did. I went through the evening and the return to the hotel and then the love making that Ian and I shared. Maman wanted particulars, so I gave them and she gave me tips on how to improve the experience in the future. She and Portia had both been married, so had experience with men, and they shared their own likes, dislikes, experiences and techniques. For Maman and me that was not unusual, but I think at first Portia was a little surprised at our candour and the explicit nature of our conversation, but she was soon enough sharing her own experiences. It is interesting to note that much of our conversation would today probably be found in some form in the pages of Cosmopolitan Magazine, but in 1970, it would have been censored if it had been printed anywhere. The talk was useful and I promised myself to apply some of those lessons with Ian when he returned to me on Sunday. I also told them about the ladies at the hotel who had sent their emissary to talk to me first about the Saint Laurent ensemble, and then about their incorrect identification of me, confusing me with either Juliet Berto or Françoise Hardy. Both Portia and Maman commented that they were unable to see any resemblance to either. During a lull in the conversation I did ask Maman for a favour.

"What do you need?" she asked.

"Can you make a poster sized print of this picture of Ian?" I asked her, showing her my favourite picture.

"I can try," she said. "I don't have paper or any equipment large enough, but I know a studio that does, and I'm sure they will help."

"I'm going to put it on the wall in my bedroom," I said, wistfully. "Then he'll always be with me."

"I thought it was only love-sick teenagers who had posters of their idols on the wall or ceilings of their rooms," Maman laughed.

"The ceiling," I said. "I hadn't thought of the ceiling, now there's an idea."

"So, you can lie in bed and indulge your most base fantasies," Portia laughed.

"You're just jealous," I said.

"No, I have the real thing here," she said, hugging Maman. "I don't need to fantasise."

"You're looking really good Portia," I commented. "Have you been doing something different?"

"I've been running with Brigitte," she replied. "I play tennis and swim, but I'd never really run before, I'm enjoying it a lot. We race each other around the property, I've managed to beat her once."

"She's catching up fast," Maman said. "I have to work hard to stay ahead now."

"So, I shouldn't run with you in the morning?" I asked.

"Of course you should," Maman and Portia said in chorus. Then Maman added, grinning slyly. "We'll go slowly for you."

"Hah," I said, rising to the bait. "We'll see!" It was good to see Maman happy; after she and Dad had split, she went through a period of unhappiness and I had been concerned for her. But clearly she and Portia were happy together, I could tell by the little things that passed between them, the smiles, the touches, the things they did for one another, it reminded me so much of what passed between Ian and myself. Further conversation was interrupted by the telephone ringing. Maman got up and answered it and called out to me. "Bébé, it's for you."

"Hello," I said.

"*Chérie*," Ian said on the other end of the line. "I'm ready to come home. I'm getting a night train to London and will be in Henley at nine tomorrow morning."

"Oh, that's super," I said, thrilled that I would see him again. "I'll be at the station to pick you up."

"Okay *chérie*," he said. "Must dash, I don't want to miss the train."

"He's coming tomorrow morning," I told Maman and Portia when I rejoined them in the sitting room. "He gets into Henley at nine."

"We'll still have time for a run in the morning," Maman said. "Then you can take a shower and we'll all go and meet Ian."

145

"All of us?" I asked.

"Yes," she confirmed. "All of us, you can hold hands in the back seat while I drive. So, if we're to get up early and run, bath and bedtime I think!"

I was awake at seven the next morning. It was still dark, what on earth had I been thinking to agree to go on a run. I dressed and went downstairs and found Maman and Portia ready. I wondered how we were going to see to stay on the path, but then it became obvious, Maman had had lights installed around the entire perimeter, so there was light enough to see. She set off, setting the pace and I was gratified that I could keep up. She and Portia traded the lead a few times then on the back side of the second lap I decided to take the lead and see if I could lose them. Fat chance, they stayed right with me until we were in sight of the house, then it was a free for all to see who would arrive first. It was a very close thing, but I did manage to pip them both at the post, fine thing it would have been if I had been beaten by my mother! Our time, forty-five minutes, which for eight miles was pretty good, better than the last time I had done that two laps around the grounds. We all discarded shoes and went to wash off the mud and warm up in the showers. I had used my brains and laid out clothes the night before, so did not have to hunt around and decide what to wear. I put on jeans, a light sweater and a heavier sweater and socks to go with my ankle boots. When I went downstairs, Maman and Portia were waiting for me, both dressed in black leather cat suits, they looked like two versions of Emma Peel. They both had hats too, like the kind that chauffeurs wear. We went out into the garage and took Maman's new Land Rover, me in the back, like Lady Muck, and the two in the front like chauffeur and bodyguard.

We arrived at the station a little before nine, just as the sun was coming up. That was one of the things I did not like about England, the short winter days, the sun only coming up near nine and going down again at about five in the afternoon. I walked out to the platform, while my entourage hung around the Land Rover looking menacing. The train was on time, for once, and there he was, hanging out of a door in his

146

eagerness to see me. Before the train had even stopped, he was in my arms and I was kissing him.

"Oh, Fiona, I've missed you," he breathed when we finally broke apart. "I've missed you too," I said. "I'm so happy that you're here. Come, let's go home and make up for lost time." I walked him to the car, and Maman saluted and opened the door for him, and Portia opened the door for me and we were bundled inside. He looked at me and grinned and I just shrugged my shoulders. I wondered what the other passengers thought, it looked like he was being picked up by some agents of some description. In the car he held my hand all the way home and whispered little endearments in my ear. By the time we got home, there was only one thing I wanted and I think he had the same idea.

"Portia and I have to go out for a while," Maman said. "We'll be back around noon, and we thought we might take you to lunch." I blessed Maman, she was giving us some space and time to spend in bed. Ian and I went into the house and Maman and Portia went off on their errand, whether it was real or contrived I had no idea.

Upstairs I did not quite tear Ian's clothes off, but I helped him get undressed quickly and took him to the bathroom and turned on the shower. There was room under for two, so we both got in and between kisses managed to clean each other off, then it was back to the bed. I pushed him down on the bed and climbed on top of him. We were both so ready that I was able to quickly dress him up with a condom and then guide him in. That first time was passionate as we both sought to release our pent-up desires for one another and the climax was monumental and for me, at least, loud, as I cried out in sheer joy. The subsequent two more times were much more relaxed and we spent the time savouring each other, he on top first and then me sitting on the dresser, while he stood between my legs. I thought about what Maman and Portia had shared with me and put those lessons to good use, so that both times the experience was better for both of us, and for me noisy. I heard Maman and Portia downstairs and reluctantly suggested to Ian that we might find some clothes and join them.

"Ah, is that better?" Maman asked as we joined them. I wondered how long they had actually been back, because they had changed clothes into something less intimidating.

"Much," Ian said, grinning his usual happy grin.

"Good," she said. "Fiona has been unbearable since you've been gone."

"Maman, I have not," I protested. "Where did you and Portia scurry off to?"

"We had to take care of a couple of things at her cottage," Maman replied. "Portia has a new tenant moving in, so we were there to hand over the keys and see them in. So, Ian, I doubt that Fiona has asked you about your trip, she's had baser things on her mind, how was your trip?"

"Not the best," he sighed. "It seems that I keep running into issues and I'm sure that Ambrose is going to whine and complain and cavil at every detail."

"I'm so sorry," I said. "Will this affect your thesis?"

"I don't know," he admitted. "But I've decided that that is for next week, today is today and is to be enjoyed."

"Good for you," Portia said. "Now, I'm going to take you all to lunch and you can give us your version of the dinner and dance."

"By the way," Maman said. "I've got some prints here of you two before the ball. I just wish that colour photography was a little easier and then I'd use more colour, I really wanted to capture the different colours in the ensemble that Fiona had on. Slides are all very well, but the films have to sent away and I don't like the idea of my subjects being pored over by some unknown lab technician."

"These are super, Maman," I said, looking at the prints she had given us. "What do you think *chéri?*"

"I like this one of us on the stairs," he said. "I still can't get over how gorgeous you look in the dress."

"She probably looked even better out of it," Maman said dryly.

"True," he grinned. "Mrs Barclay, I love Fiona, I really do."

"Please call me Brigitte or Maman, as Fiona does," she said. "Shall we go, Portia has a surprise for us?"

Portia drove and she took us, eventually, to a very impressive country house near Newbury. "My friend, Charles, has opened a restaurant here," she explained as we went up the mile-long driveway. "It's become very popular and reservations are hard to come by, but I called Charles and he invited us today."

When we got to the house it was built along the lines of Syon House, and was very imposing. We parked our Land Rover among the Jaguars, Rolls Royces and Bentleys and went inside. A very superior being met us and asked us if we had a booking. Portia did her thing and told him that we were there at the invitation of Charles Fielding. The superior being excused himself for a minute, then came scurrying back, as obsequious as they come, and escorted us to a delightful table by the windows looking out onto the lake that was in the grounds. Already seated at the table was Rachel Adams and another woman.

"Portia, Brigitte," Rachel said. "Lovely to see you, hello again Fiona, this is Vittoria, she's visiting me from Milan."

"Vittoria," Portia said. "This is my partner Brigitte, her daughter, Fiona, and her partner, Ian."

"Are you all in fashion?" Vittoria asked.

"No," Portia said. "I practise law, Fiona is a mathematician, Ian is an anthropologist and Brigitte has a number of interests, including a lingerie boutique, Bridget and Brigitte."

"So, how did the ensemble work out?" Rachel asked.

"It was absolutely gorgeous," Ian said, before I could get a word out. "And Fiona looked just divine in it, I have here a picture of her."

"And the ball?" Rachel asked, picking up the photograph and looking at it, then passing it on to Vittoria, who murmured, *bellissima*.

"Not so well," Ian admitted. "But things looked up after we left and went back to the hotel."

"So grrrr managed the laces then?" Rachel asked of Portia.

"I think he did," Portia confirmed.

"Grrrr?" Ian asked.

"I will explain later," Portia promised. Menus were handed around and the waitress gave us a description of each dish, then handed out glasses of champagne.

"Chef Charles wanted you to have these and he said he will be out shortly," she explained. I sipped on my champagne and looked around the room and saw someone I knew, Adam Hill, from my mining working group. He saw me and waved.

"Will you excuse us for a minute?" I asked. I took Ian's hand and we walked across the room to the table where Adam was seated.

"Dr Barclay," he said. "What a pleasant surprise."

"Mr Hill," I said. "This is my Rhodesian, Ian Hartley."

"Dear, this is Dr Barclay," he said, introducing me to his wife. "She is the mathematician who has been guiding us for the past few months. Dr Barclay, my wife, Audrey. Ian, I understand that you're from Mashonaland?"

"That's right, Sir," Ian said. "If I recall correctly, Fiona said that you were from Bulawayo."

"Many years ago," Adam said. "I see you mix in heady company, Dr Barclay, one of the most expensive solicitors in the country, a renowned fashion designer from London, the other two I don't know."

"One is my mother," I said. "The other, all I know at the moment is that her name is Vittoria and that she is from Milan." Audrey Hill turned around and looked and then gave us the answer.

"That's Vittoria Blengini, a really well-known fashion designer."

"Well, please excuse us for interrupting your lunch, I just wanted Ian to meet you," I told them.

"Ian, nice to meet you, if you're ever in London, here's my card, call on me and we'll have lunch and talk about cabbages and kings," Adam said.

"Thank you, Sir," Ian said. As we walked back to our table, Ian commented that Adam may have been doing some fast talking to explain to his wife why he had never told her that Dr Barclay was a young gorgeous woman, I think he may have been wrong, I got the sense that Adam did talk to his wife and had probably told her about me. Back to our table and I explained to the others that Adam Hill was one of the sponsors of my Fellowship.

Charles Fielding then made his appearance, he quickly walked among the tables stopping here and there to enquire about the food and to explain an item or two, then he came to us.

"Portia darling," he said. "So nice of you to grace us with your presence."

"Charles," Portia said in greeting. "These are my friends and guests, Rachel, Vittoria, Brigitte, Fiona and Ian."

"Welcome all," Charles said. "I have a treat for you today. If you will go off the menu, I have a venison dish that I think you'll really enjoy. Would that be something you would all wish to try?" There was a chorus of assent and Charles beamed and went back to the kitchen to supervise. I looked around the table and thought that it was really an eclectic group. Maman was French and Tahitian, Portia was British and Italian,

Rachel I think was British and Chinese, I was another hybrid and Ian was of British extraction, but African raised. As far as I knew, Vittoria was all Italian, but quite a group for an English restaurant.

While was just sat and chatted, waiting for the first course, Portia produced a folio, I thought I had seen her carrying something, but was distracted by Ian and not concentrating on anything else. It seemed this was to be a business meeting as the four ladies started discussing lingerie designs, the conversation quickly switched to Italian, and I felt some pity for Ian as he spoke no Italian. But he looked happy enough watching us. Portia took pictures out of the folio and handed them to Maman, Rachel and Vittoria. I caught a glimpse of them and saw that they were pictures that Maman had taken of Portia, Bridget, Ashley, Anna and myself, but she had marked them up with a grease pencil to show possible modifications. Maman then launched into voluble explanations of the changes and the reasons for them. Then Portia handed out more pictures and I saw Rachel and Vittoria both look up and at Ian. I craned over and saw that they were pictures of him in various types of underwear and wondered how Maman and Portia had talked him into that. Further discussion was delayed by the arrival of our first course. For the next hour we ate and talked and, I have to say that the venison dish was superb. Charles came out and talked to us again and his cooking in general was praised by all, and the venison dish in particular. He left us a happy man. Then it was back to business and then they finally roped me into the discussion. What they wanted were some models of potential sales, based on population, and specifically segments of the population. I told them that I would be happy to create the models, but needed more information as to target groups. Rachel suggested that the next time I was in London that I set aside some time to spend with her and we would decide what her target markets were and how best to size them.

The bill, when it came, was actually paid by Rachel and a date was set for another meeting, when Vittoria would next be in England. In fact, Maman suggested that could come and stay with her, as she had plenty of room at her house. Both Rachel and Vittoria agreed to that, quite enthusiastically. We left, and Portia drove us back to Henley.
"So, you're thinking of a new venture?" Ian asked.

"I am," Maman replied. "I have some ideas and Rachel and Vittoria are the best ones to make them a reality, and I will get early releases before products go on the general market."

"How did you work that out?" I asked Ian.

"Well, I saw they were discussing marked up prints, so they had to be ideas for new designs, and you have a boutique owner, a lawyer and two designers, it was a logical deduction that a new venture is being considered," he explained.

"You are the most lovely man," I said, squeezing his hand.

"Who are the three in the pictures that I don't know?" he asked.

"That would be my business partner, Bridget and two of our models, Ashley and her daughter, Anna," Maman replied.

"What I would like is an unaltered copy of the photo of Fiona in the lace," he said.

"I'll make one for you when we get home," Maman promised.

"Maman," I complained. "I don't know what he's going to do with it."

"Well, if you like, we can give you a similar one of Ian," she said.

"I suppose that's fair," Ian said. "But we also have the flip book that we haven't shown Fiona yet."

"Of course," Maman said. "Let's see what she thinks of that."

When we arrived home, I discovered what the flip book was. Ian gave it to me with great ceremony. The cover was the picture that I really liked, him dressed for Africa holding a coffee cup. I flipped through it, and it was obvious that that was what I supposed to do, because it was like a cartoon, as I flipped past each page Ian had less and less on, he was stripping bare as I flipped through the book, it was like watching a short film of him do a striptease. Somehow, Maman and Portia had persuaded him to strip off articles of clothing one by one, until he was left with his hat and coffee cup and nothing else and the hat and coffee cup hid nothing. I hugged the book to my breast and blushed.

"Exhibitionist," I said. "How on earth did you do get them do that for you?" I asked him.

"It was not my idea," he said. "Your Maman and Portia suggested it, then they were very patient while we were shooting, but the worst part was trying to do everything in the same place so that we could the proper still shots so that the movements would be smooth and it would not look like I was jumping around from frame to frame," he said.

"I suppose you want one of me the same way?" I asked.

"Only if you want to," he said. "I am happy with the photos that I have and if Brigitte gives me one of you in the lace, I'll be thrilled."

"I could shoot the pictures for you tomorrow," Maman suggested. "We would have to keep Ian away, or you'd be distracted and not be able to concentrate. Ian is right, this does take hard work and a lot of concentration to undress and stay in the same place each time."

"I'd be happy to wander around the garden," Ian volunteered. I thought about it and then decided, why not?

"I'll do it," I said. "I'll pick out something to wear tonight and we can shoot the pictures tomorrow."

"Fine," Maman said. "I'll show you the one of Portia that I made for me to give you some ideas?"

"How would the legal profession react if they knew such a series of pictures existed?" I kidded Portia.

"They would feign apoplexy, then they'd all trample each other to death trying to get a copy. I'm afraid the public image of upstanding members of the community is a façade, it has to be one of the most sexist professions, replete with bullying, condescension and archaic views. I'm sure that there any many members who would be thrilled if women were barred from practising law," she replied. "It's difficult, but I can also be difficult and I tend to win, which annoys them."

"Who's hungry?" Maman asked.

"Not me," was the universal response, so she settled for wine and grapes, in case anyone had any room left after our luncheon.

When Ian and I went to bed that night, we talked about the flip book, then he admitted to me that it had been difficult. He had had to overcome his natural reserve, particularly as the photographer was the mother of his girlfriend, and as he stripped off more, he became more aware of his body and more embarrassed. It had taken tact and patience on the parts of Maman and Portia to relax him so that he could finish the shoot. He was happy with the result and was happy that I liked the book. So, Maman and Portia had seen him naked before I had, I would have to have words with them about that. I told him that I would pose for a similar book for him and asked him if he had any particular dress that he liked.

"You know," he said. "I haven't seen you in that red Chinese dress that I saw a picture of the other day, would you do that one?"

"The cheongsam?" I asked.

"Is that what it's called?" he asked. "Then, yes, that would be super."

"Now, what about a bath and then bed?" I asked him. Bathing was fun and let us explore each other's bodies more. I washed him and he washed me, both revelling in touching the other, and being touched. By the time we got into bed, we were both ready and we enjoyed the intimacy that making love can bring. Afterwards, he cuddled up close to me and I was thrilled to feel his body next to mine, all the way from our feet, up our legs, our lower torsos and his chest against my back and him nuzzling my neck. What could be better?

The following morning, I was awakened by Ian bringing me coffee. How he had got up without waking me, I'll never know. He climbed back into bed with me and asked me to get on top of him. I did as requested then he slowly inched his way down until his face was under me. We had not tried that before, but I have to say it was a wonderful way to start the day. After he had brought me to a climax, I moved my way down his body and found him erect, sheathed and ready and guided him in and then rode him to his climax. I was really enjoying making love with Ian. Each time brought something new. Sometimes I regretted not having tried sex earlier in my life, but then that would not have been with Ian and as I had had no feelings for any man before Ian, it would have been simple sex and not making love. I sat on the bed with Ian and drank my coffee and drank in my vision of him, his body, his grin, his scent, it was a lovely morning.

Breakfast was crêpes suzette, and I was amazed at how many Ian could eat. He saw me watching him and grinned. That grin just turned me to jelly, it was him, it was one of the endearing things about him that I truly loved. My thoughts were interrupted by Maman who brought me back to earth.

"When you've finished mooning over Ian, perhaps you'll answer my question," she said.

"I'm sorry, Maman," I said. "I was miles away."

"I could see that," she said. "Now, what dress will you wear?"

154

"The red cheongsam," I replied. "Ian and I talked about it last night and he thought that that would be nice."

"Good," Maman agreed. "Now, Ian, there is plenty of coffee here, or if you want tea, everything is over there. There are snacks to eat here, is there anything else you might like?"

"No, thank you, Maman," he said. "I'll be here working on my thesis, I've got plenty to do."

"Okay then," Maman said. "Bébé, have you finished breakfast?"

"I have Maman," I said.

"Then, to work," she commanded. I kissed Ian farewell and went off with Maman and Portia to the studio, making a brief detour on the way to collect clothes. In the studio, Portia supervised dressing while Maman set up her cameras and lights. Before we got going, Portia showed me the flip book that Maman had made of her. I really liked what they had done, and then she showed me the one of Maman. I guessed that they had had fun making those books because the smiles were real, not forced. For my book, I decided that as well as the cheongsam, crimson lace underwear would work, with black stockings and a garter belt, we might as well give Ian the works. Once ready, Portia took charge of making sure I was in the right place, while Maman took the shots. Ian had been right, it was hard work to get the pace of things right so that the still shots could be taken close enough together so that the resulting flip book would not be too jerky. Twice we had to stop because I had messed things up. When that happened Portia wheeled in a frame of clear Perspex with a grid marked on it which she positioned behind me and then she sketched where I was, arms, legs, head, et cetera, so that when we restarted, I has pushed, pulled, and moved into exactly the same place as I had been when we stopped. It was quite late in the morning when we finally got to the last shots, of me standing stark naked.

"Good," Maman announced. "Now it will take me a little while to finish this, so expect to be able to give it to Ian for Christmas."

"Thank you, Maman," I said. "And thank you, Portia for your help. Now you two, I want to know how it is that you both got to see Ian in all his glory before I did?"

"We wondered if you had," Portia replied. "But having seen him, we were happy for you. You were going to enjoy that lovely body."

"You're right about that," I said, thinking about him. "Now I should put some clothes on and go and see what he's doing."

"Wouldn't he prefer it if you went with no clothes on?" Maman teased.

"Probably," I agreed. "But he's supposed to be working."

When we joined Ian in the kitchen, he was looking despondent.

"What's the matter?" I asked.

"My thesis is a disaster," he said. "All the conclusions I reach can be questioned, by me, let alone anyone else."

"Can you fix it?" I asked.

"I don't know," he said. "I'll have to talk to Ambrose in the morning, but I'm afraid, he will reach the same conclusion that I have just done. This just won't work."

"What will that mean?" I asked.

"Good question," He said. "If I'm fortunate, then a major rewrite, if I'm less fortunate then more research to back up my basic premise."

"What would that mean?" I asked.

"I'm not really sure at this time," he said. "I should talk to Ambrose as soon as possible and see if he can't provide some sort of guidance as to how to proceed."

"I'm so sorry," I told him. "You've worked so hard on this, what made you rethink things?"

"Oh, the visits to the Neander Valley, the trip last week, they all made me rethink things, and I realised that this is not original work and is basically a restatement of others' work, with a few extras thrown in," he explained. "The annoying thing is that I think Ambrose has been sending me subtle hints for the past few months and I have been too focused on my own ideas to get the message."

"I hope I haven't distracted you," I said, appalled by the idea that I may have created a problem for him.

"No, it wasn't you," he assured me. "I got off on a tangent and lost the thread of my thesis, my own fault, I should have reviewed what I had written more critically than I did. Damn, damn, damn."

"Is there anything we can do to help?" I asked.

"No," he said. "This is my mess, and I have to clear it up. But it will mean long hours for me between now and Christmas and we may not be able to see much of one another."

"Take the time you need," I told him. "Perhaps we can have Sundays together?"

"That would be super," he said. "It will probably also mean no more coffee mornings for a while."

"I can still call you," I promised. "And, you still have to eat, so I could bring you lunches."

"Would you?" he asked. "That would be great. I'm going to need a lot of support between now and Christmas."

"Well, you got just under three weeks," I said. "Is that enough time?"

"That will depend on whether or not I can rewrite my ideas so that they make more sense," he thought. "I'll talk to Ambrose and see."

"Is there anything more you can do at this minute?" I asked.

"Not really," he said. "I really need to talk to Ambrose and see where I stand. Damn, damn, damn."

"Don't be too hard on yourself," I said. "You'll work this out."

Maman prepared lunch which was eaten in relative quiet. I think we all understood that Ian was wrestling with what to do about his thesis and we all by silent agreement were determined to give him the space and time to do that. Ian spent the afternoon making notes about what he wanted to discuss with Professor Ambrose, and we left him to it. Maman, Portia and I spent the afternoon going through the proposals for the new venture that Maman was looking at. It really all hinged around getting the well-known designers on board and then having some period of exclusivity when the products hit that shelves. At the speed at which copies were made, I estimated that there would be about six months after a new line came out before copies were available. Protecting the designs was the forte of Portia, but even she told us that suing over trademark and or patent infringements was costly and time consuming. There were patent infringement settlements that could be huge, but they typically came after years of legal wrangling and hearings, so did nothing for day to day operations.

At dinner, Ian told us that he had a plan. He would talk to Ambrose the next day and propose changes to his thesis that brought it more in line with the actual research he had been doing, and the findings that he had made. I suppose that made sense, but if he had started his research with a particular topic, I would have thought that it would be expected that he stay with that topic. Ian admitted that that was true, but said that he would try anyway and see if Ambrose was willing to listen to his arguments. After dinner Ian and I packed and I drove him back to his digs.

"I'll call you tomorrow," I promised, when I dropped him off.

"If I'm not in, it's because I'm still closeted with Ambrose," he said. "Oh, Fiona, what a mess, I just hope I can sort this out."

"I'm sure you'll be able to," I assured him. I kissed him goodbye and watched as he went inside the pub. I was not sanguine about his chances of altering the topic of his thesis, but that all depended on the views of Professor Ambrose. I did not really know the man, so had no sense of how he would see things. My own thesis advisor had been a man of very fixed ideas, and it had taken real work on my part to demonstrate that my economic theories would actually work in real life. He had resisted all the way, and it had only been at the orals that others had listened and agreed with me. That had soured an already poor relationship, but his criticisms were overruled by the academic committee, who all agreed that I was more correct than my advisor and that his theories had been proven, by me, to be unworkable. That had been a very trying time, one that I did not wish to repeat. As I drove home, the thought that somehow, I had distracted Ian from his work still nagged at me. No matter what he said, I could not dismiss the idea. He had seemed to be doing well until I came on the scene, and then we had spent a lot of time together, time that perhaps he should have been spending critically reviewing his work. That plus the fact that if he was anything like me, he would have been day dreaming half the time. I had had to discipline myself a few times to drag myself back from noonday fantasies about Ian, to asset valuations.

When I called Ian's office the next day, he was still with Professor Ambrose. So, I wondered whether that boded ill or well. I waited until lunch time before trying again, and this time I went in person, with a box lunch in hand.

"Fiona, *chérie*," Ian said when I arrived. "How are you today?"

"I think a better question is, how are you *chéri?*" I countered.

"Pissed off," he said. "Ambrose is being difficult, he said that he'd take what I had written so far and see if anything could be made of it, which was a positive, then he said that I might have been more focused on my work if I had not been pursuing a noted Fellow romantically, that's you, and wasting my time on pleasures of the flesh, so that's a negative."

"Do you think I've distracted you?" I asked, hoping that he would not say yes and want to rethink our relationship.

"Absolutely not," he assured me. "I even told Ambrose that on our first date I'd actually fallen asleep on you because I was worn out from the work I had been doing. I don't think he believed me and even suggested, in a very round about way, that I had fallen asleep because I was physically spent after intercourse, not that he actually said that, but he inferred it in so many ways."

"Well, come and sit with me in the gardens and have your lunch," I suggested.

"Isn't it cold outside?" he asked.

"Not too cold," I assured him. "Wrap up well and you'll be fine."

We took our lunches and went and sat on a bench and agreed that we could not hold hands and eat sandwiches easily. I watched him eat and saw the worry lines in his face and the look of deep concern, bordering on despair. I had no idea what to do, this was something I could not fix. He looked at me and gave me a half-hearted grin.

"Sorry to be such a wet blanket, Fiona," he said.

"I'm just sorry I can't help you fix this," I said. "What you do is not something that I have any knowledge of, let alone expertise, so don't know what to do."

"Just having you here with me is enough," he said. "You light up my days. I would have been really in the dumps if it wasn't for you. I keep thinking if it's actually worth continuing, or should I just dump it all and go and do something else."

"We could make it between us," I offered.

"No, I think I have to finish this, one way or another," he said.

"I love you *chéri*," I told him. "I hate to see you down. Will you have time on Sunday to come and spend the day with me?"

"Sunday, I'll make time," he said. "I just can't do this all the time, I need time away from it just to clear my thoughts."

"Well, I'll make Sunday a day when you don't have to worry about anything," I told him. "Why don't I pick you up when you're done on Saturday afternoon?"

"I like that," he said. "Look, so sorry to do this, but I have to go, I'll call you tomorrow. I love you *chérie*."

"I love you," I told him. "But I'll have to find a way to call you, because I'm in London for the next three days, I'll be back here in Oxford on Thursday night, so we can have lunch again on Friday."

"Friday, I'll be looking forward to seeing you then," he said.

"Kiss me *chéri*," I told him. Kiss me he did, the we parted and he went back to his labours and I went back to my algorithms and researches.

I made contact with Ian the next day, I had tried him at his office a few times, but it was in the late evening at his digs that I finally managed to talk to him. His day had been filled with discussions with Professor Ambrose and the upshot was not good. He would have to either scrap his doctorate and be satisfied with a master's degree, or he would have to do more research. Fortunately, there was funding available to provide for him for the whole of 1971 and there was money for travel. Where all this money had magically come from, I had no idea, but suspected Maman. What I needed to know was how much work could be done in Oxford and England and if he would need to go back to Tanzania. That, Ian did not know at that time, he was going to have further discussions with Professor Ambrose to lay out a course of study and action. For the immediate he was going to be busy setting out the details of his course of further study and researches, and that would entail frequent sessions with Professor Ambrose who seemed to be finally taking his job as thesis advisor seriously. I wondered if this could not have all been avoided if the proper reviews had been done after each field session in Tanzania. It seemed to me to be a little late in the day to be taking a real interest. My own thesis advisor had had me present to him on a regular basis my progress, my theories and the work that supported my theories. That is not to say that we did not disagree on much of the work that I had done, but his reviews and critiques ensured that I had supporting work that proved my theories, no matter how much he questioned them, or how they conflicted with his own theories. My talks with Ian left me to believe that Professor Ambrose had agreed a course of research some three years earlier and had only now taken the time to review things and it had been found wanting.

Whilst I was in London, I did take the time to have lunch one day with Portia. The receptionist at the law firm recognised me and I was greeted cordially and she had called Portia for me without me having to ask.

"Fiona, *chérie*," Portia said when she joined me in the foyer. "Where shall we go?"

"You choose," I suggested. "My own knowledge of places to eat in London is limited."

"I know a place, within walking distance," she suggested. "Shall we go there?"

We walked to a place that was just off the Victoria Embankment. It was quiet, I suppose the low season for tourists. The few others that were there, I put as business or academics.

"So, how are you?" Portia asked when we were seated.

"I'm doing really rather well," I told her. "And you?"

"I'm doing wonderfully well," she said. "I bless the day, every day, that I met your Maman, I'm so happy."

"I'm so glad," I said. "When Dad left, she went through a rough patch for a while, but now, I've not seen her so happy in a long time. Thank you, Portia, for making her life so good again."

"Believe me, the pleasure is all mine," Portia said, smiling to herself. "I had never imagined a relationship with another woman, but find it satisfying, challenging, fulfilling and rewarding. Is that too confusing?"

"No, I think I can understand that," I told her.

"I love Brigitte," Portia said. "I know that may be odd for you to hear, that another woman loves your Maman, but I really do, she makes my life so complete. Now tell me about you and Ian."

"Ian has a problem," I told her. "He has to do a lot more work on his research, I'm convinced that it will mean a trip back to Tanzania, but he's hedging on that at the moment."

"I can understand that," she said. "If I were him and I'd just found you, I wouldn't want to go tripping half way around the world. He's just head over heels about you."

"Do you really think so?" I asked.

"I know so," she confirmed. "When we did our photo shoot of him you were all he could talk about."

"I was afraid of that," I told her. "Part of me wants him to finish his research, but part of me is afraid of losing him."

"He loves you, and I don't see a separation as affecting that," she said.

"So, what do I get Maman for Christmas?" I asked Portia.

"I was going to ask you the same question," Portia laughed. "What do we do? What are you getting Ian?"

"A new camera," I said. "I've already got it, it's a Nikon, and I got him a set of different lenses to go with it."

"That's a good idea," Portia agreed. "But for your Maman?"

"I'm stumped," I confessed. "I'll think about it a little more, but I need ideas, if you have any, please tell me."

"If I come up some brilliant idea, I talk to you," Portia promised.

"I also have the problem of what to get James and his girlfriend," I added.

"I met her the other day," Portia said. "She's really cute, her name is Charlize Cillie, she's at the Institut français in South Kensington studying French, apparently they met at a party given by the French Consulate on Cromwell Road, how James got himself invited I have no idea."

"Well, perhaps we'll find out more at Christmas time," I said.

"I would hope so," Portia said. "Now, we need to eat lunch!"

I also made arrangements to have lunch with Rachel and we talked about markets, general markets and more targeted markets. I had created some algorithms that I showed Rachel and she was delighted. To me they were a natural look at the world we lived in, but I do not think that Rachel had ever looked at things in quite the same way. Rachel gave me her views as to the demographics that she saw as potential markets and I promised her some revised numbers within a week. It was actually quite a simple set of calculations and it was something that could be done without in any way interfering with my main project. She did make me a present of one of her designs, which I was thrilled with. As Maman was wont to remind me, I had never really taken much of an interest in clothes, but since Ian, I had started to look at myself and my wardrobe more critically.

Ian and I were unable to have our lunch date on Friday; when I got back from London there was a message for me to the effect that he and Professor Ambrose would be off on a trip to London of all places. I should have just stayed there and arranged to meet him for lunch there. So, it was quite late Saturday evening when Ian finally called so tell me that he was done for the day. I quickly drove into Oxford and collected him and his small suitcase.

"Thank you for rescuing me," he said. "I needed to get out of there."

"How are things going, *chéri?*" I asked.

"I have a plan, but I'm not sure that you'll be thrilled," he said. "I'll need to go back to Tanzania right after Christmas to start work in the New Year and stay until June and then come back early July. They've arranged for me to spend some time at the Leakey dig as well as ours. After that, I should be able to write everything up in the summer and be done by September."

"I see," I said. Well, I had suspected that this might be the outcome of his discussions with Professor Ambrose. "You must go," I told him. "I want you to finish what you started."

"But I'll miss you," he said.

"I'll miss you too," I added. "I'll write every week and the time will pass, I'm not going anywhere."

"Oh, *chérie*, I wish there was another way," he said.

"You haven't found one, so this is what it must be," I told him. Inside I was crying out in horror, to be without him for six months was going to be a trial. It was bad enough when he was gone for three weeks, but six months, that was an eternity. The selfless part of me was telling me that he needed to do this and to support him, but the selfish part of me was screaming, no, no. When we got to my house, I let him in and showed him around, the kitchen, living room and most importantly, my bedroom.

"So, what would you like?" I asked him.

"A glass of wine, a bath and most of all you," he said.

"I'll get the wine, you run and bath and then I'll take care of you," I promised. When I came back with the wine, he had the bath running and had stripped off his clothes. I spent a good minute looking at him and lusting after his body before I announced myself and gave him his wine. He climbed into the bath and I quickly shed my clothes and joined him. I had come prepared and had a condom in hand and some extra lubrication. I had surmised that I might need it as he looked as if his need was immediate. It was, I took care of things, then sat in his lap and guided him into me and we just sat there slowly moving my hips back and forth. It did not take long for him to climax and when he had I just sat on him and hugged him.

"Oh, Fiona," he sighed. "I'm not sure if I can go without you for six whole months."

"You'll need to stay busy, really busy and then the time will fly," I assured him. "That's what I plan to do. I'm going to miss you, I'm going to miss your smile and grin, talking to you, feeling your hands on me and not to be forgotten, you inside me, like now."

"If you keep talking like that, I might just not go," he said. "You will be always playing on my mind. I love you Fi."

"You never called me Fi before," I said. "Is that a new pet name?"

"I suppose it is," he replied. "Either that or *chérie*."

"You're falling asleep," I said. "Let's get you into bed." I got off, removed the used condom, then dried him and led him to the bedroom. I had barely pulled back the covers when he collapsed onto the bed and dropped off. He was exhausted, goodness knows what kind of hours he had been working. I arranged him a little then climbed in next to him and cuddled up close, waking him as I did. He murmured a little in his half-awake state and draped an arm over me and promptly fell back to sleep.

The next morning, I carefully disengaged myself from him and went to the kitchen to make coffee. I confess to having a good weep. I needed it, the thought of being without him for six months was overwhelming. Still, now was not the time to feel sorry for myself, time enough for that when he actually gone, now was the time to be supportive and help him, if I could. I composed myself and then took coffee into him.

"Fi," he said. "You look lovely today. I really want you, I want to kiss you, run my hands all over you, taste you, smell you and enjoy every part of you."

"You're only saying that because I've got no clothes on," I said.

"Is this house heated throughout?" he asked. "I must try the day with no clothes on, it must be so liberating."

"It is," I confirmed. "I have underfloor heating throughout, so don't need clothes to stay warm, only to comply with convention if there are people here. So, I'm ready, if you are, how do you want me?"

"God, I don't know, Fi," he said. "I just want you, put the coffee over there and lie down on the bed and let me look at you." I did as requested and he sat up and studied me. Finally, he suggested a position and we quickly came together, not only that way but another way after that.

Then it was time from breakfast. I went through to the kitchen to start making it and he came after me, as naked as they come.

"Can anyone see in?" he asked, looking at the floor to ceiling glass that was the wall to the kitchen, dining area.

"No, I've been out and looked back carefully," I told him. "I've walked out quite a long way with binoculars and it is possible if you're in just the right place, but it's not an easy place to get to."

He came and stood behind me as I cooked, I could feel his body down the whole length of mine and it was lovely. I felt his hands under my apron and sighed with pleasure as he ran his hands over my breasts and then down my body, past my belly. I moved my legs apart and let him go farther down and cried out quietly as he found me and gently brought me to a climax, the pot moved off the stove and breakfast abandoned. Then he lifted me up onto the counter, spread my legs, equipped himself with a condom that he had managed to secrete somewhere about his person and introduced himself to me.

We finally had lunch, breakfast having been abandoned for more hedonistic pursuits. We took lunch sitting at the table unclothed, just feasting our eyes on one another. I was trying to drink in as much of this as I could, so that I would have memories when he was gone.

"You know what would be nice," he said, looking at me with lust in his eyes.

"I can't guess," I laughed. "Sex, yes, but how?"

"Let's sit on that chair over there and see how many ways we can manage," he suggested.

"Your mind, is it always on sex?" I asked, laughing at him.

"Only today," he said. "Otherwise all this week it's been *homo sapiens, homo erectus, homo habilis* and a host of other humanoid species."

"I looks as if I have *homo erectus* here in this room," I commented, looking pointedly at him.

We tried the chair, and got inventive and it was fun. We had sex just for the sheer fun of it and the enjoyment of being with one another in the most intimate way and learned a lot about each other. The more I learned the more I loved him. He really was an interesting, kind and thoughtful man, who always seemed to manage to put my wants and desires ahead of his. The only dark cloud on the horizon was his future departure to Tanzania. But there was still another weekend before the term ended, then there was the Christmas break, and he had already committed to spend that with me at Maman's house.

Ian goes back

On the twenty-first of December, the temperature dropped, it really dropped and snow was actually forecast for later in the week, so a white Christmas was possible. As Ian was going to leave from Henley to go back to Tanzania, we were going to move all his stuff in a day or so to Maman's house and store it there, at least for the next six months, so I drove over to Henley and traded my Mini for Maman's Land Rover. I was not sure just how much stuff Ian had and if it would fit in the Mini.

Two days later, in the afternoon, I called Ian to see when we might leave and he told me that we could leave at any time. He had his schedule now and would discuss it with me. I called Maman and asked if it was too soon to come, and she assured me that it was not, and to come before the snow arrived. I set the oil feed settings on my stove to ensure that my house stayed warm for the next weeks and went around looking for possible problems that might arise as temperatures fell even further. Satisfied that all would be well, and that my oil tank had enough for a month, I packed up clothes and presents and set out to collect Ian. When I got to the Billy Goat it was clear that fitting all Ian's stuff into the Mini would have been a challenge. We loaded everything in the Land Rover and then he said goodbye to April and Paul, after which we set off for Henley. When we arrived, we first went into the house to announce ourselves and to recruit James to help move luggage.
"Maman," I called.
"In here, Bébé," she replied from the living room. "Come and meet Charlize." Ian and I went in and there was James grinning away.
"Hey, Fi," he said. "Charlize, this is Fiona, Fiona, Charlize and you must be Ian."
"I am," Ian confirmed.
"It's so nice to finally meet you Fiona," Charlize said. Her accent reminded me a lot of Ian's accent, which I suppose was logical, they were both from Southern Africa. "James has told me so much about you."
"Only the good stuff, Fi," James said. I looked at him and wondered just what he had been telling Charlize, James could be thoughtful, but he

was also a younger brother and, in the past, had delighted in embarrassing me.

"I wonder, James, if you'd give us a hand with Ian's luggage?" I asked.

"Sure," James said. "I understand that you're leaving from here to go to Tanzania?"

"That's the plan," Ian confirmed. We trooped out to the garage and unloaded the Land Rover.

"Which room has Maman put us in?" I asked James.

"Your old room," he replied.

"Okay, let's lug all this stuff up there," I suggested.

"No," James said. "Ian and I can manage this, you go and chat to Charlie."

I went back to the living room and Charlize was trying out her French with Maman.

"Fi," Maman said, she continued in French, the translation of which follows. "When the Land Rover is unloaded would you go to the station for me and pick up Portia?"

"Of course, Maman," I said. "Would you like to come with me, Charlize?"

"Of course," she said. "Is everything unloaded?"

"It is," I said. We went out into the garage and there were still the boxes sitting by the door, waiting to be moved upstairs, but nothing to stop us from taking the Land Rover, so Charlize and I got in and left for the station.

"James hasn't told me much about you," I said. "Where in South Africa are you from?"

"Franschhoek, it's in the Cape," Charlize replied. "My folks have a winery there. The Cillie family were French Huguenots and arrived in South Africa in 1687. They started a winery in 1790 and it has been in the family ever since. It has grown over the years and it now more of a corporation than a family business, but it is still privately owned and we are all directors or managers."

"I understand you met James at a party at the French Consulate, how did James get an invitation to that?" I asked.

"I've no idea," she said. "But I thought he was one of the consular staff for quite a while, his French is really good, thanks I understand to your Maman."

"He uses it less than I do," I commented. "But it's still pretty good."

"I'm learning French so that I can deal with the people on the vineyard we bought in France," she said.

"Why didn't you go to university in France?" I asked. "You could have gone to Paris or Lyon, why London?"

"We do have all native French speakers as instructors, so we get the accents, the common usage and the colloquial expressions," she replied "But I also needed to improve my English, because at home we speak mostly Afrikaans, so my English is okay but not great. If, I'd gone to varsity in France, the English I heard would have been largely French English, I needed to be somewhere truly English speaking."

"That makes sense," I said. "We were lucky, with Dad it was always English and with Maman, French."

"The minor complication, now that I've met James, is that the course is only for a year, then I'm supposed to go to France to the vineyard for training for at least a year, maybe longer," she said.

"Well, France is a lot closer than South Africa, and we do have aunts and uncles and cousins in France," I told her. "So, weekend visits are not out of the question. Where's the vineyard?"

"It's in the Loire Valley near Orléans," she replied. "So, not too far south of Paris."

"So, a ferry ride and then a train ride," I thought. "Not a long weekend, but possible. It seems we're both destined for separation, but at least I know that Ian is coming back in July When James graduates I would have expected him to get a job with one of the major mining houses, which would mean Africa, Australia or the Americas."

"It looks that way, doesn't it?" she said. "Well, we'll see what happens in the next three years."

"True," I agreed. "A lot can happen."

"Is it true what James told me, that you once put three *ouks* in hospital?" she asked, changing the subject.

"I'm sorry, *ouks*?" I asked.

"Oh, sorry, men, blokes, chaps, people," she explained.

"It's true," I confirmed. "The one time in my life when I was truly scared for my life and instincts took over, flight was not possible, so it was fight and I went at it with everything I had. What kinds of grapes do you grow in South Africa?"

"Most of the famous varietals," she replied. "Pinotage, Shiraz, Cabernet Sauvignon, Merlot, Chardonnay, Sauvignon Blanc and Crouchen Blanc."

"What's the last one?" I asked.

"It's also known as Cape Riesling," she explained. "We've several vineyards around the area, because the different varietals do better on different soils and, you don't really want to hear me go on about grapes, soils, slopes, water and all the rest."

"No, please, I'd like to know more," I said. "We're here at the station, so let's just sit and you can tell me about grapes until the train arrives." We sat and she told me about grapes, it was clear that she knew her grapes and the growing conditions that suited each varietal. It was Charlize who brought the conversation to an end when she pointed out that the train was pulling into the station, only ten minutes late. I saw Portia and waved.

"Fiona," she said. "Thank you for coming to get me. Charlize, so nice to see you again."

"And you, Portia," Charlize replied. "Are you finished for the week or will you be working until Christmas Eve?"

"Sadly, until the last minute," Portia replied. "But if the forecasters are right, I'll be leaving early on Christmas Eve to beat the snow, perhaps I'll even take the whole day off."

"Well, let's get you home," I suggested. We drove back to the house and found Ian and James deep in conversation about something, what we did not discover as they both fell silent as we walked in.

"That probably means that they were talking about us," Charlize remarked.

"Possibly," I agreed. "Look the guilt is written all over their faces."

"Boys," Portia said, walking by then and cuffing them both lightly. "You don't know how lucky you are! Where's Brigitte?"

"Mum went to her studio for something," James replied.

After Portia had gone, James looked at me and asked. "What do you think about Mum and Portia?"

"I think they're lucky to have found one another," I replied.

"You don't think it's weird?" he asked.

"No," I said, quite simply. "I like Portia and she loves Maman and Maman loves her, and that's enough for me."

"I'm still having a hard time with it, though," he said. "I accept that they're close, but do they, you know?"

"Do they what?" I challenged, knowing full well what he meant, but not letting him off the hook.

"Do they have sex?" he finally asked, blushing like a beetroot.

"What do you think?" I asked. "Of course they have sex."

"It's quite normal," Charlize chimed in. "I have an aunt in Jo'burg, who is my favourite aunt, and it took me an age to work out that the one who lived with her was her lover. But just because my aunt was in love with another woman did not change my feelings towards her."

"I suppose," James grudgingly admitted. "Still, I'm just finding it hard to acccpt."

"Well, does Maman seem happy to you?" I asked.

"She does," he admitted. "Actually, happier than I've seen her in years."

"So, isn't that a good thing?" I asked.

"You're right," he said. "God, I hate it when you're right."

"Anyway, Ian and I have things to discuss, so if you don't mind, we'll leave you and Charlize to your own devices or vices," I said.

Ian and I went up to our room and he had stacked his belongings in one corner. I kissed him and then asked what his schedule was, when was he actually going to leave for Tanzania.

"I have a flight on BOAC on the 28th to Nairobi, I'm to meet some more of the dig team there, and transport is arranged for the 29th," he said. "From Nairobi, we'll drive down to Arusha, there I'll do all the admin stuff I need to do before I go out to the dig in January."

"So, how do I contact you?" I asked.

"This is the address in Arusha," he replied, giving me a sheet of paper with an address on it. "That's the address of the office the dig maintains in Arusha. All the admin stuff gets done there, and mail is collected and sent from there. I expect to get back into Arusha at least once a month, but there are often people going back and forth almost every week, and they usually bring mail and supplies. The flight schedule is at the bottom of the page there, out and back."

"I'll take you to the airport on the 28th," I promised, looking at the airline schedule and crying inwardly that that meant it was serious, Ian was actually going to leave and be gone until June. "That is if I don't kidnap you before then. I'll miss you *chéri.*"

"I'll miss you too, *chérie*," he said. "But I'll be back in July, then I'll have no reason to go off again."

"I've never asked this, but what do you think you'll do after your doctorate?" I asked.

"To be honest I'd not thought that far ahead," he confessed. "Right now, I'm so focused on getting this finished and done, I've not given too much thought to afterwards. I think before I met you, I had seen myself as leading my own dig somewhere and furthering my researches, but now I doubt that I will."

"I'm sorry to have put a spanner in those works," I said.

"Don't be," he said. "You've made me so happy these past couple of months, I'll figure something out just to be with you."

"How long does it take mail to get from here to Arusha?" I asked.

"About a week to two weeks," he replied. "It depends on flights and how quickly things get sorted out in Dar and then sent by road to Arusha. If you send something big and heavy and it goes by sea, then think in terms of a month, maybe even longer."

"So, you'll write to me?" I asked.

"Every week," he promised. "Will you write to me?"

"Of course I will," I said. "I'll write at least once a week, I've already got airmail letters, so am ready. Is there a telephone there?"

"Sadly, no," he said. "We don't warrant a telephone, the phone people there are trying to expand their service, but need more wires strung and more switchgear, so it's going to take a little while before telephones are as universal there as here. If you need to contact me urgently, send a telegram."

"Maybe I will," I thought. "Ian, stop, love you, stop, come back to me, stop."

"Fiona love you, stop will do, stop," he said. "That's what, seven words, so the minimum for a telegram, so 12s and 6d."

"Is there anything else I need to know about your trip?" I asked.

"I don't think so," he said. "You have my return date and flight number, just check with BOAC to see if there are any delays before you go trekking out to Heathrow."

"I will," I promised. "I could be selfish here and say that I don't want you to go, but you should finish what you started. I'll have your picture on my wall, Maman has a poster sized one for me."

"Oh, that's a thing," he said. "I'm only going to take the portrait picture of you with me. I don't want nosey customs people, or people at the camp poking through and leering over pictures of you, so could I leave the rest of them here?"

"Of course," I said. "We'll keep all your stuff safe until you return."

"We should probably join the others downstairs," he suggested.

"We should," I agreed. "But what were you and James talking about when we came in?"

"Just comparing notes about you and Charlize," he said. "We were both wondering how we were so lucky."

"James always seems to get really cute and beautiful girls," I said. "I often wondered what it was about him."

"He does seem a little less enthusiastic about your Maman and Portia," Ian said.

"I know," I said. "In many ways he's like Dad, and Dad had no time for queers, nancy boys, sapphists and dykes as he called them. But I think even James had to admit that Maman is happier now than she has been in ages."

Downstairs Maman was preparing dinner and James was hanging around, trying to be helpful, but really only just getting in the way. Charlize was in the living room talking to Portia about wine and what it took to protect brand names and appellations. Portia had some experience with that as she had represented several major French clients in a fight over appellations. Ian and I had nothing to contribute to that conversation, so we repaired to the kitchen and tried hard not to get in the way.

"You could make yourselves useful by setting the table," Maman suggested. Ian and I took the hint and got knives, forks and the rest and set them out on the dining table. We also set out wine glasses, water glasses and condiment cruets. Finally, I found side plates and serviettes and placed them at each setting. Maman called everyone to dinner and there was a free for all as we tried to decide where to sit. I could not decide whether to sit next to Ian or across from him. In the end I decided that across would be better, that way I could see him without having to turn my head, and I could also play footsie with him under the table. Maman brought out some wine and we watched in great anticipation as Charlize swirled, looked, smelt and tasted it.

"Excellent," she announced. "I would say a 1966 Chateau Latour."

"Quite right," Maman said, beaming. "James you should take lessons from Charlize, she might be able to teach you what I could not."

"You mean he wouldn't listen?" Charlize asked.

"He's more of the swig your wine rather than the savour it type," Maman laughed. "But he does have the basics."

Dinner was excellent, as usual, and conversation ranged from wine to mining to fashion. We all wanted to know how Maman's new venture was going. She announced that it was going very well, an agreement had been reached, designs hashed over and approved and goods were due to appear on the shelves by the end of March. She did have some samples that she said that she would be happy to show us. In the end that was an actual fashion show, so sadly, Ian and James were banished to the library while Maman showed off the new creations. For Charlize this was a new experience, having a live model show off lingerie, and the fact that it was her boyfriend's mother made it even more unusual. But she did relax and enjoy the show and joined me in our critique of the products, not that there was much to complain about, the designers had done an excellent job and form, fit and function had all been addressed, without losing allure.

Ian and James were summoned back when Maman was modestly dressed again, agog to know what we had seen and what we thought. We gave them general descriptions and Maman actually handed them the items for them to look at and imagine what they might look like on. I could see Ian eyeing me and seeing me in the various items and I was sure that James was doing the same with Charlize. It was Portia who broke things up, when she announced that she had to go to bed, as unlike the rest of is, she actually had to go to work the next day. She and Maman went upstairs, leaving us to clean up and do the washing up. Then Ian asked if I was ready for bed, and James quickly followed suit with Charlize. I was more than ready and happy to be off for a bath and bed with Ian. We had not seen each other since the previous Sunday, so had days of missed love making to catch up on.

"I like Charlize," he told me, when we were in the bath together. "James is certainly smitten."

"He is isn't he," I agreed. "I wonder what they'll do next year when Charlie is in France, and then what happens when James graduates and has to look for a job?"

174

"That's a few years away," Ian reminded me. "A lot can happen between now and then. So, when do you get some of the new items your Mum has coming to her boutique?"

"Probably not until March, unless I can get some preproduction test articles," I replied. "What's Arusha like?"

"It's quite a small town, maybe 35,000 people," he said. "If you've seen the Hatari film, you've actually seen quite a bit of the town. They shot many of the final scenes there in 1961, when the baby elephants are chasing after Dallas. The Safari Hotel does exist, and there are a couple of others now, so there are places to stay. Why are you thinking of coming?"

"I was wondering whether when you get done in June If I should come for two weeks or so, and then we could come home together in mid-July," I said.

"That would be great, I'll meet you on Nairobi and we'll do a small safari," he said. "I'll change my tickets tomorrow to two weeks later and maybe you could make a booking yourself."

"Let's do that," I said. "Now, are you ready for bed?"

"I'm ready for you," he laughed. "See, *homo erectus* is with us again!"

He was ready, as was I, so we enjoyed the next hour or so, just lazily making love and relishing the touch and feel of each other.

The following day I told Maman my plan, and she thoroughly approved. She also took me aside, away from Ian and handed me a whole fistful of money.

"Buy him a first-class ticket," she told me. "Buy one for yourself as well, where would you fly into?"

"Ian suggested that he meet me in Nairobi, and that we do a short safari from there," I explained. "Are you sure about the ticket, Maman? I have enough to buy my own ticket."

"Consider it a Christmas present," she said. "What will do you, go to the travel agent here?"

"No, I thought we'd go to the ticket office at Victoria," I said. "Then I'll know that everything is properly booked."

"Good, I wonder if James and Charlize might want to go with you?" she suggested.

"I'll ask," I promised. "But they may want to just stay here."

"Judging from the noise we heard last night," Maman said. "Those two are getting along famously and perhaps they'll need a rest today, before more amorous adventures tonight. She's as noisy as he is."

"Who's noisy?" Portia asked, as she came to find Maman.

"I was telling Fiona how much noise James and Charlize made last night," Maman explained.

"They did rather," Portia said. "It was good though, they drowned us out."

"They did, didn't they, *ma beauté,*" Maman said, with a smile.

"I need to go," Portia said. "Will you run me to the station *chérie?*"

"Of course," Maman said. "If anyone gets up before I'm back, start some breakfast would you Fi?"

When James and Charlize finally showed themselves, Ian had made breakfast for us and we had eaten. He volunteered to make some for them, but Charlize said that she would make theirs. I told them that Ian and I were going up to London to the BOAC office and asked them if they wanted to tag along. They both declined, I think they had other pursuits in mind. Maman returned from the station and I made arrangements with her to drop us at the station later, we would take a train to London, do our business with BOAC, then have lunch and spend some time sightseeing, before returning on the same train with Portia. Ian and I had some more coffee and traded small talk with James and Charlize until we had to leave to catch the train to London. I had considered driving up, but parking is always such an issue, that it was far easier to take the train and use the Tube once in London. Maman made another trip to the station and dropped us off. I got us tickets to Paddington and we boarded the train that was standing there. We changed trains at Twyford, for a fast train to London. From Paddington it was a quick ride on the Circle Line to Victoria. There it was but a short walk to the BOAC offices on Buckingham Palace Road. When we walked in, I saw a familiar face at the counter, it was Adam Hill.

"Dr Barclay," he said. "How nice to see you again, and you Ian, are you here to make a booking?"

"We are," I confirmed. "We need to make an adjustment to Ian's ticket and also buy one for me for next July."

"Ah, I see," he said. "Well, Mrs Jennings here has always taken very good care of me. Mrs Jennings, Dr Barclay is a colleague and friend and I would be much obliged if you would help her in any way possible."

"Of course, Mr Adams," she replied.

"Dr Barclay, are you free for lunch?" he asked.

"We've no other engagements or errands beyond this," I replied.

"Then, do me the honour of joining me for lunch, I will be waiting just over there," he said.

"Now, how may I help you," Mrs Jennings said.

"My friend, Ian has a ticket for Nairobi on Monday the 28th of this month," I explained, handing her the ticket. "I would like to see if I can change his seat to one in First Class, also I would like to change his return to the 21st of July and also change that to First Class."

"Of course," she said. "How will you be paying?" I thought that was a little rude, but I produced a stack of twenty-pound notes and held them ready. She departed for a few minutes and came back with a new ticket. While she was gone, Ian started to protest about the cost, but I shushed him telling him that this was a Christmas present from Maman, and that she was most insistent about it.

"That will be £240 12s," Mrs Jennings said, when she returned. I counted out the notes and handed them to her and accepted the change.

"Now, I need to make a booking for myself," I said. "I would like to fly to Nairobi on the 4th of July and return on the same flight as Ian, on the 21st, also a First-Class ticket."

"Of course," she said. She disappeared again and came back with a ticket for me. "That will be £533 4s," she said. I counted out more notes and waited for the change. Tickets in hand, I thanked Mrs Jennings for her help and Ian and I went to join Adam.

"All done?" he asked.

"Yes," I replied. "Ian is going back to Olduvai for a while and leaves after Christmas on the 28th. Then I'm going out for a short visit in July and we'll come back together."

"I'm sure you'll have a wonderful time. Look, I'm meeting my wife for lunch and then we're leaving for Jo'burg tonight, shall we go and join her?" Adam said.

"Of course," I said. Adam led the way to a restaurant that was close to Victoria Station.

"Dr Barclay," Audrey said, when Adam ushered us in. "How nice to see you again."

"It's so nice to see you again, Mrs Hill," I replied. "I hope this not an imposition, I understand you're leaving tonight."

"No, no, I'm delighted to see you again," she assured me. We sat down and she and I were soon deep in conversation while Adam and Ian, shared stories and tales of Rhodesia. They seemed to have a lot to talk about and had been to many of the same places, albeit some years apart. I was delighted with this, it was good for Ian to have contacts outside the sometimes stuffy atmosphere of Oxford. We ate and talked and over coffee Ian confessed that his thesis was less than impressive and that he was returning to gather more data to do a rewrite. Adam and Audrey both sympathised, and Audrey asked the obvious question, how were we both going to weather the time we were apart.

"You two young people are so much in love, that is obvious, so how are you going to manage the separation?"

"With difficulty," I said, holding his hand. "But we'll manage and I'll see him in Kenya in July."

"That's still a long time," Audrey said. "I remember when Adam was still in the RAF and he was in Korea for a year, that was difficult. So, when we get back from South Africa, if you need any advice, please come and see me."

"Thank you," I said. "Forgive me for the changing the subject, when do you need to leave?"

"I think soon," Adam said. "We're going to take the bus from the terminal here out to Heathrow. It has been delightful talking to you Ian, I wish you well and make sure that Dr Barclay has a good time in Kenya next year."

"I will, Sir," Ian said. "Mrs Hill, it was a pleasure today, I hope we meet again before too long."

"Go well, young man," she said. "Do good things in Tanzania, but don't forget your sweetheart here."

"I won't," he said, looking at me with such affection I could have kissed him right there. We said our goodbyes, then Ian and I just walked the streets, hand in hand, taking in the sights and sounds. It was cold, but that did not bother us, being together was what mattered. We did find ourselves outside an antique shop, and I noticed a French sommelier's tasting cup. I thought it would make a nice gift for Charlize, so we went in and negotiated the price until I was happy. We also stopped at a bank and bought travellers' cheques. British exchange control regulations limited the amount of money that could be taken out of the country in the form of cash, £25 would not get one very far, so travellers' cheques were necessary. Banking done, we made our way to the offices where Portia had her practice, told the receptionist that we were there and waited in the lobby for a few minutes until she came down.

"Fiona, Ian, how delightful, what brought you to London?" she asked.

"We just got me a ticket to out to Nairobi in July and Ian can take me on a safari," I explained.

"How lovely," she said. "Are you ready to go home, because I've finished for the day." We took a taxi to Paddington and found our train. On the ride to Henley we told Portia about our day, about our changing Ian's ticket and about our lunch with Adam and Audrey Hill. Portia knew the Maman was going to tell me to change Ian's ticket to First Class and was pleased to hear that there had been a seat for him to take. I did complain about the question that Mrs Jennings had asked, it suggested that I might not have the means to pay.

"Well, *chérie*," Portia said. "Forgive me, but you do look as if you're barely out of your teens, and where would one so young looking get so much money?"

"Barely out of my teens," I protested, until I met her questioning look and subsided, she was right, twenty is barely out of one's teens.

"But your friend Adam Hill had introduced you as Dr Barclay," Ian said. "So, I would have thought she would have taken that into account."

"Anyway," I said. "We're set now for July, you'd better get us a room in Nairobi," I told Ian. "We're going to need it!"

"I would think so," Portia agreed. "Now here we are, almost home."

James and Charlize were at the station to meet us and were full of their tales of going to Maman's boutique and the items Charlize had got there, Maman had given her carte blanche to get whatever she wanted, Maman's gift to her. I actually caught sight of James blushing when Charlize describe some of the things she had got. I guessed that there was going to be a private fashion show that evening.

Maman was delighted to hear that all had gone well with the ticket exchange and was really thrilled when Portia told her that she was not going to her office the next day, she had taken Christmas Eve off, in fact she was not going to her office again until after the New Year.

179

Apparently whatever legal issues that might arise over Christmas could wait until the New Year. Portia may have had the gift of foresight, because the next day it snowed, creating chaos around the south of England. Fancy, snow on Christmas Eve and unless temperatures increased dramatically, it was going to stay, meaning a white Christmas, not a common occurrence in England. We all stood at the windows and watched as the snow came down, thanking our lucky stars that we were warm and dry and that we had done whatever shopping that was needed in the days before. We had food and drink for at least two weeks, so come what may, we would not go hungry or thirsty. Maman then issued instructions, first she told Charlize and Ian to book calls to their respective parents. Those were the days when one could not simply dial an overseas telephone number, the call had to be arranged through operators, and the best way to do that was book the call for a specific time. Both South Africa and Rhodesia were two hours ahead of us, so the calls were arranged for six and six-thirty the next morning, both Charlize and Ian being confident that their parents would be home at that time. James and Ian were given the task of bringing in the Christmas tree that Maman had in a pot in the garden, and then they were told to chop wood into reasonable sizes and bring it into the living room to put on the fire there. Charlize and I were given the task of decorating the tree, while Maman and Portia would be busy in the kitchen. I decided that the best way I could help was hand things to Charlize, my previous attempts at decorating trees had been met with anything from amusement to less than muted criticism.

Lunch was served and then we were all able to just relax and enjoy the day. James took Charlize outside to build a snowman, something I had no interest in. I had built snowmen in the past with James and it had usually led to me getting snow pushed down the neck of my jacket, so regarded his invitation with a degree of suspicion. Ian, though, accepted the invitation, even after I warned him about the perfidy of James. I was proved correct, the snowman building turned into a snowball fight, which was fun to watch from the warmth of the house, but in which I had no desire to participate. When they all came back inside, they were quite wet from the snow and dry clothes were called for. Ian came in and quickly ran upstairs to change, when he came back with dry clothes, I had coffee ready for him, fortified with a decent shot of whiskey, to really warm him up.

"Did you have fun?" I asked him.

"Oh yes," he said. "I haven't been in a snowball fight for years, not since I first came to England. Snow was just not something we got at home."

"The snowman looks a little lopsided," I commented.

"He does, doesn't he," Ian said, laughing. "That was my doing, I was in charge of the body, but I got distracted by snowballs, so only did a quick job of building the base. When Charlize had the head ready, I was still trying to pack snow into the body and dodge incoming missiles."

"He's a demon with a snowball," James said as he joined us.

"That's all the cricket I played growing up," Ian explained. "I could throw a mean cricket ball."

"How's Charlize?" I asked James.

"She'll be down as soon as she gets some dry clothes on," he replied.

"I'm surprised you're not up there helping," I said.

"Ha, ha, Fi," he said. "It's not all about sex. You should have come out and helped us with the snowman."

"Not a chance," I said. "I know you James, I would have had snow down my neck before I could move, I remember at least three times when we tried to build snowmen and it just ended in a fight and tears."

"Yes, but we were just small then," he said. "I've matured since then.

"Oh, really, I doubt that," I laughed.

Maman then announced from the kitchen, that she wanted the table set for dinner, a little early, but she said that after a day of cooking she was going to go and soak in a bath, and that we were in charge, of setting the table, organising wine and also getting ourselves decently dressed. She had a long-standing tradition of dressing nicely for Christmas Eve, the observance of which typically ran into the early hours of Christmas Day. Ian asked me what that meant for men and James gave him some advice, to which I listened carefully, I would not have put it past James to set Ian up for embarrassment. But he did give good advice, describing what he had worn in the past, that was acceptable. We divided up duties and Ian and I found a tablecloth and matching serviettes, and then, cutlery, plates and the like. James was on glass detail and Charlize examined Maman's collection of wines until she found some that she thought would be appropriate. James also told her to dig out champagne and to

181

chill it, champagne in the early hours of Christmas morning was a French tradition that Maman maintained.

Table set, Ian and I then went upstairs to bathe and change. I liked bathing with Ian, it gave me the chance to be with him without there being anyone else around, and also just to savour his body. There was also the opportunity to get intimate, which we did, me sitting on his lap in the bath, my legs stretched out either side of him, and my arms tight around his body. It was such a wonderful opportunity to make love, something that I was taking every chance I could while he was still with me. The six-month separation was like a sword of Damocles hanging over us, threatening to sever us at any minute. When we finally got out of the bath, I asked Ian if he had any preferences about what I should wear.

"I've not seen you in that Chinese dress you have," he suggested.

"The cheongsam?" I asked. "I suppose I could wear that."

"From the picture I have you in it, I'm sure it will be lovely," he said, gallantly.

"What underneath?" I asked.

"I don't know," he said. "Bra and panties, what about stockings or tights?"

"I hate tights," I said. "They're a pain if you need to go to the loo, and the skirt is slit too high for stockings to work, unless you want me looking like a lady of the evening, showing stocking tops and bare thigh above them. So, calm your lecherous self, I'll forego tights and stockings, and just go bare-legged, but I will wear the red lace bra and panties. I also have a nice pair of silver slippers I can wear with it."

"That sounds super," he said. "What should I wear?"

"Well, you heard James, nice trousers, a white shirt and that blue vee-neck pullover you have," I suggested.

"That does seem rather a double standard," he commented. "Here you are going to get dolled up in a really nice dress, and the best I can do is trousers and a pullover."

"That's the price we pay for being women," I said. "You might add a tie to your ensemble, that will go about one per cent to equalling things."

"No, I'll go with a jacket and tie," he suggested. "I have a nice pair of slip-on shoes, would that be acceptable wear in the house?"

"That will be fine," I assured him. "It's just outside shoes that have to stay either outside, or in the foyer."

We joined the others downstairs and Maman handed us each a wineglass with a very nice light white wine.

"A toast," she said. "I have Portia in my life, which makes me so happy, Fiona has Ian and James has Charlize, I think we're all very lucky to have such wonderful partners, here's to our partners, lovers and friends." She made the toast first in French and then for the benefit of Ian, she repeated it in English. Her toast was sentiments that we all shared, and we were all happy to raise our glasses to her. I had not seen Maman so radiant in a long time, Portia was clearly good for her and I saw the look of that Portia gave Maman, they clearly shared a deep and binding love and affection for one another. I looked at Ian and he was looking at me and our eyes met, and there was that same electric thrill that ran through me. He was the one for me. With James and Charlize, it was a little harder for me to judge, but they did go well together and they were certainly all over one another, whether or not that was purely physical I could not judge. We had all taken Maman's instructions to heart and I noted that Charlize had obviously dressed up for the occasion. She had on a plunging evening halter top with wide leg Palazzo pants in black. It looked as if it would drive James to distraction. She had no bra on, but then she could get away with it, she was still young enough that things were still firm. Portia had picked a Burgundy dress that bared one shoulder and draped around her body. It also bared much of her legs when she moved, altogether most alluring. Maman had an outfit that was new, or at least new to me. It was a silver jacket top paired with form fitting trousers, and under the jacket she had on a Burgundy top that matched the colour of Portia's dress. I just hoped that when I got into my mid-forties that I looked as good as either of them. Ian had gone with a jacket and tie, and to my great surprise, so had James. Perhaps Charlize had told him that if she was going to dress up, then he could as well.

Dinner was served and we took our time. We were not going anywhere and I think we all appreciated just how lucky we were. We were warm, had food and drink and were in the company of those we loved. When the clock struck twelve midnight, Maman served champagne and we drank to our good fortune. We lingered a little longer, then the party broke up for the night. We all helped with the clearing up, the more hands there were, the quicker we could all get to bed and the pleasures that lay there, which I could see was on all our minds. Upstairs, Ian unzipped my dress and helped me out of it and I stood in front of him, dressed only in the lace panties, while I removed his clothes. By the time I got to working his underpants down his legs and off over his feet, he was erect and alert for me, so I equipped him with the necessary protection and led him to the bed. He helped me down and then slipped my panties off and knelt between my legs, where he practised his magic on me until I was crying out for him. We made love, tenderly and slowly, relishing the moment, with me silently wondering just how I was going to last six months without this. We made love again a little later, but this time I tried something different, right out of the Kama Sutra, I am not sure what the position would be called in English, but in my French version of the book it was *la caverne*. It was very erotic and I promised myself that I would try some more positions like it in the few days before Ian left.

Ian had set an alarm and was up at the ungodly hour of six to make his call to Rhodesia. He was on the line for about twenty minutes, then he came back to bed and snuggled up close to me and we both went back to sleep. When we all surfaced later on Christmas Day, we all looked as if we had had a good night, in every way one could imagine. Now it was time for gifts and a late breakfast. I gave Ian his camera and he was delighted. I gave Charlize the sommelier's tasting cup and she cried a little. I do not think she expected anything, certainly nothing so personal to her life. James, I gave a geology hammer and all the gear for collecting samples of rocks and minerals in the field, plus an eyeglass for close examination. He had told me that he had a field trip coming up at the Easter vacation, so that had seemed a suitable gift. For Maman and Portia, I got matching gold lockets, with both their portraits inside. It had taken me some time to find the right photographs, but I had finally managed and they were both thrilled with the gift. Ian gave me a locket with his picture and mine in it, and I was just over the moon. Now I had something that I could wear daily and if I ever needed to be reminded of him, all I had to do was look inside. Portia had already given me the

Saint Laurent ensemble, so I did not expect anything else, but she surprised me with a really beautiful new leather briefcase. My old one was much the worse for wear, so that was really appreciated. Maman gave me a pair of emerald earrings, which surprised me, because I had never had my ears pierced. She told me that if I did not want them, she would be happy to exchange them, but she thought I might like them because they came from Rhodesia. That decided it for me. These were something that would also remind me of Ian, so I was determined to get my ears pierced at the earliest opportunity. James and Charlize had gone in together and had got two picture books, one of Rhodesia and the other of the Cape Province of South Africa. I was delighted with both books and hugged and kissed them both.

Other gifts were exchanged and then we ate a late breakfast. The balance of the day was spent talking about anything and everything. Charlize was a mine of information about wine and she and Maman had some spirited discussion about the merits of various varietals and which wine growing regions were better for each. Ian spent a great part of the day learning about his new camera and even got me to pose for him, fully clothed. James and Charlize disappeared for a while and came back smiling. I thought that was a good idea and dragged Ian off with me to the bedroom, where we tried out two new positions, and our favourite. I think that Maman and Portia also took time out as we met them coming out of their bedroom hand in hand, both looking very pleased with themselves. Dinner was eventually served and it was a traditional French dish, roast goose stuffed with chestnuts. Maman long ago abandoned the foie gras that usually went that, as she disapproved of the methods used to produce the foie gras, to her, force feeding ducks was inhumane. As a dessert we had a chocolate *buche de Noel*, something that tasted as good as it sounded. We all actually had an early night, the speed at which we cleared the table and washed up was impressive. We had been up at the wee hours of that same day, we had eaten well, drunk well and bath and bed called.

Boxing Day it snowed again, but there were no takers for a snowball fight or another attempt to build a snowman. I was counting down the days until Ian left, and was determined to spend as much time with him as I could, each waking moment and that time when we were asleep. Ian and I spent some time going through his clothes and gear that he would take with him to Tanzania. Some clothes we put aside to be laundered and then packed away pending his return, others we stacked ready for packing in his suitcase, or rather his rucksack. He was going to travel with a large rucksack that would be easy to carry no matter what transport he was on in Tanzania. The rest of the family were giving us time together, not studiously avoiding us, but not intruding on our time together. It was an odd time, we were in limbo, the time was flying by, down now to hours that could be counted, but there was not enough time to embark on any new project or adventure, we just had to enjoy the moments as they were. We did retire to the bedroom early on Boxing Day and spent as time as we could making love, until we were both spent and fell asleep in each other's arms.

The day before Ian's departure, we awoke early, but did not go downstairs for some time. There were other priorities. I had been determined to make it through as much of my illustrated version of the Kama Sutra that we could, but in the end, we just stuck to our favourite positions and learned more about each other's likes, dislikes and preferences. I think I was more adventurous than Ian and more willing to experiment, but was still happy with whatever he wanted to do, I just wanted to be with him. It was almost ten in the morning when we finally admitted that hunger and thirst were things that needed to be addressed and went downstairs.

"Ah, you are up," Maman said. "Would you like some breakfast?"

"That would be wonderful, Maman," I replied, speaking for both of us. "Ian, would you get my slippers for me, I left them upstairs." When he had gone, Maman put her arms around me and asked.

"Bébé, how are you doing?"

"I'm struggling, Maman," I admitted. "I don't want him to go, but I realise I must and I hate it."

"I know, I know," she said, holding me close. "The time will pass, and you'll be able to enjoy him again, but in the tropics where it is warm."

"I'm looking forward to that," I said. "It will be fun, but it's the time between now and then that frightens me."

"It will pass," she assured me. "When I married your Dad, I had to wait in Paris until he made arrangements for me to join him in London, that was a difficult time. I had to keep convincing myself that the marriage was real and that I was not just another wartime romance that would end in misery."

"How did you manage?" I asked her.

"I kept busy," she said. "There was plenty to do, and I also wrote to him, sometimes as often as three times in a week. It helped when the letters from him started to arrive, then I could read his words and imagine him speaking them to me, it took a lot of effort because his French was only passable and my English was almost nonexistent."

"Here you are *chérie*," Ian said, when he returned with my slippers. Maman let me go and I put my arms around him and hugged him close.

"It's okay, *chérie*," he said, guessing that I had been bemoaning my fate. "The time will go by and I'll see you in Nairobi."

"But you leave tomorrow and that is too soon," I protested.

"I know, *chérie*," he said, holding close and stroking my hair. "I'll be thinking of you tomorrow night when I'm on the plane, and I'll write to you as often as I can."

"And, I'll be thinking of you," I promised. "Was that your stomach?"

"I'm a little hungry," he admitted.

"I'd better feed you two, before you faint away on me," Maman said.

We ate, not so much a late breakfast as an early lunch and learned that James and Charlize had taken the old Land Rover and gone looking for a suitable hill with snow on it. James had dug out a sledge we had in the garage and they were going to see if he remembered how to avoid crashing at the bottom of the hill. Portia had taken the new Land Rover and had gone to check on her cottage to see that her tenant was all right. She came back a little after one, satisfied that all was well. She had also stopped by a garage and filled the Land Rover with petrol so that the next day there would be plenty for the drive to Heathrow and back. Maman quickly made her something to eat and they then retired, ostensible for a nap, but I think they had other plans, leaving us to our own devices and desires. In the end we just sat by the fire in the living room, me sitting in his lap, head on his shoulder, kissing as the mood took us.

"So, snogging again," James commented, waking us both from our semi reverie. I had not heard them come in, so he startled me a little.

"Did you manage to avoid crashing?" I asked him.

"We did land up in a couple of snowdrifts," Charlize said. "But that was fine, the snow was not packed down, so it was soft enough."

"Did James put you in the drifts deliberately, or was it just poor driving?" I asked.

"I rather think it was deliberate," Charlize replied. "We went down the same hill three times, and it was only on the last run that we went into the drift, so, if you'll excuse me, I need to get some dry clothes, are you coming James?"

They went off, and I was sure that in time dry clothes would be donned, but full expected them to indulge other passions first.

"So, what do you want to do on our last night?" I asked Ian.

"I want to spend it in your arms," he said. "What else?"

"I was just wondering whether you wanted dinner first," I said.

"I suppose we do need to eat to keep up our energy levels," he laughed. "I'm going to have plenty of memories of you to keep me going for the next few months, but I can only preserve those memories if I have enough energy to do so."

"Good," I said. "Let's see if we can find something to eat."

"For just us, or everyone else?" he asked.

"We'd better feed everyone," I thought. "Or we'll get complaints."

We did prepare dinner, or rather Ian did, with me scurrying about on his orders to do this and that. He could cook, which surprised everyone else when they came to see what the delicious aroma was emanating from the kitchen.

"Marry this man, Fiona," Portia said, as she tucked into the meal that Ian had created. "Marry him, before I forget how much I love Brigitte and marry him myself, this is wonderful Ian."

"Thank you," he said. "I learned from the cook we had at home, he could create masterpieces from a simple fire, one pot and some imagination."

"So, you don't starve on your digs?" James asked.

"No," Ian said. "We manage, there's actually quite a lot available in the bush, and with some knowledge and creativity you can eat quite well."

"So, when Fi visits you next year, you'll be cooking?" James asked.

"I will," Ian said. "I'm the host, so will look after her."

"See that you do," Maman reminded him severely.

"I'll be fine, Maman," I assured her.

"All you have to do…" James started, but he stopped as he received a well-aimed kick on the shin from Charlize.

"Naughty, naughty," she said. "I know what you were going to say, and if it applies to Fiona, it applies to me, so be careful what you think and even more careful what you say."

"But," James protested.

"No buts," Charlize scolded him.

"Remember we're severely outnumbered in this house James," Ian commented.

"Now, as Ian and Fi cooked, then I think the rest of us will clear up and wash up," Maman announced. I took that as a hint and took Ian's hand and led him off upstairs.

We got up late again the next morning, that was the dreadful day when he was scheduled to leave, flying out of my life, hopefully for a few months only. Maman had prepared breakfast, which we ate in silence, each, I think, lost in his or own thoughts. I know mine were on how I was going to deal with the upcoming months and had already planned out a series of projects over and above my main asset valuation project, that would keep me really busy. James and Charlize had gone off again, not looking for snow covered slopes, but to explore the country lanes and enjoy the winter scenery. Portia and Maman tried not to hover over us too much, but they were clearly trying to make our last hours together as pleasant as possible. Ian and I excused ourselves and went to pack Ian's rucksack, it looked to me so little for someone going for so long. But he pointed out that they did have camp staff who would do laundry, on a daily basis if necessary, plus there was no real need for too much in the way of formal clothing, so he could pack fairly light. Lunch was loud and raucous as James and Charlize recounted their adventures in the back lanes, of getting through snow drifts, towing a few cars out of drifts and almost getting stuck themselves. I welcomed the hilarity; it took me out of my dumps and made me laugh. After lunch, Ian and I had a leisurely bath, then made love for the last time that year. For me it was a need to get all of him that I could, so I did, I kissed him, fondled him and clung to him while we made love.

We left for the airport at about four that afternoon. Maman told me that she was going to drive us there. She probably did the best thing, as I knew I was not going to be in a good state to drive home, seeing past tears is difficult. The roads were clear, for the most part, indeed the motorway was quite clear, it had been well ploughed and was even drying up a little. At Heathrow, Maman and Portia stood discreetly aside while I went with Ian to check in at the BOAC counter. The First-Class ticket netted him some immediate attention and he selected his seat and was presented with his documents. Then it was time for him to go. I was not allowed past the immigration desk that guarded the entrance to the departure gates, so we hugged and kissed for quite a few minutes, before we heard over the tannoy an announcement with the gate number for the flight and the first call for passengers to proceed to the gate. I said my final farewell to Ian and watched him walk away. The immigration officer flicked through his passport, glanced at his boarding card and waved him on, and then he was gone, lost to view in the maze of corridors beyond. I had tried to be brave, and had only sniffled a little when I kissed Ian goodbye, but when he was lost to sight, I bawled, with tears running down my face. Maman came over and held me, and just let me cry. She understood what it was like and knew to just let me cry it out. I knew that I should see him again in a few months, but like Maman, I had that nagging fear of permanent loss.

On the drive back to Henley, I was seated between Maman and Portia in the front of the Land Rover. I think that they were both concerned that I would descend into the pit of self-pity if I sat alone in the back, so they kept an eye on me. By the time we arrived home I was done with the crying and was already, in my mind, writing my first letter to him. When we went into the house Charlize had prepared a meal, but most of all, what I wanted was alcohol. I got myself a large Scotch and told Charlize about the trip to the airport and the pangs of loss I felt when Ian disappeared from view. She told me about her leaving South Africa to come to England and the loss that she felt saying goodbye to parents and friends. Obviously, I was not alone in this, all of us had gone through it, so, for all my self-pity, I was not the first to be separated from a loved one. For some reason that made me feel better. I suppose misery really does love company. By the time I went to bed, I was feeling much better, I think because I knew I had the support of my family and friends and people I could turn to when I felt the blues descending upon me.

The next day there was more snow and traffic was snarled all over the place, with snow drifts on high ground of up to six feet. Not a good day to be driving over Dartmoor or anywhere else exposed to the winds that were beating across England. It was a good thing that Ian had left on the 28th, otherwise, he would have been faced with delays at the airport not that I would have complained. As it was, he was in the sunshine, probably motoring south towards Arusha as I ate my breakfast. I sat down after breakfast and started my first letter to Ian. I skipped over my emotions after he had left, and instead, talked about the new snow and how fortunate he had been to leave when he did. I filled the aerogramme page and, like many others, added little notes in the margins, anywhere where the glue that held the letter together would not obliterate the writing. I missed the post for that day, but was assured that it would go on the morrow.

Despair

The New Year came and went and I returned to Oxford, my office and work, and I got my ears pierced and acquired a set of gold studs to wear when I was not wearing the emeralds, but I took to wearing the emeralds as often as I could. I had written two more letters to Ian and had posted them off, wondering how long it would be before I had any replies. I had only been back at work for a few days when I decided it was time to let my sponsors know that I had completed their project and would now just be taking their money for idling. I arranged for the team to meet in London and made a trip there on the 6th of January, not thinking until later that Epiphany was a good time to reveal all to them. I travelled up to London and met with the assembled team and painstakingly went through the whole process, the algorithms and the results.

"How is it that you've managed this so quickly?" Adam Hill asked.

"The algorithms are not that complex, we're not dealing with unknown variables like vibrations in the sound board of a violin," I replied. "And thanks to the generosity of those of you who have given me computer time, I have been able to validate the models. I am now in the position to make all the models available to each of you and will be, of course, ready to work with your accounting and technical people to help each of you set up the models in your own systems."

"How is that we grossly overestimated how long it would take to develop these models?" Barry Tyler asked.

"I think the algorithms came together quicker than we thought," I replied.

"I think we owe you a lot," Barry said. "I also think you're selling yourself short, Dr Barclay, we didn't realise when we selected you, just high a calibre of economist we were getting. What's the next step?"

"I think we should present our findings and approach to the Inland Revenue and to the Institute for Chartered Accountants," I suggested.

"Yes, we need to do that," Adam agreed. "Harold you have contacts with the accountants, could you set a meeting soon and tell them what we're going to present. Who has the best contacts with the Inland Revenue?"

There was general laughter around the room. Each one of those present had had encounters with the Inland Revenue before, and none of those encounters could be said to be amicable. In the end it was Paul Carter who volunteered that he had as good as relations as any of them, and he would set things up.

"So, what will you do now, Dr Barclay?" Selwyn Allen asked.

"I'm not sure," I admitted. "I do have a couple of small projects lined up in the fashion industry, but I need to know how we will proceed, I cannot in good conscience take your money for the Fellowship, now that the project is essentially complete."

"Perhaps," Selwyn agreed. "But let me make a suggestion. Stay on as a Fellow on our support at least until the end of this year, then if we need technical support or someone to come in and explain to our boards what we're doing, then you'll be available. Meanwhile, if you find other projects that interest you, pursue them, recognising that we have first call if we need you. Add to that, if anyone in this group has a project, we can ask you to work on it, understanding that it would be for that member only and not to be shared with the others."

"I can do that," I agreed.

"There's a little problem with that," Harold Flint said. "If you have a big project that takes up all her time, then we're paying for your work."

"I accept that," Selwyn said. "So, any project we individually ask for cannot be more than a fourteenth of Dr Barclay's time for the year, let's say 125 hours of her time, we must provide for some time off in this."

"Can you work on projects concurrently?" David Cowan asked.

"I can," I said. "I find it useful to have different things to work on, often I get an idea that will apply across different industries and markets."

"We need to keep you busy, Dr Barclay," John Wells said. "If the Inland Revenue people or the Treasury ever got you working for them, we'd be in deep trouble."

"I can compartmentalise very well," I said. "How these algorithms work is your property and I would not share them with anyone outside this room without your express permission."

"No, I didn't mean that," John said. "I meant that if someone like you worked for Treasury, the Government might actually know what happens in the economy, and I'm not sure that would be such a good thing. I've met some of the Treasury Civil Service economists and you'd run circles around them, God forbid that you'd join them."

"Hear, hear!" George Montague said. "With those that I've worked with, I can jolly them along to the position I want, I suspect that with you, Doctor, that would not be so easy."

"So," Adam said, interrupting this love festival. "If Harold you could let us all know when we should meet with the accountants and Paul likewise with the tax wallahs."

"I'll do that," Harold said, and Paul nodded agreement.

"Okay, then perhaps we should adjourn?" Adam suggested.

The team members all trooped out of the room, leaving Adam and myself.

"So, have you heard from Ian yet?" he asked.

"Not yet," I said. "I'm expecting a letter any day now."

"Mails from anywhere in Africa can be unreliable, so be patient," he advised.

"How was your trip?" I asked.

"It was really nice," he said. "We did a wine tour in the Cape."

"My brother is dating a Charlize Cillie at the moment, she's from Franschhoek, her family have a winery there."

"I know it," Adam said. "We went there, I gather they picked up a vineyard in France."

"They did," I confirmed. "Charlize is in London at the Institut français studying French before she goes to that vineyard. I'm going to have lunch with her when I leave here."

"You know, John was right, I'm afraid we all underestimated your intelligence, we had heard the reports, but we dismissed them as publicity from the college, we had also assumed that you would have to learn how to read a P&L and balance sheet and that we would have to spend far more time than we did explaining the concepts of proven probable and possible," Adam said. "We had no idea how good you were at this kind of project."

"I think algorithms and mathematics just come to me," I said. "I never really saw it as anything special. When I was younger it used to annoy me that others couldn't see what was so obvious to me, it used to get me into trouble when I was at school. I also have an investment banker as a father, who saw to it that I could pick up an annual report, or a quarterly report, and make sense of it and guess what lay unsaid behind the report."

"I can imagine," Adam said, dryly. "So, Ian, you like him?"

"I think a little more than like," I admitted. "The separation is really hard, but I'm looking forward to seeing him in Nairobi in July."

"I'm sure that you'll have a wonderful time," Adam said. "Make sure that Ian shows you the Ngorongoro Crater as well as the Serengeti."

"He mentioned those," I said. "I'm sure they'll be on the itinerary."

"Well, I'll be in touch when we have dates for the accountants and the Inland Revenue," Adam said. "Go well, Dr Barclay."

"Thank you," I replied. I was sure that there was a response to the go well, but needed to ask Ian what it might be.

I made my way to the Victoria and Albert Museum, they had a nice place for lunch on one of the upper floors, nothing special, but the atmosphere was relaxed and probably in keeping with the museum. Charlize was already there and waved to me.

"Charlize, *ça va?*" I asked.

"Bon, très bon," she replied. "How was your meeting?"

"Good," I said. "I told them that the project was done, bar some technical issues around transferring the models to them, and that I felt that I was taking their money for nothing. We came to an agreement for the rest of this year, and then I'll see what to do. And, you, how are your studies?"

"Much better," she said. "The time I spent with all of you at your Maman's house made a huge difference. Even the professors noticed and asked if I had been to Paris over the Christmas break. Have you heard from Ian yet?"

"Not yet," I complained. "But one of the members of the team I have been working with is also from Rhodesia and he cautioned me to be patient as he reminded me that mails from Africa can take a little while. I think he was trying to tell me in a nice way, that the infrastructure is not always that well developed."

"I really like James," she said. "But I'm not sure what we might do in the future. I have to go to France this August and when he graduates, he's likely to get a job in Australia or South Africa."

"Well, you have a little time to see what transpires," I reminded her. "See what comes later in the year, you may not like James by then."

"How can you say that?" she asked, but then realised that I was teasing her. "I think I would always like him," she said. "The question will be, do I love him? When I saw you and Ian together or your Maman and Portia, the love was obvious. I'm getting there with James, but we're both so young, with so little experience of the world, are we both grasping at the first promising relationship that develops?"

"I'm afraid, only you can answer that," I said. "And, I'm not one to give advice on that, Ian is my first relationship of any kind. What did you tell your folks about James?"

"I just told them that I'd met a family that spoke really good French and that I had been invited to spend Christmas with you. I skipped over the bit about James," she admitted sheepishly. We got food, we ate, we talked and laughed, I really liked Charlize, she was fun and had had a completely different upbringing to mine, so it was interesting to hear her stories. She finally excused herself, she had classes to go to, whereas all I had to do was make my leisurely way home.

When I got home there was a surprise for me, a letter from Ian. I tore it open and scanned the contents quickly, then got myself some coffee and read it again, slowly, lingering over every word. I tried reading it aloud, imagining him talking to me. I was just thrilled. He had made it to Nairobi on time and had met the others he was going to be working with and they had travelled down to Arusha in the back of a lorry taking supplies. He told me that there were four new people, two women and two men, Rosalind, Angela, Tom and Edward. They were all Americans, and it was, for all of them, their first trip to Africa, so Ian said that he was in great demand as a translator and also as a cultural guide. Apparently Rosalind was to be based in Arusha doing administration work, so how she would fare without a working knowledge of Swahili was a question. Ian had not received any of my letters when he had written his, so they probably passed each other, either in the air or on the ground somewhere in Tanzania. I put the letter aside and took pen and paper and wrote to him. Four times I referred back to his letter to answer some specific point that he had made. I was so happy to have heard from him, I hugged myself with joy and then danced around the house. I sat back down and put the finishing touches to my letter, including a drop of Rive Gauche on the paper. I had no idea how well that would travel or dissipate before it got there, but it was worth the try.

I made dinner for myself and poured a glass of wine then propped up Ian's letter against a glass and read it again as I ate. I have an eidetic

196

memory and can recall precisely what I have read or heard, so could have recited the contents of Ian's letter at any time, but it was not the same as reading his words. He talked about the heat, the dust, the blue skies, the animals, the herdsmen and their cattle, the vast expanses of Africa and his delight to be back, already planning what he was going to show me in July. I got my atlas out and found Nairobi, then Arusha and then the Ngorongoro Crater. The dig was close to that, so I knew roughly where he was, half a world away, but next to me in my heart. When I went to bed that night, it was with fantasies of Ian, made very real by the use of the vibrator that Maman had sent me, and I fell asleep thinking of him and his arms around me holding me close.

I received a call at my office the next day, to let me know that meetings had been arranged for the Wednesday and Thursday of the following week. I had thought about crying off for the meeting on the 14th, the idea of a meeting on my birthday was not the most exciting, but decided to let it go ahead, then they were over and done with. I called Maman to let her know that I would be in London for the 13th and 14th and she suggested staying over on the night of the 14th as well and that we would celebrate my birthday in London. She would book rooms for us all at the Park Lane, which was convenient for me as that was where the consortium normally got a room for me when I needed it. She said that she would contact James and Charlize and let them know the plans. I told Maman that I had heard from Ian and that he was well and getting back to work. The next week dragged, I did a few things to my models, mostly minor changes to make the output more elegant, and I waited. I waited for time to pass before the next meeting and I waited for the postman to see if there was another letter for Ian. I even saw him one day and asked if he had seen anything from Tanzania. He was sympathetic, but unable to oblige. I would just have to have patience and wait. I satisfied my longing for Ian by reading his letter again and again, until the folds were becoming more fragile and the letter was in danger of falling apart, so I took it to work and made a copy. The original I stored in a box of things that I had that related to Ian and me, the copy I kept with me in my briefcase.

The meeting with the accountants was at their place of business in Moorgate Place. I went there with Harold Flint and Charles Mudd and Mrs Fletcher, who had been present at all our meetings and had been charged with taking the notes. We made our presentation, then fielded questions, all of which, I am pleased to say, I was able to answer quickly and easily. The grilling that the team had given over the past few months had helped me iron out all the issues. There were no disagreements with the valuation treatment methodologies and I even left with an offer of a job. There was one surprise, one that had been kept from me very carefully. It seemed that the members of the team had had my work reviewed by two eminent economists and had been passed as meeting all the requirements set out in the scope of work. I had great respect for one of the other economists, and would have given the other a passing grade at best. I suppose at first, I was a little irritated that they had done this without letting me know, but rationalised it to myself that they were just protecting themselves against future questions and queries from the accounting profession and the Inland Revenue. Harold and Charles thanked me and said that they would take care of letting the others know about the meeting as soon as Mrs Fletcher had typed up her notes. I was then at a loose end and wondered what James was up to. It took a chance and got a taxi to South Kensington and went to his hall of residence. I found him in the bar, with four others.

"Fi," he said, when he saw me hovering at the threshold. "Come and have a drink." I went over to the group and kissed James hello.

"Who's your friend Barclay?" one of the others asked.

"My sister, Dr Fiona Barclay, Bill Wilson, Gerald Henderson, Simon Black and Robin Webb," James said, making the round of introductions.

"Doctor, of what?" Gerald asked.

"Mathematics," I replied.

"So, one of those pure science types," Robin said.

"Not really," I said. "I've a project at the moment for a group of major mining houses working out how to value ore reserves, so I've been doing more with economics lately."

"So, what do you want to drink, Fi?" James interrupted.

"I'll have a white wine," I replied. "Are you all in the same class as James?"

"Yes," Simon said. "Where did you get your doctorate?"

"At Oxford," I replied. "I'm currently a research fellow there funded by the mining industry."

"Now that's the kind of job I'd like," Gerald said. "Pay me to think about stuff, no sweating away underground."

"So, Fi," James said when he came back with my wine. "Mum tells me that we're going to get together for your birthday tomorrow?"

"That's the plan," I said. "I have a meeting with the Inland Revenue people in the morning, but otherwise I'm free for the rest of the day."

"You've got a birthday tomorrow?" Gerald asked.

"She does," James said. "Twenty-one tomorrow."

"And you already have a doctorate?" Robin asked. "Wow."

"She does," James confirmed, speaking for me, looking at me with great pride, as though he had a hand in it, not that I minded, James has always been a supporter, when he was not privately tormenting me. "Two degrees and a PhD, makes me look like a real dodo. Have you had dinner yet, Fi?"

"No," I said. "You have a suggestion?"

"There's a curry place just down the road," he said. "We could go there. You blokes want to come?"

"No, James, you go and spend time with your sister," Bill said. "I've got stuff to do and we wouldn't want to intrude."

"You're sure?' I asked. "I don't mind, really."

"No, you go and talk to James," Bill said. "I know when my sister comes to see me that it's nice to talk to her alone."

As we left, I overheard Gerald say to Robin, "I wonder if she has a boyfriend, I never thought of James as having a dish for a sister." It was nice, if a little sexist, to be thought of as a dish. Since Ian, I had become much more aware of myself and the image that I projected. I was happy with my body and liked the way I looked and tried very hard to stay fit and in shape, particularly now that I had a boyfriend. I wanted to look my best for him.

"So, Fi," James said as we walked the short distance to the curry house. "Heard from Ian?"

"I have," I confirmed. "I got a letter last week, I'm waiting for the next one. How are you and Charlize doing?"

"We're fine," he said. "You'll see her tomorrow night. We're going to be staying at the Park Lane with you."

"Have you introduced her to your friends?" I asked.

"Yes," he said. "They're jealous right now that I have a girlfriend like Charlize."

"They'll get over it," I assured him. "So, apart from beer, how's it going?"

"Not bad, actually," he said. "Nothing I can't handle yet, but I may come to you for some explanation of a couple of math items."

"Anything that I can do," I promised him. "Is this the place?"

"It is," he said. "The food's not bad and we haven't been thrown out yet."

We talked over dinner, about his classes, about Charlize, about the food at the restaurant and about his field trip that would be held over the Easter vacation. It seemed that the mining students did not get much in the way of real vacations, the Easter vacations were going to be the geology field trip, a mine surveying trip at the copper mine that the college owned in Cornwall and a visit to various mining operations in Europe. The summer vacations were similarly occupied, with work experience scheduled. To graduate James had to have worked so many hours in a mine. I was thankful that my degrees and doctorate had had no such requirements. After dinner I hailed a taxi to go back to my hotel, leaving James to walk the short distance back to his hall of residence.

On my birthday I went to Somerset House, which apart from being the repository for records of births, marriages and deaths, was also the headquarters of the Inland Revenue Service, otherwise known as the tax man. There I met Paul Carter, Neil Pain and Mrs Fletcher. We were shown to a meeting room and cooled our heels for a few minutes before a bevy of intense looking men came in. These were the tax men, no tax women, perhaps that would come in time. I went through my pitch again and answered the questions that they raised. More than the accountants, the tax men wanted to know about my qualifications. How was it that I had been selected to create the algorithms and models and what other experts had reviewed the work. Paul went through the selection process that had used to pick me for the job and also trotted out the names of the two other economists who had reviewed my work and that satisfied that question. To me the really interesting item came towards the end of the meeting when one of the tax men said that the real test would come in a dispute between a company and the service over the tax treatment of assets, and would I be available to testify. I danced around that one, it would depend on when and where and who would pay for my time. Paul said that if a mining company called me as an expert then they would pay, he asked the tax people if they would be prepared to pay. That led to a lot of umming and aahing, on their part, which led me to suppose that none of them wished to stick his neck out and commit to spending money. It was an interesting difference between the meetings, the accountants had been more concerned with the methodology of the valuations, the tax people were more concerned with how someone might rule if there was a dispute, and how well qualified I was to create the models. We finally left, and as I was leaving I was approached by a man who introduced himself as being from the Treasury, and asking me if I would be available to work on some economic models that would predict tax revenues, so that the government would have some idea of how to balance the budget, or at least know how out of balance the budget would be and how much they would need to borrow. I gave the man my card and told him that I did have some time available. He said that he would be in touch.

I had the rest of the day to myself, so called Rachel to see if she might be available to discuss her project. She was and suggested that we meet for lunch. She named a restaurant that was near Harrods, so I took a cab there and waited only a few minutes before she also arrived.

"Fiona," she said. "I was about to call you in Oxford when you called. I wanted to talk about our project."

"I've made progress," I said. "How are you?"

"Well, thank you," she replied. "And you?"

"I just came from a meeting with the Inland Revenue," I said. "There's a bastion of male chauvinism if there ever was one. A great way to spend one's birthday."

"It's your birthday today?" she asked.

"It is," I confirmed.

"What are you twenty-five, twenty-six?" she asked.

"Twenty-one," I said. "Twenty-one has rather lost its significance after the voting age was lowered last year, I was rather looking forward to getting a key to the door."

"You can't be just twenty-one," she said. "But we should celebrate." She called over a waitress and ordered us a glass of champagne each. While we waited for that I went over the models that I had that related sales to particular demographics and she said that that was most useful as it helped her focus on those markets likely to be most profitable sooner rather than later. We were interrupted by the waitress bringing champagne and menus. Rachel toasted what would have been my coming of age, then we looked over the menus and made choices. She was in no hurry, so we sat and talked, then ate, then talked some more. Her views on the trends in the fashion industry were fascinating, an altogether different business to the mining of metals. When we finally left the restaurant, it was with a date set for our next meeting. Before that I would have to try and get some more computer time to run simulations. Sadly, the college was a little behind in acquiring and building computing power, so, although we had a machine, time on it was at a premium, we really needed another machine because the demands on the one were overwhelming. I thought that I might try and persuade one of my other clients to let me have some time on their machine. It was a long shot, but worth the try.

Maman was already at the Park Lane when I got back. She expected Portia a little after six and thought that James and Charlize would be there around five.

"So, Bébé, how are you doing?" she asked.

"I've taken your advice," I said. "I'm staying busy. So far, I've only had the one letter from Ian, but I'm hoping that when I get home there'll be another. I miss him, Maman, I miss his silly grin, I miss his touch, I miss the scent of his aftershave."

"I know, Bébé," she said, hugging me close. "I cannot say that it will get better with time, but you will learn to deal with the separation."

"I suppose so," I said. We talked more, essentially killing time until the others arrived. When they did, we had dinner, but it was a subdued party. I think they all realised that I was missing Ian a lot, and although I was not actually sulking, I was not the best company. James tried to liven things up by reminding me of things I had done on past birthdays, and I admit, I did start to laugh. When I looked back, we had got up to some real pranks and was surprised that one, we survived them all, and two, that either Maman and Dad did not know what we were up to, or chose to ignore things. I rather think, in retrospect, that it was the latter. Like most parents who were deeply involved with their children's lives, they had a pretty good idea of where we were and what we were up to, but there were some things that I knew they were blissfully ignorant of.

James got Charlize laughing at some of the things we did, and that triggered memories for her, so we learned quite a bit about her upbringing. By the end of the evening I had put my sulks behind me and was planning my next letter to Ian, to tell him things that had happened in the past that I thought would amuse him. By the time we all went to bed I was a much happier person and went to sleep fantasising about Ian and what I would do to him when I saw him in July.

Maman and I travelled back together at least to Twyford, then we split, her to catch the connecting train to Henley, me to go onward to get the train to Oxford. When I arrived home, there on the floor by the front door was a letter from Ian. Not an aerogram, but a real letter, three pages long, written on both sides of the paper. I dropped my bags and took the letter to the kitchen and quickly scanned through it, then got wine and sat down and read it again, word by word, line by line, to myself, then aloud, to get every nuance of what he was saying to me. My first letter to him had arrived, which was good to know and he said that he was looking forward to getting more. Well, there were several on the way. He told me about the dig, the sun, the dust, the people, his tent and the meals he was getting. I tried to imagine it all from his words. I sat in bed looking at the poster sized picture I had of him and read it aloud, trying to project what he was saying onto the poster so that it would seem that he was there telling me all about his adventure. I got pen and paper and wrote back to him, telling him about my meetings, my birthday party where I had been less than the soul of the party, because he had not been there to share it with me. I finally went to sleep with his letter safely stored under my pillow.

The next week disaster struck. On the 20th of January the postal workers went on strike, no collections, no deliveries, no parcels, no stamps, no telegrams, nothing. In the intervening week since I had received his last letter, I had posted my reply to Ian and had been waiting for another one from him, but until the strike ended, there would be apparently be nothing. I called Maman in a panic.

"Maman," I cried. "Did you see that the bloody Post Office has gone on strike?"

203

"I did," she said. "I was just talking to Portia. She has a few cases in Europe, so she's trying to set up a system for sending and receiving letters."

"Don't they have an office in Paris?" I asked.

"They do," Maman confirmed. "Portia was thinking that they would have a courier fly over a couple of times a week until the strike is over. Then letters can be posted from there and received there."

"That's a great idea," I said. "Can you get the address for me, that is if Portia doesn't mind me sending letters through their office?"

"No, that's fine," Maman said. "In fact, Portia suggested that. Do you have a pen and paper handy?"

"I do," I said. I wrote as she dictated. I had an address to which Ian could send letters and if I got mine to Portia, she would include them in the pouch that the courier would take over to Paris. I was annoyed with the Post Office, I took it as a personal affront that they would go on strike and affect my mail. I knew that there was a pay dispute between the union that represented the workers and the Post Master General, but that was their problem, not mine. So, I would have to wait for word from Ian until, either the strike ended or, he got my next letter that would be routed through Paris, so at least another two weeks before I heard from him again, perhaps longer. I did wonder if I could get a telegram sent from Paris and asked Maman that.

"I should imagine so," she said. "They have a telegram service as we do. Why don't we call Mémère Monique and have her send a telegram for you, at least with the address of the Paris office?"

"Brilliant," I said. "Do you think she'd send another for me, telling him that I love him?"

"I'm sure she would," Maman said.

"Why don't you have her send the message in Tahitian?" I suggested. "I told Ian once that I loved him in Tahitian, so he knows what it means."

"I like that," Maman said. "That would be a very private message, there might be a telegraph operator in Paris who speaks Tahitian, but I doubt that there are many, if any, in Tanzania." The strike was a nuisance, but at least we were taking some action and trying to get mail sorted out so that Ian and I could continue to send each other letters.

"When you have your next letter ready, bring it over here and I'll make sure Portia gets it to put it in the pouch," Maman said. "Meanwhile I'll call Mémère Monique and ask her to send the telegrams."

"Thank you, Maman," I said, much relieved. "You're a life saver, I don't know where I would be without you."

For the next six weeks until the 7th of March, I wrote letters and diligently took them over to Henley for Portia to take and include in their courier pouch. I kept busy with Rachel's project and with three of the consortium members who needed guiding through the process of setting up the asset valuation models, otherwise, I waited and waited for something back from Ian, but there was nothing. I would have thought that with the Paris address he would have written there and that letters would have reached me. I read and reread Ian's first two letters, wondering why I had had nothing more. Perhaps the telegrams that Mémère sent did not get there and his letters were piling up somewhere. I wondered just what the Tanzanians did, did they hold letters in Dar es Salaam, or did they put them on a plane, which meant they could have been sitting in a growing pile of mail bags at Heathrow airport. It was frustrating and alarming, what if I did not hear from Ian, had something happened to him, had I offended him in some way. I reread his letters and there was nothing in them that suggested he was in any way unhappy with me, so had something happened to him.

I visited the anthropology department at the college and asked them if they had had any communication with the dig team, and they had not. They had not been as creative as Maman and Portia and were just waiting for the strike to end. So, they were no help. It was so frustrating, difficult for people today to understand. In a time when telephones are almost universal, it is hard to look back to a time when the main mode of communication was by letter, and there were no letters, because the service that moved them was on strike. Also, at that time there was no FedEx, UPS or DHL, no e-mails, so no alternates. The Post Master General did issue authorisations for people to set up private mail delivery services, but that did not help me, my saviour was the Paris connection, at least it should have been. In the middle of all this decimalisation came into effect, by that I mean that the United Kingdom switched from pounds, shillings and pence, to pounds and new pence, so no more twenty shillings to the pound and twelve pennies to the shilling, now it was one hundred new pence to the pound. This change was brought into final effect on the fifteen of February, and included changing postage stamps as well, if we could ever buy any, so aerograms were now four new pence instead of nine pence.

A couple of days after the strike ended, there was a letter from Ian. Only the one, but I thought that perhaps there were more in the backlog of mail that was being sorted after the strike. I read Ian's letter and read it again. He talked about his daily life and he talked about missing me. He said that he missed seeing me laugh, he missed smelling the perfume that I used, he missed my touch, he missed my kisses and he missed my body. He described in eloquent terms running his hands over my body, the mounds and dells that he discovered and the secret places that were mine to share with him. I propped his letter up against a wine glass and read it aloud, running my own hands over myself as he described things. It was very erotic and on the one hand very comforting, but on the other hand made me miss him more, as I wanted to feel those hands on me and have him joined with me. I sat down and wrote a reply, that would have been banned if I had offered it as a novel, Lady Chatterly's Lover was tame stuff compared to my letter, mine was more along the lines of Delta of Venus by Anaïs Nin, only more so. I wrote describing in intimate detail what I was going to do to him when we were together in Nairobi. I read my letter through and the urge was too strong, so I got my vibrator out and used it as I read my letter aloud. When I got to Nairobi, Ian was in for an exciting time!

I waited a week and there were no more letters from Ian. I talked to the postman and he told me that the backlog of letters was just about cleared. I talked to Portia, and nothing had arrived at their Paris office, so what was the problem. I went to the anthropology department and talked to them and they told me that they were getting mail from the dig site, including an occasional update from Ian. I sent a telegram to Ian, asking him if everything was all right. I waited and waited for a reply and nothing came. I wondered what I had done or said, that he did not contact me. I stuck it out until the end of March then took his letters and went to consult with Maman and Portia.
"Bébé, what's wrong?" Maman asked when I arrived in Henley.

"I haven't heard from Ian," I sobbed. "His last letter was written in January and there hasn't been one since. The postman says that the backlog from the strike is about cleared, so there aren't any letters waiting to be delivered, something's gone wrong, but I don't know what."

"You've had some letters from Ian?" she asked.

"Three," I said, through my tears. "Here, read them, tell me if I missed something in them that should have told me that he was unhappy with me, have I said something that has driven him away?" I handed her the letters and she and Portia quickly looked over them.

"These are very personal," Maman said. "Are you sure you want me to read them?"

"I'm sure, please read them, study them and tell me if there are any clues there that will tell me what has gone wrong," I begged. "I know he's still there and working, the college confirmed that, he does send an occasional report to them, but since the last letter written in January, I've had nothing. I've sent telegrams begging for a reply and nothing, nothing in reply. What's happened?" Maman took each letter and read them carefully, and when she had done, she handed them to Portia who also read through them.

"I don't know Bébé," Maman said. "What I read are words from a man who loves you and is missing you. His last letter really tells me he misses you, he describes in such intimate detail missing your body, if that was written to me, I could only conclude that it was my lover who had written those words to me. Do you remember what you wrote to him?"

"Mostly," I said. "I've written two a week since he left, so that's twenty-five so far, a lot to remember, and I've had three back, and they were written one a week. In my letters to him I told him about my days, my meetings, my missing him, I don't think I said anything that anyone could take offence to. Am I trying too hard, sending too many letters, am I smothering our relationship?"

"I wouldn't have thought so," Maman commented. "Portia?"

"I agree," Portia said. "I can see nothing in his letters that hints that he's at all unhappy with you, he's unhappy about not being with you, but that's not the same thing. From what you said about your letters to him if I were him, I'd be happy to get them, I'd go and sit in a quiet place and read them, then read them again to linger over every word, so that I could see you in my mind."

"That's what I do with his letters," I said, sniffling a little. "I read them, then I get a glass of wine and read them again, then I try and read them aloud using his voice, so that I can hear him say the words."

"And you say that the college does hear from him?" Maman asked.

"They say they do, occasionally," I confirmed. "He doesn't send much to them, but they have heard from him, so he's alive and I presume well enough to work, so why not well enough to write?"

"I've no idea," Maman admitted. "I don't know what to tell you Bébé, other than wait and see if there are more letters. I would keep writing to him, perhaps once a week instead of twice a week in case he is feeling smothered by your affections for him, why he might think that I don't know, but you never know. I can't believe we were so wrong in our estimation of Ian. I would have staked my life on his love for you, I cannot imagine what has changed or gone wrong."

"Can I stay here tonight?" I asked. "I don't want to go home to my empty house now."

"Of course, Bébé," Maman said. "You can always stay, whenever you like."

"We're happy to have you here," Portia added. "We'll be here to help you, whatever you need. I'm also confused about what might have gone wrong. Like Brigitte, I would have staked my life on his love for you, I can't imagine what must have happened in Tanzania that he stopped writing to you."

I stayed with Maman and Portia for the rest of the week, driving over to Oxford each day. I was frustrated, feeling lonely and sad and confused. I could not imagine what had gone wrong. I would have said that we were meant for each other, was I wrong. I cried a lot and wrote drippy letters begging him to reply and tell me that he loved me. I finally went back home and settled into a work routine. The Treasury man did contact me and they gave me a very lucrative contract to develop more sophisticated models of the economy and projected tax revenues, so I was busy, in fact I was really busy as four more of the consortium members also had projects for me, so I was working long hours each day, which was good, because it kept me from brooding. The days ran into weeks, and I wrote each week, and the weeks into months and I still wrote each week, and still nothing from Ian. I wrote about my work, I wrote about what was sprouting and blooming in my garden, I wrote about the day I borrowed the boat from April and Paul and rowed up to the Trout Inn to visit the place where we had had out first picnic. I wrote about sitting in the coffee shop where we had met so many times, hoping to see him walk through the door and grin at me like he did. I wrote about going back to the Randolph and spending the night, trying to remember all that we had done there, I wrote about that in detail hoping to kindle a spark in return. But it did not seem to matter what I wrote about, there was no reply.

I was trying hard not to think it, but was coming to the stark reality that perhaps this relationship was over. If that was so, why did he not have the character to actually tell me and not just leave me hanging. I had written faithfully, first two letters a week, and then once a week like clockwork, with no replies, beyond the three letters I had received early in the year. I had tried letters to elicit a reply, I had tried telegrams, but even with them there was no reply. I would have thought a telegram would have garnered some kind of reply, even if it was, leave me alone. It was driving me to despair. How could things have gone so wrong. What was it that I had done to drive him away. I suppose like most, I thought it most likely that it was something that I had done, or said, or not said, that had caused him to sour on our relationship, but what that may have been, I was at a total loss. The things that really tore at me were the memories, it seemed that almost everywhere I went there was something that would trigger a memory and all of our shared memories would come flooding back to haunt me. I would sit alone in the coffee shop where we had spent so many hours and hope that he would walk through the door and all would well again. I confess to shedding more than a few tears there, such that I finally gave up going there, it was just too painful.

I started to spend more time at Henley and Portia was the one who suggested that I just sell my house and move back. I demurred telling her that I did not wish to come between her and Maman, but she insisted, telling me that she had come to look upon me as the daughter she had never had, and that she loved me. In fact, I had on a couple of occasions when I had been feeling particularly down, climbed into bed with them and had literally come between them. But they both understood and cuddled me close so that I did not feel abandoned, but cherished and loved. We had a conference then, the three of us and Portia told me and Maman that she would be happier if I moved back, she would worry less about me sinking into a depression if I stayed on my own in Oxford. Maman agreed with her, and I accepted their offer and decided to move back. Portia was right, I had become moody and sad, and depression would soon follow if I did not address the issues. It was hard, I had never really loved another, outside my family, before, and had put my heart and soul into the relationship, which now was looking more and more that it was over. The sense of loneliness was powerful and there were times when I felt as though I was truly alone in the world, which was foolish as I had Maman and Portia who truly loved me, even James and Dad were supportive.

We put my house on the market and within two days I had four offers. That surprised me and made we wonder if I had priced it appropriately. But the estate agents all assured me that the price was generous and that I would do well from the sale. I picked one of the offers and the process moved forward, in fact the estate agents were startled at the speed at which the process did move. Normally these things could develop a life of their own and it could be weeks, dragging into months. By the middle of June, I was out of the house and it was sold and I had the money in the bank. Now I had another decision to make. I had my trip to Africa planned and paid for, at least the airfare, but the question was, would Ian be there to meet me, in fact did he even want to see me. That question was resolved quickly. I went to the anthropology department and they were in a turmoil. Apparently, Ian had left the dig and gone back to Rhodesia. He had received some communication from someone, packed his bags and left the next day. I could only presume that meant something had happened to his parents, but there was no more information forthcoming. So, I wrote no more letters, I had no idea where to send them, except perhaps to Ian Hartley, Mount Darwin, Rhodesia and hope that they might get there. But would I be deluding myself. If he had not written to me in five months, why would he start again.

So, now it was a reality. I had lost the love of my life. Something had happened and he had stopped writing to me, did that mean he had met someone else. That was my worst fear. I knew that he was alive and well, but could find no other explanation for his dropping me. I toyed with the idea of talking to Adam Hill and having him find out for me where I could contact Ian, but decided against it. Part of me was still desperate to rescue the relationship, but part of me was smarting from the rejection that seemed patently obvious. I still had enough pride, that I had grown angry over the situation, and was not about to go begging. One day, perhaps, I might find out what had happened or who it was that had taken him away from me, but for now I was beginning to accept that I had loved and lost. There were times when I felt so alone and could have easily descended into a pit of self-pity, but there were also times that I was angry, angry that he had made no effort to at least let me know that things were not right and give me the opportunity to fix whatever the problem was. Even with the acceptance that I had probably lost him, deep in me I still had the longing for him and for all I thought I hated him at times for rejecting me, I still loved him. I began to understand some of the emotions that I had seen Maman go through after Dad left to be with Felicity the floozie. She had been hurt, then angry, then sad, then depressed and it had taken a while to get over things. But I also saw from Maman's experience that it was possible to get over these things and that she was deliriously happy with Portia. So, perhaps one day there would be someone else for me. As for my trip to Africa, I went to see the BOAC people and tearfully told them my story and cancelled my tickets to Nairobi, I was not going to go on my own.

The balance of that year came and went and I stayed busy, really busy, I was gaining a reputation and companies were calling me in sufficient numbers that I could pick and choose the projects I wanted to work on, and I could charge outrageous prices. By the end of the year, I had built up enough of a clientele that I really no longer needed the Fellowship, and the consortium that had funded me terminated their support, as we had agreed that they would, so decided that I would leave the college and set up on my own. It was logical that a good place to do that was in London, so I contacted Dad and had him help me find an office from which I could work. For a while, I joined Portia as another of the commuters, who travelled back and forth to London. I would travel with her, which I think we both enjoyed, I even started to laugh again. Portia suggested that I get a flat in London, there really was no need for me to travel back and forth every day. She did it because there was Maman to come home to, but for me, there were no such ties and she was now comfortable that I would not sink into a depression over the loss of Ian. She helped me find a flat, on Cadogan Place, and negotiated the lease for me. I moved in and also moved all Ian's belongings that had been left in Henley, even though there were times that I considered throwing the whole lot in the bin. I sold my Mini Cooper, there really was no need for a car in Central London. I studiously avoided places where Ian and I had spent time out, so I did not set foot again in the Trout Inn, nor in the Randolph, there were too many memories there, particularly at the Randolph. What did surprise me was that I had no particular interest in other men, no matter how many well-meaning people threw in my way. I think part of me now distrusted men as fickle, untrustworthy and interested only in one thing, no matter how well they dressed up the seduction. Was I being unfair to Ian. I did not know then and wondered if I would ever find out. I looked back often on the experience and delighted in the pleasant memories and avoided dwelling on the negative, but put it down to part of growing up and thought often of the Tennyson quote:

I hold it true, whate'er befall;
I feel it, when I sorrow most;
'Tis better to have loved and lost
Than never to have loved at all.

Personally, I thought that Tennyson was full of it, I wondered if he had actually loved and lost and gone through the heartbreak. I could find nothing in the histories of Tennyson to tell me that he had endured a loss, perhaps he had and I was being unjust. There were times when I thought it would have been better to have never met Ian, then the heartache would not be so bad, but then I thought of the wonderful times we had spent together and dreamed of a reconciliation, and kept deep inside me the hope that he would come back to me.

The family got together for Christmas, James and Charlize were still seeing one another, which surprised me, as I did not see distance relationships working well. But it seemed that James had managed to cleverly arrange trips to France on weekends, and yet still keep his studies going well. Charlize was enjoying her stint at the vineyard in France and she and James were often in a corner talking about the future and how they might manage things. It struck me that I could see James changing his career and shifting from mining to grapes, either as the grower or the processor. I think given the choice, I would have gone with grapes, particularly if Charlize came with the job. I admit I felt pangs of jealousy, Maman had Portia and was deliriously happy, James had Charlize and they seemed to be working things out, even at a distance, whereas I had nothing, just memories that with the setting sun would come flooding back to haunt me, again and again. I saw the little gestures and touches of affection that passed between them, but I had no one whose touch I would feel and respond to, I longed for his touch, but knew that I was never likely to feel it again.

Over dinner on Christmas Day, Maman dropped her bombshell. She and Portia were going to retire to the south of France and sell the Henley estate. I was dumbstruck, this was the house I grew up in. Now it was to be sold. Maman told us that she had been approached by an American company who were looking for a country house to convert to a conference and education centre for their executives. Apparently, the wife of one of the top executives had been in Maman's boutique and had bought a ridiculous amount of clothes and Maman had invited her to dinner at the house. She had come with her husband who had fallen in love with the place and had sounded her out about selling. Maman and Portia had discussed it and had made the decision to sell, for Portia to retire, and for both of them to move to the Riviera. I could hardly cavil at that, given the choice of Henley or the Riviera, I would have picked the sunshine any day. The heads of agreement of the sale were already done, all that remained was the details and the transfer of funds. What made that even more attractive to Maman, was that they were quite happy to transfer funds to France, so Maman would have a financial base there as well as one in London. She was also selling her share of Bridget and Brigitte to Bridget, and the new lingerie line that she had developed with Rachel would go as part of that. Maman told James and I that if there was anything in the house that we really wanted then we should take it. I could not think of anything that was there that I really wanted, all the material items that I had long ago coveted, I either already had, or they were Maman's and she was moving them to France, what I really wanted I could not get back, I wanted the love of my life to walk in the door and tell me that he loved me, but that was not going to happen. I had already moved all the belongings that Ian had left with us when he had gone back to Tanzania, to my London flat, so there was really nothing in the house that I really wanted. Portia then added that she had sold her cottage to her tenant, so she no longer had any ties. Her firm were disappointed that she was leaving, but she thought secretly relieved. She had become quite vocal about the lack of women in the ranks, and pointed out regularly the fact that she was the only partner who was not male.

The close on the Henley estate took place at the end of January of 1972 and James and I were invited to a farewell party with Bridget and the other ladies from the boutique as well as neighbours. It was difficult to leave for the last time, knowing that I would never be back. So, another chapter closed, I had loved and lost, now the ancestral pile was gone and Maman and Portia gone to another country. They had found a villa close to Cannes and the furniture would be moved there as soon as the party was over. Maman had traded in her Land Rover for one that was left-hand drive and had sold her Lotus and replaced it with an Alfa Romeo Spider. She and Portia were going to drive to Cannes as soon as the furniture left and they received word that the funds had been transferred.

So ended the Henley on Thames period of my life. I had had a wonderful childhood there; I had been lucky with my parents who had understood early on that I was going to be a challenge and who had risen to that challenge. I had returned there after I had loved Ian and lost Ian. I had been nurtured through that difficult time by Maman and Portia and was now mostly satisfied with life, if that could be said for someone who spent most of their time working with little time, or even inclination, for a social life.

An expedition

It was early May in 1975 when life changed again for me. When I had been a teen I had gone to the cinema in France and seen the Spaghetti Western film, *C'era una volta il west (Once upon a time in the West)*. It had made an impact then and I had enjoyed it and been moved by it, particularly the music. The sound track of the film had been released in 1972 and then in 1974 words were put to the main theme music of the film and were sung by Mireille Mathieu. I had always been a fan of Mireille, but for some reason had not immediately bought the album on which the song was recorded. When I got home the day of my purchase, I played the record and collapsed in tears, sitting on the floor, just crying my heart out. I started out just sniffling, then I cried, I bawled, I howled, my body wracked with sobs as I let out all the emotions that had been bottled up for so long. The first track, *Un jour tu reviendras,* one day you will come back, had really hit home. The music was bad enough, it had a haunting quality that had always brought a lump to my throat, now the lyrics talked about memories, and the hope that her lover would come back to enjoy a life together as they had before. It brought back memories of Ian and the time we had spent together, of his grin, his touch, his ready wit, the way he talked and the way he made me laugh, the times we spent making love and the closeness that that brought, both physically and emotionally, it also played to the part of me that, deep inside, always hoped that he would return, as the song said, *l'espoir de ton retour.* I could hardly stop crying, the memories crowding my mind, and the pain of my loss flooding back, I could almost feel his touch, which, as in the song, I longed for still. It took a while, but finally I was cried out and now filled with a new resolve. I was going to find out just what had happened. There had to be someone who could give me some clues. What we had had was just too precious and valuable to not try and rescue, I loved him still and thought that I would always love him, no matter what happened. I should have done something before, but I think my pride was hurt and I had not been about to go traipsing around the world looking for him. But now I realised just what I had lost and it was worth a try to see if that could be found again.

I called Maman to talk to her about my idea and to see if she and Portia would come with me. I say that because I was determined to go to Africa and to Arusha in particular to see what I could learn there about what had happened.

"Bébé, how are you?" she said, when she answered the telephone.

"I'm okay, Maman," I replied. "And you and Portia?"

"We're both just fine, what's up Bébé, you've been crying?" she commented, as sensitive as ever to my moods and disposition.

"I bought a new record by Mireille Mathieu, it's music of Ennio Morricone," I said. "If you get it and listen, you'll understand. It's from the sound track of *C'era una volta il west*, and first track is *Un jour tu reviendras*."

"Ah, I think I understand," she said. "It brought back memories?"

"Oh, Maman, so many memories, they all came flooding back and the hurt came back as well, it was overwhelming for a while and I just sat on the floor and cried and cried and cried, but I have decided to do something," I explained.

"What are you going to do?" she asked.

"I'm going to go to Arusha to see if I can find out what happened," I said. "I wonder now if I shouldn't have gone as soon as his letters stopped coming."

"Are you sure?" she asked. "It's been a couple of years now, there may not be anyone there who knew Ian."

"I think there will be," I said. "I'm going to try no matter what."

"We'd love to come with you," she said. "When are you thinking of going?"

"I was thinking of June or July," I said. "From what Ian told me, that is a good time to see animals and it's in the dry season, so no rain to worry about."

"Do you need help organising a trip?" she asked

"Would you?" I asked. "I'm really busy at the moment, but I should be able to take two to three weeks off in late June to July."

"If you give me dates, then I'll get us flights to Nairobi and then a car to take us on a safari and to Arusha," she said. "We might also go on from Nairobi to Johannesburg, then by train to Cape Town to see how James and Charlize are doing."

"That's a good idea," I thought. James had kept up his romance with Charlize and after he graduated had switched over to grapes and wine and had taken to it like a duck to water. He and Charlize were managing the French vineyard, but they were both going to be in the Cape in July for more education about wine making. There was even talk of a wedding, so perhaps the knowledge that we would all be there would precipitate that event.

"How much time can you take?" Maman asked.

"I was thinking of two to three weeks, but I could take as much time as I wanted," I replied. "Why?"

"I was thinking we could come back by boat, unless you have a pressing engagement in June or July," she explained.

"Let me take a look at what I've got on and when I'll be able to finish the various projects I'm working on now," I promised. "I'll let you know in a day or two what my timetable looks like. How long is the boat trip?"

"I'll check," Maman promised. "But I think about twelve days."

"What would you do, come to London and then we'd all fly to Nairobi?" I asked.

"I think that would be best," she agreed. "Portia and I could come over a day or two before we go and stay with you."

"That would be lovely," I said. "I need to go now and start clearing up all my projects so that I can take time off."

"I'll start checking on things," she promised. "I'll call Charlize and James and tell them of our tentative plans, and, perhaps, we'll have their wedding to go to in the Cape."

"That sounds good, thank you, Maman, I love you," I told her. "Tell Portia that I love her."

"I will," she promised. "I love you, Bébé."

I spent the next two days carefully reviewing my projects and estimating how long each would take to finish. It looked as if I could clear my calendar by the twentieth of June. I called Maman and told her that I would be free any time after the twentieth. I also told her that I could take as long as a month off. That gave her some dates to create a trip around. Then I decided to go and see Adam Hill. I had never told him what happened, but he might be able to get some information for me from Rhodesia that would help me. I called his office and asked to speak to him. The gatekeeper asked me my name and my business, so I told her that I was Dr Barclay and that I wanted to talk to Mr Hill. I got the usual Mr Hill is a very busy man speech, so I suggested that she just take my message to him and if he chose to speak to me that was fine, and if he did not, I would try again on another occasion. The wait was only about fifteen seconds and then he was on the line.

"Dr Barclay," he said. "How nice to hear from you, how are you?"

"Well enough," I said. "And you?"

"In the peak of health," he said.

"And Mrs Hill?" I asked.

"She has a few arthritis problems, otherwise is well. I gather you picked up another doctorate, one in economics, congratulations. To what do I owe this pleasure?" he asked.

"I need your help," I told him. "I need to find Ian and I don't know where to start."

"Why don't you come to my office and tell me all about it?" he suggested. "Where are you now?"

"I'm only about fifteen minutes' walk from your office," I said.

"I'll expect you then, shortly," he said.

"Thank you," I said. I hung up and got my coat and walked the mile or so to the office block that was the London Headquarters of his company. The gatekeepers downstairs must have been warned of my coming, because as soon as I announced myself, I was directed to the tenth floor. When I exited the lift, I was met by Andrea. She was new to me, but introduced herself and led me to the inner sanctum where the top executives were quartered. I was shown straight to Adam's office.

"Dr Barclay, so nice to see you, coffee, tea?" he asked.

"Coffee please," I said.

"Andrea, could you get us some coffee and please hold my calls?" he instructed. "Now, what's up, what do mean you can't find Ian?"

"I'm so sorry, this is a long story," I said.

"Take your time," he said. "Ah, Andrea, put it over there would you and bring some Kleenex, thank you."

"Well, it all started when Ian went back to Tanzania in 1971," I said. "I wrote to him and got letters back. Then the letters stopped and I heard nothing. Then I learned that in June of that year he had received some kind of communication and he packed and left the next day to go back to Rhodesia. I got three letters from him, that's all, written in January, after that nothing. I tried sending telegrams, but got no replies. At first, I thought it was the postal strike, but even after that mess was all cleaned up, there was nothing. I have no idea what happened, I've shown his letters to my mother and she can find nothing in them that gives us a clue as to what happened."

"So, why start looking now?" he asked.

"You're probably going to think I'm crazy," I said. "But it was a song, *Un jour tu reviendras*, that brought back memories, and I just have to know what went wrong. I'm going to Tanzania to Arusha to see if anyone there can shed some light on what happened, I just have to know."

"I'm so sorry for you," he said. "How have you managed?"

"It was very hard," I said. "My mother and her partner were very supportive, without them I would have probably sunk into a deep depression. Even now I find it hard, so I have to go, I have to find out."

"How can I help?" he asked.

"Would you use whatever contacts you have in Rhodesia to find out if he's still there, or if not where he might have gone?" I asked.

"Of course," he said.

"I miss him," I said, sniffling a little, and then crying real tears. Andrea appeared and brought Kleenex tissues and hovered.

"Andrea," he said. "We have a mission, we need to find out anything we can about Ian Hartley of Mount Darwin. He may have been in the Rhodesian Army, he may still be in Mount Darwin, or he may have left, he went back there in June of 1971 and has not been heard of since."

"Yes, Mr Hill," she said, then she put a comforting arm around my shoulders and said. "Don't worry, Dr Barclay, we'll find him."

"Thank you," I said, between sobs. "I have his picture here," I said, proffering it to her.

"He's a very handsome man," she said. "We'll find him, don't worry."

"Oh, he once told me he has a sister, Irene Hartley, she's a doctor, in 1970 she was a resident at Groote Schuur in Cape Town," I added.

"We'll start there," Andrea said.

"Thank you," I said. "I'm sorry to be a bother."

"It's no bother," Andrea said.

"No bother at all," Adam echoed. "My older daughter has just gone through an emotional break up with her boyfriend, so I have some sense of what you are going through. When do you leave for Arusha?"

"In late June," I replied. "We're going to fly to Nairobi and then drive, we'll visit the Serengeti and the Ngorongoro crater while we're there, and then we plan to go south to Cape Town and visit the Cillie winery."

"Who's going with you?" he asked.

"My mother and her partner," I explained. "We're debating now whether to fly back or come back by boat."

"If you have the time, try the boat," he suggested. "The service will probably end soon as the new Jumbo jets have taken much of the market."

"If you learn anything, here's my card with my office address and this is the address of the Cillie estate in the Cape," I said. "If I'm gone to Africa, then that will be the best place to send things. Thank you for helping me."

"It is my pleasure," he said. "Andrea and I will dig around and see what we can learn, Andrea is also from Rhodesia, from Salisbury, and she has more recent contacts that I do."

"Yes, but not so highly placed," Andrea added. "If you want senior army officers, then Mr Hill knows more than I do."

"Well, thank you again," I said. "I've taken up too much of your time."

"Not at all," he said. "Have you been busy lately?"

"Very," I replied. "I'm just clearing up projects at the moment so that I can take some time off."

"Would you be available when you return to take on a project for us?" he asked.

"Of course," I promised. "What are you looking at?"

"The economics of agriculture," he said. "We're looking at our farms and trying to decide which products to grow more of, and which to scale back."

"That sounds interesting," I said. "I do have a relationship with the Cillie vineyards, so if grapes and wine are involved, I may have a conflict there."

"No grapes, no wine, rum maybe, but not wine," he assured me.

"That would be fine then," I thought. "Should I contact you when I get back?"

"Please do," he said. "By then we'll have a better idea of what we're looking for and also will have collected production figures and costs, so that you'll have something to work with."

"Good," I said. "Well, again thank you for your help, I'll call as soon as I get back."

"Thank you, Doctor," he said. "We'll be in touch when we have something to report. Andrea, will you take Dr Barclay to the front desk?" Andrea went with me down the lift to the front door and assured me that they would leave no stone unturned for me and gave me the direct line numbers for herself and for Adam, so no gatekeeper switchboard to get through.

Andrea called me the next day to confirm that Irene Hartley had once worked at Groote Schuur, but she had left in June of 1971. It was thought that she had gone to Rhodesia, but the people that Andrea talked to were not certain of that. Of Ian, Andrea had no news yet, but assured me that Adam was doing all he could. My surmise was that whatever had taken Ian back to Rhodesia had also taken Irene back. My suspicion was that it was likely to be a family matter, possibly concerning their parents. The war in Rhodesia was heating up, and farmers were targets, particularly in Mashonaland. Maman called with a possible itinerary, she dictated dates, times and places to me and also told me that she had put it all in a letter which she had posted that day. The itinerary looked simple enough, we would fly to Nairobi on BOAC, perhaps stay at the Norfolk hotel for one night, then pick up a safari that would take us to the Masai Mara Game Reserve and then south through the Serengeti National Park, to the Ngorongoro Crater and finally to Arusha. From Arusha we would take the main road back to Nairobi and then fly to Johannesburg and then take a train to a place called Wellington, which was a little way out of Cape Town. James would meet us in Wellington and drive us to Franschhoek. We would then get the boat back from Cape Town. All in all, the trip would be one month, I decided that I could afford to be gone that long and called Maman back to tell her to go ahead and make the bookings. I also made arrangements to get smallpox and yellow fever jabs, I was not certain that I would need them, but better to be safe than sorry, I also get malaria medications to take. The other thing I did was go back on the pill. With no sex life, I had not bothered with it for a couple of years, but one of the nice things about the pill was that if you kept taking it there was no period, no nothing to mess up our trip.

A week after Maman had started on the bookings she called me again with the news that Charlize and James had set a wedding date of the 13th of July, and the honeymoon would be on the same boat we were taking back to Southampton. That gave them plenty of time to organise things and apparently the family were happy with that. James had been to South Africa a few times and knew the family. I had met Charlize's father twice in France when they engaged me to do some work for them, Maman and Portia had also met those members of the family who had travelled to France, but there were others in the wider family that we had not met. James contacted Dad and invited him and Felicity, we would have to be on our best behaviour around her, we did not want to embarrass James. A wedding meant an event, which meant clothes. I discussed this with Maman and we decided to take two extra suitcases each, one just with wedding attire and other clothes to wear in the South African winter and the other for fancy clothes for the boat trip. We would make arrangements with the safari operator to leave those suitcases in Nairobi at their offices while we were out on safari. I decided to talk to Rachel about what to wear and called her to see when it was convenient to go to her studio. The next day worked, so at ten in the morning I was there.

"Fiona," Rachel greeted me. "Lovely to see you again."

"Nice to see you, Rachel, how are you?" I asked.

"Well, busy as always, but busy is better than not, so, what brings you here?" she asked.

"James is getting married in July to Charlize," I told her. "The wedding will be in South Africa, so I expect the weather to be cool."

"Where in South Africa?" Rachel asked.

"Franschhoek, it's in the Cape," I replied. "The Cillie family has vineyards there and an estate."

"So, conservative Afrikaners," Rachel thought. "We'd better not go too avant-garde, don't want to upset their sensibilities. You'll want something to wear to the wedding itself, and then at least one other outfit, for the other socialising, anything else?"

"Well, Maman, Portia and I are going on a safari in late June," I told her. "We plan to leave suitcases with the wedding clothes with the safari operator in Nairobi while we out looking at animals. Oh, and we're coming back by boat so probably should take some clothes for dressing for dinner."

"Sorry if this brings back old hurts, but whatever happened to Ian?" she asked.

"That's a mystery and part of the reason we're going to Africa," I replied. "We're going to stop in Arusha and see if we can learn anything."

"Well, I hope you find something," she said. "Come back in a week and I'll have something for you."

"Thanks, Rachel," I said.

A week later I picked up my clothes from Rachel and paid her. I also bought some more safari clothes and a new pair of binoculars and got my hair cut. I had my regular hairdresser give me a pixie cut, nice and short, so that long hair would not become annoying in the tropics. It might be winter in South Africa, but on the equator, there was probably not that much difference in temperatures throughout the year. My projects I got done in record time and had them all finished two days before my self-imposed deadline. That gave me four days before we left for Nairobi. I gave final instructions to the service I used to take messages for me and who collected my mail for me, and then I was set for the holiday. I got a call from Andrea, they had had word from a contact in Rhodesia. Ian's parents had been killed in an ambush on the road, their car had hit a landmine, and then they had been gunned down. Ian and Irene had both gone back to attend to their funeral and to dispose of the family farm. After that was done, Ian had joined the army and had gone off on a series of clandestine missions, until late 1972, when he told the powers that be that they were fighting a losing battle and that he was leaving. He had then just disappeared. Irene had stayed long enough for the funeral and the disposition of the family farm and she too had disappeared. It was thought that they had both gone south to South Africa, but whether or not they stayed there no one knew. Andrea did say that the farm had not fetched the highest price, but it was known that they had converted the funds into gem stones, which suggested that they circumvented Rhodesian rules about taking money out of the country. The army command was unhappy with Ian, they felt that he was a deserter, but were not in a position to do anything, as they had no idea where he was. So, I knew a little more, but nothing that would really help me.

Maman and Portia flew over from Paris two days before we were to fly to Nairobi. I had seen them on holidays but not as much as I would have liked. We had discussed their relationship and how countries in Africa might view it and had all concluded that for the purposes of this trip that Portia was simply a friend of Maman. What might go on behind closed doors was no business of anyone's save theirs. I took a taxi out to

Heathrow to meet them and joined the throng waiting at the arrival's hall. I saw them before they saw me and was thrilled to see that they were still in the mode of holding hands, even in public, not caring what people thought about them. I waved and Portia saw me first and pointed me out to Maman, who steered their luggage trolley in my direction.

"Bébé," she said as they joined me. *"Ça va?"*

"Bien merci," I replied. *"Et tu, et tu, Portia?"*

"We're both well, thank you," Maman said, replying for both.

"You're both looking really good," I said, as I looked them both up and down. They really did look good; the Mediterranean living must have been agreeing with them.

"We've been quite active lately," Portia said. "Henley was flat, but our villa, as you know is perched on a hill, so running involves a lot of up and down, so we're fitter than we used to be."

"Is this all your luggage?" I asked, stupidly, as I thought about it, because they had just cleared customs, so of course it was all their luggage.

"I think we have everything," Maman said.

"Okay, we'll get a taxi," I suggested.

The day was hot and my flat had heated up in the afternoon sun so was doubly warm inside. I opened windows, but that did not cool things much, so Maman started the trend by stripping off. She spun around and announced that that felt much better, so Portia and I followed suit. The windows may have been open, but the chances of anyone seeing in were next to impossible. My flat looked out onto the gardens and I could not see flats on the other side, so similarly they could not see me.

"You've been sunbathing nude," I commented to Maman and Portia, noting the complete lack of tan lines on either of them. I also thought, as I had done in the past, that I hoped I looked as good as they did when I was approaching fifty.

"Why not?" Maman asked. "You know that courtyard at our villa, well, it's the perfect place, lots of sun, no wind and no peeping Toms."

"So, are you ready?" Portia asked.

"Yes," I said. "I know a little more about what Ian did after he left Tanzania, but still want to know what the hell happened there."

"We'll see what we can find out," Maman promised. "Now, do we die of thirst in this place?"

"No, Maman," I said. "I'll get something to eat and drink, you and Portia make yourselves comfortable and stop nagging me."

"Yes, Bébé," Maman said, coming up to me and hugging me close. I melted, as I always did when she held me like that, there was something very primal and comforting to have my naked body touching hers, it brought out the child in me and I revelled in her touch. I loved her and I knew that she loved me. It also made me think of Ian and the deep feelings that I got when I had felt his naked body against mine, different to those when Maman hugged me, much more sexual and arousing, I missed that.

We spent the next day making sure that we had everything that we needed for the Africa trip and each packed three suitcases, one for the safari, one for the wedding and one for the boat trip. On the appointed day we got a taxi to Heathrow to begin our expedition. British Airways, as the new combination of BOAC and BEA was called, flew the new Jumbo jets to Nairobi, they were huge and whereas the mathematician in me knew why they flew and could run the calculations, it was still awe-inspiring that this huge thing actually flew, lumbering its way into the skies. We had seats in the very front of the Jumbo jet, row 1, A and B, and row 2, A, which were quite comfortable and the service was extremely good. Our flight was going to include a stop in Zurich, before going on to Nairobi. The flight to Zurich was quite short, only an hour and forty minutes, then there was a brief stop and then we were on our way to Africa, late at night, so that, if awake, we would see the dawn come up over Africa. I did see the dawn come up, and it was spectacular, and it was not long after that the captain made his announcement that we would be landing shortly in Nairobi. We cleared immigration and customs and then spotted our guides, they were holding up signs that read Barclay, and I doubted that there were too many Barclays on the flight. We introduced ourselves as the Barclays, and learned that our guides' names were Henry and Julia Conway, they came with three helpers who took our bags.

"Jambo," Henry said. "Welcome to Kenya, we'll be with you for the next week or so, anything you want, any questions, just sing out."

"Thank you," Maman said. "I'm Brigitte Barclay, this is Portia Harding and this is my daughter, Fiona."

"Great," he said. "I understand that you want to leave some bags at our office?"

"We do," Maman confirmed. "We've a wedding to go to in South Africa after this, and then we're taking the boat back from Cape Town."

"Okay, let's go then," he said, leading the way to their vehicles, where three more staff were waiting. There were two vehicles, one for us and the other, a Bedford lorry for all the camping gear, we were going to do this old style as a mobile safari. He made us comfortable and quickly drove into town and stopped at an office long enough for us to use the loo, change into more comfortable clothes and to deposit the bags we were leaving. The bags we were taking with us we identified as to which belonged to whom, and Julia took charge of those. Then we were on our way, we had decided that there was really no need for an overnight stay in Nairobi and would just head off on our safari. Henry and Julia had coffee and tea in flasks, that Julia handed around, depending on preference, plus some biscuits.

"We'll stop for lunch on the way," she said. "There's a few nice places between here and the Maasai Mara. Your first trip to Kenya?"

"First trip to Africa, except for Portia, who was actually born in Tunis, so I suppose is African," Maman replied.

"True, but I always thought of Africa as beginning south of the Sahara," Portia interjected. While Maman and Portia made small talk with Julia, I took stock of our guide. In many ways he was like Ian, tall, slim, tanned and spoke with a similar accent, not the same, but still an accent that one would associate with Africa. Our caravan drove out of Nairobi and soon we got a view of the Great Rift Valley. Henry explained that we would be going into the valley and were on our way to a place called Narok. The view of the valley was amazing, it was vast, stretching out forever. I knew Africa was a big continent but had no idea how big until I realised that I was looking at a small part of one country in the continent. We descended and raced out across the floor of the valley, if racing was the right word, given the state of the road. Not far past Narok, we passed the Game Department barrier at Nwaso Ngiro, then we travelled on until we stopped among some trees, which Henry explained signalled the existence of a periodic watercourse. While he chatted to us, the team went into action and had tables and chairs set out, plus a canvas awning to keep the sun off and had the table set with food and drink in short order. I have to say I was impressed with the team, they knew just what to do and how to do it. I saw Maman ask something of Julia, who gave an instruction to one of the staff and he quickly went off into the thicker bushes and then came back and nodded, then Julia handed Maman some tissues, who suggested to Portia and myself that we use the facilities before lunch. That was my first experience of peeing in the bush. I lingered a little longer than Maman and Portia and when I went back, I saw them in conversation with Henry and Julia, which ended as I arrived.

"What's up?" I asked.

"We were just talking to Henry and Julia about the schedule for the next few days," Maman said.

We ate lunch listening to the sounds of birds chattering away in the trees and bushes. I had taken Ian's letters with me and had read them again on the plane, and now could begin to relate to some of the things he had talked about. The wide-open expanses, the smells of the earth and the people, the birds and the sense of the place. Henry talked about what we might see in the way of animals in the coming days, but was curious as to why we wanted a whole day in Arusha. Maman told him that we had some enquiries to make at the offices of one of the Olduvai digs and left it at that. Portia asked Henry how had got into the safari business, so we got his life story. His grandparents had emigrated to Kenya and had tried farming, but had quickly decided that life in the bush was preferable to grubbing in the dirt, so had set up a mobile safari business. His parents had taken the business over and now ran it. He and his brother ran the trips and their parents did all the bookings, managed staff and ordered supplies. Henry had been educated in England at a small boarding school in Hampshire and had skipped university, opting instead for an education in the bush at the feet of two of their local Kenyan guides. He had met Julia when she came out to Kenya to be the manager at one of the fixed lodges, they had met and she had decided that mobile safaris could be fun so had joined the company, then married Henry.

Lunch done, we continued on our way, and we split, Julia went with the lorry, presumably to set up camp, while Henry took us on a game drive.

"Anything in particular you'd like to see?" he asked. "The big five?"

"We're not fussy," Maman said. "We'd just like to enjoy the day and whatever we see, we see. I expect that there will be other trips to Africa in our future, so we don't have to rush all over the place trying to find everything, let's just take our time and see what comes."

"You didn't bring any cameras," Henry commented.

"We do have one," Portia said. "But this trip is about the experience that can sometimes be lost if you spend all your time behind the viewfinder, time enough for that on another trip."

"What are those antelope over there?" I asked, interrupting.

"Impala," Henry replied. "We'll see plenty of them on the trip. If you look past them, you can see a cheetah on that rock over there just watching them. If you look to the right, there are also some giraffe walking towards us."

We all watched the cheetah for a while, but he did not seem that interested in chasing an impala just then. The giraffe walked behind us and ambled off into the distance. We drove on and Henry pointed out topi and gnu and some lions. Portia asked him about some of the birds we could see, and he quickly identified ten species for us. I was awe-struck at the majesty of the place and the sheer abundance of nature and deep in me regretted that this was not with Ian, as we had imagined those few years ago.

We drove slowly on, stopping every now and then to look at birds and animals, it was absolutely enchanting and I was delighted that I had decided to make the trip, and also that I was able to share it with Maman and Portia. The only thing that would have made it better was if Ian had been with us. We finally came to a place where there were tents set up.

"Here we are," Henry said. "First camp. Julia has some refreshments for you and let us know when you want a shower and we'll fill the bucket showers that you'll find behind your tents."

"How was the trip?" Julia asked, as she came to greet us. She had a tray in hand with glasses of champagne, that she handed around.

"It was wonderful," Maman said. "I'm so glad we came."

"Let me show you to your tents," Julia said. "We have one for two and a single, who do I put in the single?"

"That would be me," I spoke up. "Put Maman and Portia in the other tent." Julia led the way and one of the staff followed with my bag. The tent was roomy with a cot in it already made up as a bed. There was also a chair and a small side table. Attached to the tent was a canvas enclosure in which was a shower and a wash basin.

"The loo we have set up over there," Julia explained, pointing to a small tent set up a little way from the sleeping tents. "If you need to go in the night, blow this whistle and one of the staff will go with you to make sure there's nothing around. If you need anything, please just let me know and I'll see what I can do. When would you like a shower?"

"Would now be inconvenient?" I asked.

"Not at all," Julia replied. "Brigitte, Portia, what about you"

"Now sounds wonderful," Maman said for both of them. "I'd like to get the dust off before dinner."

I made myself comfortable and two minutes later two of the staff came with a large bucket of hot water. They lowered the bucket shower and filled it with the water then hoisted it up and secured it. After they had gone, I stripped off and stood underneath and opened the valve in the bottom of the bucket. The stream of hot water was wonderful, washing away the fatigue of the journey and the dust of the day. I dried myself and dressed in clean clothes, then went to see what I could see. The camp was set on a small rise among some large trees. It had a commanding view of the area below and I could see groups of antelope, some giraffe and some zebra. It was absolutely enchanting, something out of a story book or Hollywood epic. Maman joined me and she put her arms around me and we just looked out at the majesty in front of us. "Missing Ian?" she asked.

"I am," I confirmed. "This would have been so wonderful with him, I'm more determined now than ever to find out what the hell happened. Things I see, smell and hear remind me of things he said in his letters, and that brings back other memories. Oh, Maman, I should have come out here as soon as his letters stopped to find out what was wrong."

"Well, we'll see what we can find out in Arusha," she said. "Come and join the rest of us for a sundowner."

Portia had stolen a march on us and already had a glass of wine in hand and was munching on some small pastries. Julia asked what we would like to drink and we opted for the white wine that Portia had. It was very good, a light French wine that we all recognised. Julia asked us about ourselves and we each gave a much-redacted life story. She was also curious about our desire to spend a day in Arusha and I told her that I wanted to try and find out what had happened to a friend of mine who had worked on one of the Olduvai digs and with whom I had lost contact. Julia also asked about the wedding and Maman gave her the basics, James marrying Charlize, then going back to France to manage the vineyard. Portia interrupted to point out the sunset, it was beautiful and we were all amazed at the speed at which the sun dropped below the horizon. I had not realised that in the tropics that happened and it was only in the higher latitudes that it seemed to linger much longer. With the setting sun, memories of Ian came flooding back and it was hard to hold back the tears. Dinner was then announced and we went to be seated at the dining table. The amount of furniture and crockery that must have been stowed in the lorry was impressive. Plus, the fact that it was packed well enough that nothing was broken, even after traversing rough dirt roads. Dinner was superb, Ian had told me before how the chefs in Africa could work magic with the minimum of equipment, and he was right. Over coffee around the fire later, while everyone else was busy chatting, I did have a moment of self-pity, and silently shed tears as the others laughed. I excused myself early and went to bed and cried myself to sleep, dreaming of finding Ian again and renewing a life together.

I was awakened the next morning by one of the staff bringing coffee. It was hot and surprisingly good. I listened to the camp noises, the birds and animals, and was sure that in the distance I heard lions. Henry confirmed that when I went for breakfast. There was a pride not too far away and they were announcing their presence to the world, or at least the world of big cats. Our lives for the next week or so settled into a pattern. We would get up, have breakfast, then leave for the day, knowing that when we reached our destination that the tents would already be up and ready for us, and that dinner would be served and would be superb. Henry spent some time with us talking about the stars and the constellations that we could now see that were not visible in the high latitudes of the northern hemisphere, so I got to know the Southern Cross and would look for it each night. Crossing the Serengeti was something right out of the film Hatari and I could see John Wayne and the others chasing around in Jeeps, bouncing through gullies and dongas and catching animals. We were not interested in catching animals, just in enjoying what we happened upon, which actually turned out to be very rewarding as we saw so many animals it was impossible to even begin to try and count them. We went down into the Ngorongoro Crater and marvelled at this natural enclosure that kept so many species in semi captivity. The skies were blue every day, it was cool at night, but warm in the day, the camp staff were cheerful and friendly and I enjoyed myself, probably more than I had since Ian went away. Finally, we came to Arusha. We made camp outside the town and sat around the camp fire and made our plans for the visit to the office.

Henry and Julia drove us into town and we found the offices of the college dig and went in.

"Good morning, how may I help you?" a very proper English girl asked.

"We were wondering if you could help us, we're looking for some information about a man who worked on the dig a few years ago?" I said.

"I'm not sure that I can be of much help," she said. "My name's Alison, by the way, who are you looking for?"

"Ian Hartley," I said. "He worked here from 1967 to 1970, then came back in the first part of 1971, I have a picture here of him." I showed her the picture that Maman had taken of Ian dressed for the bush.

"Let me see," Alison said, opening up a filing cabinet.

"I'm sorry," I said. "I should have introduced us, I'm Fiona Barclay, this is my mother, Brigitte Barclay, our friend, Portia Harding, and these are Julia and Henry Conway, they're our safari guides."

"So nice to meet you," Alison. "I should get you some tea, Tega," she called. A man appeared and Alison gave him instructions. I saw Henry wince a little and then he excused himself and went out to talk to Tega. We could hear a rapid conversation taking place in what we assumed was Swahili.

"I suppose my Swahili might one day be nearly as good as that," Alison said, a little wistfully.

"It will come in time," Julia assured her. "Henry grew up here, so spoke it from a child."

"I've only been here a month," Alison told us. "The one who would have known about your friend Ian, would have been Rosalind, but she left just a month ago, when I arrived." Rosalind was a name I remembered from Ian's first letter.

"What about an Angela, or a Tom or an Edward?" I asked.

"The rest of the all-knowing, everything is bigger and better, American contingent?" Alison smirked. "They all just left as well, all gone back to the States."

Tega came back in with tea and Henry helped pass it around, then he asked me, "You're Fiona Barclay, Doctor Fiona Barclay?"

"That's right," I confirmed. Henry looked at Tega, who then started to volubly expound about something. When he finished, Henry asked a couple a quick questions, then explained for our benefit.

"I'm a little confused, but it seems Tega may be able to help," he said. "I need to take him to his house to collect something, we'll be gone about thirty minutes, is that okay, Alison?"

"Of course," she replied, as intrigued now as the rest of us.

"Oh, before we go, I saw that you had a picture of Ian Hartley there, may we look at it?" Henry asked. I gave it to him and he showed it to Tega who nodded yes and launched into another long discourse.

"Tega confirms that, yes, he knew Ian and that that is a really good picture of him, we'll be back soon," Henry said.

While they were gone, we made small talk and I explained that I was not another anthropologist, even though I was Doctor Barclay, but an economist, and Alison told us that she had just got a degree in English and was wondering what to do with her life, and had taken the job as administrator just to get some work experience. We were all quite relieved when Tega and Henry returned. Tega was carrying a cardboard box, which he set on the table and then launched into a long explanation of what was in it. Henry stopped him and, I think, basically told him to start at the beginning, so with Tega talking and Henry translating this is the story we got. Tega knew Ian, he had worked out at the dig once, before he felt that he was too old for the physical work involved. Then he had taken the job in the office. He had seen Rosalind the American arrive and she had taken over the office, managing all the communications in and out, that included letters, reports, grant requests, in fact anything that passed through the office she saw and handled. When she was packing up to leave to go back to America, she had given the cardboard box to Tega with the strict instructions to burn it and all the contents. He had taken it out to burn it and had looked inside and seen letters. Tega had had only the most basic education but he could read and he saw that there were letters addressed to Ian and letters, not stamped and obviously not posted to a Doctor Fiona Barclay from Ian. He knew Ian and did not want to burn the letters so he took the box home. He had been concerned about what to do with it. He knew that Ian had left and had heard that he had gone to Rhodesia, but he had no idea of his address, similarly, he had no idea if Doctor Fiona Barclay still lived at the address on the letters, and that was made worse by the fact that some of the letters had an address in France. He opened the box and gave me a whole stack of letters, all those I had written to Ian, unopened, save one, and another stack of letters that had been written to me. There were even the telegrams that I had sent, received, but not forwarded to Ian and not replied to. I did note that the two telegrams that Mémère Monique had sent for me, were not there, so possibly Ian got those, which explained the French address on some of the letters.

I picked up the bundle of letters from Ian and burst into tears. He had written to me so many times and I had seen nothing.

"*La connasse,*" I heard Maman say. It had been a long time since I had heard Maman swear, but I could tell that there was more to come. "*La pétasse, la salope, la poufiasse,*" she added with venom, roughly translated as motherfucker, slut, bitch and whore. Portia added a few words of her own, but they were all in Italian, a really good language to swear in, but unnecessary to repeat here. All good descriptions of what I was thinking of this woman, this bitch and quite a few other, even more derogatory adjectives, who had completely destroyed our relationship.

"Why did she do it?" I asked Henry through my tears. He then had another chat to Tega and then reported back to us. "It seems that this Rosalind met Ian Hartley when they travelled down here from Nairobi and according to the gossip, she had the hots for him. Tega did some asking around after he found the letters and all the stories were that Rosalind was basically throwing herself at Ian, but he had this girl in England who had been writing to him and him to her, so she got in the middle of that and stopped the letters. Sadly, Tega did not find this out until after she had gone, or he would have found a way to get the letters to Ian and to post his. He also said that after Ian left, she latched onto another, one of the Brits, a Gordon Busby, that was on the dig and spent a lot of time with him."

"Where is this person Rosalind now?" Portia asked.

"I gather she's back in the States, in Ohio," Alison replied.

"Does she ever plan to come back to Tanzania?" Portia asked.

"Why?" Alison asked.

"Because, the Tanzanians, like the Brits and the Americans have laws about tampering with mail," Portia explained. "If she was coming back to Tanzania, I'm sure we could get her declared persona non grata, I have a friend in the Tanzanian judiciary who is highly placed."

"As far as I know she has no plans to ever come back here," Alison said, looking a little bemused and confused. "Why would anyone do something so mean, underhanded and just wrong?"

"We'll never know for sure, maybe she thought it was love, but it was probably infatuation in the extreme," Henry said, replying for all of us. I wanted to leave, I wanted to read all of Ian's letters, I wanted to meet this Rosalind in a dark alley and leave her broken, battered and bruised. I was angry and distraught, I was so angry that I think that if I had learned that Rosalind was still in Tanzania, I would have borrowed Henry's rifle and gone and shot her, never mind the consequences.

"Thank you for your help," Maman said to Alison. "Henry, please thank Tega for us, is there anything we can do for him, anything at all?" Henry had another conversation with Tega and then looked at us in speculation, then had a few more words with Tega.

"There is one thing," he said. "Tega has a granddaughter who wants to go to university, but is having trouble raising the money, Tega wondered if you had a few shillings to help her."

Maman reached into her bag and took out a roll of pounds and gave them to Tega, then she asked Henry to translate. "Tega, please take this to the bank and change it into shillings, there will be about three thousand three hundred shillings there that will help you with your granddaughter. You have been most kind and we are very grateful for your help." Henry dutifully translated and assured Tega that Maman meant what she said, and that the money was a gift. Tega looked at the money, then thanked us again and again and left the room in tears.

We left and Henry drove us back to the camp. I found a chair and got some coffee, then opened and sorted Ian's letters by date then started to read them. At first, they were full of his doings at the dig, his life and what was happening, but as the weeks went on his letters took on a different tone, he was confused as to why I had not written, he was asking me what was wrong, had I met someone else, what was going on. I recognised the change in tone, my letters to him had had the same change in tone over time as I was confused as to why I had had no letters from him. I cried and cried, how could someone so deliberately and callously destroy other peoples' lives. I heard Julia comment to Maman that Ian was obviously much more than just a friend. Maman gave her a little more of the story and how much she liked Ian and how she had questioned her judgement when letters from him had stopped. So, now I knew. I knew what had gone wrong, we had been deliberately sabotaged and there was no way to exact vengeance on the perpetrator and, even more importantly, no clues as to where Ian might be. It was devastating. I thought that it was as well that we had done the safari part of our trip first and left Arusha to the last. If we had done Arusha first, I would have seen nothing of the spectacular sights we had seen over the past week, I would have only seen the haze of confusion and anger. Now the only thing I had to steel myself for was the wedding. That was going to be difficult. I was happy for James and Charlize, but could not help but speculate as to what might have been if Ian and I had been together. I dried my tears and just felt angry, angry with Rosalind for sabotaging our relationship and angry with myself for not coming out to Tanzania as soon as Ian's letters stopped. I joined the rest of the party who were gathering for lunch.

"Well, Bébé?" Maman asked.

"At least now I know what happened," I said. "Now I have to find him and see if this can be fixed."

"And Rosalind?" Maman asked.

"If I ever meet her, I might just have the beat the living daylights out of her," I said, quite bitterly.

"You know, it's as well you came when Rosalind had gone, if she had been here when you came, then she would have made sure that she burned the box of letters and you would never have known," Julia commented.

"Julia's right," Maman agreed. "As soon as you told her who you were, guilty conscience would have made her bury, or burn, all the evidence."

"I don't understand why she put them in a box, why not just burn them as they arrived?" I wondered.

"I doubt we'll ever understand that," Maman said.

"I think I'm going to drink to Ian, who clearly wasn't the bastard we thought he had become," Portia said. "We'll find him, Fi, we'll find him, bet on it."

"I wonder why one of your letters to Ian had been opened?" Maman mused.

"My guess is that she wanted to find out if this was a romantic letter or an anthropology letter," Portia said. "Once she read it, then she knew and the rest of the letters that came went straight into the bin. Let's face it, Doctor Barclay could have been an associate, or an advisor."

"Well, here's to Ian," I said, holding up a glass of wine. "Here's to finding him now, wherever he may be."

"Ian," Maman echoed. "I wonder what the bitch made of your telegram in Tahitian? At least we know Ian would understand."

In the afternoon, I put aside my letters and was more sociable and we spent the time talking about our trip through Serengeti and the Ngorongoro Crater and the sheer numbers of animals that there were. Henry commented that the old contemporary accounts of travels in South Africa and other places had described not being able to move for two or three days because of the vast herds of animals passing. That must have been truly awe inspiring, all that was left of those huge herd movements was the annual wildebeest migration in the Serengeti and Maasai Mara reserves, a truly awesome sight, but also a bloody, brutal and smelly one as dead bodies piled up at river crossings. By the time sundowner time came. I was more composed and able to watch the sunset without bursting into tears as the memories of Ian came flooding back as the disappeared below the horizon. I had a mission now and was filled with a resolve to leave no stone unturned until I found him again.

The next day we drove back to Nairobi and Henry dropped us off at the Norfolk Hotel and promised to bring our other suitcases by later. Maman invited he and Julia to dinner, an invitation which they accepted with alacrity. They duly came with the rest of our bags and we enjoyed dinner together. They were full of stories about prior safaris and the antics of guests. They both told me that they hoped I would be able to find Ian and rekindle our romance and said that if we did and we wanted a romantic trip to Kenya, then they would be more than happy to organise it for us. I liked that idea, but first I had to find him. Henry took us to the airport the next day to catch the British Airways flight to Johannesburg. The flight took us over Tanzania, then the top of Lake Malawi, then I suppose roughly along the border between Malawi and Zambia, then Mozambique and across the Zambezi and over Rhodesia. When we crossed the Zambezi, I tried to see as much as I could outside through the window. I had picked a seat on the right-hand side of the plane, so most of Rhodesia was visible, I even saw Salisbury as we flew over. Rhodesia struck me as dry, I could see where the farming areas were by the green of the irrigated crops, but the greater part of the country was brown and looked dry and dusty. Not long after Salisbury we started to descend and eventually landed in Johannesburg.

The train only ran south two days a week in the winter, so we had to stay overnight in Johannesburg. We picked a hotel near the railway station and bided our time until the following day when we went to the station to catch the train. Maman had spared no expense and she and Portia had taken the one suite on the train. It took up half of one carriage and had a sitting room, bedroom and its own bathroom, with an actual bath, very elegant. She had got me a luxury compartment adjacent to the suite, and it came also with its own bathroom, complete with bath. That was luxury, to be able to languish in a bath, not have to spin around under a bucket shower. The train was quite new, it had only gone into service in 1972, replacing much older carriages. I must say that it was a very nice way to travel, if the budget would stretch that far. After we made ourselves comfortable, we all repaired to the lounge car for a drink before dinner. They had a wide selection of wines, several of which we knew were from the Cillie vineyards, so we stayed with them, supporting the family to be. Dinner, when it was served, was excellent, so many courses, that I decided to skip a few, or I would have surely ballooned up. After dinner, we retired and my bed had been made up. I had never slept on a train before, this was a new experience for me and the noise of the wheels on the rails was actually very soothing and I soon dropped off to sleep.

The morning was announced by a steward bringing me coffee. I got mine and knocked at the door of Maman's suite. Portia opened the door a crack and when she saw it was me, invited me in. Maman was still in bed, but got up and put on a gown when I went in. It was obvious that she and Portia had shared the one bed, as the other was quite undisturbed and Maman had been naked before donning the gown. A pity really that the suite did not boast a double bed. Portia rumpled the second bed, so as not to give the staff too much to gossip about. We drank our coffee and opened the blinds on the windows and looked out on the world flying by.

"So, only a boat ride left and then we will have done the trains and boats and planes," I commented.

"I hadn't thought of that," Maman said. "Glad you came?"

"Yes," I said. "I know what happened now, and am more confident that when I find Ian that we can rekindle things."

"You're confident you'll find him?" Portia asked.

"If I can't use this supposed great intellect of mine to work out where to look and who to get to help me, then I should just hang up my consulting sign and retire," I said.

"But what if he has met someone else or is married?" Portia asked.

"Then, I've no idea what I'd do," I admitted. "I haven't thought about that, I think because I've been afraid to. If he is married, then I'll just give him my letters and tell him I'm sorry it ended the way it did and try and get on with my life."

"Well, we'll be there to help you, no matter what," Portia said.

"Thank you, *chérie*," I said. "When do we get to Wellington?"

"About a quarter to eleven," Maman said. "Hopefully, James will be there to meet us."

"How far is from Wellington to Franschhoek?" I asked.

"About fifty kilometres, so forty-five minutes or so," Maman replied. "Now, I suppose I should get dressed and go for breakfast."

"I'll see you in the dining room," I said, and left them to themselves. I had at one time wondered whether Portia would be jealous of my closeness to Maman, but she was happy that we were close and, in truth I had got almost as close to her. She had been admitted to the bathing and chatting circle and we three got on famously. I was just delighted that she and Maman still obviously loved each other and I loved them both.

I was mulling over what to eat when Maman and Portia joined me. A steward appeared at the table and we ordered coffee while we considered the menu. It was interesting, printed in English and Afrikaans. I looked at many of the words, and wondered how much progress James was making learning to speak the language. We ate breakfast and then returned to the suite to enjoy the rest of the trip. South Africa was quite different to Kenya or Tanzania and I thought that at some time I would make another trip there and spend some time just exploring. We started to descend through mountains and there were times we could see the end of our own train as the line curved around. Eventually things flattened out and straightened out and we came to Wellington. James was there to greet us, along with George, James's best man, his longtime friend from school and college.

"Hey, Mum" he said. "Portia, Fi, how was the trip?"

"Delightful and instructive," Maman replied.

"Instructive, how?" he asked.

"Some American bitch by the name of Rosalind intercepted all my letters to Ian and his to me," I said. *"La connasse!"*

"Wow, Fi, haven't heard you use words like that since we were kids and Mum threatened to wash your mouth out with soap," he said. "So, he wrote to you and you wrote to him but neither of you got the letters?"

"That's about the size of it," I confirmed. "If I ever meet that bitch, I might have to just beat the living daylights out of her. Anyway, that's for another day, how are you George?"

"I'm well Fiona," he said. "Sorry to hear about your problems. I'm well, haven't married yet, still looking, I took time off from the mine to come down here."

"Dad arrived with Felicity a few days ago," James told us. "They're going on to Kruger for a safari after the wedding. They're staying with one of Charlize's aunts, and you'll be in the guest house, with me, got to preserve the appearance of propriety, at least 'til we married. Shall we go?"

"Of course," Maman said. James waved over a porter who loaded all our suitcases on a trolley and followed us out to the car. James was driving a Land Rover that belonged to the winery, it was just like the one Maman used to have in Henley, but this one was a light cream colour, with the winery name painted on the doors. He supervised the loading of the luggage into the back and onto the roof rack and then we got in. He drove us out of Wellington and into the hills beyond until we came to Franschhoek, a delightful small town with Cape Dutch houses, all painted white and with thatched roofs. He turned off on a side road and took us to the family estate. It was quite a place, a main house, a smaller guest house and several buildings that were all part of the wine making process, and all around there were vineyards, with neat orderly rows of grape vines.

"I'll let you get settled," James said. "Then, there's a family *braai* planned?"

"What's a *braai?*" Maman asked.

"Afrikaans for a barbecue," James explained. "Lots of meat and beer, not a vegetable in sight, but fun all the same, it will be a family affair, so you'll get to meet more of the relatives. Most of them speak some English, but if you get stuck grab me or Charlize to interpret, or one of her brothers, or even George."

"How is your Afrikaans, James?" I asked.

"Improving," he said. "Look, I'll leave you to get settled. I have to go and talk to Charlize's Dad about some new vats for France. George has his eye on one of the bridesmaids, so he's going to be busy."

"Piss off, James," George said, laughing. "I'll admit, she quite a looker."

We looked around the guest house and it was obvious which room James had taken, he was never the most tidy of people. Maman and Portia took the room that had the double bed and I took the last smaller room that looked out onto the mountains behind. It really was very nice, if a little chilly. I changed into jeans, a sweater and a jacket and put on the boots I had brought and was ready. Maman and Portia had also both changed, into very conservative looking skirts and tops, also with jackets. We walked over to the main house and found James with Mr Cillie, both busy with barbecue fires.

"Mrs Barclay, welcome," Mr Cillie said. "And, Mrs Harding, so nice to see you again, Fiona, we're so happy you came, how was your trip to Kenya and Tanzania?"

"Spectacular," Maman replied for all of us. "Thank you for putting us up, it must be a great burden on you to have all of us visit."

"No man, it's no problem," he said. "Go on into the house and see Anna, she's in there somewhere with Charlize." Maman and Portia went into the house and I stayed talking to James and Mr Cillie. It was not long before people started to arrive. Dad and Felicity came with the aunt, and I was on my best behaviour. When Maman and Portia came out with Charlize they were polite, but kept their distance. I think both Maman and Dad were really happy to see James happy and to be married, but that did not mend any bridges between them. I noted that Maman said only the briefest words to Felicity. It was as well that Dad and Felicity were going on to the Kruger Park after the wedding, I could not imagine all of us on the boat together, the close quarters for eleven to twelve days would be difficult. I watched James throughout the evening, he was quite comfortable with the Cillie family and chattered away in Afrikaans, translating for me once or twice when those I was talking to ran out of English. George also helped me out a couple of times, he was working on one of the diamond mines and had learned Afrikaans so that he could talk to others on the mine.

The next day, we were taken on a brief tour of the vineyards and the surrounding area by Frikkie, one of Charlize's brothers. He was a good tour guide and took us to a really nice restaurant for lunch and said really nice things about James. Frikkie also explained the form of service to us, the church was the Dutch Reformed Church and the service would be in Afrikaans, but he gave us a printed form of service that had both the Afrikaans and English words, so we would know what was happening. He drove as back into town and took us to the church and showed us around. It was a beautiful building, white walls outside, and inside wooden vaulted ceilings, that really were breathtaking. Frikkie showed where we would sit and basically ran through the service with us. I thought that was very thoughtful of him. When we were leaving, I caught a glimpse of Dad and Felicity being brought in by Hansie, the other brother. He had obviously been roped in to be a guide as well. I thought it very nice of Charlize to organise things, and how sensitive to keep Maman and Dad apart. That evening there was a dinner for Charlize and James and their respective parents, plus George, as the best man and Jenny, the chief bridesmaid. Portia and I roped Frikkie into taking us to a local restaurant and we learned from Frikkie that Hansie was taking Felicity somewhere else.

The line up in the church pew on the day of the wedding was Dad, Felicity, me, Portia and Maman, keeping the exes well apart with me in the middle. We were all thankful for the English version of the service as we knew then what was going on. It was fairly simple and over quite quickly, then there were the requisite photographs and finally the reception. Maman did shed a tear or two in the church, as did I, but for different reasons. Maman because she was happy to see James married and me for that a little, but also because Ian was not there to share the moment with me. Charlize really did look like a bride, I felt quite eclipsed by her, but then it was her day to shine. James actually looked good as well, and he breezed through the ceremony as though he had spoken Afrikaans all his life. The reception ran on late and I excused myself long before it was over. I was tired and just wanted a bath and bed. I heard Maman and Portia come in not long after I did. James and Charlize had been given a cottage for the night, so we saw nothing of them.

We spent one more day at Franschhoek, mainly sampling wines and getting to know Mr and Mrs Cillie, John and Anna, a little better. They were very nice and belied a lot of the stories I had heard about Afrikaners. They could not have been more welcoming and made us promise to go back and visit them in the future. They talked about grapes, soils, wine vintages and the problems that farmers encountered there and in France. Dad and Felicity had left already, on their way to the Kruger Park. James and Charlize did finally put in an appearance, and took some ribbing from her brothers, both of whom were married with families. Charlize, like me, took after her mother, but the two brothers clearly favoured their father, as did two of the grandsons. Of the other children, I would have said that they took after their mothers. We spent the afternoon packing for the boat trip. Frikkie and Hansie were both going to take us and all our luggage, five of us plus a mountain of suitcases. We, who had come down through Africa, had three each and James had two and Charlize had four. The plan was to load all the luggage into one vehicle, *bakkie* as Frikkie called it, and we as passengers would go in relative comfort in the Land Rover. I did hang on to my leather shoulder bag, apart from my passport and money, it had all Ian's and my letters, and I was not going to lose them again. John and Anna

Cillie were also coming to see us off, I think particularly to see Charlize off.

Dr Morrison

Our cavalcade left Franschhoek at seven-thirty the next morning to beat the rush hour traffic into Cape Town and get us to the docks in plenty of time. We were on the dock by nine and Maman made our presence known at the first class check in desk. Porters were swiftly assigned and our bags whisked up to our cabins. James and Charlize had been put in a de-luxe cabin, A23, 'Green Leaves' on the same deck as us, but at the other end of the luxury rooms. That was probably a good thing, they were noisy in bed, so someone else could listen to them, not me. My cabin, A3, 'Dragon Fly', was adjacent to the suite occupied by Maman and Portia, they had the one suite, 'Almond Blossom', of the boat which boasted two rooms, twin berths and a host of other amenities, including two baths, not just one, but two, luxury indeed. Maman and Portia made some noise in bed, but nowhere near as much as James and Charlize, so I did not mind having the room next to theirs. With bags stowed in our rooms we all repaired to the suite for a sendoff drink. John and Anna were going to stay in Cape Town that night, they had business to conduct, so were in no hurry to leave. John told us that on board the boat were 20,000 gallons of wine from their vineyards. He explained that in 1968 bulk wine tanks had been installed in the Windsor Castle, a total capacity of 81,000 gallons, and they would ship wine to England to be bottled locally. It saved on the cost of shipping glass across the Atlantic. But he was concerned that the steady decline in business on the mail boats, and the rise of cheaper air travel, meant that that capacity would go away in a few years. As it was, he was prophetic as the last mail boat sailed from Cape Town to Southampton in late 1977. But back to my story, when the first steamer blast sounded there was an announcement that all those not sailing should leave the boat, so we said good bye to the Cillie family and went out on deck, streamers in hand to say goodbye again, but this time with streamers that we would hold until they broke. At one on the dot, lines were cast off and the steamer blast sounded again as we were pulled away from the dock by the tugs. I had thrown my streamer to Hansie and we both held it until the boat moved far enough away that it broke. After that I just waved to all the family as we were pulled out into the open water of the harbour and started to sail away under or own steam.

Lunch was now served. We trooped down to the dining room and found our assigned table, number 72. It was a table for six, but the boat was not full and there were quite a few empty seats, including the sixth at our table. I looked around the room and decided that it was mostly an older clientele. I would have guessed that for the most part the passengers, at least in first class, were older, fifty plus, but there were a few younger passengers here and there. A steward took our lunch orders and scuttled off to get things and soon returned with bowls and plates. After lunch, we went our separate ways, agreeing to meet again at four for afternoon tea. I thought then that I would have to be careful, or I could gain weight easily on the trip, and resolved to get some kind of exercise while I was on the boat. I went back to my cabin and collected my shoulder bag and went upstairs to the first-class lounge and found a table looking out over the bow. I set out my picture of Ian and all his letters and read them through again, one by one, taking in all he said and trying to see him saying the words. I thought that I should not read them aloud, particularly while trying to imitate Ian, the other passengers might end up calling the ship's doctor, thinking that I had lost it.

I sat and marshalled my thoughts as to what I knew of Ian. He had grown up on a tobacco farm, but that was now sold. He had a degree in anthropology, and was almost to his doctorate, but I was not sure whether or not he would return to Oxford to finish it. So, Professor Ambrose would be on my list of people to call when I got back to England. I added to that list Chris at the Trout Inn and April and Paul from the Billy Goat. I knew that his sister had worked at Groote Schuur, but that she had left. Because she had worked there, that suggested that she had a permit to work in South Africa, so she could have returned to South Africa after her trip to Rhodesia and be working somewhere else, or she could have gone to England to work, perhaps a call to the British Medical Association would yield something. There was probably an equivalent in South Africa, so I thought that I would write to them and ask if she was listed as working in South Africa. I should have called them before we left. As far as I knew Ian had no permit to work in South Africa, but he did have a British passport, that meant that he could return to England and work, if not study. If he had returned to England after 1972, then he had to fly or go by boat. If he had gone by boat, then Union Castle would have a record. The purser would be the person to ask about that. Sadly, I had no contacts at British Airways or South African Airways, so no real hope there of learning anything from either of them. Ian spoke Portuguese, Shona, Ndebele and Swahili and had a good knowledge of the bush, so perhaps he was working as a guide somewhere, that would be hard to track down. He knew a lot about tobacco, so even though he personally did not like smoking or tobacco products, in a pinch he could get a job working in the industry as a buyer, or even a farmer.

I called over a steward I saw and asked for some coffee and asked when it might be convenient to see the chief purser. He said that he would check. The coffee was brought in short order, and so was the chief purser.

"Dr Barclay," he said. "How may I be of service?"

"Mr Dermot, you didn't have to come, I only wanted to know when it would be best to come to your office, won't you please join me?" I said. I suppose having one of the de-luxe cabins and being related to the occupants of the suite counted for some more personal treatment. "Coffee?"

"Thank you," he said. "Now, how can I help?"

"I'm not sure how much trouble this would be," I started. "But I'm trying to track down someone, he may have taken a boat north to Southampton, sometime between late 1972 and now. I know that's a lot of sailings, but wondered if the company keeps records that go that far back?"

"Is this him?" Mr Dermot asked, picking up the picture of Ian I had placed in front of me on the table.

"It is," I said. "His name is Ian Hartley. This is something of a gamble, because I don't know if he stayed in South Africa, or went to England, and if he went, I don't know if he went by air or by boat. I know that he did travel by boat many years ago in the mid-sixties when he first went to university, and he told me that he had really enjoyed the trip, so I'm gambling that if he did go, it would have been by boat again. If it's not too much trouble could you also check on a Dr Irene Hartley, I suspect that she may have travelled north in late 1971?"

"Let me see what I can do," he promised. "How is your cabin?"

246

"Super, thank you," I said. "This is my first trip to Africa, so it was plane out, boat back, and I'm glad I did this."

"Are you a medical doctor?" he asked.

"No, I'm a mathematician and economist," I told him. "I typically create mathematical models for markets, economies and the like."

"So, you're the one to talk to about the daily wager on distance travelled," he laughed.

"I confess that that does intrigue me," I said. "So, perhaps, I'll put in an entry or two. I could always cheat by borrowing a sextant and taking some star shots then calculating our position."

"You know how to do that?" he asked.

"I do, but I'd have to borrow the sextant and the star charts," I said. "So, perhaps I'll just stick to estimating and turn in an entry."

"I look forward to it," he said. "Thank you for sharing your coffee with me, let me see what I can do for you."

"Thank you, Mr Dermot," I said. When he had gone, I drank the rest of my coffee and pondered what else I could do.

I looked outside at the brave souls who had braved the weather and wondered when we would be far enough north for the temperatures to improve. I thought about it and calculated that at twenty-two and a half knots, it would take us about a day and half to be inside the tropics, then the temperatures would probably rise enough for me to venture out and bask in the sun. I packed up my letters and took them back to my cabin, then went down to the dining room for afternoon tea. Maman and Portia were there already, and had poured tea.

"Are James and Charlize coming down?" I asked.

"They said no," Maman replied. "We should leave them to their honeymoon. And, what did you do this afternoon?"

"I asked the chief purser to check back records for me, to see if there is any record of Ian sailing north since 1972, I also asked him if they could find out if Irene, his sister, sailed north in 1971 or later," I said.

"Good idea," Maman thought. "If they did, then you'll know they're probably in England. What if they flew?"

"Then I don't think I'll have much chance of getting anything from BA or SAA," I replied. "But I have to start somewhere."

"What about his sister, isn't she a doctor, she should be easier to track down?" Maman asked.

"I thought I'd call the BMA when we get back to see if she's at any of the hospitals in England," I replied. "I'll also write to the South African equivalent of the BMA to see if she's practising there. And what did you two do this afternoon?"

"We explored the ship a little," Portia said. "We looked in on the lounge and saw you, then we looked at the smoking room, horrible place, then the card room, the library, the cinema and a few other places. We saw the people out in the sun decks, but I don't think I'll be joining them until the weather warms up a little."

"I have to say that I like this form of travel," Maman commented. "It's more relaxed than by air, you get the chance to walk around, bathe, sleep and do nothing for a few days. I know it takes longer, but if you're not in a hurry, this is the way to go."

After tea I found a route to walk around the decks and up and down ladderways and get some exercise, and did the appropriate number of laps to amount to a mile. I felt better for it and returned to my cabin refreshed. I spent the afternoon in the library browsing among the books there until it was time for dinner. Apparently, it was tradition that on the first night out one did not dress for dinner, so no need for fancy dresses. James and Charlize had made it out of their cabin, looking very smug and pleased with themselves. Charlize wanted more practice with her French, so we all obliged and spoke French at the table, except when the stewards came for drink and dinner orders. James wanted to know more about our trip to Kenya and Tanzania, so between the three of us we gave him an account. Charlize wanted to know more about what we had learned in Arusha, so I gave her chapter and verse, but refrained from describing Rosalind in too harsh terms, in case someone else in the dining room spoke French and was offended by my language. I did hear a couple of old codgers comment about those damned French people and why did they not learn to speak English. The chief purser stopped by our table to ask if all was well, and we were able to assure him that indeed all was well and that we were being well taken care of. He added as an aside to me that he had sent a radio message to the company asking after Ian and his sister. I thanked him for that. It was most considerate, he was under no obligation to check on past passenger lists.

The next day there was the obligatory lifeboat drill and we all mustered at out stations, life jackets in hand, then life settled into a routine, early morning coffee, followed by my kata routine on the sun deck, using it to calm myself and lose the anger that I often felt when I thought of Rosalind. Following my kata, I ate breakfast, then did some activity, followed by lunch, quiet time, afternoon tea, more quiet time, then dinner, for which I did dress, going through my evening dresses in rotation. I had taken six with me, so they would all get worn twice. Maman, Portia and Charlize all had plenty to wear, so I think they only rotated three dresses for a second wearing. Even James dressed up, he had a white dinner jacket that he wore, very tropical looking. For the men, it was easy, one jacket and appropriate trousers, whereas we women were loath to wear the same dress four or five times, so generally overpacked by the standards of today. When we made it to the tropics, I actually ventured out onto the sun deck once or twice to bask in the sun. I had taken a bikini with me, and actually got to use it. It was not quite as skimpy as the one Charlize had, but for me, skimpy enough. The first-class sun deck was actually quite small, I estimated that it was about 1,540 square feet, plus another few hundred square feet on each side, which with 191 first class passengers worked out to about 10 square feet per passenger, if they were all there at the same time. The tourist class deck area was more complex, there were promenade and dance areas on the Promenade Deck and A Deck, there were also games areas and a lido, so trying to calculate how much space there was for actually just lying out in the sun was difficult, with the time and inclination I could have done it, but I confess my interest waned quickly. When I went to the sun deck, I would stay long enough to get some sun, then retire to my cabin or the lounge. Using the lounge meant putting on extra clothes, so I typically went to my cabin anyway, then made the decision to just idle there or go for a walk about the ship and end up in the lounge.

We were probably a day short of crossing the line when the chief purser tracked me down in the lounge.

"Dr Barclay," he said. "How are you today?"

"Very well, thank you, Mr Dermot, and you?" I asked.

"Capital," he said. "I have news for you. According to our records a Dr Irene Hartley took the Windsor north, sailing on the 30th of November in 1971, and an Ian Hartley took the Pendennis Castle north, sailing from Cape Town on the 5th of December in 1972. There are no records of either of them returning south on one of our ships."

"Thank you, Mr Dermot," I said. "I really appreciate the effort you went to. Thank you."

"Is he an old boyfriend?" Mr Dermot asked.

"He was," I admitted. "We lost touch with one another, but I recently had news of him and want to get in touch again. But I had no real idea of where to start. This has given me something to go on. I think his sister as a doctor may be easier to find, if she's registered with the BMA. What does it cost to send a radiogram?"

"Give me the message and I'll let you know," he said. I quickly wrote a short message to Andrea and included the cable address that they used. He looked it over and seemed happy with the form.

"I'll get the radio room to send this," he said. "I'm happy that we could be of some help in your search. Enjoy the rest of your day." After he had gone, I sat back and took stock of things. I now knew that Irene had gone to England late in 1971 and that Ian had gone to England and that he had arrived on the 18th of December of 1972. As far as I knew, he had made no effort to contact me in any way, but by then I had moved to London, Maman had sold her house and moved to France, so contact would have not been that simple. I also had to presume that he felt that I had abandoned him, so why would he try and contact me. Here I was nearly four years later, trying to find out how to mend things, if I could, but there were risks. As Portia had already pointed out to me, he could, of course, have found someone else, he could even be married, a prospect that just horrified me, as then I saw no hope of ever recovering our relationship. Was I setting myself up for disappointment and more heartache, was this a fool's errand that would end badly, was it even worth it. I think I had already answered that last question, if I did not think it was worth it, I would not even have begun, or taken the trip to Arusha.

The daily routine was broken when we did cross the equator and there was a big crossing the line ceremony by the tourist class pool. The crew had approached several of the passengers to be participants and I had been terrified that they might ask me. I had no idea what kind of antics were planned, but had no real desire to be on public display, perhaps a little childish on my part, or perhaps because of my basic introverted personality. I admired those who did take part and allowed themselves to be smeared with shaving soap and put through all kinds of things designed to amuse the crowd.

As we steamed our way north, I was approached three times by male passengers who wanted to buy me a drink, but I'm afraid I rebuffed them all, not wanting their company or the complication in my mind of another person. I am glad to say that they all took it in good part and that I did not have to reinforce my polite refusals with anything more drastic. If I wanted male company, I had James to talk to, when he was not canoodling with Charlize. I tried to stay out of their way and not intrude, giving them space to enjoy their honeymoon. I similarly avoided being overly intrusive of the time of Maman and Portia, but they were kind and entertained me often in their suite. I had read and re-read Ian's letters so many times that I could quote them word for word. I had taken our guide books from our trip and found places that Ian mentioned. I also found a couple of books in the ship's library that had wonderful pictures of some the places Ian mentioned, so could see in my mind what he was talking about. I was struck but the way his change in tone of his letters mirrored mine. As time went on and there were no replies, each of us put more desperation into our words, it made me cry each time I thought of it. I had no idea what the other passengers might have thought, a young woman sitting in the lounge reading and reading again the same letters and crying. I was surprised that no one ever came up to me and asked me if I was all right, but I suppose they saw Maman and Portia sit with me at times, and when they did, my tears went and I smiled.

When we put into the port at Las Palmas, we were on the downhill leg of the journey, with only another 1,700 miles to go, about three days, and 4,287 miles already gone. I learned that the reason for the Las Palmas stop was for fuel, it was cheaper than in either Southampton or Cape Town, so the boats made stops southbound and northbound to replenish their bunkers. We arrived into Las Palmas at sunset, so shore excursions were somewhat limited and none of us had any real desire to just go to a bar and drink, we could do that on the boat. I gathered from the steward that southbound trips included a longer stop in Las Palmas in the daytime, so longer excursions ashore were possible. We departed Las Palmas after dark and I noted that the Southern Cross was no longer visible, we had lost it at about 25°, a little way north of the Tropic of Cancer. We were now on the last leg of the journey and reality was beginning to hit home. I had set out on this adventure full of hope and determination, probably in a romantic mode, thinking that I would find Ian and he would sweep me off my feet and things would return to the way they were before he went away. But now as we were nearing Southampton, I was apprehensive about continuing my search for Ian, as I had thought a few times on the voyage, was I setting myself up for heartache and pain. Part of me still wanted to do it, I needed to find out if there was a chance of rekindling the romance, or was it dead forever. I did not have a real plan as to how I was going to go about finding him, but thought that the best place to start would be with his sister. If she was still working as a doctor, and if she was in England, then the BMA would have a record and might be disposed to tell me where to find her.

The last night before docking was the farewell dinner, and as with the first night out, tradition had it that it was not necessary to dress up, but Maman had other ideas and we were informed that a nice turnout would be appreciated. I think it was for her rather than for the steamship line. When we arrived back into Southampton, the likelihood of another holiday where we would all be there was low, so she wanted to make the most of the occasion. I picked my red cheongsam as my dress of choice with red heels and a red clutch bag. I checked myself in the mirror and was pleased with what I saw. The dress had lost none of its appeal, and I had stayed almost the exact same weight as I had been when I had bought it, so it still fitted well. The heels and the line of the dress did make me look a lot taller than I actually am.

I made my way to the dining room and found James and Charlize there, James looking very dapper in a blue blazer with khaki coloured trousers, and Charlize in a dark purple trouser suit that really looked good on her, such a pity that it clashed a little with the purple of the chairs at our table, but it was either the red of some chairs or purple of others, quite who had picked the colours and why was a mystery to me. Maman and

Portia arrived soon afterwards and they had gone to town, Maman had on a Dior evening dress in purple and silver and Portia wore a black and white halter culotte by Galitzine. They had to be the two best dressed in the dining room. I had not seen either dress before, so presumed that they were acquired for the trip.

"A toast?" Maman suggested when we were all seated. "Here's to us, to James and Charlize and their vineyard, to Fiona, may she find happiness, and to Portia, may our life together stay as wonderful as it is now."

"To us," we echoed. It was moments like that that were the most difficult for me. James and Charlize were happy and had a career in wine making to look forward to. Maman and Portia had each other and they were deliriously happy together, and there was me. I had a successful career, but I would have traded that in a minute for Ian. Perhaps I would be lucky, perhaps not.

"Have you ever thought about setting up shop in France?" James asked me.

"Not really," I said. "It's hard enough to be taken seriously in London, I can't imagine the French being any more enlightened."

"Maybe," he said. "But we could always use a good person at the vineyard."

"What could I do for you?" I asked. "I'm not an agronomist, or an expert in wine making."

"True," he agreed. "But you do have this way of reducing problems to a set of conditions that can be solved for, be it sunlight, water, pruning, whatever."

"Let me see what happens in the next few months," I said. "I can always find work in London, I'm well enough known now."

"I would be really happy if you spent a little more time with us," Charlize added. "And we're not that far from the Riviera."

"I'll try," I promised. Charlize's invitation was welcome; before we had gone to Africa, I had done little else but work, taking few holidays, even working on Saturdays and Sundays. There was really no need to do that, so taking time off to visit them in the vineyard and to visit Maman and Portia in the South was enticing.

We sailed up the Solent in the morning of our last day and docked in Southampton just before noon. Then there was the rigmarole of immigration and customs and we were finally back. For me it would be just a train ride into London, but for the others it was a plane ride to Paris, then they would go their separate ways. The easiest way for them to get to the airport was to actually go into London and then back out again, so we travelled together on the boat train to Waterloo. Once in London, I took a taxi home and the others to a taxi to the British Airways terminus in London to get transport to catch their flight to Paris. They were going to stay the night in Paris and then go on from there. When I arrived home, I pushed the front door open, over the mountain of letters, flyers and other stuff that had been shoved through the letter box. The flat was hot, it had been a warm day, so I threw open all the windows and let the flat breathe a little, and then picked up all the letters and put them on the kitchen counter to be sorted out later. My adventure was over, time to return to reality and everyday life. The boat trip had been a kind of limbo, the holiday over, but not yet over, as we steamed north. It had been a time of reflection and to some extent avoidance, I had avoided coming to grips with my real goal, that of finding Ian, and I had avoided the possible reality that Ian was married. If I had flown back, I would have been back a week already and may, or may not, have made progress in finding either Ian or Irene. I may have already been disappointed or even heartbroken. But now that I was really back, it was time to decide, to continue or not. I got a glass of wine, then sat and sifted through the letters and mulled over my problem. It was a note from Andrea asking me to call her as soon as I got back that decided me. Andrea might have something, so I would pursue it, to the end, even if it was a bitter end.

I had no groceries in the house, so went out to dinner. I frequented a small bistro that was close and got good food and service there. They greeted me like the proverbial prodigal son and wanted to know where I had been, so I gave them the short version, I had been to Africa on safari and had just returned. The next day I stopped at the service that took telephone messages for me and where my business mail went. There was a mountain of telephone messages and quite a number of letters, so I took them all to my office and sorted them. There was a message from Andrea and another note. She had made sure to try all avenues to ensure that I did contact her as soon as I returned. I called her and was put on hold for about a minute before she came on the phone.

"Good morning Andrea," I said. "It's Fiona, I got your message and your notes, what's up?"

"Oh, Fiona, so nice to hear from you, are you busy at lunch time?" she asked.

"No," I said. "I've not been back long enough to set up anything, so where do you want to meet?"

"What about the Provençal on the Victoria Embankment at twelve thirty?" she suggested. "Oh, and Mr Hill wanted me to set up an appointment with you to talk about a project."

"Well, you're the first, so pick a date and time," I suggested.

"What about Thursday at ten?" she asked.

"Fine," I confirmed.

"Good, then I'll see for lunch soon," she said.

"I'll see you then," I promised. I wondered what that implied, did she have information for me about Irene, or even possibly Ian. I would find out later. I went through the telephone messages again and sorted them into some sort of priority and started returning calls. I had set up eight appointments by the time I needed leave for lunch, which boded well for future earnings. The Provençal was only a short walk away and I arrived there at the same time as Andrea.

"Fiona," she said. "Nice to see you back and in one piece, how was your trip?"

"Kenya and Tanzania were amazing," I said. "I learned something about why I got no letters from Ian, and my brother's wedding was very nice. How are you?"

"I'm fine," she said. "I'm going on my holidays soon, I'm off to New Zealand for two weeks to go skiing."

"That's a long flight," I commented.

"Long," she agreed. "Let's get a table, shall we?"

After we were seated and had placed an order for food, Andrea told me why she had wanted to see me.

"I have done some digging on Ian," she said. "I tried Directory Enquiries and learned that there are quite a few Ian Hartleys, the operator I talked to went down the pages and she guessed at least 8,000, so unless you want to spend a month on the phone, that's not going to work. Then I tried Irene Hartley and there were 2,500 or so, so, again not much luck there. I did what you asked and the BMA had no current listing for an Irene Hartley."

"You've been busy," I said. "But you didn't have to do all that, Andrea."

"No trouble at all," she assured me. "So, the BMA was no good, so I wondered if she'd got married. So, I called the Times and went through old marriage announcements for Irene Hartley and found ten since 1972. I then called the BMA back and found forty-four names that matched my list of married names, twelve Smiths, three Jones's, and so on up to ten. I started calling those on the list and got lucky at Charing Cross Hospital, there the lady I talked to asked me if I meant Dr Morrison who had been Evans or Dr Morrison who had been Hartley. I told her Hartley and she told me that the Doctor was on holiday at that moment but due back next week, she also pointed out that Dr Morrison was a surgeon and should be addressed as Mrs Morrison. So, then I called the BMA again and said that I was considering some surgery and that Mrs Morrison of Charing Cross had been recommended to me and could they give me her medical training and experience history. They told me that she had been at Groote Schuur, so it had to be her."

"So, do you think I should talk to her?" I asked.

"Of course, you should," Andrea said. "What do have to lose? If she's Ian's sister, she might throw tea in your face for apparently dumping her brother, but she might listen to the story, what did happen?"

"There was a woman in Arusha," I said. "Apparently, she had a thing for Ian and didn't like him getting letters from me, or sending letters to me, so she intercepted them and dumped them in a box. We were lucky the African she told to burn the box when she left, looked inside and kept the letters. So, I have them all now."

"The bitch," Andrea said. "Where is she now?"

"In the States, Ohio, I think," I said.

"A pity you didn't get to meet her and knock her block off," Andrea said.

"I was angry enough that I'm not sure what I would have done, if she'd still been there," I admitted. "Probably just as well she'd gone back to the States. We should eat, before this goes cold." We ate, and talked, Andrea trying to convince me that I should talk to Dr Morrison, and me, finding reasons why it might not be a good idea. That was something I was going to have to sort out myself, to steel myself to face the possible scorn and dislike of Ian's sister, unless of course, she did not like her brother. But I had no way to know or gauge that. Ian had told me a little about her, but not that much and I had never met her, or even seen her picture. When we had done with lunch and split the bill equally, I went back to my office to continue returning calls. I had to give up just after five because most of the people I was calling had gone home.

On Thursday I went to the office of Adam Hill, he told me that he was now managing all the non-mining interests of the company and he had a project that was intriguing, but I was not sure could actually be done. He wanted a model of their agricultural enterprise that would predict revenues based on weather predictions and subsequent crop yields. I promised that I would give it a try and he signed me up for a year, at a higher rate than I would normally charge because he wanted to limit who else I could work for in that time. He did not want me to take any other projects that related to agriculture. I did not expect any others, but it was always a possibility, I did get him to agree to an exception, the Cillie winery was already a client and did not compete with any of the agricultural businesses that Adam managed. The project sounded really challenging, I would have to start at the Met Office to see what models they used for forecasting. I would also talk to Charlize and others about soils and see what I could learn.

Friday I was done with all my calls and had only one appointment, so after that was done, I was free for the day. So, I hired a car and drove out to Oxford. I called at the college and talked to the people in the anthropology department, including Professor Ambrose, but they had not heard from Ian since he left in June of 1971 to go back to Rhodesia. Then I drove next to the Billy Goat, hoping that April and Paul were still there, they were.

"Fiona," April said, when I walked in. "I haven't seen you in ages, how are you?"

"I'm okay, April, thank you, and you?" I asked.

"I'm doing fine," she said. "Busy now, summer season, you know how it is."

"You haven't heard from Ian, have you?" I asked.

"Not since he left to go back to Tanzania,' she said. "Why what happened?"

"It's a long story," I said. "I'll come by one day and tell you all about it." My next stop was the Trout Inn, where I hoped I would find Chris. He was there, now the manager.

"Fiona," he said. "Where've you been, haven't see you since you were here with Ian?"

"I moved to London," I explained. "How are you?"

"I'm fine," he said. "Got married, to Heather, you know her, was the barmaid here forever."

"Congratulations," I said.

"Where's Ian?" Chris asked.

"I was hoping you could tell me," I said. "I've lost touch with him."

"Wow, didn't see that coming," Chris said. "I would have bet my life savings on you two, what happened?"

"Have you heard from him lately?" I asked.

"Not for a couple of years," Chris said. "I got a postcard from him from Rome, but since then, nothing. So, what happened?"

"In the words of my new sister in law, a *gemors*," I replied. "I wrote to him and he wrote to me while he was in Tanzania, but neither of us got the letters, they were intercepted by another woman and thrown into a box that she kept in Arusha."

"How did you find that out?" he asked.

"I went to Arusha and one of the African staff who was the cleaner in the office had been told to burn the box when she left, but he knew Ian and kept the letters, so I have them now, all of them, mine and his," I explained.

"What a *does*," Chris said. I knew from Charlize that that was really not a nice word, but guessed that no one in the bar understood.

"Do you have a room available?" I asked. "I don't fancy driving back to London tonight."

"I do," Chris said. "Nice room looking out over the river, a couple had booked it and then I got a call this afternoon to cancel, it seems he had been caught with her best friend, so the romance is off. Oh, sorry, I didn't mean to upset you."

"That's okay, Chris," I said. "I'll take the room for two nights if that's okay?"

"Fine," he said. "You want breakfast in the morning?"

"Yes, please," I said. "What's on the dinner menu tonight?"

"We've got lamb, chicken, beef and rabbit," Chris said. "What do you fancy?"

258

"I think I'll try the rabbit," I said.

"Okay, I'll get you a table, here's the key, room four, around the corner and up the stairs, need help with your bag?"

"No, thanks, Chris," I said. "I'll be down in a few minutes for dinner."

I ate my dinner on the terrace by the river and thought about the first date Ian and I had had. That had been such a magical day, and the memory of it just brought tears. Chris must have been watching, because he brought a box of Kleenex and a glass of brandy.

"Are you okay?" he asked.

"It'll pass," I said, through my sobs. "We had our first date here and it's hard."

"Well, if you need anything, just yell," he said. "I'm sorry, but I have to go, I have a crisis in the kitchen." He left and I gained control of myself and hated myself for being so emotional. I was supposed to be the cold logical one who could compartmentalise things and suppress nasty things like emotions. I went to bed early and fell asleep to the sound of the river, dreaming of Ian. I spent most of the next day where Ian and I had had our picnic, I got a packed lunch from Chris and a bottle of wine and just went to relive the moment. I enjoyed just watching the river and the birds and animals, it was actually very soothing, the sound of the water was almost hypnotic and very conducive to relaxing, and the birds did not intrude that much and the odd splash of an animal in the water was enough to bring me back to the present. I was also working on my approach to Irene, what I might say and how I might respond to her criticisms, sarcasm, denigrations, or whatever she threw at me. I stayed until late and then had dinner on the terrace, more at peace. The memories were still there and would come flooding back with the right triggers, like the river, but I saw them now as memories to be cherished and enjoyed, not suppressed and bemoaned. I drove back to London the next day and returned my hire car, glad I had made the trip and more prepared to face Irene.

On Monday I called the Charing Cross Hospital and asked to speak to Mrs Morrison, the surgeon.

"Good morning," a voice said. I recognised the accent, it was just like Ian's.

259

"Good morning Mrs Morrison, my name is Fiona Barclay and I wondered if you might have five minutes to talk to me?" I asked.

"Why should I talk to you?" she asked.

"Please, if you'll give me five minutes in your office, I would be happy, if after that you wish me to leave, I will," I promised.

"Very well, eleven o'clock sharp," she said, very snippily. This was not going to be easy. At eleven I presented myself at her office, shaking with nervousness. I was frightened that she would just look at me and show me the door. I was actually surprised that she agreed to see me at all, perhaps she just wanted to look me in the eye and tell me to my face what she thought of me. I screwed up my courage and started into my prepared speech.

"Thank you for seeing me," I said. "As I said on the phone, I'm Fiona Barclay and Ian and I once went out together."

"I know who you are," she said curtly. "What do you want?"

"Last month I went to Arusha," I started. "There I found these." I pulled out the packet of my letters to Ian. She picked up the bundle of my stamped and delivered and unopened letters and the telegrams that had been sent which had been opened. She leafed through the letters one by one, realisation beginning to dawn as she did so. The letters all had either French or British stamps and all had post marks dating from 1971.

"These haven't even been opened, except this one," she said, picking out the earliest one in the bundle. "Does that mean that Ian got your letters, but didn't even bother to open them? Does that mean he's been lying to me and that he's the one who walked away?"

"I don't think so, I don't think he ever saw them. There's more," I said, and placed on her desk all of Ian's letters to me. She then looked at Ian's letters, which she obviously recognised as being written by him, none of which had been stamped and therefore logically not posted. I could see on her face a look of horror as the full impact of what that meant hit. She then called out to her secretary, "Janice, what do I have this afternoon?"

"A gall bladder and an appendix," came the reply. "First one at two."

"I'll be back by then," she said. "And call Tom for me and tell him to join me at The Corner Café for lunch."

"Yes, Mrs Morrison," Janice replied. Then Irene looked at me and said. "I think we'd better go somewhere quiet and you'd better tell me all you know."

She led the way to the Corner Café, small café close to the hospital and got us a table in a corner and some coffee Then she sat and looked at me and said, "Why don't you start at the beginning."

"Well, as you probably know, Ian was having trouble with his thesis," I said. "We agreed that he should go back to Olduvai for more research. He left at the end of 1970. We agreed to write to each other. So, I wrote, at first two letters a week, then later one a week. I got two letters back from Ian, then there was the postal strike. So, I sent him a telegram with an address in Paris to send letters to. You can see he did that with these letters here, and I had mine sent over by courier and posted there, that is this pile."

"How did you manage that?" she asked.

"My mother's partner, Portia, worked in a big law firm and they had the courier, all I did was add my letters to the pile already going," I explained. "During the strike I got no letters from Ian and when it was over, I got one and no more. I wrote and wrote and sent a couple of telegrams, but still nothing in reply. By the time June came I was convinced that he had met someone else, then I heard from the college that Ian had just left the dig and gone to Rhodesia, then I subsequently learned the reason why, I'm so sorry about your parents."

"That was a bad day," Irene said. "But go on."

"Well, I was devastated, and debated about trying to contact him in Rhodesia, I have a client with contacts there. But I'm ashamed to say now, that I was angry with Ian and decided not to, and have heard nothing from him since. Earlier this year I decided that I needed to know what happened and thought that the best place to start was Arusha. So, I went to Arusha and spoke to a person there, who told me that the person who would have best known was a Rosalind, but she had just gone back to the States," I continued. I noted that Irene looked up sharply at the name, Rosalind.

"To continue," I said. "While we were talking, one of the Africans, Tega, who worked at the office as a cleaner and a maker of tea, said that he had something that we should see. Our safari guide took him to his house and he came back with a cardboard box with all the letters. He told us that this Rosalind met Ian when they travelled down from Nairobi in January of 1971. He told us that the gossip was that she wanted Ian and when she worked out that there was girl in England who was writing, she intercepted all the letters incoming and outgoing. When she left, she told Tega to burn the box and everything in it. Tega looked at the letters and recognised them as to and from Ian, who he knew, so didn't burn them but kept them. He then didn't know what to do with them as he had no idea where to send them."

"May I?" Irene asked, pointing to the pile of letters.

"Of course," I said. "They're a little personal, but please do." She picked the last letter Ian had written to me and my last one.

"May I open this one?" she asked, holding up my last letter to Ian.

"If Ian won't mind," I said. She opened it and laid it beside his last one and read them both, then cried, and because she cried, I could no longer hold back the tears that had been there all along.

"Oh, Fiona," she said. "I'm so sorry, I'm sorry for all the names I called you, I'm sorry for hating you, I'm sorry I mistrusted you, I'm sorry I was so rude to you today, I'm so sorry for both of you, what you lost and why, how you must both hate one another."

"You weren't to know," I said, through my tears. "I thought I hated Ian for a while, because I couldn't understand what had gone wrong, but I don't hate him, I'm just lost without him. The one I do hate is Rosalind, how could anyone do such a thing?"

"I've no idea," she said. "It's hard for me to understand anyone doing something so underhanded and cruel, I'm sure that in her own mind, she was doing what she wanted, and the hell with the impact it had on you. I'm sure you miss him, Ian was devastated, and confused, he couldn't understand why you'd stopped writing."

"I was devastated and confused as well, and I couldn't think what I'd done to push Ian away," I said. "I cried and cried for quite a while, then I had to get on with my life. I thought I was over it, but as I said, earlier this year I felt compelled to find out what happened."

"What on earth compelled you to go looking now?" she asked.

"You'll probably laugh, but it was a song," I explained. *"Un jour tu reviendras."*

"Ian told me that you were part French, let's see if I remember, one day you will come back?" she asked.

"That's right," I said. "I listened to it and just sat on the floor and bawled, all the memories of the times we spent together all came flooding back, it was painful. Then I decided that I had to know and that the best place to start was Arusha."

"You said that Rosalind had gone back to the States when you went to Arusha?" Irene asked.

"That's what we were told," I confirmed. "I wanted to kill her, I was so angry."

"I'm not surprised," Irene said. "So, what do you want to know?"

"I'm almost afraid to ask," I said. "Perhaps because I'm afraid of what the answer will be. But is Ian seeing anyone now, is he married how is he doing, where is he, what happened in Rhodesia, life this past few years has been empty without him?"

Irene looked past me for a short while, as if recalling things and formulating a reply, then she started on her narrative.

"I got the message that Mum and Dad had been killed, so quit my job at Groote Schuur and went north to see about the funeral and the farm," she told me. "Ian was already there, I think he must have gone to Nairobi and caught a flight from there to Jo'burg, then gone to Salisbury, but that's by the by. He looked as if the world had just collapsed around him. After the funeral he told me all about you, he showed me your picture, then he told me about getting a few letters, then two telegrams, one with an address in Paris, which I now know was to get around the Brit postal strike, the other he showed me, but I didn't know what it said and he wouldn't say."

"It said, *ua here vau ia oe,* it's Tahitian and means I love you," I explained.

"Well, then Ian said he got no more letters, he kept asking at the office if there were any and Rosalind assured him that there weren't and was a great support and comfort to him," Irene continued.

"I'll bet she was," I said, quite bitterly.

"He had, like you, thought that the relationship was over, why, he just couldn't work out, so was quite bitter," she added. "Neither of us wanted the farm, so we sold it for what we could get, I decided to come to England to look for a job and Ian joined the army as a way of striking back for the death of our folks and to work out some of his aggression because you had apparently dumped him. Because he spoke excellent Shona and Ndebele, the army used him in an experiment with pseudo terrorist groups, like the Brits had done in Malaya and the Kenyans had done during the Mau Mau crisis. But he told me that he came to realise that it was a losing battle. Contact for contact the army would win, but the army command wasn't up to the job and there just weren't enough soldiers in the field and the politicians in Salisbury were out of touch, So, he walked away from it all and came to England."

"I found out that you'd sailed here in late 1971 and that Ian had sailed here in 1972," I said. "But I didn't know if he'd gone back again or not."

"How did you find me?" Irene asked.

"A friend of mine here checked with Directory Enquiries and found out that there are some 2,500 Irene Hartleys, she also checked with the BMA and that there was none. So, she had the brain wave of checking for marriages, and scoured the Times announcements between 1972 and now and came up with ten possibles. Then she called the BMA back and got forty-four potential matches, and just started calling, going down through the married names, Smith, Jones, and so on, getting possible contacts by subtly getting an approximate age," I explained. "When she called Charing Cross, she was asked was that Morrison who was Evans or Morrison who was Hartley."

We were interrupted when a man came up to the table. Irene looked up and greeted him. "Tom, this is Fiona Barclay, Fiona, my husband Tom."

"Fiona Barclay aren't you the b…" he started to say, but he was interrupted by Irene who held up her hand and said. "It seems that there was another in this who connived and engineered the breakup by withholding all the mail." She pointed to the piles of letters on the table. Tom picked them up and leafed through them and the telegrams, which he quickly scanned.

"You mean that someone kept all the letters to Ian so that he never saw them?" he asked. "All these letters were delivered to the office, but never passed on, not even opened, except these two?"

"That's about the size of it, oh, I opened the last one," Irene confirmed. "And, if you'll look, you'll see that Ian's letters were never posted."

"Who?" he asked.

"Rosalind," Irene said.

"But Ian said that she was really kind and understanding," Tom said.

"I'll bet she was," Irene said. "Apparently the gossip among the people at the dig was that she had the hots for Ian, so she used her position as the office admin to control things. She has to be the worst bitch I've ever heard of."

"God, you must have hated Ian," Tom said to me.

"I thought I did for a while," I admitted. "But I was really confused, I thought we had had something very special and I couldn't imagine what had gone wrong, I thought that I'd done something to drive him away, but couldn't think what. My greatest fear was that I had lost him forever, he had found someone else."

"That's exactly what Ian said, he was devastated by the idea that you had someone else," Tom added. "So, now what?"

"We were coming to that," Irene said.

Encore Ian

"To answer the question that probably uppermost in your mind," Irene said. "Ian is not married. He's had a couple of on again, off again, relationships, but nothing that serious. He's still in England, he got a job as a civil servant with the Foreign and Commonwealth Office, and has moved into the Diplomatic Service."

"Do they have him working on African things, or did they do the typical government thing and assign him to South America or Russia?" I asked.

"They, for once, actually did the right thing and he is in the Africa office, particularly the Central and Southern African office," Irene explained.

"Does he live in London?" I asked.

"He does, he has a flat in Notting Hill," Irene said. "It's not the nicest place I've seen, but it's adequate. Are you seeing anyone else?"

"I've had exactly three dates since I said goodbye to Ian," I said. "In each case I was set up by friends and in each case, something was wrong, he didn't laugh like Ian, he didn't talk like Ian or make me laugh like Ian, there was always the comparison there and no one else matched up. I ended all the dates early by making an excuse, headache, stomach ache, and the best one of all, I needed to go and fix a computer program and that was the only time available to me. Two of them called to see if we might try again and I told them no thanks."

"Where do you live now?" Irene asked.

"I have a flat in London, on Cadogan Place," I replied. "It's very nice, fourth floor, so a bit of a climb with suitcases, but overlooks the gardens and is close to the centre of London."

"How on earth did you deal with the lack of letters from Ian?" Tom asked.

"I wrote more and I sent telegrams and I cried a lot," I said. "By the time June came I was in a bad way, then I heard from the college that Ian had left because your folks had been killed and knew that I'd probably never to be able to find him."

"He was really pissed that he didn't hear from you," Tom said. "He just didn't understand what had gone wrong."

"Well, we know now," Irene said. "Do you want me to give these letters to Ian, or do you want to do it?"

"I should do it. Part of me wants so desperately to see him again, and part of me is terrified to do so, what if he hates me, what if he just doesn't want to see me, what if he really does have someone else, but just hasn't told you?" I replied.

"Look why don't you come to dinner with Tom and me on Friday?" Irene suggested. "And, I'll make sure that Ian is there. I can't guarantee his reaction, but I can referee."

"That would be wonderful, but I'm scared, I'm afraid that he'll leave me again, and it will be for good," I admitted.

"Why, you weren't scared to come and see me?" Irene commented

"I was," I admitted. "I was shaking, I was terrified that you'd just show me the door and not listen to anything, which is why I pulled out the letters so quickly."

"I admit I was ready to give you an earful," Irene said. "But when you said you'd been to Arusha and you had all those letters, I didn't know what to say. I couldn't imagine what you and Ian must have gone through, each thinking that the other had found someone else and just ended things without even as much as a goodbye. When I read your last letter to him and his to you, they read almost exactly the same, confusion, despair, longing and hopelessness."

"Ian was my first love," I told them. "In every way, and he still is, I've not been really happy since he left. I've spent good times with my family, but I'm feeling like the odd one out, my brother is married now, to the girl that Ian met, and Maman has Portia, but I sit like a wallflower at family affairs. I keep thinking back that I should have just gone to Arusha in March or April of 1971, and then none of this would have happened."

"You couldn't have known what was going on there," Tom said. "And from what I understand this Rosalind person managed all the communications, so even if they'd had a phone, you'd have been given the brush off. Going there would have probably saved the day, but only if you stayed there, as soon as you left, I'll bet it would have gone back to what it was, and if you'd gone this Rosalind would have made sure to get rid of the evidence, so you'd both be accusing the other of not writing and recriminations would have flown back and forth."

"When we were there earlier this month, I got the impression that the new girl, Alison, didn't like Rosalind much. One thing we couldn't work out is why she didn't just burn the letters when they came, why save them at all?" I said.

"Who knows what goes on in the mind," Irene said.

"So, how do I approach things on Friday?" I asked.

"Probably just like you did with me," Irene said. "Ian's much like me, he'll come out swinging, then he'll see all those letters and all his preconceived ideas will go flying out the window. He'll be as shocked as I was, and more so for him, because he was there and didn't see what was going on. When I saw them I realised that something was seriously wrong and that whatever I may have thought about you was seriously flawed. It's going to be hard for him, don't be surprised if he runs out early. He's going to need a little time to understand what happened and to rethink everything."

"I can appreciate that," I said. "I had the boat trip back from Cape Town to read each of his letters and to read them again and again. I did cry quite a bit on that trip. It was just so heartbreaking to read his words and see that he had been getting more desperate by the week, as I was. Are you going to tell him that I'll be there this week end?"

"No," she said. "I want him to be there, so I'll tell him it's a blind date, I've set him up with a few, and he's humoured me so far, plus, we don't want him showing up with some girl on his arm."

"God, no," I agreed. "I can't imagine just how awkward that would be. Where do you live?"

"We live in Taplow, just outside the village, the best thing for you to do is come and stay the weekend," Irene suggested.

"Won't that be difficult if Ian also stays?" I asked.

"We've plenty of room," Irene assured me. "You won't have rooms next to one another, you'll be at different ends of the house."

"How do I get there, I sold my car a while ago, should I hire a car?" I asked.

"Don't do that, just let us know what train you'll be on and we'll meet you at Taplow station," Irene suggested. "Or you could just take the train with me on Friday evening."

"I like that idea," I said. "If it's not too much trouble."

"No trouble at all," Irene said. "I'm atoning a little for my rudeness today and all the nasty things I've said about you over the past couple of years."

"Look, I don't want to break things up too quickly," Tom said. "But I need to have some lunch and go back to work and I suspect that Fiona does too, and you must have someone who needs cutting up Dear."

"You're right," Irene said. She called over the owner who took lunch orders and brought more coffee.

"So, Fiona," Tom said. "Ian once told us that you'd outshot him in a rifle match, is that true?"

"I did, but only after the range master ruled on one shot," I said. "I had gone with Ian to a college event, members plus girlfriends in a shoot-out, highest aggregate score wins. We won easily, then it got silly and people were betting on who was the better shot, Ian or me. The best part about it was that it was the first time we really kissed. I had just shot a one hundred, so leaned over and kissed him. It was magical. We also won £40 on a private bet, so that bought us a very nice lunch."

"He did tell us that you're a mathematician," Irene said. "What do you actually do?"

"I've created a number of mathematical models for industry and government, mainly to do with economics," I explained. "I've even done some for the Treasury. I actually met the Chancellor of the Exchequer once. He wanted to see who had created this one taxation revenue model I had done for them. I don't think he believed it was me that had done the work, I was a woman, too young and it wasn't possible that I could have done it. But the tax people all stood by me and assured him, that yes, it was me. Where did you two meet?"

"At a hospital dance," Irene said. "Tom was there as a benefactor, and we just hit it off."

"I'm in the City," Tom said. "And, on occasion I have funds to spare that I donate to the hospital, they took great care of my first wife, before she died and I'm eternally grateful."

"My Dad's in the City as well," I said. "He's an investment banker."

"Not William Barclay?" Tom asked.

"Yes, do you know him?" I asked.

"We've done quite a bit of business together, funny that he never mentioned you," Tom said.

"I spend more time with Maman," I said. "And, I'm not the best of friends with Felicity. Dad and Felicity are in South Africa now on holiday."

"Sorry to eat and run," Tom said. "But I do need to get back, I'll see you Friday night Fiona."

Irene and I finished our lunches and then went our separate ways. I had work to do and Irene went back to the hospital to her gall bladder. She did give me her direct telephone line which would let me call her without going through the hospital switchboard. I returned to my office, happier, but yet still full of apprehension. I now had a date and time when I would see Ian again. How would he react, what would he say to me, if anything, it was going to be a long week. I thought myself lucky that Irene had so quickly grasped that all had not been well in Arusha and wondered if Ian would see it so quickly.

The next day I took a taxi to Waterloo Station and caught a train to Bracknell, where the Met Office, the Meteorological Office, the official body that kept weather records and who issued forecasts, was based. It was a quick taxi ride from the station and once there I announced myself and said that I had an appointment with a Dr Kevin Black. He was one of the mathematicians who created weather models and I wanted to learn how I could adapt what they used to my purposes. I met Kevin and he quickly worked out that I was actually quite good at mathematics and understood the concepts he used and the mathematics that he had developed. I think he had been prepared to give me a polite hearing, then make an excuse to show me the door, because when someone came to him with a message, he told them that all was well and that he would be a little while yet. I knew that the science of meteorology was complex and was quite ready for the possibility that I would get nowhere. But between us, we came up with some ideas for models that might give me what I wanted. I think he was quite excited by the idea that I was someone he could talk to in the most esoteric terms and not be lost by it all.

I treated Kevin to lunch and we returned to his office and continued our discussions. I talked with Kevin until well after six, and then pointed out the time to him, but he waved it off with the comment that he did not mind at all, and was in fact waiting for his wife to arrive. She worked at Selfridges and did not usually arrive until just after six. His wife arrived soon after and he introduced me to her, her name was Anthea and she was a manager at Selfridges, in the cosmetics department. She was curious about me and Kevin waxed lyrical about finding someone with whom he could have a good discussion about models and the mathematics behind them. I did not want to intrude upon them, so excused myself and left them to themselves. I had noted on occasion before that when older men introduced me to their wives, there was often a look of suspicion as they saw this young, potentially flighty competition, and no amount of effort on my part would ever sway that initial reaction, so I had learned that the best thing to do was leave as quickly as was polite to do so. The exception to this rule, I have to say was Audrey Hill, perhaps Adam and she had a very stable and understanding marriage and she did not see competition in every younger woman. On the train back to London, I reviewed what I had learned from Kevin, the most exciting part of which is they had a nice really fast powerful computer, but getting time on it was probably out of the question, unless I could come up with a model and give it to Kevin to run as one of his.

My next trip was to Nottingham, to the university there, particularly the school of agriculture at Sutton Bonington. I took the train from St. Pancras to Loughborough, and then it was a short taxi ride. I met a professor there whom I bombarded with questions about growth rate influences. We talked about sunlight, daylight, water, altitude, temperature, soils and other factors that would affect growth and yield rates. He also talked about other influences, like insect pests, worms and other underground agents, fungi, moulds, bird losses, the impact of local, but not direct, application of pesticides and herbicides, all in all, it was almost as complex as the weather. I explained that I was trying to build a comprehensive algorithm that would include weather factors as a prediction tool for yields and he wished me good luck, but had little confidence that it could be done. He was informative and I did get a lot of useful information from him. He also took me to lunch in the staff dining room, which was nice, but I did feel a little like a prize animal that was being led around the show ring for all to see and admire, as we took a circuitous route around the room to the table. I suppose it boosted his ego and his standing in the academic circle that he had a not unattractive visitor. After lunch, he gave me a tour of the facility, which was fascinating, all kinds of plots of different plants being raised. I asked about pollination and he pointed out plants pollinated by bees and those that used a different insect. I thanked him profusely for his time and promised to keep him apprised of anything groundbreaking that I might come up with. On the train back to London, I wrote up my notes and wondered, not for the first time, whether I had not bitten off too much this time.

Wednesday brought me a new client. The Ministry of Transport was looking at congestion in cities and how to model traffic flows. I think they were working with about twenty large cities and towns to help them improve their traffic light synchronisation to get the best flow and least wait time. I tried models similar to those used for gas dynamics as one approach, and also suggested a few different ideas. I got a contract from them that would last about six months and that was actually quite lucrative. The one aspect that I was not keen about is that they wanted me to partner with a large consulting firm, with whom I had not worked before, but who had a reputation for winning government contracts then turning them into lifelong employment for some of their staff. It would be an interesting job, but I would have to find a way to work with the consulting firm as I did not, as was often said about me, play well with others.

I was becoming more apprehensive about seeing Ian again, it was all very well for Irene to say, just show the letters to him what if he just threw them back at me and refused to listen. Enough time had passed that memories could start to fade, or even become coloured by subsequent events. He might actually have found someone else, despite the assurance that Irene had given me that there was no one. I was wavering and considering cancelling my trip when Maman called.
"Bébé, how are you, I've not heard from you in a few days?" she asked.
"Maman, how are you, how's Portia?" I responded.
"We're fine, but what about you?" she pressed.
"I'm okay, Maman," I said. "I met Ian's sister, Irene and she's set up a meeting between Ian and me on Friday, but I'm scared to go."
"So, how did you find Irene?" Maman asked.
"A friend of mine tracked her down and I went to see her, I was really nervous that she would yell and scream at me then throw me out of her office," I said.
"And did she?" Maman asked.

"I said hello, then told her I'd been to Arusha, then I showed her the letters," I replied. "After that, we went to a café and I told her the whole story about Rosalind."

"What was her comment?" Maman asked.

"That she had to be the worst bitch she'd ever heard of," I quoted.

"So, why are you scared to see Ian again?" Maman asked.

"What if he really doesn't want to see me again, what if he has someone else, what if he hates me so much, he can't see logic and truth?" I asked.

"You won't know until you meet, and does he have someone else, what did his sister say?" Maman asked.

"She said not, she said he had had on-again, off-again relationships, but nothing serious," I replied.

"So, that probably means that he's not over you," Maman said. "Go, Bébé, see him, give him the letters, tell him the story, then if he still hates you, you should leave him, because things will never be the same again."

"Do I ask him if he slept with this Rosalind?" I asked.

"Do you really want to know?" Maman asked.

"I don't know," I admitted. "Part of me just doesn't want to know, but the idea of Ian with someone else just is unbearable."

"When you first met Ian, did you ask him about anyone from the past?" Maman asked.

"No, what was in the past could stay there, buried forever, I didn't want to know," I said.

"Then, you should look at this the same way, after he gets the letters and if he talks to you again, treat it as though it's a new relationship, which it is, because things have changed," she advised.

"That makes sense," I agreed. "What do I wear?"

"Where are you going to meet?" Maman asked.

"At Irene's house," I said. "She invited me to spend the weekend with them, her and her husband Tom Morrison."

"So, casual, but nothing too short that makes you look like a tart," Maman suggested.

"Maman," I protested. "When have I ever dressed like a tart?"

"I'm not saying that you have, Bébé," she said. "Just don't start now."

"No, Maman, yes, Maman," I said. "The weather people say that it's supposed to be hot this weekend, so maybe I'll just wear shorts."

"Check with the sister before you do that, she may have conventions that she follows," Maman suggested.

"I'll do that," I said. "I'll call you when I get back here on, maybe Friday night late if things go badly, or maybe Sunday if things go well."

"Good," she said. *"Bonne nuit, Bébé, j t'aime."*

"Je t'aime aussi," I replied.

I called Irene the next day to get the lie of the land. Because the forecast was good, with temperatures up in the 90s, she planned to eat outside, so suggested shorts and sandals. I giggled to myself briefly, despite my apprehensions about going, that she had not mentioned shirts or tops, but did not pursue that, I did not know enough about her to gauge her sense of humour. So, the first night was simple, I would wear the shorts and shirt I had worn on when Ian had taken me for the picnic at the Trout Inn. I picked out a few other things and packed a small suitcase, hoping that I had enough. I even put in my bikini, if the weather was going to be as hot as predicted it might even come in handy. I pondered underwear and, in the end, picked a wide selection from fairly conservative to quite risqué, it would all depend on how things went. I took my large floppy hat and my film star sunglasses, I might as well take the whole ensemble I had worn when Ian and I had gone on our boat ride.

On Friday I met Irene at Paddington and we got seats on the train, fast to Slough, then stopping thereafter. We alit at Taplow and Irene led the way to her car. It was a short drive to their house, a nice-looking place, not quite the pile that Maman had had in Henley, but big enough, with four bedrooms, plus the usual downstairs rooms. Tom was already there. He had come down earlier in the day, he explained, to prepare dinner. It seemed he liked to cook and took every chance he could to show off his prowess in the kitchen. Irene showed me to a room and I quickly changed into my shirt and shorts. I went downstairs with my shoulder bag that had in it the all-important letters. Those would be the making or breaking of any chance of reconciliation. While Tom cooked, Irene walked me around the garden, sensing that I was a bundle of nerves, not knowing how this was going to go.

"Don't worry," she assured me. "It'll be all right."

"Thank you," I said. What I was actually thinking was, easy for you to say, but I did not want to appear ungrateful for the effort she had gone to. Irene got us both a glass of wine and we sat out in the garden waiting. The waiting seemed interminable and I had to force myself to relax. Irene had told Ian to come at seven, but seven came and went with no sign of him. I wondered if something, or worse, someone, had come up and that he was not going to come. It was almost a quarter to eight when I saw Tom go to the front door and let someone in.

"So, who's it this time?" he asked Tom. It was Ian, I heard his voice and tears welled up in my eyes and a lump formed in my throat.

"Come and see," Tom said. They came out onto the patio and Ian looked at me, and shock, then disdain ran across his face.

"What the hell is this, Reenie, some kind of bad joke?" he asked. "I'm leaving."

"Sit down!" Irene commanded, and it was a command, of that there was no doubt, she probably used that voice in theatre when things were not going well. Ian did sit down, probably much to his own surprise, not happy but compliant, I have to admit that I would have sat down too if Irene had spoken to me like that, my guess that was the big sister voice that she had developed over the years.

"This is no joke, Ian Arthur Hartley, you will sit and listen," she said quite angrily. I was reminded of Maman, when she was really angry with us, or wanted to really get our attention, she did what most mothers do and used our full names. "Fiona," she invited me to start.

"I went to Arusha last month," I said, barely getting the words out, hurt by the look he had given me. "There I met Tega."

"So, you met Tega, so what?" he said.

"Well, Tega gave me these," I said, digging into my bag and handing over to Ian the bundle of letters that I had written to him, and the telegrams that I had sent. He took them and looked at them in shock. He rifled through them and then said. "So, you wrote a load of letters recently and put stamps on them to make it look as if they'd been mailed in 1971."

"Don't be such an ass," Tom said. "Get down off your high bloody horse and look at what you have there, your bitch friend Rosalind stopped all Fiona's letters to you and yours to her, show him Fiona."

I pulled out the other bundle of letters and he recognised them as his own and saw that they had never been stamped or posted and that even he had to admit that my ability to forge in his handwriting my own name and address on the envelopes would be pushing the bounds of credence just a little far.

"I don't understand," he said.

"Rosalind withheld all my letters and telegrams, bar the few that are not here, and she withheld all your letters bar the three that I did receive," I explained.

"But she was so understanding," Ian protested.

"Wake up you idiot," Irene said quite sharply. "As people say, you were played like a bloody violin and you never saw it."

"But how did you get them?" Ian asked me.

"I told you," I said. "I went to Arusha last month and Tega had them."

"How did Tega get them?" Ian asked.

"When Rosalind left in June, she gave Tega a cardboard box and told him to burn it and its contents. We were lucky that Tega looked inside and saw what was there, and that he knew you. So, he didn't burn them he kept them, but he didn't know what to do with them, so it was fortunate that we went when we did. We also learned that after you left in June to go back to Rhodesia that Rosalind took up with Gordon Busby." I knew that was mean, but I was still smarting from the look he had given me and the tone of voice he had used when he first arrived.

"I don't know what to say," Ian said. I actually felt a little sorry for him, I had had time to read all his letters and think about things, he was just being handed it all and was learning what kind of person Rosalind really was.

"You might start by apologising for your rudeness just now," Irene said. "I've had to do my apologising, so it's your turn now."

"Why have these two been opened?" he asked, neatly skirting the subject of apologies.

"I opened one and one was already opened," Irene said.

"We surmised that Rosalind wanted to see if they were professional letters about the dig, when she saw that they weren't she started withholding them," I replied, a little more in control of myself now.

"Why did you open one Reenie?" he asked.

"I wanted to see what it read like, and I put it next to your last letter to Fiona to compare the two. You two were really badly served by the bitch Rosalind," Irene said.

"But after all this time, why go to Arusha now?" Ian asked me.

"It was a song," I said.

"A song?" he asked.

"I can explain," Irene interrupted. "After Fiona told me that, I wondered just what the song said, so I bought the record and listened to it, and then to really understand it I asked one of our orderlies, who's Moroccan, to translate for me. It brought tears to my eyes, so God knows what it would do to a French speaker, especially one who had experienced the loss Fiona had."

"Okay, we can continue this later, but now my dinner is going to spoil, so let's eat and we can talk at the same time," Tom said. He went inside and brought out knives and forks, then plates of food.

"I want a drink," Ian said. "A bloody big one. God, what a mess."

Over dinner Ian asked questions that I tried to answer, I decided that I would have my turn later, perhaps even the next day.

"You said, we went to Arusha, who did you go with?" he asked. That was a logical question, I might have gone with a new boyfriend.

"Maman and Portia," I said.

"They're still together then?" he asked.

"They are, they live on the Riviera now, Maman sold her place in Henley and Portia sold her cottage and resigned from the law firm," I elaborated. "Oh, and James and Charlize got married last month in South Africa, and they live in France now on the vineyard."

"You went to Arusha; how did you get there?" he asked.

"We flew to Nairobi and took safari through the Serengeti and the Ngorongoro Crater and ended up in Arusha," I explained.

"I really wanted to show you those places," he said, tears welling up in his eyes. "What the hell do we do now?"

"I think you should start by reading all the letters that Fiona sent you," Irene said, and that was obviously more of a command than a suggestion. "Then in the morning you two can talk and see how things go from there."

"God, I hated you," Ian said to me. "I was hurt and confused, but I suppose, given all this, you hated me as well."

"For a while," I admitted.

"Hell," he said. "Are you staying the night?"

"I am, Irene was kind enough to invite me for the weekend," I said.

"How was Tega when you saw him?" Ian asked.

"He was fine, his granddaughter is going to go to university," I told him.

"I always liked Tega," Ian said. "I can't believe that bitch hid all your letters and telegrams. How the hell could I have not seen it?"

"No comment," Tom said. There was a lot not said in that simple statement. But I was not going to add fuel to the fire. Tom and Irene were deliberately making Ian see the situation for what it was and making him face his own gullibility. I think both of them felt guilty that over the years they had vilified me and not forced Ian to look at himself.

"Do you still work at the college," Ian asked me.

"No, I've gone out on my own," I said. "I have an office in London."

"Good, for you," he said. "Look, I'm going to need some time here, I'm going to go to my room now, I've a lot to read and think about, I'll see you all in the morning."

After he had gone, I looked at Irene with an unspoken question.

"So far so good," she said. "He's got a lot to read and a lot to think about, particularly how he could have been so trusting and gullible and let the bitch convince him that you'd moved on."

"I wanted to meet and beat the living daylights out of her," I said.

"Could you?" Tom asked.

"Easily," I said. "Maybe Ian didn't tell you, but I am a karate black belt and have also other skills in kung fu. I once put three creeps in hospital for trying to attack me. So, probably better for me that she had already gone, or I might be languishing in a Tanzanian prison now. I was a little surprised that Ian stayed, when he first came, I was sure he was going to walk right back out of the door."

"He would have," Irene said. "I haven't spoken to him like that for a long time, I'm just glad he still listened."

"What was he like growing up?" I asked.

"The typical Rhodesian," she replied. "Lots of interest in the bush, firearms, hunting, went to boarding school in Salisbury and made a name for himself as a rugby player and cricket player, then off to varsity. He and I used to fight a lot as kids, but as we got older and were away at boarding school, then varsity, we grew closer. We both worked out early on that tobacco farming was not for us, which I think disappointed Dad, because he thought we'd carry on the family farm."

"I'm sorry about your parents," I said. "It must have been a shock and difficult for you."

"It was," she said. "But it also made us both realise that Smith is living on borrowed time, this is a war he cannot win. It's a shame that Dad didn't sell the farm sooner, because when we came to sell it, we got the lowest price for it."

"I heard that you'd converted the proceeds to gem stones," I said.

"You heard that, where from?" she asked.

"One of my clients originally came from Bulawayo and his secretary comes from Salisbury, they both still have contacts there and they told me about the ambush, the farm sale, and the fact that you'd both left, Ian after serving with the army for a while," I explained.

"You're well informed," Irene said dryly. "Yes, we did buy stones, they were easy to shift out of the country and when I got here, I sold most of mine. You said you went to Arusha with Maman and Portia, I presume Maman is your mother?"

"She is," I confirmed. "Portia is her partner, they met after they both got divorced and are really happy together."

"What did your mother think when you found the letters in Arusha?" Irene asked.

"She used a lot of bad language," I replied. "I've not heard her use such language since Dad left to go off with Felicity the floozie." Tom almost choked on his drink at that comment. I think he had met Felicity, but had never heard her described that way. "Both she and Portia said that they were sorry for all the things they had felt about Ian."

"So, what were you like growing up?" Tom asked.

"A challenge, I think," I said. "I was super bright and had my degrees early and my first doctorate before I was twenty-one."

"You've more than one?" Tom asked.

"My first was mathematics and I picked up one in economics about two years ago," I explained.

"But along the way, you learned how to shoot?" Tom asked. "I know Ian is a crack shot, I've been out with him, but when he told us that you'd beaten him I was really surprised."

"I went with Dad to his gun club and became interested in the mathematics of bullet trajectories, so had my first paper published before I went to college. In the process I shot off thousands of rounds and am pretty good," I explained.

"I like the picture that Ian had of you," Irene said.

"That was one Maman took for us," I said. "I have more here. Ian left them with me when he went back to Tanzania." I showed them some of the pictures Maman had taken of me, but not the flip book. I was not going to share that with anyone, perhaps not even Ian if things did not go well.

"Your mother has a good eye for this," Irene said.

"These are some she did of Ian," I added, pulling out more pictures.

"These are super," Irene said. "Do you have any than I could have?"

"Pick which ones you want," I said. "I'll get Maman to print some more for me."

"Thank you," Irene said. "All the pictures we had of us as kids went up in smoke when they burned the farm, so we really don't have much."

"Do you mind if I go to bed?" I asked. "It's been quite draining, and I'm nearly falling off the chair here."

"Go," Irene said. "Get a good night's sleep and we'll see what the morning brings."

I did not wake with the birds the next morning, dawn comes early to the northern latitudes in August, but I did awaken fairly early and saw that it was just after seven. I smelled coffee and went down to the kitchen and saw Tom there.

"Morning, Fiona," he said. "Sleep well?"

"After a while," I said. "It's still very emotional. Do I smell coffee?"

"Coffee, yes, my specialty, here try some," he said, handing me a cup with coffee in it. "Milk, sugar?"

"Just some milk, please," I said.

"Ian's out in the garden with Irene," Tom said. "Big pow wow out there."

"Do you know what they're talking about?" I asked.

"You, I should think," Tom replied. "Ian's a much chastened lad this morning, keeps telling us that he should have suspected shenanigans from the bitch, but she was so nice, so understanding, always there to help and be supportive, you get the idea. I'm making omelettes for breakfast, want one?"

"That would be lovely," I said. "Thank you."

"Take your coffee and join the others, I'll bring your omelette out," he said. I took my coffee and went out onto the patio.

"Good morning Fiona," Irene said. "Did you sleep well?"

"After a fashion," I said. "How are you this morning Irene and you Ian?"

"I'm sorry Fi," Ian said, not waiting for Irene to answer. "I'm truly sorry, I'm sorry I was so rude yesterday, I'm sorry that I didn't even try to contact you when I arrived here in 1972, all that time wasted. I read your letters last night and that was really hard, I didn't get much sleep, maybe an hour, two at the most. I was stupid, I should have gone to the post myself. I should not have trusted Rosalind, the workers in the office tried to tell me that she was no good, but she was very persuasive and so reasonable and accommodating."

"Posting your letters yourself wouldn't have really helped," I said. "All my letters to you went to the office, so you would have sent letters to me and got none in return. I'm sorry too, I'm sorry I didn't come out there in March or April when your letters stopped coming, but I was confused, I thought I'd said something in one of my letters that had driven you away, but I couldn't work out what, so I was angry, angry with you for not writing, angry with myself for becoming so emotionally attached to you that separation hurt and I didn't know what to do."

"What do we do, Fi?" he asked, looking at me, almost pleading with me for the answer that I thought that he wanted, and that I wanted so badly. "What do we do now?"

"Do we try again?" I asked, dreading that he would say no, but hoping and praying that he would say yes.

"Do you still want to?" he asked.

"Yes," I said. "I wouldn't have gone to Arusha if I didn't want to try and rescue things."

"Thank God," he said, I think relieved. "Yes, I do want to try again. When I saw you last night, I was really confused, and then I saw the hurt in your eyes and wondered what had happened. I didn't know what you knew, but I still so desperately wanted you to not be married or going out with someone else. What do we do now?"

"You eat breakfast," Tom said, plunking plates down in front of us all. "My specialty, Western Omelette, got everything in it. What about some champagne to go with it?" That sounded to me like a really good idea, and I took my glass with enthusiasm. I chinked glasses with Ian, then Irene, then Tom and took a swig.

"That's good," I said. "Cheers."

"Cheers," Ian echoed. "There is a complication."

"Already?" I said, in distress again, how complicated was life going to be with Ian, did he have a girlfriend that he had to break things off with, or

God forbid, did he have a child from some liaison, had he joined a monastic order, just what was the complication?

"I'm sorry, it's my job," he said. "I've just been ordered to a posting at the High Commission in Nairobi, I would go out there as the Third Secretary. If I decline the posting I need to give them an answer at the end of next week."

"You really know how to complicate things," Irene commented. "What happens if you turn it down?"

"I'm not sure," he admitted. "But it won't be good."

"If you said yes, when would you go?" I asked.

"Four months, or so, I'd go out a few days after Christmas," he replied. Four months I thought, well in four months we ought to know if things were going to work. I was afraid that the same thing would happen again, he would go, we would write and the letters would be lost, stolen, mislaid, undelivered, or something. I was on the verge of crying when the whole absurdity of the situation hit me, it was something that you would see in a West End farce. There was a solution, but was I ready for it, was he ready for it, would it even work?

"Well, if you think you're going off again on your own, you'd better think again," I said.

"You're right, I can't lose you again, I'll tell them I can't go," he said.

"No, that's not what I meant," I said. "I'm going to go with you, I can't trust you out of my sight not to be waylaid or stolen from me."

"But" he said, looking at me stunned. "That would mean…"

"Maybe," I said. "We'll have to see how things work out, we've a lot to talk about, and I need to learn to trust you again, as I'm sure you do me."

"Didn't see that," Tom said. "Look you two need to be alone, why don't you take the boat and go for a picnic up the Cliveden reach, it's quiet, and you can start to get to know one another again?"

"Just as long as you don't fall asleep again," I said.

"What?" Tom asked.

"Ian can explain later," I said.

"I'll put together a lunch for you, take as much time as you want, we're not going anywhere, and I thought we'd *braai* tonight," Irene added. She went into the kitchen to pull things together while Tom looked at me, then at Ian, and shook his head. "You two," he said. "You two, you didn't deserve this. I hope it works out this time, but take it from someone who lost someone they loved, and then found the love of his life, take your time, get it right, but when you do, commit, no wishy washy stuff, try and work things out so that you accommodate each other, but don't sacrifice your relationship for a career, in the end it's not worth it, your love is what's most important, like Irene is to me."

"I need to go and change if I'm going out in a boat," I said. "I'll be down in five minutes."

I went upstairs to change and thought, what have I done. It was a spur of the moment thing, but deep inside it was something that I had dreamed about for years, but was it real, was it the right thing to do, was it sensible or just a romantic fantasy. It seemed that Ian was amenable to the idea, but we would need to talk seriously and also see how we got on together, there were hurt feelings to get past, there were trust issues, all of which I thought we could manage, but I needed to know if Ian felt the same way. I needed to take his hand and see if the same magic was still there, look into his eyes and see if the same electric thrill ran through me, I needed to do those things before I went to the kissing stage and finally back into the bed. That was something I was determined not to rush. It would come as we built our relationship back up. But I had to drag myself back to the issue at hand and change for a trip on the river. For clothes I picked what I had worn on our first date, shorts, shirt, sandals, big floppy hat and sunglasses. I did not bother with a sweater or even a rain jacket, the day was already warm and it promised to get hot, and no rain was forecast, and, for once, it looked as if the forecasters had it right.

Irene had a lunch basket ready when I went back downstairs. "I've put everything in you might need," she said. "Hope this works out for you."

"Thank you, Irene," I said. "Thank you giving me a hearing and thanks for getting Ian here."

"Go, get to know one another again," she said. "Don't rush things there's a lot of hurt and distrust to get over." Ian came and took the basket and led the way. Irene and Tom had a small boat house on a branch of the river that had been a mill stream at some point. I tentatively reached for his hand and was delighted when he took mine and held it as he used to. The same thrill was there as it had been when we first held hands at the Trout Inn. The boat house was a short walk across the fields to a lane, then up the lane a little way. Ian helped me into the boat, a small motor launch with seats for four, then he started the engine and eased us out of the boat house and into the stream. There was enough room on the back seat where he sat for both of us, so I sat next to him. There was no traffic on this back water, so all we had to do was keep straight upriver. Soon enough we joined the main branch of the River Thames and mingled in with all the other boats going upstream.

"How are you, Fi?" Ian asked, looking at me with worry lines and concern.

"Happier now," I replied. "I was terrified that you'd walk out last night."

"Stupid me, I almost did," he admitted. "When I first saw you, my heart was in my mouth, but I was still smarting from what I thought was you abandoning me. I'm glad Reenie made me sit down, she hasn't used that tone of voice in years, reminded me of my Mum, disobey at your peril."

"I'm so glad I went to Arusha," I said. "If I hadn't, I doubt that we'd ever have found each other again. I'm just sorry that I didn't come out in 1971, then all this could have been avoided."

"Yes, but when I got back here the next year, I could have tried to find you," Ian said. "But probably like you, I was pissed, I couldn't work out what I'd done wrong. So, did you mean it when you said you'd come to Nairobi with me?"

"Yes, if we manage to work things out between us," I said. "What do you have to tell your bosses?"

"Just that I'll go," he said. "What do I tell them about you?"

"Tell them that you're working up the courage to ask me to marry you, but that you expect that to happen before you go, then they can check me out, or vet me, or whatever it is they do," I suggested. "That may be easier than might think, because I've done work for the Inland Revenue and the Treasury and I've met the Chancellor of the Exchequer."

"You have, wow, a bit above my level?" he asked. "Do you have clients and contracts now?"

"I do," I confirmed. "But one of the contract clauses is travel time and expenses, and there is no restriction on where I work or what it cost to go to meetings. I'm sure everyone presumed that I'd be living and working in London. So, I live in Nairobi, work there and fly back for meetings."

"Won't they baulk at the cost?" he asked.

"Maybe, but then they can terminate the agreement and pay costs," I said. "So, we've got four months to work things out between us. Any entanglements?"

"No, no wives, girlfriends or other impediments," he said, basically repeating what he had said when we had had our first coffee together. "And you?"

"None," I said. "What do you think about children?"

"I try not to," he spluttered. "You're as direct as ever. Do you want a family?"

"At the moment, no, not really," I said. "If you really want a family, then I'm sure we could manage it, but I'm not that thrilled."

"Thanks for the honesty," he said. "I can live without children, I was just not sure how strong the maternal drive was that you either had or didn't."

"I was sorry to hear about your folks," I said. "That must have been hard."

"It was," he said. "The bastards mined the road, then shot up the folks when they crawled out of the car, then they burned the farm to the ground. I found the people that had done it and took care of them. That took me a while, but after that I had no heart for the operations and could see that it was a lost cause, so I walked away. God, Fi, it's so good to see you again, it's been a hard few years, I've missed you at all kinds of odd times and places."

"I went to see Chris at the Trout Inn last weekend," I told Ian. "He told me that he'd had a card from you from Rome, but otherwise, hadn't heard from you."

"Rome," Ian said. "Ah, that's when the Foreign Office sent me as an errand boy to the embassy there."

"Do you like what you're doing now?" I asked.

"I do," he said. "It's interesting and could get more so as I move up the ladder."

"Would I help or hinder that?" I asked.

"They'll have misgivings that you have your own successful career, but will appreciate your languages," he thought.

"I got another doctorate," I said, then felt guilty. "I'm so sorry, that was insensitive, I know you didn't finish yours, Ambrose told me."

"No worries," he said. "I wasn't that keen on it anyway, and if I hadn't gone back to do more work, I wouldn't have lost you. So, what are you working on now?"

"I've a contract with Adam Hill to develop some algorithms to predict crop harvests, based on weather forecasts, and I've got a job with the Ministry of Transport to develop some methodologies to better synchronise traffic lights in towns for more even traffic flow, and I've a couple of jobs that I'm thinking about," I replied.

"So, busy?" he asked.

"As busy as I want to be," I said. "I make enough that I can pick and choose."

"What will you do if we're married? You're probably more successful now than many of the spouses, usually when a successful woman marries a diplomat, she gives up her career, because she can't carry on in the places she's sent to, I think many of the men in the service are still hanging on to the notion of the supportive wife hanging onto the arms of the British diplomat and saying nice things about the host country, or else serving afternoon tea," he said.

"Is it really that bad?" I asked.

"Bad, enough," he admitted. "There's an organisation you should look into, if not join, the Diplomatic Service Wives Association, the DSWA. They're becoming much more vocal about issues that wives face when their husbands get posted."

"I'll do that," I promised.

"If you wanted to work locally, then we'd have to look into things like work permits, and there is also the issue that immunity is not preserved if something happens while you're working locally," he said.

"I'd probably work out of my London office," I said. "I don't have to live there, just have a business address there. I have a service already that handles mail and phone calls, so if I get a new project, I would see them when I flew back to London. The actual thinking part of any project can be done anywhere, even in a tent on safari."

"Oh, Fi, I'm really pleased that I found you again," he said. "I'm just so happy."

"Is it really this easy?" I asked him. "Aren't we supposed to drag up all the hurts and fill our conversation with recriminations and back biting? I can't believe it's going to be this simple, are we missing something?"

"I don't know, if anything, you should be the one with the recriminations, I was closest to the problem, but didn't see it," he said.

"I've never done this before. Let's just accept things and see where it leads us."

"I agree," I said. "And if I had my heart set on recriminations I wouldn't gone to Arusha, so put that out of your mind."

"We do need to agree on something, if we don't hear from each other for more than a week and the normal channels are not working we need to have another channel, one people would not expect," he said.

"I like that," I said. "Let's not use family, let's use your friend Chris at the Trout."

"Good idea," he agreed. "We'll go and see him soon and tell him what we want. I doubt that we'll ever have to resort to that, but it would be a good thing to set up. If we going to act like spies, then we need code names, what do you fancy?"

"Fifi L'Amour," I joked. "No, maybe not, what about Victoria White?"

"Sounds good," he said. "What about Victor Black for me?"

"That makes it easy," I agreed.

"Shall we take the side channel that goes up past the old Hedsor Mill and stop for lunch?" he asked.

"You know this part of the river better than me," I said. We did take the side channel and pulled over and tied up along the bank next to a large field that had been mown for hay and in which there were those big round hay bales still. I jumped out onto the bank and made us fast, then he handed me the picnic basket. He brought a blanket to spread out for us, but before we laid out our picnic, I put my arms around him and held him close, then all the emotions of the last week, the last month, the last four years came pouring out and I burst into sobs. It was cathartic, I really needed it and I needed him to hold me while I cried. I think my tears released his emotions too, because I heard him sniffle a little, then start to cry and felt his tears on my neck as we held each other close. I've no idea what other boaters might have thought, two people standing on the river bank crying their eyes out.

It took a while, but finally my sobs lessened and I looked up at him and the tears running down his face, and knew that I loved him, I did not care what had gone before, I did not care that he had been gone from my life for too long, I just loved him. He kissed away my tears and looked deep into my eyes and said the magic words that I had been longing to hear again and again. "I love you," he said. "I really love you.

Life without you has been empty, thank you for finding me and bringing me back to my senses and you back into my life."

"I love you," I told him, and I really did, the thought of going through life without him was almost unbearable, particularly as I had now found him again and was able to be in his arms and feel the comfort of having him near me. We just stood in each other's arms for a while, just enjoying the closeness and the security that a loved one's embrace can bring. It was a cow that brought things to a halt, she came wandering over, curious to see what was going on and if there was anything a cow might like, she tripped over our picnic basket then frisked away a few feet, before snuffing at it. She brought some friends and soon we were surrounded by about fifteen cows, all looking at us. As we looked back at them, they began to get a little skittish and backed away, but not too far. When we broke apart, the cows moved farther away, but still hung around watching. I had no idea that cows could be so curious. We watched them, and as we shook out the blanket to spread on the ground, they skipped away from us a few more yards, then stopped again and turned around to watch us, and moved back again closer to form a ring around us, all the time carrying on whatever kind of conversation cows have with one another.

"Nice audience," Ian said.

"I suppose they're just curious," I said. "Want to know what we're doing in their neighbourhood."

"Shall we have some lunch?" he asked.

"Good idea," I agreed. "What did Irene give us?"

"Pork pie, lettuce, tomato, potato salad, white wine and chocolates," he enumerated. "Some of each?"

"Please," I said. I sat on the blanket and watched him put things on a plate for me. I studied his face and noted that he had not been out in the sun as much, because he no longer had that deep tan that he had had when I first met him. He saw me watching him and grinned, that grin that I had missed so much. I know I grinned back, this was going to be the beginning of a beautiful life, if we did not mess it up again by separation and lack of communication.

We finally made our way back downstream just before four, not saying much, just sitting in the boat arms around each other. I had not been so happy for ages, I had Ian back in my life and it looked as if he was there to stay. It still surprised me that we had been able to make up so quickly, was I missing something, was reality going to hit later and things fall apart, were there recriminations yet to be brought to the surface, or had we both decided that that was a waste of time. For my part, I was just so thrilled that he was back, that I was not about to raise old hurts, I had had my dig about Rosalind, but was determined that that would be the one and only one. I think if we had not both seen and read the letters that each us had sent, then it would have been far more difficult. We both saw that we had been victims of a predatory person, who had connived and engineered the complete lack of communication and that lesson was well learned, we needed to communicate and ensure that we never lost that.

By the time we got back to the house we were chattering away about all kinds of things, me about what I had seen in the Serengeti and he about things he had encountered in diplomatic circles. I think Irene and Tom had spent an anxious day, wondering how we would fare and whether or not we would resolve things between us.

"Everything okay?" Irene asked as we entered the house.

"Great," Ian said, for both of us and grinned at me. I flashed him a grin back and hugged him.

"I'm so glad," Irene said. "Ian, will you help Tom with the *braai?*" After he had gone, Irene looked at me and asked, "How are you?"

"I'm in seventh heaven," I said. "He still loves me, we both cried a lot, or at least I did, and we agreed that we can't allow this to ever happen again. We've got to find a way to keep in touch always."

"Can I have a hug?" she asked. I hugged her and we both shed a few tears, I think for relief, happiness and regret. I could have got to know her years ago if Ian and I had not lost touch and I regretted that, I had come to like her, for all her initial frosty reception.

"What are you two crying about?" Tom asked, when he came into the kitchen for things to cook.

"Just girl stuff," Irene said, looking over my shoulder at him. "I'm happy, they're happier than they were and it looks like a real reconciliation."

"Well, good, about time," Tom said. "Ian's blithering on about Fiona this, Fiona that, I should meet her mother, I should meet her brother, we should all get together some time. I blame Fiona for all this, she opened up a floodgate, and he's talked more today than the whole of the past month."

"So, you're not happy with them?" Irene asked, kidding with him.

"Of course, I'm happy with them, for them and for us, we won't have to look at Ian's long face anymore," he said. "As I said, about time. Now what do you want me to cook, who else is coming, can Ian and Fiona stand company?"

"No one else is coming," Irene said. "And, there's the meat I want you to cook, I've made it up into *braai* packs." Tom left to go cooking leaving Irene and I still with our arms around each other.

"Irene, would it be possible for me to call my mother?" I asked.

"Of course," she said.

"It's a call to France, but I can pay you for the call," I said.

"Don't be silly," she said. "Call her, tell her your news."

"Thank you," I said. "Please don't be offended, but we'll probably speak in French, is that all right?"

"Of course," she said. "Ian told me once that you and your Maman, as you call her, typically use French when it's just the two of you, and this is a private conversation. The phone is in the hall."

Maman answered the telephone and I was delighted to hear her voice.

"Maman," I said. "He loves me, he told me today, he hugged me, he grinned at me and he cried for me."

"So, he loves you, good, and you love him?" she asked.

"Oh, Maman, more than ever," I said. "Oh, and Maman, I think he may ask me to marry him soon."

"Are you sure?" she asked.

"Maman, I'm sure, I wasn't certain this morning, but we spent the day together and the time melted away and the hurt was washed away with tears, when he cried when I cried, I knew," I told her.

"Bébé, I am happy," she said.

"I'll call you tomorrow when I get home," I promised. "But now there is a family *braai*, tell Portia I love her, *je t'aime* Maman."

"Je t'aime aussi, Bébé," she replied.

"Everything fine?" Irene asked, when I went back to the kitchen

"Everything is better than fine," I said, smiling from ear to ear. "I love your brother, Irene, I really do love him."

"I know," she said. "I could tell when you first came to see me, I was angry with you, but as the story came out, I felt such sorrow for both of you, now you're happy again and so is he."

Better each day

It took Ian a week to propose, he called me and asked me if I would like to take a trip to the Trout Inn for the weekend. Of course I did, I could not think of a better way to spend the weekend. We had called each other every day since spending the weekend with Irene and Tom, and had had lunch or dinner each day as well, now all that remained was to spend the night together. I spent hours agonising over clothes to take and called Maman three times for advice. If we were going to be spending the weekend together, that meant that sex was on the table and I was definitely in the mood. I had waited for over four years for this and I was going to make the most of it. In the end I probably took far more than I needed for a simple weekend. Ian hired a car and picked me up at my flat on the Friday afternoon and we joined the early rush hour traffic out of London onto the A40, towards Oxford. All through the drive, I took sideways glances at Ian, imagining us together, until I was almost at the point of just telling him to pull over into some private place when we arrived at the Trout Inn. Chris saw us come in and came to greet us.

"Fiona, Ian, great to see you again," he said. "I have your room for you, room four up the stairs to the front."

"Thanks, Chris," Ian said.

"Here, let me help you with your bags," Chris said. He took my bag and led the way upstairs. The room was the same one I had had when I had been only a couple of weeks earlier, but this time the bed would not be the lonely place it was then. "Dinner at eight?" Chris suggested.

"Eight," I agreed. Chris left and I looked at Ian and held my arms out to him. He came to me and put his arms around me and kissed me. I returned his kiss and then undid the waist band of his trousers and pushed them down onto the floor. He felt around my skirt looking for the zipper, or something to undo it. I showed him where it was and my skirt joined his trousers on the floor, quickly followed by his shirt, my blouse, my bra and panties then his underpants, then we were on the bed together, body to body, the whole length of us touching. He was ready, oh, was he ready, and so was I, I could feel myself anticipating what would come, so I equipped him with the necessary protection and climbed on top of him and guided him into me. The feeling was incredible, I had him back, I was once again whole, feeling him inside me, we tried as hard as we could to make things last, but the need for both of us was urgent, so the climax for both of us came quickly.

"God, Fi," he said. "I've missed you."

"I've missed you," I said. "I've missed this, I've dreamed of this, I've fantasised about this, but nothing is like the real you. Are you ready for more?"

"Please, oh please," he said, reaching for my body and running his hands everywhere over me. I had missed that, his touch, his caresses, the sheer eroticism of body nestled close to body. We took longer that time and spend more time just slowly and lazily at first, then building as the passion built with more frenzied motion, with the bed squeaking and creaking in sympathy, until the climax came for both of us, which I have to say was quite noisy, at least for me, almost rivalling the noise made by Charlize.

It was approaching eight, so we put clothes back on and went down for dinner. The couple who had the room next to us came out almost at the same time as us, and he looked at us and asked us to keep the noise down. We let them pass and go downstairs and when they were gone I started giggling, then laughing and Ian looked at me and grinned, then started laughing as well, until both of us were standing there convulsed in gales of laughter, we laughed at the humour of the situation, we laughed for the happiness of having found one another again and we laughed for the sheer joy of living. The laughter was almost as cathartic as the tears had been the week before. So nice to be enjoying one another so much that it annoyed the neighbours. Chris saw us come down and showed us to a table on the terrace, overlooking the river. He gave us menus and brought us a bottle of Sauvignon Blanc. "On the house," he said. "It's great that you're back together."

"What's your suggestion for dinner tonight?" I asked him.

"Trout is good tonight," he replied.

"Trout it is for me," I said. "Ian?"

"Same please," he said. Chris went off to relay the order, then Ian reached over the table and took my hand. "Fiona, will you marry me?" he asked.

"Yes," I said. "Yes, yes, yes." He then pulled out a ring and put it on my finger, it was a huge emerald, emerald cut in a simple platinum setting. "This is part of what I got for the farm, I want you to have it," he said. I held the ring up to look at it, I had never been much of a jewellery person and the only other things I had were the sapphire pieces that Portia had given me and the emerald earrings that Maman had given me, but my ring I would cherish forever. Chris came over to see how we were doing and Ian gave him the news.

"Congratulations," he said. "You should have done this years ago and not put me through all the heartache."

"You?" Ian said. "What about me?"

"Never mind you," Chris said. "Let's see the ring Fiona." I held out my hand in the time honoured fashion, palm down, fingers extended so that the ring was obvious.

"Nice," he said, "Rhodesian emerald not Colombian, can tell by the colour, emerald cut, I'd say fifteen carats. You going to invite me to the wedding?"

"It will be in London, we can't do it in France unless at least one of us has been there for thirty days, which is not practical," I said. "Would you and Heather come?"

"Absolutely," he promised. "Where in London?"

"Probably close to where I live," I said. "So, somewhere around Chelsea I should think."

"Church wedding?" Chris asked.

"Probably not," I said. "A register office do."

"One thing," Ian said. "Would you be my best man?"

"Sure, sure, just let me know the date and I'll try and make sure you show up sober. I'll tell Heather, she'll want to come over and see you," Chris said. The neighbours who had objected to the noise were seated at the table next to us and she smiled sweetly and said something to the man, I presume husband. He looked over at us at scowled and I wondered what she was doing with such an unhappy man. Heather came over with the trout and wanted to see my ring. I wondered why it was that women always wanted to see engagement rings, was it to assess the worth the man placed upon the woman, or the depth of his bank balance or the level to which he was prepared to go into debt. Heather waxed lyrical about the ring and said that she was already picking out what she would wear. I told her that the wedding would be in early September, the actual date not yet fixed. She went off to huddle with Chris and presumably start working on time away so that they could go to London, without leaving the inn unattended.

"What did you tell your bosses?" I asked Ian

"Just what you suggested," he replied. "I told them that I had a girlfriend and that I was working up the nerve to propose."

"When they vetted you, didn't they go into your deep and dark background and ask about girlfriends?" I asked.

"They skipped over that, surprised me," he said. "I was ready with a story, but maybe the bloke wanted to get home early, because the vetting seemed to me to be pretty cursory."

"So, will I be getting a call soon as part of your vetting process?" I asked.

"Probably," he thought. "So, you think we should get married early next month?"

"Well, we have to post banns, where ever we do it, and that's two weeks, and we should give people a little notice," I said. "But beyond that, why wait? Who do you want to invite?"

"Irene and Tom, Chris and Heather and April and Paul," he said.

"That's all?" I asked.

"That's all," he confirmed. "We have some odd aunts and uncles, but we never had anything to do with them, they were here and we were in Rhodesia, so I don't know them at all. And you?"

"A few more, Maman and Portia, James and Charlize, Dad and Felicity, Mémère Monique, Rachel Adams, Adam and Audrey Hill, and Andrea, works for Adam and helped me track down Irene," I listed.

"So, what do we need to do next?" he asked.

"I think go to the local register office and sign up and get a date," I said. "I think there's one on Kings Road in the old Chelsea Town Hall, why don't you meet me there at noon on Monday and we'll do that?"

"Great, if there's any issues with me getting away, I'll call you," he promised. "Maybe we should eat, before it gets too cold."

After dinner we went back upstairs to the delights of the bedroom. First, we bathed, which was not as much fun as it could have been, because the bath was really only big enough for one. So, I bathed while he sat and chatted, then I went and lay seductively on the bed and waited for him. It was still warm, although the day was coming to an end, the temperatures were not dropping, so there was little need for any kind of bedclothes. He came to me and we enjoyed each other as only lovers can, finally falling asleep in each other's arms in the early hours of the morning. When I awoke, I could feel his body next to mine, and the little rivulets of perspiration running down between us, all very erotic. It had been a hot night, in all senses of the word. We returned to love making and only went down for breakfast late, after we had each taken a quick shower to be all sweet smelling before joining the rest of the world. Chris was there in the dining room, it struck me that the hours of an inn keeper were quite onerous, and I wondered how one found staff that could be relied upon absolutely to manage things properly in their absence.

"And how are we this morning?" he asked.

"Wonderful," I said.

"I should think so," he laughed. "The couple next to you left early and he was complaining bitterly about all the noise you were making. I should probably look at that bed some time and see if I can fix the squeaks and creaks."

"Sorry," I said.

"Don't be," he said. "I think the woman was quite jealous. So, what's the plan today?"

"Do you have any events on the island today?" Ian asked.

"None," Chris replied. "You want a packed lunch and some wine and go and have a picnic?"

"That would be super," I said.

"Just don't fall asleep on her, this time," Chris cautioned.

"I won't," Ian said.

Ian did not fall asleep and we spent a most pleasant afternoon watching the river and listening to the birds and animals. We did find a place, hidden from view where we could shed our clothes and make love in the sun, which we did three times, once before lunch, once during lunch while we fed each other food and other delights, and once again after lunch, before finally getting dressed again and returning to the inn to get washed and dressed for dinner. We were making up for lost opportunities and we were making up with a vengeance. Dinner we took on the terrace again, until the rain came. It poured, there was thunder and lightning and rain, huge drops of rain, soaking everything. I felt sorry for poor Chris, he had to try and accommodate all those who had been in the terrace into an already full dining room. In the end he managed it by appealing to all the guests and asking them if they would share tables. We shared with a couple from Scotland who were touring the South on their honeymoon and who were almost ready to return home at the end of their trip. It rained steadily for an hour, then stopped as abruptly as it had started and the sunset was dramatic, to say the least. We retired to the bedroom and engaged in more love making, which to detail and describe would become tedious and serve only to titillate. Suffice to say that we explored every inch of each other's bodies and ways to connect and returned to the Kama Sutra for ideas. We had no neighbours that night, so there were no complaints in the morning about too much noise, which was as well, because we did manage to actually physically move the bed across the floor a little way.

We drove back to London on Sunday morning and I asked Ian if he would move in with me.

"I'd love to," he said. "Let me drop you at your place with our luggage and then I'll turn the car back to the hire company and take a taxi back. I'll pick up the rest of my stuff in the week."

"Good, just don't be too long about it," I told him. "I have designs on you."

"Can't wait," he said. He dropped me and the luggage off then went to return the hire car. While he was gone, I called Maman.

"He asked me to marry him," I blurted out when she answered the telephone.

"And did you say yes?" she asked, teasing me.

"Oh, Maman, you know I said yes, I think I said yes four times," I assured her. "We go to the register office tomorrow to post banns and get a date, probably the 6th of September."

"Good," she said. "Portia and I will come over a week before. Have you decided how many guests and where you will have a reception?"

"At the moment, fewer than twenty," I said. "Neither of us has long lists. Will you bring Mémère Monique with you?"

"I will," she said. "When will you send out invitations?"

"As soon as we can confirm the date and the place, for both the ceremony and the reception," I thought. "Then I need to go and see Rachel about something to wear."

"What did you have in mind?" she asked.

"I'm not sure, but I don't want one of those big fancy wedding dresses with trains, veils and flounces," I said. "I want something that I can wear afterwards."

"It's up to you Bébé," she said. "I suppose you'll have to invite your Dad and Felicity the floozie."

"Yes, Maman, I will," I said. "Ian is moving in with me, he's out now dropping off a hire car we had for the weekend, but he'll be back soon, he'll collect the rest of his stuff this week and vacate his flat."

"And the sex is as good as it ever was?" she asked.

"Oh, Maman, it was, is good, I think better than ever, we were busy this week end," I told her. "And for you and Portia?"

"Oh, very good," she said.

"I hear Ian coming, do you want to talk to him?" I asked.

"No, that's fine, Bébé," she said. "Go to him and ravish him for me and we'll talk later in the week when you have dates and places, *je t'aime Bébé.*"

"Je t'aime aussi Maman," I replied.

Ian spent the night with me, the first of what I hoped would be a lifetime of nights together. The next day we met at the closest register office which was the old town hall of Chelsea on Kings Road. We signed up for banns, paid our fees and booked a date for the 6th of September at ten in the morning. Then we went looking for venues for the reception. Situated neatly between my flat and the register office was the Sloane Square Hotel, so we visited them and got the requisite information and booked a room for the day and agreed to contact them shortly for catering arrangements. I was going to hand that off to Maman, she could negotiate with them and get the service terms and the best service, between her and Portia they made a formidable team. Ian and I then split, he to go back to work and me to my office. There I started calling people, first I called Dad and told him that Ian and I were getting married and gave him the date. He had not actually met Ian, so suggested that Ian and I go to dinner with he and Felicity the floozie, my words, not his, on Wednesday evening. I promised to be there and asked him if he would be at the wedding. He told me that he would be there, nothing would keep him away, and he asked me if he could give me away. It was still fairly traditional in England then so that would be expected, even though my preference would have been for Maman to do the honours. He asked who was invited and I gave him the list, short as it was. I also told him that he knew one of the guests, Tom Morrison, and explained that Tom was married to Ian's sister, Irene. He was surprised by that, but then hummed and hawed, and asked if we were going to invite various and sundry distant aunts and cousins, none of whom I actually really knew. I had probably met some of them in my lifetime, but could not actually place any of them. He asked who was paying for the wedding and I told him that I was. He demurred at that and insisted that he paid. I agreed, but only on the condition that he did not go expanding the guest list to include all the waifs and strays of the far-flung family, and said that the hotel would be in contact with him shortly.

My next call was to Andrea, to give her all the news and to invite her to the wedding, plus one, she had just returned from New Zealand and was getting back to work slowly. I also made calls to Adam Hill and the Ministry of Transport, letting them know that there would be a change in my status that could impact their projects. I invited Adam to the wedding and told him that I would be moving to Nairobi at the end of the year and that if he wanted to terminate our agreement then I would understand. He told me to go and see him and we would work out a travel schedule built around meetings he had. He did not want me to stop work on the project. My call to the Ministry of Transport was entertaining. I do not think they had ever been faced with a similar situation in the past and had no idea how to proceed. They tried to tell me that my contract said that I would live and work in England, but I told them to read it and note that the only stipulation was that at the time of signing I lived and worked in England, there was no language that covered subsequent domicile, and that the contract specifically covered all travel costs without limitation. Someone had dropped a clanger on that one. I was asked to go and sit down with them to discuss where we were on the project and could my part be completed before I left. Next, I called James and Charlize, to tell them about the wedding and to ask Charlize if she would be my maid of honour. Finally, I called Rachel to invite her and ask her about clothes for the wedding. She suggested that I stop at her shop at five that afternoon and we would discuss ideas.

"So, what do you have in mind?" Rachel asked me when we were ensconced at her showroom.

"I'm not really sure," I said. "The only thing I do know is that I don't want a typical wedding dress with flounces, trains and miles of material, I don't want it to trail around on the ground, something much simpler that I can wear afterwards."

"What about a simple Empire line dress in white with matching buttonless coat?" Rachel suggested. "Or you could go back to pre Victoria and wear red, it was only after Queen Victoria wore white to her wedding that the fashion switched from red to white."

"Maybe I'll stick to white," I thought. "I do have a maid of honour, could we do the same design, but in a colour for her?"

"Of course," Rachel said. "I'll need her measurements, but it should be simple enough."

"What do I wear underneath?" I asked.

"A full slip, then whatever you want, bustier, matching white bra and panties of some sort, lace, thong, whatever you fancy," Rachel said.

"And shoes and stockings?" I asked.

"For this dress, low heel pumps, plain white, as for stockings, do the wedding thing, white stockings and garter belt, no pantyhose, or else no stockings at all, just bare legs," Rachel suggested. "And for your maid of honour, same shoes, but colour to match the dress, if you wear stockings, then she should too, also white."

"I'll get the measurements for Charlize," I promised. "When should I come back for a first fitting?"

"A week," Rachel said. "Is your maid of honour going to be around before the wedding?"

"I'll check," I replied. "She comes over quite regularly for wine events and to work with large customers, so she should be able to fit a visit here into her plans."

On Wednesday Ian and I made the requested visit to Dad and Felicity. They had a flat in Mayfair, very swanky, right on Park Lane with a view out over Hyde Park. They had five bedrooms, quite why I was never sure because they rarely had overnight guests. They did have a live-in maid, one Gabriela, an Italian girl, who hailed from Genoa. She cooked, cleaned and generally looked after them. We took a taxi to Park Lane and announced ourselves. We were buzzed in and went up to the top floor where Dad and Felicity were.

"Good evening, Dr Fiona," Gabriela said, as she opened the door to us. "Please come in."

"Is that Fiona?" Felicity called.

"It is Signora," Gabriela confirmed. Felicity came to the hall and introduced herself to Ian.

"Nice to meet you," Ian said, shaking her hand.

"Come in, come in," she said. "Bill, Fiona's here," she called out. I heard a door close and footsteps down the hallway and Dad came to greet us.

"Fiona," he said, giving me a kiss on each cheek. "Thanks for coming, and you are Ian?" he said, holding out his hand.

"Yes, Sir," Ian confirmed.

"Come in, what can I get you to drink?" Dad asked.

"I'll just have a glass of white wine if you have one open," I said.

"A Scotch, if that would be okay," Ian said.

"Water with that?" Dad asked.

"A little," Ian said.

"So, Gabriela, a Cabernet and a Glenlivet with a splash, Felicity, what are you having?"

"I'll have a Cabernet," she said.

"And I'll have a Glenlivet as well, no water thank you Gabriela," Dad said, passing on our drinks order.

"So, you're the chap who almost broke my Fiona's heart," Dad said.

"I'm afraid so," Ian confessed. "But then I thought she'd broken my heart. It seems that we both wrote madly but another intercepted all our letters and left us both wondering what had happened."

"Nasty thing to do, did you meet her Fi?" Dad asked.

"Fortunately, no," I said. "Or I might be in a Tanzanian prison now."

"I heard the story from James," Dad said. "Sad thing to do to anyone, but you're back together and going to get married. Not letting him get away again, hey, Fi?"

"No, I'm not," I confirmed. "We will be going overseas though, Ian has a posting to our High Commission in Nairobi, so we would leave at the end of the year."

"Won't that affect your clients?" Dad asked.

"Some," I confirmed. "But there are others who are happy to pay the air fare to have me come to London for meetings, and I can work anywhere.

Thank you, Gabriela." I took my glass of wine and tasted it, it was a very good vintage, Dad did not do things by halves.

"So, date and place confirmed, I've talked to your mother and we've agreed upon a menu and I'll foot the bill, I gather from James that he and Charlize are providing the wines from the Cillie vineyard," Dad said. "Anything else we need to know or do?"

"I've taken rooms at the Sloane Square Hotel for myself and Ian for the wedding night, and for Chris and Heather, April and Paul and Tom and Irene, Ian's guests and for James and Charlize. Maman and Portia will stay at my flat with Mémère Monique, would you like me to get a room there for you and Felicity, or will you go back to your own flat after the reception?" I asked.

"We'll come back here," Dad said. "It's close enough, but I'll foot the bill for the rooms, I presume night before the wedding and night of, before everyone goes their own way?"

"I think so, thanks Dad, I appreciate that," I said.

"So, tell me about yourself Ian," Dad invited. Ian then gave a quick précis of his life up to the death of his parents and his time in the Rhodesian army. Dad wanted to know about the farm and what had happened to it, and Ian told him that he and Irene had sold it and taken the funds that it had generated.

"Sorry about your folks," Dad said. "Terrible thing to happen to anyone, do you think there'll be more?"

"Sadly, yes," Ian confirmed.

"Terrible thing," Dad repeated. "So, tell me Ian, apart from digging up ancient people what other interests do you have?"

I sat and watched and listened as a bystander as Ian talked to Dad and Felicity about music, art, politics, travel, economics and all manner of things. As I knew from before, Ian had a much broader knowledge of music and art than I did, and I had wondered before how much he actually knew and how good he was at stringing me a line. Well, it seemed that his knowledge was real, as he was able to more than hold his own with Dad and Felicity. Conversation was interrupted by Gabriela who announced that dinner was served, but over dinner, it continued. Finally, Dad threw out an invitation.

"Look," he said. "I've got a box at the Albert Hall, why don't you and Fiona join us for the last night of the Proms?"

"Fiona?" Ian asked me.

"That sounds like fun," I said. "When is it?"

"On the twentieth of next month," Dad said.

"Then, thank you Sir, we would love to come," Ian accepted.

"Good, we'll meet at the Albert Hall at six thirty, that should be plenty of time to get seated and comfortable," Dad suggested.

"I'm sorry to break things up," I said. "But I have an early train to catch tomorrow."

"Thanks for coming Fi," Dad said. "Ian, don't be a stranger."

"Thank you, Sir," Ian said. "Good night, Sir."

"Night to you both," Dad said as he showed us to the door. "Talk to you in the next couple of days to confirm wedding plans, Fi."

"Thank you, Dad," I said. "Love you, Dad."

"Love you, Fi," he said.

On the Friday of that week I had a visit from a Mr Appleby of the Foreign and Commonwealth Office, he had come to do the vetting that Ian and I had expected when he told them he was going to get married. He was a fussy little man and asked all kinds of questions, but spent much of his time on the incident when I put the three in hospital. I simply told him that I had been attacked and had defended myself and that the incident had been witnessed by a Chief Constable. Of course, Mr Appleby knew all that and he had the court transcripts as well. I suppose he just wanted to hear my version of the story. I gathered from his questions that they were looking for something that an unfriendly power might use to pressure Ian into revealing something or spying for them. Mr Appleby was a little surprised at my finances, he could not understand how anyone so young could have amassed so much. I pointed out to him that mathematical models were my bread and butter and that I modelled the markets regularly and invested accordingly. I also reminded him that I had done work for many people including the Treasury and that I had met the Chancellor of the Exchequer. He, of course, also knew that. He wanted to know if my loyalties lay with Her Majesty's Government or with France. I pointed out, that although my mother was of French origin and currently lived in France, that I had been born and raised in England and considered it home, and that, yes, my loyalties were to Her Majesty. He knew I spoke Mandarin and wanted to know if I had been approached by anyone from the People's Republic. I was able to answer that one with a definite no. He did ask if I intended to continue working after I was married, and I told him, yes.

I pointed out that some of my contracts would require me to continue working well into the next year and that I would, from time to time, be travelling back to the UK for meetings. All this took the better part of the afternoon and I was quite glad to see the back of him.

Maman, Portia and Charlize came over from France and had meetings with the hotel staff to finalise the wedding luncheon menu and inspect my wedding dress. They were happy with both, which was a relief as I had anticipated much discussion. Portia also organised flowers and met with printers to get the order of service done and formal invitations which I then sent out. Charlize met with the hotel catering staff and worked out an arrangement for the wines, and I rather think she also negotiated a longer term relationship for the supply of wines generally. She also went to see Rachel and was fitted with her dress for the occasion.

Time marched on and the day of the wedding came. Ian decamped the night before to the Sloane Square Hotel to a suite there that we would occupy after the wedding, leaving my flat to Maman, Portia and Mémère Monique. I was primped and prepared by Maman and Portia, who made sure everything was right, before leaving for the Register Office, leaving me to await Dad, who did arrive in good time and who was more nervous than me. I failed to understand his nerves, I was the one getting married, all he had to do was get me there on time. He had engaged a fancy Rolls Royce for the short drive, complete with the usual white ribbons stretching out from the front of the bonnet to the tops of the front doors. We were on time and Chris had done his job as well, as Ian was there, sober, well dressed and fidgeting. The ceremony itself was fairly short and sweet and we signed the registers with Chris and Charlize as witnesses, that saved squabbles between Maman and Dad. We got a few copies of the marriage certificate and I also knew that I could get more from Somerset House, should I need them. I would need one right away, along with my old passport, to get a new passport in my married name. Chris pointed out that we would now be, Mr and Dr Hartley, much to the amusement of everyone.

There followed the photographic session, in which every possible combination of family member and guest were grouped together and told to smile. Maman had engaged a photographer she knew and who met her standards. I was quite glad when it was all over and we could move on to the reception. Ian and I were delivered to the hotel and then waited to greet our guests. Dad had organised a fleet of Rolls Royces and they made quite a procession from the town hall to the hotel. The staff at the Sloane Square Hotel were well prepared and the room was ready for us, decorated and tables set. Ian and I had discussed seating and we drew names out of a hat, the only exception being seating Maman and Portia away from Dad and Felicity. I expected them to be on their best behaviour, but why tempt fate. I noticed Mr Appleby lurking in the foyer of the hotel and asked him if he would like to join us. He thanked me, and said that he would stop for a drink and piece of wedding cake later. The wedding lunch was excellent, the hotel had done a good job, but it was made simpler by the relatively small party, only twenty-one of us. The wine all came from the Cillie vineyards and was in abundance and I noted drunk with appreciation. We had a wedding cake, three tiers, from Harrods, who I learned actually got it from a convent at Parmoor, not far from Henley. We cut the cake and had all the requisite toasts and speeches, even one from Dad, who did admit that he had despaired of me ever finding the right man, but was thrilled with Ian, in whom he saw as someone who could put up with me. I was not sure that I really appreciated that, but had to admit that was some truth to it, and I think it was really only Dad trying to be funny. I took a piece of cake and a glass of wine out to Mr Appleby, who I believe was there to see if in fact Ian really did get married and to whom, and who was on the guest list. Ian and I escaped the festivities around three in the afternoon and went up to our suite.

"Well, Mr Hartley, are you ready to do your conjugal duty?" I asked him.

"Oh, yes," he said. "Shall I help you with your dress?"

"Unzip me," I told him. He ran the zip all the way down and I stepped out of the dress and pulled down the shoulder straps of the slip and let it fall to the floor, and stood in front of him in the white bustier, briefest panties and white stockings.

"I wish I had a camera," he said. "That is a picture I would carry with me always."

"Enough talk," I scolded him. "Off with your clothes." He did a strip in record time, discarding clothes in a pile of the floor. I led him to the bed and pushed him down onto it.

"One change," I told him. "I'm on the pill, so no need for any more condoms, I've insisted until now more as a double protection. So, we can be a lot more spontaneous."

"I like the sound of that," he said. "Are you going to just stand there and look gorgeous, or are we going to do anything?"

We consummated our marriage, and for good measure we consummated it again just to be sure and I felt that I was now definitely wedded to Ian, body and soul. It had all been a little whirlwind since I had got back from Africa, but there had been no reason to have an extended engagement or delay for any reason the marriage. Once we had established that we both still felt about the other the same way, then there was no reason not to proceed.

We made good use of the suite, breaking from our amorous time to order an evening meal to be served in the room. The bed in the suite had a squeak to it, just like the one at the Trout Inn, and we made it squeak a lot, particularly when things got really heated. I was never sure if anyone in adjoining rooms could hear the noise or not, but we did get a few looks the following morning when we went down for breakfast. We saw James and Charlize there and joined them.

"So, Fi," James said. "What's it like to be married?"

"Wonderful," I said. "And you, are you and Charlize still talking?"

"We are," James grinned. "We're loving it, wouldn't have it any other way."

"We're doing just great," Charlize added. "When do you and Ian leave for Nairobi?"

"Not until the end of the year," Ian said. "We leave after Christmas, so perhaps you could come and spend it with us?"

"Or, you could come and spend it with us," Charlize suggested. "We've got the big chateau on the vineyard, and Maman and Portia could also come."

"Ian?" I asked.

"Sounds great," he said. "Only this time when we go to the airport, you're coming on the plane with me, I'm not losing you again!"

"I'll be hanging on to you," I promised. "Do we have flights yet to Nairobi?"

"We do," Ian confirmed. "We take the BA flight London, Nairobi and the FCO has put us up front, row 2, seats A and B."

"Nice of them," James said.

"We've been asked if we want to send luggage ahead," Ian said. "That might be a good idea."

"Okay," I agreed. "We'll sort out what goes early and what can stay in my flat."

"You're not letting your flat out?" James asked.

"No, I decided that it would be handy to have a place to stay in London when I come on business," I explained. "And if you and Charlize want to use it at any time, I'll give you a key. Ian, do you want me to get us flights from here to Paris and back?"

"If you would," he said. "I'll get dates tomorrow and let you know."

We checked out of the suite at lunch time and went back to my flat. Maman, Portia and Mémère Monique were still there and awaiting our return before they left for the airport to go back to Paris. We talked about getting together at Christmas and they all thought it a capital idea, even Mémère. I would leave her travel arrangements to Maman. We talked about the impending move to Nairobi and Maman wanted to know about the bombings that had happened earlier in the year. Ian told her what he knew and said that since March there had been no further incidents. He said that embassy officials were all well briefed about what had happened and where and had a list of places to avoid, or at least treat with caution. After Maman and the others had left to go to the airport we sat back and listed all that had to be done before we left. I had already arranged with Dad for the property manager who looked after Dad's flats and houses that he had around London, to do a monthly inspection of my flat and had met the people who were going to do the inspections. I had taken a safety deposit box at my local bank and was going to lodge a number of documents and pictures with them, that I did not wish to leave lying around in my flat. It was not that I did not trust the management company people, but why leave temptation in their way. Language was the next item on my list. Ian was going through a four-month course on Swahili, which he really did not need as he spoke it well enough, but standard procedure was that you got the fourth months of language before heading off, then you got a month in country to cement the language then you went to work. I asked Ian if he would help me in the evenings get some working knowledge of Swahili, and we came up with a plan.

I also asked Ian if foreign assignments were at all risky and he, not surprisingly, said that would depend where. That made sense, Washington or Canberra were likely to be less risky than Beirut or Kabul. Ian told me that there would be a briefing session for me at the FCO to tell me what to do, what not to do, how to dress, how not to dress and all the issues that might arise in Nairobi. I was thankful for that, it would be terrible to be in a foreign country and blithely offend all and sundry through sheer ignorance. I would also get a sense from them as to what would be expected of me, as I gathered, officially nothing, it was Ian who was the paid member of the diplomatic service and I was just along for the ride, but there was an expectation that I be at his beck and call if and when he needed me to host events, dinners or whatever the embassy deemed appropriate. Well, we would see how all that worked. Ian suggested that I ask some of the members of the DSWA about their experiences.

When I got home from my office on Monday, I was greeted with *Jambo*, and thereafter Ian used only Swahili. I was completely lost, but with hand gestures, nods and other clues eventually understood what he was talking about. By the time we went for a bath and bed, I was exhausted. The mental exercise of trying to understand this new and foreign language was quite trying. I knew that it would get easier with time, so steeled myself for the task to come. One thing he had done, that really helped, he had put stickers on things around the house, so I could see what a table was called, what cups were and so on. We did take a break from Swahili when he told me what he knew about the others in the High Commission in Nairobi. The High Commissioner himself was fairly new to the post, he had only taken over that year, he was Stanley Fingland, who had been the High Commissioner in Salisbury that Ian and his family knew, and had been in Rhodesia from 1964 until 1966 when the Smith régime expelled him, his posting before Nairobi had been Cuba. Ian went through what he knew about the others so I had a clearer picture of what the staff looked like. It struck me that it was all male, and Ian confirmed that women in the service got a raw deal in his view. It had only been in 1972 when the rule that a woman in the service had to resign when she married, was repealed. He told me that the posting in Nairobi was likely to be four years and then we would be moved somewhere else.

I sent in all my paperwork for a new passport in my married name and for a diplomatic passport, also in my married name. The regular passport I would use when travelling back and forth to London on business and the diplomatic passport only when Ian and I were travelling on official business, so our trip out to Nairobi would be official business, but our trip to France at Christmas was not, so we would both use regular passports for that.

For the next three months, I diligently worked at my Swahili and also finished up my contract with the Ministry of Transport and picked up three new contracts, each of which would probably take me three to four months and each of which were quite happy to pay my way back and forth from Nairobi for meetings. My fees were now outrageous, or at least to me they were and after I had paid the mortgage on the flat, left me with a good deal to invest or spend on something frivolous. I did not belabour the point, but my earnings far exceeded those of Ian, and probably would always do, even as he progressed up the ladder of promotion. I had a reputation and was enjoying the financial benefits that came with it. I went to a briefing on Kenya and learned quite a bit, apart from what I had gleaned by reading up on the place. I met four women from the DSWA and got two quite different views. One more liberal in outlook and the other more tied to the traditional rôle of husband support in a foreign place. Because I was committed to contracts I would probably by default fall into the former group. Because I saw myself travelling back and forth from Nairobi quite regularly, I duplicated my wardrobe and got two of everything, so that all I would have to travel with was my work briefcase and a small overnight bag. I did expand my wardrobe a little and add some more lightweight summer dresses for the warm climes, but I even bought two of each of those. I made arrangements with a laundry and cleaning service, so that when I left London to go back to Nairobi, I would just drop off a bag with the laundry and it would be delivered back to my mail and telephone service, where I would pick it up the next time I was in London. That was the theory, I had to actually try it out before I knew it would work or even be convenient.

Ian and I flew to Paris on the 21st of December. We had both taken the Christmas week off and would be ready to fly to Nairobi the next week. Maman had prevailed upon me to collect Mémère Monique on the way, so we stopped by her flat and collected her and her luggage and then went to Gare d'Austerlitz to get the train to Orléans. An hour and forty minutes later, James was driving us from the station to the chateau. Maman and Portia were already there, they had come up by train the day before. I felt sorry for Ian, most of the conversation was in French a little of which he understood, so I tried hard to remember to translate things for him. When he was alone with me, we did speak English, or on occasion Swahili, as he was determined that I have some facility by the time we arrived in Nairobi. The weather in Orléans was dismal, temperatures in the forties and rain, with more rain forecast. Nairobi was looking rather attractive with the thought of sunshine and warm temperatures.

Charlize took us all on a tour of the vineyards and the winery and storage vats, the bottling line and the warehouse. I had seen all this before, but it was all new to Ian, who was fascinated. Charlize kept up her patter and talked about varietals that they grew, yields per hectare and litres of wine produced and what that translated to in bottles and revenue. The winery was profitable, quite happily so, and she and James were looking at acquiring some more property. There was some money available from South Africa and I gathered from James that Dad had even expressed an interest in financing the purchase. That might be a good idea as the South Africans were beginning to clamp down on hard currency leaving the country and the French would not take Rand in payment, it had to be Francs, Pounds or Dollars. After dinner, I sat down with James and Charlize and we created a financial model of the new property, including the costs of financing. It showed how much they could afford to borrow, at rates that I set. I also created a model that

I was sure would be very similar to the one Dad would use to negotiate with. That gave James and Charlize what they needed to go into the negotiation. James might be Dad's son, but Dad was still an investment banker and that would drive his thinking, family ties notwithstanding. Ian was in awe of all this, he had never seen me produce any of the algorithms that I used, or mathematical models and he commented on how easy I made it all look. For me, it was a straightforward simple model of an enterprise, that had some risk, driven mainly by the weather and other imponderables, but that could be accommodated with factors that allowed for such variability.

Christmas, when it came was fun, it was like the first Christmas I had spent with Ian, full of laughter, good food, wine and lots of time in the bedroom. I was still in the mode of making up for the four years we had been apart. I did not hear any complaints from Ian, so he had to be enjoying our lovemaking as much as I was. It was far too cold to make love outside, but I did wonder if we would get the chance in Kenya. I asked Ian and he thought that we would be able to, but that we would probably have to go out of the town and away from people. His comment was that people in Africa had a habit of popping up when and where you least expected them, so making love in the bush always had an element of the unexpected. We had spent Christmas Eve in a very traditional style, so had gone to bed late, or early depending on your viewpoint, so no one was up at the crack of dawn on Christmas Day. When Ian and I surfaced, Charlize was already about, preparing breakfast, with James as her fetch and carry person.

"Fiona," Charlize said. "Did you sleep well?"

"Like a log," I said. "And you?"

"Really well," she said. "I have crêpes for breakfast, would you like some?"

"Please," I said. "Ian, are you having some?"

"Please," he said. "So, James, are you still enjoying the wine-making business?"

"I am," James confirmed. "I've learned a lot in the past year or so, and I know there's lots more to learn. Charlie and I are planning a trip to the States soon to visit some California properties and see how they operate."

"Will you come and see us in Nairobi?" I asked.

"That would be fun," Charlize said. "We'll let you get settled and maybe next year we can come for Christmas."

"That would be great," I said.

"Are you looking forward to Nairobi?" James asked.

"I am," I confirmed. "It's a new adventure."

"It's my first real overseas posting," Ian added. "So, it'll be interesting to see what the job really entails. But at least I get to go with Fi, so there will be someone to share it with."

"So, life is good?" James asked.

"Life is good," Ian confirmed. "Don't you think so Fi?"

"It's good," I said. "In fact, it seems to me to get better each day," I said, echoing a phrase from the song, *Un jour tu reviendras,* which says, *la vie me semblera plus belle chaque jour.*